He just fell into it.

Thomas Laurie was already much needed; a village policeman and an honourable man, he kept the peace at home, even in war.

Yet driven by conscience and filleted by the stares of strangers, he'd entered an army enlisting office in Worcester and jumped.

Now, owned by King and country he was thousands of miles from his wife's love, holed up in a rat-infested carpet shop in a darkened Cairo backstreet, intent upon a plan. Somewhere opposite within the gloom of a tired hostel was the spy. He and Corporal Nooney had become a great team. They would sort it, they always did.

But still the doubts nagged: Mildred Lowthian, his senior officer at the Arab Bureau, was unlike any other woman he'd known, but she too seemed burdened by the duplicity of superiors. And the ignorance and disdain of those with power had shocked.

Who was he really helping?

At the same hour in her farmhouse on the island of Menorca, the formidable self-made landowner Llucia Quintana sat fearing for the safety of Oriol, her only son and heir. His routine trading trip to Cairo was to be his last; Mediterranean passage had become increasingly hostile and British control of the city increasingly unpredictable. He'd not made contact; but how could she rely upon the support of others, given her past?

In these colliding worlds a moving, tragicomic tale unfolds of adventure, conflict, trust, and fairness. Surely we would learn? There could be a better world.

THE POET LAURIE ATE

ASH JAMES

Copyright © 2024 Ash James

The moral right of Ash James to be identified as the author of this work has been asserted in accordance with Section 77 of the Copyright, Designs and Patents Act, 1988.

Apart from any fair dealing for the purposes of research or private study, or criticism or review, as permitted under the Copyright, Designs and Patents Act 1988, this publication may only be reproduced, stored or transmitted, in any form or by any means, with the prior permission in writing of the publishers, or in the case of reprographic reproduction in accordance with the terms of licences issued by the Copyright Licensing Agency. Enquiries concerning reproduction outside those terms should be sent to the publishers.

This is a work of fiction. Names, characters, businesses, places, events and incidents are either the products of the author's imagination or used in a fictitious manner. Any resemblance to actual persons, living or dead, or actual events is purely coincidental.

The Poem 'I Met A Man Today' Ch 17 is ©Ash James 2024

Troubador Publishing Ltd
Unit E2 Airfield Business Park,
Harrison Road, Market Harborough,
Leicestershire. LE16 7UL
Tel: 0116 2792299
Email: books@troubador.co.uk
Web: www.troubador.co.uk

ISBN 978 1805143 826 (Paperback)
ISBN 978 1805148 678 (E-book)

British Library Cataloguing in Publication Data.
A catalogue record for this book is available from the British Library.

Printed and bound in Great Britain by 4edge Limited
Typeset in 12pt Jenson Pro by Troubador Publishing Ltd, Leicester, UK

CONTENTS

About The Author	ix
Chapter 1	1
Chapter 2	21
Chapter 3	40
Chapter 4	60
Chapter 5	82
Chapter 6	104
Chapter 7	124
Chapter 8	148
Chapter 9	171
Chapter 10	187
Chapter 11	218
Chapter 12	242
Chapter 13	259
Chapter 14	288
Chapter 15	309
Chapter 16	320
Chapter 17	345
Index Of Characters	357
Llucia Quintana Family Tree	361
Index Of Historical References	363
Acknowledgements	368
Bibliography	369

ABOUT THE AUTHOR

Ash James has always written, though other works had to come first. He has been Deputy Head of a Secondary School for which he was paid, and variously a Music Promoter, Conference Organiser, Adviser, President, Musician, Charity Fund Raiser, mini-Vicar, centre-page spread and Chair of Governors: for which he was thanked. He is now free to graze his imagination and *The Poet Laurie Ate* is his first published novel.

www.ashjamesarts.co.uk

CHAPTER 1

There is a time in every life when the simple certainties of the self overpower and sing their triumph. Faced by our folly we stumble, desperate for space, any space, for peace.

"Three hours a day for the next four weeks will be spent on parade duties," barked the voice.

So much for the peace.

"Men who are disciplined are men who can follow orders. You will drill, fight, and if necessary, die together. Our enemies are a complex beast. They are many-headed and devious. But the last thing they want, indeed the thing they dread the most, is to be faced with an adversary who knows how to march."

Honour is a noble virtue. It respects the giver and brings joy to the tribe. But it stamps hard upon those closest and the left-behind.

Thomas Laurie was indeed an honourable man. That he was driven was beyond question. Rarely could a duty be nobler than to King and country. But at this moment, all he felt was the sickening paralysis of fear and self-pity. What had he done?

Together with a hundred or so other men, he was sat bolt upright on hard wooden benching, incarcerated within a dimly-lit briefing hall. His eyes scanned ahead. The words shoved his way barely registered though the source was clearly visible.

"Two hours every day will be spent in stripping each item of equipment. That means not only cleaning your weaponry but also your boots, your belts, your trouser pockets and linings, your caps and straps, and especially your bedding. You will ensure fastidiousness in every element of your being. The reason should by now by patently clear."

There was a pause.

"Sand."

He sank further into blackness. The smell of sweat drifted about the room like a nauseous river fog. Move a haunch and his heavy woollen trousers oozed moisture. Edge an arm and pearls of water trickled below his shirt. His neck was stiff, razor-washed by wetness upon the grazes from an ill-fitting collar. The discomfort was intense.

There were fans on the ceiling, droning out a monotonous belly hum in a limp effort to circulate air around the foul, stifling vacuum. But he didn't take notice nor much care. All he saw was his wife, pleading with him to stay, and the tear-filled faces of his children as he'd waved goodbye.

"Yes, sand. Get's everywhere, the bloody stuff. There are only three things that will cost us this war: sand, hygiene, and water. Too much of the first will block your weapon, too little of the second will lay you out, and not enough of the third will likely kill you. Can you imagine the Ottoman carping that they defeated the greatest empire the world has ever seen by denying their people the efficiency to fire a gun, wipe their arse and wash their hands? We'd be a laughing stock. You men have a duty to your masters, your nation, and to each other, to remember the mantra, 'sand, hygiene, water.'"

Captain Hillary slammed the table with his stick and the room of men sprung from their seats, releasing a fresh plume of odour. Laurie began to rally.

"'Sand, hygiene, water,'" repeated the Captain, "'sand, hygiene, water'. Come on, together with me." He banged his stick in time like a deranged conductor, as the company of Worcestershire's joined in as ordered.

"Sand, hygiene, water, sand, hygiene, water." The louder he shouted and thumped, the louder the men chorused, and the wider the grin that appeared on his face.

Laurie started mouthing the words too, his eyes now focussed more determinedly forward. There were at least four officers, one of them distinctly top brass with an air of familiarity about him. Behind them was a woman dressed smartly in full uniform, a military administrator or medic, he assumed. In front of them all was the performing Captain Hillary, from whose armpits deltaic fingers of perspiration were beginning to emerge.

He was unmissable in his desert-issue uniform, baggy shorts and lightweight long socks, quite a contrast to the woollen jacket and full-length trousers worn by the men. His legs, at least from Laurie's vantage point, appeared extremely thin, matching the sculpted moustache that hung below a sharpened nose. He would have made the perfect music hall dandy had he been wearing a toff's top hat. Instead, his head was adorned by an ill-fitting cap, which he regularly adjusted.

Despite the mildly absurd appearance, there was a certainty and a bearing about him, both in the way he spoke and the manner with which he bore himself. And it was with this that he'd discharged a dismissive mix of indifference and invective towards the men.

"Sand, hygiene, water," they all shouted, "sand, hygiene, water."

How they would have been delighted to wear the proper desert clothing he displayed. They'd been promised light khaki kit within the month, but six weeks into their posting they remained glued into the heavy-duty gear issued back home. Useful though this was during the cold of the Egyptian night, for the majority of the time it was unbearable. Unlike Hillary, they were already scorching away in the heat of the Egyptian day.

"Sand, hygiene, water," they all shouted once more, "sand, hygiene, water."

And the proper bloody uniform, thought Laurie.

Captain Hillary raised his hand and the chanting stopped.

"You men are probably wondering about the mission to which you will devote yourselves. You might be thinking that your three months' training in England and the pretty little boat and train trips you took to get here, have earned you the right to call yourselves soldiers. Well, I can tell you with certainty that soldiers you are not. What I see before me is a mob of indiscipline. We need brains and heart to finish this job off, but what we've been sent is the backside of the British Empire."

To demonstrate the point, he spent the next few minutes brow beating individuals, their backgrounds, breeding, and general ignorance, whilst simultaneously encouraging mocking laughter from those otherwise safely ignored. But there must have been something about Laurie. There was always something about Laurie.

"You, man."

The Captain pointed directly at him, anonymous though he'd thought he'd been until now.

"Stand Up."

Laurie looked around momentarily, shocked by the attention and uncertain that this really meant him.

"Yes, you man, hurry up with it."

He shot to attention, suddenly upright, exposed and isolated. A bolt of cold sweat shot down his back.

"Do you know where you are?"

"Yes, sir," he replied crisply, whilst silently berating himself to pursue caution.

"Well?"

Laurie paused nervously, "Barracks, sir."

"Barracks, did you say, barracks?"

The Captain feigned bemusement and a few of the men obliged with laughter.

"No, you fool, the place. What's the name of this place? Where the hell are you?"

Be very careful, thought Laurie, *be very careful*. But as ever, there was an uncontainable ire, and it was rising.

"Not sure, sir."

"Not sure, not bloody sure? Well, haven't you spotted any clues?"

"Clues, sir?" replied Laurie.

"You know, camels, the heat, the Arabs, the lingo."

"Oh yes, sir, but…"

"But what man?" demanded the Captain.

"We were told to keep shtum, sir."

"Shtum?"

"Yes, sir, in case of loose talk."

"Loose talk? Who told you that?"

"We were all told it, sir, before we left England, on a poster, by General Haig."

There was some nervous foot movement amongst the Company. To this point, few men confronted by the Captain had braved anything beyond the briefest response, concluding reasonably their subservience was as de rigueur in a fighting force as it was back home in their place of employment.

"Loose talk you say, loose talk, well I'm your fucking Captain, so I think you're safe to be loose with me."

There was a further ripple of uncomfortable laughter, though not entirely directed towards Laurie whose sacrificial resistance they were beginning to admire. But it was clear to a man that Captain Hillary's sarcastic wit was merely the prelude, particularly if challenged, to something much worse, and none of them fancied him as an opponent.

Laurie prided himself upon his hard work, determination and honesty. Born with nothing and bereft of advantage, these at least were tools he could use, qualities he admired so much in others. That he imposed them so severely upon himself had been a constant sense of burden. That they were often lacking in the feckless creatures who assumed authority over him frequently led to challenge. And this was limiting, dangerous even, for a boy born into struggle.

He'd led a solitary childhood. As he grew, such isolation drove him to become incautiously independent. A hot head needed a cool heart, but after a year in apprenticeship, he'd fled the town that bore him, threatened by a foreman for answering back. Speaking honestly towards a superior had its consequence.

"I'm waiting, man." Captain Hillary banged his stick.

"Can you maybe remember the journey you made to get here? Perhaps that would help," he suggested, mockingly.

Laurie fixed the Captain's gaze with an adjudged degree of facial supplication. Of course he could remember the journey, every aching last inch of it, from the enthusiasm of enlisting, to the appalling reality of his current circumstance. Still more, the journey from those loneliest of times to the man he'd become, respected by those he helped, loved by his wife and six children. Two years into the war, he was still safely at home, protected from conscription by his occupation. But it had provided poor protection from the taunts. No one directly accused him of cowardice but he saw it in their faces and it haunted. So, in the honesty of his guilt, he enlisted and gave himself to his country. He would travel, serve, and return with honour, conscience assuaged.

And in so doing, he laid upon his family a burden that would batter their very existence, and a personal guilt that would never leave.

"Yes, sir. Twelve weeks' basic training in England, sir; boat from Devonport to France, train to the Mediterranean, boat to Alexandria, acclimatisation training at Camp Minia and then the train here to Cairo, sir."

"Well, well, so you can speak?" replied Hillary, barely hiding a sneer.

"Be so good if you would to tell me therefore," and he paused as if to inquire of the most indelicate of matters, "did you and the men have a lovely time in France?"

There were smiles from the ranks. Unpleasant though the Captain seemed, he certainly had good timing.

"Passable, sir."

There was a gentle hiss of amusement.

"Passable? What do you mean, passable?"

"I believe it's French, sir."

"French?"

"Yes, sir, French… *passable*…" he intoned with his best comedic accent, "the adjective for passing tolerably through the country."

The Worcestershires broke into a belly hoot. Even the officers laughed. The men may have been the armpits of the Empire, but here was an excuse for brotherly fraternity. This bloke knew something, and blimey, he was going to cop it.

"Silence!"

Captain Hillary banged his stick with such a force that it risked destruction.

"So we have a clever arse here do we?"

"Sir?"

"Fluent in the francaise, 'le double entendre'?"

"No, sir." Laurie affected shock, hurt and complete sincerity, a skill at which he was well practiced. "That's what we were taught by some of the French we met, sir."

"So you met a lot of the French did you on your 'jolly' through their country?"

"No, sir, we learnt to keep away."

"Keep away?"

"Yes, sir, they didn't seem to like us."

"Like us? They are our main ally, you bloody idiot. Why on earth would they like us?"

"Well, we all rather thought that if these are our friends, sir, we'd hate to see what the enemy were like."

There was more muffled laughter, and by now even Captain Hillary was aware of the dubious merit of further interlocution. In addition, there was awkward movement behind him from the senior officers and their staff. He stared hard at Laurie.

"What's your name, man?"

"Private Laurie, sir."

"Well, 'Private Laurie sir', unusual though that name is," and some of the Company smiled at his wit," I shall remember it when I need a pedantic literalist to be sent behind the enemy lines. But in the meantime, stay where you are when the men are dismissed so that I can brief you about your undercover work in *la lavatoire* for the next week."

"Sir?"

"The shit house, Laurie, something to get stuck into whilst you 'acclimatise' in Cairo."

A slow gator smile crept across the Captain's face as he fixed his prey.

"Do you understand me now?"

"Yes, sir," responded Laurie, sufficiently pliant.

"Now sit down," he spat.

Laurie did as instructed. He'd alienated an officer, but in the process felt confirmed by his peers. He'd stood up for himself and for the men. Most of them would have taken the blows subservience required. But he'd felt a sense of duty to some misty personal morality, to engage with Hillary; better 'to jump than be pushed'.

Captain Hillary touched his cap in a nervy attempt to re-align it, as if trying to remind himself of who he was, and returned to addressing the whole troop.

"As you may know if you were still awake when you arrived last night," and he glowered at Laurie, "these…" he gestured to the walls of the building, "are the Bab El Hadid barracks in Cairo."

He waited for the words to sink in. He doubted if any of the men had ever been further than their next street.

"Shambles that you were," he continued, "you would have had no idea that as you fell out of the stinking waggons that bore you here and shuffled across the square to your billets, that you'd actually arrived in the greatest city in the whole of Africa."

He raised his voice for emphasis.

"And not just 'in it' but in the very heart of it, the main bloody square indeed, Midan Bab El Hadid, just alongside Shari el Maddbuli, one of the main bloody streets. So, when you are finally trusted to leave this building, remember those names in case you get your silly little selves lost because unlike at home, you won't be able to ask a policeman."

Laurie blinked. *Did he say policeman?*

"Yes, thank you, Hillary."

The voice from the officer behind him momentarily flustered the Captain, but he quickly composed himself, realising its source.

"I think the men can have their geography lesson a little later on," continued the voice.

"Sir," replied Hillary, somewhat chastened, and he turned, clicked his heals obediently, and took his place with the other officers.

This was the top brass Laurie had spotted earlier, and he rose slowly and moved awkwardly, dragging a leg.

He was a tall man, towering well above Hillary as they crossed, and upon reaching the dais, stood upright, back stiff as a board. The braids that straddled his uniform, the way he removed his cap to address the men and the confidence in which he surveyed them, announced a man of authority and distinction. He was greying around the temples, though the head was full of dark greased-back hair. Laurie judged him to be a good twenty years older than himself, though there was something oddly familiar about him.

"Gentlemen, welcome to Cairo."

Laurie could almost touch the sense of relief around the hall these words brought. He spoke directly, yet with a distinct and unexpected kindness.

"I am your Commanding Officer, Brigadier Regis-Templeton, and I'd like to add just a few words to those of Captain Hillary. I know you will all be tired and probably a little confused following the long journey here from Plymouth. And I guess that for many of you, this is your first visit to Cairo."

He smiled, as did the men. Already they liked him.

"Quite so, quite so."

He moved his weight forward slightly and then gently back again, as if readjusting for some inner pain, yet remained faced firmly frontward.

"During your training at the Raglan Barracks in Plymouth as members of the proud Worcestershire 6th, you doubtless expected to become part of the push to beat the Germans in France. I hear from one of you men..." and he motioned towards Laurie, "...that there was talk of your enemy. You were probably expecting to face the Hun and certainly that remains the case. So when you were placed on the troop trains through France, you must have been somewhat surprised to learn that you would soon be on another boat from Nice, sailing to Alexandria."

The men nodded, though in reality they had been told little about anything, let alone their destination. At times, it was if the army was unsure what to do with them.

"Well, whilst my officers behind, including Captain Hillary, have fought alongside me during the last two years both in Gallipoli and on the Western Front, we, and now you, find ourselves together in the British Protectorate of Egypt, a key arena in this war, fighting as part of the Egyptian Expeditionary Force."

The respect from the men was growing with his every word. Back home, both town and country were coming to terms with the maiming and appalling loss of life these places evoked. The horrors of the front were on show everywhere, and the dreadful stories of the suffering at Gallipoli were just emerging.

But the Egyptian Expeditionary Force? To many, those stationed in Egypt were thought of as being on leave. All the real stories were about France.

"Gentlemen, in time and depending upon our tactical requirements, many of you will transfer from your duties here to the Western Front. You will quickly become aware that there are also Australians and New Zealanders stationed in barracks across Cairo, plus troops from India and the extended Empire. They will also be on the same boats back to France, once the final push develops. But a good many of you will also stay here to defend the British Protectorate from the Ottoman, whom you may also recognise as Turks."

Laurie felt for the first time since enlisting that here was an officer deserving of attention, and he wasn't alone. Having been assaulted and cowed by Hillary, the men were suddenly alert, their discomfort in the heat allayed for the moment by the straight talking they were hearing.

"Make no mistake gentlemen, you may never get used to the sun, the dryness, the hordes of flies, but you will need very quickly to acclimatise to the fight. The Ottoman soldier is a fearsome opponent. They believe they have rights to the whole of North Africa, and are also threatening our allies in Europe." He paused.

"I believe, as I'm sure do you, in the fundamental goodness of mankind. In the trenches on the front line, the fighting was tough, but the Germans, as did we, approached an opponent as a fellow human. The Ottoman though, seems to fight by different rules; their own men are frequently starved of rations and we have reports of appalling degradations by them towards the Armenians, Greeks and Assyrians. So, you can gather that defeat and capture by such a foe is not an option."

There was an intense seriousness on the Brigadier's face as he delivered this news, and none doubted its credibility.

"Added to that, strategically, we are almost fifty years on from the opening of the Suez Canal. God help the British Empire if that were to fall into Ottoman hands. Our Arab hosts need our military strength and organisational resolve to help them protect and build their country. Were we to fail, they would be overrun in a matter of weeks. So, gentlemen, your work here will be pivotal to winning the war."

He moved a hand towards his cap and winced, momentarily.

"We shall meet for briefings as events dictate, but for now, just a few important instructions."

He seemed to slow a little, as if to ensure that what followed had time to be properly received.

"Remember well Captain Hillary's directives to you, and act upon them at all times. As we speak, Army Engineers are at work in Cairo and beyond, digging wells, laying pipelines, searching for water. They have already constructed over one hundred miles of diversionary channels. Water in Egypt is more precious than gold. Abuse this notion and you will be severely disciplined."

There was visible surprise at this change in emphasis.

"You may think this stricture somewhat grave, but it is for your own good. Far too many of our young men have died for lack of water, and it's as big a danger to us as the enemy."

He stood in silence for a moment as his words flew across the room.

"With luck, one gallon of water a day will be available to you."

That was clearly a shock.

"Five pints of that will be taken for cooking and making tea. That will leave you with three for drinking and washing."

There was a collective though contained intake of breath across the room and a discernible movement amongst the men. The Brigadier could see what they were thinking: three pints a day, how would they cope? Laurie though wasn't so confronted; he'd been used to deprivation.

"See to it that these orders are followed to the letter."

Brigadier Regis-Templeton raised his cap with his left hand and placed it skillfully upon his head, holding the lectern on the dais with the other, for balance. He scanned across the room, observing the draining away of innocence. *How many more times?* he thought. He saluted the men who responded in kind, and then beckoned towards the officers behind.

"Over to you, Captain Hillary."

The officer party stood, and Hillary, caught somewhat unawares, rushed forward.

"Attention," he barked, and the men stood as one.

The Brigadier, now noticeably less upright, walked with a studied precision towards the open doorway leading to the drill square, followed by the officers. Laurie's view was, by now, partly obscured, but even so, he could tell by the gait that Brigadier Regis-Templeton was in pain. The officers behind him appeared aware too, allowing him space, curtailing their own pace. The woman in uniform was third in the line as they left, and Laurie was surprised. In his short military experience, officers generally left a formal briefing such as this in the order of their rank, yet she was close by the Brigadier.

Once the stage party had left, Hillary dismissed the men back to their billets to prepare for their first parade of the day. Laurie, however, remained behind, standing alone.

"Well, Laurie, you're not so cocky now are you?" said Captain Hillary.

He was joined by a Sergeant.

"Sir?" replied Laurie.

"All that *'passable'* shit just now, hey?"

Some spittle affixed itself to Hillary's moustache, balancing along the rim and gently elongating southward like a mucous icicle.

"You wouldn't know a French adjective if it stood up and slapped you in the face would you?"

"I think that's unlikely, sir."

"What?" shouted the Captain.

Be careful, Laurie told himself, for pity's sakes, be careful. "That I would be slapped in the face by an adject—"

"Shut it, man," bellowed the Captain, now a few inches from Laurie. The fact that he was shorter and therefore looking upward meant that further spray landed on Laurie's chin, and this together with the Captain's breath caused him to make an involuntary move backward.

"Stand still, man."

"Yes, sir."

Captain Hillary paused and turned towards the Sergeant. "You see what we are up against here?"

The Sergeant nodded. *He's a wiser man than I to keep his mouth shut*, thought Laurie. Hillary closed even more, his eyes peering from below Laurie's nose.

"Adjective my arse. Why, a man like you wouldn't know a bare infinitive from a past-participle, would you?"

"No, sir."

"Quite right," he bawled.

"Why, I'd be amazed if you could barely write your name."

"Yes, sir."

That's better, thought Laurie, *show deference, stay calm.*

"Yes, sir, indeed," lisped Captain Hillary sarcastically, parodying Laurie's reply.

"We need men here with intelligence Laurie, do you understand?"

"Yes, sir."

"Men with the intelligence to keep their scummy little mouths shut."

He paused and walked slowly around Laurie, looking him up and down as if inspecting an unpleasant obstruction. Then he signalled to his Sergeant to do the same. Odd though this felt to Laurie it was so obviously a well-worn routine.

"Do you see what I see, Sergeant Wirrall?"

"I do see it sir, yes, I do see it."

"And what is that you see, Sergeant?"

"A man who is full of shite, sir."

"And how can you tell that Sergeant, if I may ask?"

"Because he both looks and very much smells like shite, sir. And in my extensive military experience in the service of His Majesty, sir, something that looks and smells of shite is quite specifically shite, sir."

"Correct, Sergeant. And therefore where do you think him best deployed?"

"Most definitely as you have previously indicated, sir… latrines."

"Thank you, Sergeant Wirrall. So one week's lavatories shift alongside the Arab orderlies. Let's hope that does the trick. A sufficiently *'passable'* place for a clever arse like you Laurie, don't you think?"

"Yes, sir."

"A clever arse, Laurie. What are you?"

"An arse, sir."

Hillary erupted again, "I said a clever arse, damn you. What are you?"

"Yes, sir; clever, sir."

Hillary was finished, and besides, he had important work to attend.

"Keep me informed of progress, Sergeant."

"Yes, sir."

"But given the smell he will carry, please keep him away from my office. If I need to speak to him, arrange for it to be in the open. Is that clear?"

"Sir."

And with that, Captain Hillary turned sharply and headed off through the door used by the departing officers. Laurie, stinging from the unfairness, yet relieved that he'd endured and gained approbation from the men, turned to follow the Sergeant. As he did so, he caught sight of the woman who'd been sitting with the stage party. She was standing in a shaded corner of the room, but he'd studied her face sufficiently earlier to recognise that it was definitely her. She must have heard what had gone on. Hillary hadn't spotted her upon his exit, and she'd remained sheltered by the dark, making no effort to either move away or communicate.

Odd, thought Laurie, as he followed the Sergeant at the double, *quite odd*.

After a week adhering to the strictures of Captain Hillary, the Worcestershires were indeed dulled beyond numbness.

Their daily routine began at 4.30 am sharp with roll call and inspection. Dressed in full uniform and stood to attention, their bedding and kit were forensically examined for any linear misalignment. Once this was completed, they made their way in an orderly manner to the canteen and queued for tea. Breakfast was a routinely cheerless affair involving bread, bacon, cheese and the occasional egg. This was consumed sitting regularly in rows, either side of the communal tables. Talking was allowed, but at this time in the morning and with the growing realisation of their lot, the whole affair was increasingly undertaken in a stuporous silence.

The three-storey barrack block that housed them had once been a magnificent ornate municipal building, brim-full with the business of life. But now it was dark, musty and overbearing, with the smell and pallor of a dying man. There were no formal windows in the sense the men understood, merely arched openings arranged uniformly along the outside of each floor. They looked elegant enough from the street, but merely served to vacuum the dry air and attendant hordes of insect flotsam deep into their sleeping quarters.

Some arranged towels and shirts on the guard rail that ran across each arch, in the slim hope of protection. Others fashioned makeshift mosquito covers from spare clothing. But these efforts were largely futile and few slept well, not least as in one of the hottest places on earth, the nights were cruelly cold. Their heavy woollen uniforms therefore served some useful purpose under the Cairo stars.

As they sat in collective post-breakfast glumness, the heat of the day began steepening, bringing with it more of the insect life that had swamped them since Alexandria. And from outside, the noise of an awakening Cairo began to intrude, rising in intensity like a distressed steam engine pulling out of Worcester Station. Amongst it were the muezzin, calling the faithful to prayer, the hordes of traders with their impenetrable language and the bellowing protests of thousands of awkward, angry donkeys. The only recognisable sound to the ears of these newest servants of blighty was the intermittent metallic screeching of the street trams as the daily timetable of the Cairo Electric Railway and Heliopolis Company commenced.

Added to this growing sense of alienation was an unforgettable smell that would crescendo with the rising heat: a mixture of fragrances beyond the experiences of the ranks, including cinnamon and herb, sweet apple smoke, citron, date and fragrant coffee. Suffused within this was the more familiar thumping of manure, so invasive some suggested it could be sliced and served with the rations. Therefore, even in these, the earliest of days, it became essential routine outside barracks for patrols to watch their feet as well as the locals.

At 5.30 am precisely, the first drill of the day began. Each Sergeant took it in turn to pull the strings, inflicting some modification or other upon the practiced accomplishments of their predecessor, lest the sloppiness so derided by Captain Hillary appear. Exhausted by an hour of routine, the men returned to the canteen to pick up their first water ration of the day. Needy though they were, bitter experience already determined they limit their intake to just a small portion of the pint issued into their water bottle.

By 7.15 am, the sun was high enough to match the hottest summer day back home, and within moments of their return for the second drill, a wetland ecosystem of sweat and insect life festooned their uniforms. By the end of this, at least one soldier had usually collapsed and been ferried to the medical ward by Arab orderlies.

Following this second hour of drilling, it became customary for Captain Hillary to address them on what he was observing.

"Complete shambles you are, complete shambles."

Routinely, he would point to a deemed defect and insist upon further refinement.

"Makes perfect does practice," he would frequently say, accompanied by a little chuckle to himself at his quirky cleverness with words. Sometimes he would develop the theme.

"Remember, a hundred years ago the Duke of Wellington..." he paused to give suitable emphasis to his authority... "triumphed at Waterloo, thanks largely to the discipline of his southern front. Bonaparte might have lived by the maxim that *'in war morale is everything'* but the silly bugger forgot just how effective fit men in drilled lines can be. Outflanked him they did, outflanked him."

Following further marching under Hillary's occasional gaze, the men would then be dismissed to stumble exhausted, but praising Bonaparte, back to their billet. Most collapsed into sleep until their 11.30 am mug of tea.

The ceaseless monotony of the day continued with weaponry training and endless stripping down and cleaning of equipment, enlivened by the occasional briefing on tactical considerations and how to behave outside barracks.

Water rations for the rest of the day were collected at dusk, following the third and final drill practice. Any thought the cookhouse would lift spirits quickly diminished, as a dinner of stew, potatoes and soup became the staple routine. Such camaraderie as there was before lights out at 9 pm, depended upon the avoidance of the most obvious question of all: what are we doing here?

Not that Laurie had that luxury. Those last couple of hours facilitated the punishment duties prescribed by the good Captain. He'd feared the worst as the lavatories were hellish. The ranks were required to deliver their all in one of the twelve metallic basins fixed uniformly within a stone plinth running the length of an enclosed cloister. Each of the three storeys within the barrack had such a facility. Business done, primitive and yet ingenious army plumbing, transported the product of bowel and bladder from the building, eventually reaching the covered cesspit deep outside the barrack wall.

Men spent as little time as they could in the cloister, fearing the smell, mosquitoes, the occasional snake, and whatever deposit they'd unwittingly perched upon. Most quickly learnt to squat above the hole and aim for the best, and Laurie was no exception. So despite an outward bearing of confidence in the face of Hillary's admonishments, the thought of attending to the latrines had worried him. But he hadn't reckoned with Sergeant Wirrall.

"How old are you, Laurie?" he'd asked, as he'd walked him away from Captain Hillary following the dressing down.

"Thirty-four, Sergeant."

"Hmm, you'll be as old as me soon lad, and I'm nearly forty-two."

"Sergeant?"

"What I'm telling you, Laurie, is that you're older than most of the other men. From what I see, you've got brains inside that head of yours, just a pity it's balancing on your shoulders."

Laurie moved uneasily. He sensed he needed the Sergeant, and now with just the two of them there was no show to give in front of the men.

"You see, they'll look up to you, will the men. So you go ploughing through the minefield that is Captain Hillary and you'll find you end up in pieces. He can't afford an enemy amongst his own ranks, so you're not the first that's been sent to the shite house and you won't be the last. Do you understand what I'm saying?"

Laurie nodded. The Sergeant was a stocky man with a north-country gruffness, but below the prominent scars that crossed his forehead were kindly eyes that betrayed his directness.

"Family have you?"

Laurie gulped, the stiffness with which he protected himself suddenly dented.

"Thought so. Hard isn't it?"

The emotion bottled within Laurie's coping framework rattled towards the surface. His wife's face, his children's tears. Why had he enlisted? What was it that led him to believe he would be perceived a better man? What suffering he'd put them through, so that he might live.

"Difficult isn't it? For you, for me, for the Company, and even for the Captain. We've all folk we've left behind. But the thing is, I need men like you to step up to the plate, not smash it with a great big bloody mallet."

He studied Laurie thoughtfully for a moment.

"What's your work back home, farm or factory?"

Laurie hesitated, but determined that the Sergeant would find out for himself if there was prevarication.

"Policeman."

Sergeant Wirrall smiled.

"Thought it might be a cut above. Starting to make sense now."

His eyes tightened.

"Well, Laurie, you'll know better than any that staying clear of trouble is better than what you've just landed yourself in."

Laurie nodded.

"You'll think I'm in Captain Hillary's pocket following that little show in there. But I'm coping and surviving in my own way, using my wits and doing the best I can, the same I hope as every man here. Surviving Captain Hillary and his ways isn't going to be helped by whether I like him or not."

He paused, and the voice softened.

"So, because we need good men with a brain, and despite what you may think following that little show in there, I'm going to ease some of the burden that awaits you in the khazi. I'm about to save your head from your arse by ensuring you stay sane and above disease."

Laurie felt grateful for this unexpected twist, but unsure how to respond. His face must have betrayed this and Sergeant Wirrall bristled.

"What I'm saying, Laurie, is that I'll look out for you this time so long as you start to look out for yourself as well. But don't let me down, clear?"

"Yes, Sergeant."

"Remember, we all need somebody."

"Yes, Sergeant," replied Laurie again, adding, "thank you," to enforce the point. He knew Wirrall was correct.

There was no further conversation on the quick march back to quarters, but to Laurie's great relief, the Sergeant would prove to be true to his word. Each evening for a week he was required to spend just an hour supervising the removal of waste from the barracks cesspit, a duty so essential to the effectiveness of the Company that even as a punishment it seemed worthy. Consequently, any poor unfortunate upon whose shoulders this responsibility fell received prestige as well as sympathy.

Captain Hillary's delicacies prevented any form of contact by him with the sanitary areas concerned, and so he had been left to assume that those committed by him to these tasks had spent hours of drudgery late into the night. This arrangement suited everyone. Laurie and the others so engaged had no intention of repeating the experience, Sergeant Wirrall built trust, Captain Hillary convinced himself of his wisdom, and most importantly, the cesspit contents stayed below ground level.

Not that Laurie had to engage too directly with the tasks. He soon learnt from the Sergeant that his role was to protect the Arab orderlies, whose unfortunate job it was to dig out the excrement and load it onto the carts for dispatch.

At least three men of varying ages worked the shift each night. Startlingly to Laurie, two young boys no older than his seven-year-old back home, accompanied them. None of them appeared to be dressed in a way suitable for such a task, adorned as they were with white head caps, lightweight cotton tunics, billowing trousers cut to the knee, and simple sandals. The boys were barefoot.

The men methodically scooped up the surface layers using primitive wooden shovels and rakes, heaving the content onto the waggon through its open side. The boys then cleaned up and loaded the droppings, a task they performed with meticulous efficiency, as if gathering slivers of precious jewellery. Occasionally, the men would burrow deeper into the hard core of the pit, an effort requiring their full collaboration, and this could take time. But for the most part, forty-five minutes or so provided for two fullyladen carts.

Job done, Laurie then escorted the party across a deserted Midan Bab El Hadid, with its large ornate spaces, intersecting roads and tramlines, and on to the railway station at Pont Limoun a hundred yards or so away. There, the cargo was transferred to the safe keeping of a small party of Egyptian railway officials working for the British, for onward transport by rail to the Nile delta. Nothing, it seemed, was to be left as waste.

"Remember, even if you lot fail as soldiers, at least you'll have had the satisfaction of knowing that you have helped fertilise the desert," as Captain Hillary had put it, following one of his many post-drill admonishments.

There was no saluting or formality in the handover. To the contrary, there was a surliness about the officials that troubled Laurie. The team of pressed orderlies then scuttled off into the night, leaving Laurie on his own to return to the barracks at a pace reasonable enough as not to betray his fear, and in good time before lights out.

In those early days in Cairo when everything was new and strange, he cared little for the sights he witnessed or the relativities of life between the locals and the men.

"Use your rifle the first instance you sense danger; never trust an Arab," Sergeant Wirrall had warned him.

But within his subconscious, the troubling unfairness of it all was beginning to register.

CHAPTER 2

To Mrs E Laurie, Police Station, Kempsey, Nr Worcester, England.
Dearest Eve,
Arrived safely here at barracks in Cairo, having spent a few weeks in camp on the coast in Alexandria. The picture is of the square where we are stationed and the barracks. I have put an 'X' by my quarters.

It is a rum place for sure. There are sights here that would turn your stomach. I am well and managing on the rations. The men seem a solid bunch and I've a good friend in Nooney. He's from New Zealand – can you believe it?

We have just received our khaki uniforms, which are a great help in the heat, and we work hard on duties. We must be the best drilled company in the British Army. I am not sure where I am likely to settle, but will write with the address once I know.

I am longing to hear from you all.
God bless you my darling.
Ever yours my dearest love,
Thomas.

As Laurie finished crafting his message on the back of the Carte Postale image of Midan Bab El Hadid, the blackness that had eased since his punishment detail returned. It was an official rest day for the Company, but he was sitting alone in the mess, most of the men having left for R & R in town.

The isolation that accompanied a policeman had pursued him to this new continent. Back home it was frowned upon to form attachments beyond those of your work colleagues, lest it led to compromise. Similar strictures held for his wife and children. That they would also be lonely and in desperate need without him merely served to deepen his depression.

He wasn't naturally given to emotional expression or self-pity and so the water in his eyes was a betrayal.

"You alright, mate?"

Laurie flinched. He recognised the voice, but didn't turn for fear his weakness would be construed.

"Laurie, are you alright?"

"Oh, hello, Nooney, thought you'd gone into town with the others."

"No chance, mate. I've got more sense than to hang around with that lot. They'll be drunk in an hour and then who knows what?"

He was an articulate man, though his antipodean bonhomie had initially thrown Laurie. As a Lance Corporal he was senior to him, so why the friendly banter? Nobody else ever called him 'mate'. But Laurie had quickly learnt to be at ease in his company, not least as he seemed sincere and honourable, and there was an inspiring wisdom about him. Nooney, for his part, intuitively knew Laurie was wrapped in struggle.

"Reckon a good few might end up on latrines duties by dusk," he said, and Laurie turned fully round to see Nooney's wink. They both smiled.

"I mean, mate, the smell when you got back to barracks after shovelling all that…"

"Come off it Nooney, everyone was far gone by the time I turned in. I had to creep around so as not to wake anybody."

"No mate, I was there and I promise you we weren't 'far gone' as you put it. We were all under the blanket with nose pegs on. You smelt worse than a mummy's arse."

They both burst out laughing.

"Come to think of it," continued Nooney, "you'll now be such an encouragement to the blokes to behave, that instead of going to the bars and seeking out the joys of Cairo, they'll all be visiting the library at the YMCA. They'll come back smelling of roses and spouting sonnets."

Nooney was indeed a tonic. He was also intelligent and well-read. Laurie had already enjoyed jousts with him about life, love and literature. At first Laurie's combative mind had been confronted by one that seemed much sharper. Back home he'd rarely experienced, let alone welcomed, a subsidiary role in matters of opinion. But with Nooney it was different. There was no need for winners. Here was a man who shared his mind but who also listened, a man whose unassuming ways brought out the best in him.

"You're right, I must have smelt. But just a bit, Nooney, just a bit."

"Yeah, but the thing is Laurie, which bit, mate?"

"Anyhow, down to business so to speak," he continued, changing the tone, "I've got a patrol detail in a few hours and usually I'm out in the square with three of the men. You've never been lucky enough to share that joy in my company, so I thought that as you're just kicking your feet here you could do something more useful and join me."

"But it's my rest time."

"Don't look to me like you're much enjoying it, and anyhow, you can earn a few more shekels to help maintain the King's Empire." Laurie was cheered by this irreverence.

"I've no desire, from what I'm beginning to see of His Majesty's dominions, to wish to encourage that habit."

"No, mate, but the money for your extra duties will be useful at home, and there'll be more where that comes from." Nooney, as ever, was entirely sensible in his practicality.

"After all, what the hell are you going to do for the rest of the day, knit a sweater?"

"Well, as you ask so nicely," replied Laurie with a gentle glare. "OK, fine. Where do we meet for briefing?" There was a short pause.

"Er…, well, the problem you see is that Dewey, Hinds and Bonejangler, the three assigned to me today, they're all down with the belly in sick bay. Wasn't told until the rest of the men had gone into town. There's no way I'm asking Captain Hillary to lend me reinforcements from the poor buggers on drill practice this afternoon."

"That's great, Nooney. You want me to join you because there's no one else, plus, we'll be half the size of the normal patrol?"

"Not quite, Laurie. As I see it, you're worth two of any man. Anyway, it's an opportunity to gain some great learning from me without the complications of any accompanying dimwits."

They both burst out laughing again. *What the hell?* thought Laurie.

"Alright, Nooney, you've convinced me."

"Be kitted by four."

"And the briefing?"

"Come off it. We'll have that whilst we walk across the square together."

"In strict order, of course. Don't want the locals taking a fancy." Laurie was still keen for that assurance, at least.

"In strict order, mate."

Ten minutes before the due time, Laurie was standing at the appointed place, dressed in his khaki uniform and pith helmet, ready for the patrol. For him, to be on time was to be ahead of it. He detested lateness in others. It represented a sloppiness of mind that slowly infected every aspect of a life. Like alcohol and self-absorption, it must be strictly rationed and if possible, avoided altogether. His boots were clean to the point of specular brilliance, though the dust and sand of the square would soon change that. His rifle was strapped across his shoulder, his tunic, shorts and knee socks immaculate. He and Nooney would cut an impressive and authoritative pair over the next few hours.

That this was needed was beyond doubt. As he looked out from the sentry post behind the main gates, all he surveyed seemed chaotic. The square was bursting into life once more, after the relative calm that had descended during the hottest part of the day. Dozens of market stalls were setting up, selling exotic fruits, unrecognisable foodstuffs, cotton goods, carpets, clothing and livestock. Traders were beginning to vie noisily with each other; there were innumerable water sellers entreating passers-by to their services, and barbers tending to the heads of those who sat cross-legged at their feet. Nearer to his vantage point, he could make out a wide paved area, where goats were herded and penned for sale, and where their elderly minders huddled, no doubt discussing the day's prospects just as they'd done for many years past.

There was a bitter smell of coffee drifting from stalls stacked around the perimeter of the square and down along the side roads and alleyways, accompanied by a deep aromatic perfume of sweet tobacco from the shisha pipes. There were women, but they seemed a minority within the crowd and, to his unacquainted eye, there was a degree of uniformity to their appearance. They were clothed for the most part in long, dark robes, faces barely visible, and were generally accompanied by small children whose job appeared to be to help carry the day's purchases. Some of the women used their heads to balance bowls of food and goods, a task they performed with apparent ease, though all quite shocking to Laurie's way of thinking.

But what really stood out was the enormous number of donkeys tethered to trees, posts and iron stands as far as the eye could see. There appeared to be some organisation in this, though it was hard to fathom. The carts they'd borne were either stationed on their ends protecting a flimsy stall, or were propped up by haphazard cane work and operating as a makeshift shop. As people started to mill around, the cumulative effect from a distance was dizzyingly distracting, almost as if an ethereal human hive had been damaged and its workers were toiling convulsively to enable repairs.

Then occasionally into this scene strolled a European male or two dressed in fully suited civvies with an accompanying straw boater, either deep in thought or animated discussion. It was as if they were wandering along a street in the middle of Worcester. Some boarded one of the many trams that stopped in the square, using them as they would back home for carriage to the bank or office. Others strode with the purposeful confidence of the colonialist, on route to who knows where.

As anomalous as this seemed, it did rather contradict the warnings about safety the men had consistently received since arriving. What he actually saw before him were people getting on with their lives and just trying to exist, despite the presence of the barracks and the imposed sense of British order. For the briefest moment, he wondered how he'd react in their position of poverty and subservience. Would he be so accepting? And were the British really there to save the Arabs from the Ottoman, and bring them the advantages of the Empire?

Right on time Nooney appeared, also immaculately attired in his majesty's uniform and eager to get going. He nodded to Laurie, and they lined up and headed to the gate.

"Usual step, brisk, purposeful; just follow me."

He nodded towards marble steps and what appeared to be a fountain some fifty yards away. Whilst the area around it was ablaze with activity, this space was relatively free of bodies.

"First task, show them we're serious, so look the part. When we get there, anyone on that site we remove under threat of arrest. It's used during feasts and festivals for national meetings and proclamations and has been a source of unrest, so we keep those with no official authority well away."

"What happens after we leave?"

"Generally once we're out of sight those who were there creep back. But what matters is the threat we pose, so keep a look of coldness in the eye."

"Coldness?"

"You know, the sort of cautious indifference that appears on an Englishman's face when they're asked for an opinion."

Laurie thought to counter but they were off with the gate closed firmly behind them, out into the heat and dryness of the square.

"Then we'll go over by the animal quartering at the railway station to inspect a few of the passes."

Nooney was talking, eyes fixed ahead, with both men in quick march formation. To Laurie's amazement, no one seemed to be paying them any attention. It was as if they were as normal to the daily routine of the square as the donkeys.

"Passes?"

"Yep, every donkey handler has to have a pass to trade and quarter in the square: Cairo law. We get establishment reward for monitoring it, keeping order, though the Arab traders don't always like us for it."

They were nearing their first objective and a few hawkers could be seen rapidly gathering their goods and scarpering.

"Establishment reward? What do you mean?"

"Taxes, mate. We're making sure these people pay their taxes to our people."

"Our people?"

"You know, the Sultan and his friends in government and business."

"What are you saying, Nooney?"

"Later, mate, let's sort this out first."

They walked towards a small crowd gathered on the sun-browned lawn area bordering the limestone and marble heart of the square. To Laurie's surprise, the formal area beyond was nothing more than a raised platform accessed by wide steps, though admittedly a good vantage point from which to view across the whole of Midan Bab El Hadid. There were nervous looks as the two British soldiers approached the grouping. It parted to reveal a tall, bearded middle-aged man, dressed flamboyantly in flowing white robes and adorned with multi-coloured cotton scarves. He appeared to be in the middle of an elaborate performance and was in conversation with a performing monkey sat on the back end of a miniature black donkey. To his left was a tiny goat, balancing improbably on top of a bottle. Sat obediently to the rear, was a three-legged dog wearing a fez. So engaged was he by his profession that he hadn't initially noticed the intrusion by men in uniform, and the success of his work was obvious from the notes and coins that lay in the basket beside the dog.

"*Sabaah alkhayr*, Manoli," said Nooney. Both the performer and Laurie blinked in shock. "*Kayfa haluk?*"

The man stopped and turned to Nooney, a broad smile of recognition spreading across his face. He said something back and Nooney grinned.

"This is Manoli," continued Nooney, "and these are his children." He waved his hand towards the animals.

"He's a regular here, brilliant act, and I've told him before that when this lot finishes, I'm going to be his agent back in Auckland."

Laurie was open-mouthed. This was an Arab, and Nooney, unlike most of the troop, seemed amiably disposed toward him. Not only that, he also spoke his language.

"Don't worry," said Nooney, who could see what Laurie was thinking, "all I really said was good morning mate and how are you doing? Don't cost us anything, he's a good bloke."

The man smiled and bowed his head towards Laurie.

"*As-salam ayakom.*"

"He's wishing you peace, mate. We could all do with some of that."

After a few more minutes of animated discussion, Nooney and Laurie moved away, bowing graciously as they did so, and the crowd re-converged, eager for the show to continue.

"What about his permit?" said Laurie. "Shouldn't we have checked it? I mean, I know he had a smaller donkey, but it was a donkey, nevertheless."

Nooney shot him the gentle but kindly 'are you a fool or what?' look with which Laurie had become familiar, and they moved on towards the now empty steps and promontory that overlooked the square, where they stood for a few minutes, observing in silence.

"You see, Laurie, he's someone to be admired." Laurie was still confused.

"He's bloody good at what he does, keeps out of trouble, and is popular. What on earth would be the point of finding out he hasn't got a permit?"

"But those are the rules, Nooney, break them for one and you ruin them for all."

"That's the policeman in you, mate. I'm a teacher back home. You learn very quickly that rules need to be applied with a dainty shaving brush rather than a great big bloody broom."

Laurie was still puzzled.

"Look down there."

The three-legged dog was now using the donkey as an obstacle course, running between its legs and jumping up onto its back, then balancing on its one hind leg.

"Happy people are good for us all. And what's more, there's no bugger up here for us to arrest and annoy. They saw us coming, I made sure of that, and chatting to Manoli gave others the time to clear off. We avoided a confrontation."

"So we let them get away with it?"

"No, Laurie, we used our resources correctly and saved them for the important battles."

He had a point, thought Laurie, and though it conflicted with his policing experience, he couldn't help respecting the man.

They remained for a little while longer, surveying the human panorama, swatting midges, and pulling their uniforms away from their wet skin. Then as they started to descend, a fracas developed at one of the donkey ranks. The shouting quickly became louder, aggressive even, and soon pushing and a scuffle began.

"Quick, mate."

Nooney led off at a sprint and by the time they were close, a full-scale brawl was developing. Nooney shouted something in Arabic and momentarily there was a pause in the action. Unlike in the earlier meeting with Manoli, this crowd wasn't about to disperse, and Laurie could see that even with Nooney's charms, the situation was becoming threatening. He'd seen enough fights in his time to know how these incidents escalated, though he'd not experienced the minacious cursing toward them that was now apparent.

In the enfolding rage, some were pointing towards a solitary waggon under which two terrified youngsters were hiding. Laurie recognised them instantly. They were the boys from his punishment detail. A short distance away, a melee had developed. Blows were being landed on a man who looked remarkably like one of those who'd loaded the sewage carts on those nights.

The situation was about to boil over. Nooney was reasoning with the assailants but without success. Both he and Laurie were being shouted and spat at. Instinctively Laurie felt compelled to act, pulling his rifle from his shoulder. Those closest immediately moved back, but in their fury the aggressors continued to reign in fists and feet on the petrified victim. Laurie leant back and shot into the air. The shock of the crack from the rifle barrel brought an instant transformation. There were gasps, a good few cowered, some ran, whilst others glared defiantly. But the fighting stopped and a wide circle formed around the scene. Everyone apart from the semi-comatose victim looked at Laurie.

"No," he shouted, waving an arm forcefully, taking care to point the rifle above the heads of the crowd, as non-aggressively as he could.

"*La',*" translated Nooney, recovering his entanglement and now making calming gestures.

For a brief moment there was a silent standoff. Then the man on the floor groaned and mumbled something towards Nooney. A sudden realisation dawned.

"He works for us, Nooney, on the carts. Yes, I'm sure he's one of the men I guarded when I was doing the punishment detail. Those two as well." He pointed to the terrified boys.

Nooney nodded and bent down next to the agitated victim, and engaged in a brief and awkward exchange with him and his assailants.

"As far as I can tell, they claim he's selling dodgy donkey excrement from his cart. Is this madness or what?"

The man, afflicted as he was by his injuries, was struggling to sit upright. He grunted something again, though whatever it was it merely served to inflame things.

"He seems to be saying there's been a mistake. Hard to fathom this one. What's he mean, mistake?"

Laurie thought for a moment, though in the circumstances there was little time for hesitation. In a pub brawl, he always chose a course of action that singled out the weakest culprit, giving cover and saving grace to the real thugs. They could then be picked off later following reinforcements, and a confession or two harnessed. So he was drawn in an instant to the injured victim, and the likelihood that some particular artifice had inflamed the normal protocols of trade within the square.

"Think I might have it, Nooney. I suspect he's taking some of the barracks' offering and mixing it with the donkey stuff this lot really want."

Both men looked towards each other.

"This could be awkward, mate. Impurities in the donkey offering. Something of a first for us, hey?"

"Wish I could laugh, Nooney, but we're in a jam."

"Bit of an understatement, mate. Any ideas?"

Laurie stood emotionless, apparently untroubled, conveying an impressive authority towards the crowd and his colleague that confounded their true predicament.

"Arrest the man on the floor and the two boys for stealing. Then we save them and us from a beating or worse."

"And if that fails?"

"We'll have to use whatever authority the nineteen bullets left in our two rifles give us."

Nooney nodded and motioned as clearly as he could to the injured man and the boys that they were to be arrested. This seemed to go down well with the crowd, given the surprised looks. Even the chief protagonists appeared startled. The man himself protested at first, but once he recognised that Laurie was also indicating this course of action he complied, staggering as best he could onto his feet. He signalled to the boys, and they scuttled from the safety of the waggon to help steady him, taking advantage of the safest and probably only option of escape from their predicament.

Nooney placed his arm on the man's shoulder and pushed him forward. He then un-harnessed his rifle and held it towards him, taking care by this action to draw the sting of the crowd. Laurie formed in behind him, indicating to the boys to stay close, and in this tenuous association they began to walk slowly between the parting crowd and back towards the barracks.

After some twenty paces or so of distance from the agitated gathering, there was a momentary feeling of relief. They were heading cautiously, yet with growing confidence, away from a situation that could have escalated beyond control. But that was to underestimate the capacity of Captain Hillary.

Coming towards them and on the run with rifles drawn, were at least twenty men from the Company, led somewhere from behind the pack by the Captain himself. He was blowing his whistle and shouting instructions. To the front was Sergeant Wirrall, bent towards what had been the affray and rumbling along like a wayward beer-barrel. They must have heard the commotion in the square, and were coming to establish order.

"Oh, no," groaned Nooney, "just what we bloody well need."

The sight of the British Army seemed to have the opposite effect upon the crowd to that intended. The pugilists from the incident, far from retreating, formed up and began to run to confront it. Many of the other otherwise peaceful occupants of the square also moved in solidarity towards the estimated site of engagement between the two groups, as no matter what the cause of the congress, they had little to thank the British for.

"This bugger can't run," shouted Nooney, nodding at the injured prisoner, a fact already very apparent to Laurie.

"We'll have to stop, Nooney. The boys are terrified as well."

"Maybe not." Nooney replied, his voice now raised, "better to be facing our own lot than be dragged back amongst the locals."

"But he's had it, Nooney. If we leave him they'll kill him."

Nooney slowed and looked over his shoulder at Laurie.

"We gave them our word Nooney," implored Laurie, and they stopped.

"You're right, mate."

At that moment, a volley of shots whistled over their heads. This was the first time in the King's service that either man had been shot at, and they and their prisoner party fell to the ground. When they looked up, they saw that the troop had formed a defensive party of two rows, the front one kneeling with bayonets drawn and the back one standing, their rifles trained on the crowd, most of whom by now were also prostrate just a short distance behind them.

"Bloody hell, shot at by our own lot," said Nooney, barely audible, but shocked and enraged.

"So much for fearing the enemy, then?"

"Lie still, you two men."

There was a shout from somewhere behind the two Company rows, presumably from Hillary, though they still couldn't make him out.

"You heard the Captain, you two, lie still," shouted Sergeant Wirrall, more visibly central.

But the instruction hadn't travelled to the Arab hard core who, emboldened by the belief that the British would not shoot in cold blood, were now standing again, inching towards the injured man who'd robbed them. If there was to be justice, they, not the British, would dispense it.

"Take aim, men," shouted Hillary, followed by the sound of rifles engaging and pointing above the fallen guard party toward the chests of the approaching crowd.

"When I give the order, fire directly into the mob. Avoid any children and old men."

From their flattened positions, Laurie and Nooney could hardly believe their ears. They had the matter under control until the overzealous appearance of the Captain and his men. His actions were about to end lives and encourage a riot, and for what: a cartload of contraband manure?

Laurie couldn't contain himself. He knew his contribution would be unwelcome, but the obligatory requirement to remain mute when a senior officer spoke had yet to fully form within him.

"Private Laurie, sir. The situation's under control, sir." There was a short hesitation before the Captain responded.

"Well my word, it's you again 'Private Laurie sir', I might have known. What an imbecile you are. No wonder this mess has happened."

"No, sir, it really will be alright if—"

"Shut it, Laurie and lie flat. On the count of three, men."

The mob that Hillary referred to was still walking forward, though more cautiously now, their confidence diminished, as if confused by the dialogue between the British.

"One…"

"He's really going to do it…" said Nooney, pale with shock.

"Of course he's not," hissed Laurie, "he's not going to shoot innocent people."

"Two…"

"He is," retorted Nooney, his face now contorted in disbelief.

"Sir, the matter is under control."

Laurie leapt to his feet, facing the now revealed Captain Hillary, less than twenty yards away. He could see his bulging eyes and the purple rage rolling across his cheeks.

"Lie down, man, or you'll be shot."

Laurie ignored him and turned towards the Arabs who were now stationary, frozen by the sudden reality of their imminent death. He signalled to them with his arms that they should stay calm, he bowed his head and touched his heart, whilst all the time behind him Captain Hillary ranted.

Nooney also stood and joined him, and in his broken Arabic, gave further reassurance. Whether it was that or the sudden recognition and fear in the face of the overwhelming odds, it nevertheless seemed to do the trick. The main protagonists began to disband, heading back towards their donkeys, muttering obscenities. With it, the interest from the larger crowd that had gathered also evaporated and they too began to move away.

Within a few short moments the incident was over, and the life of the square returned to a semblance of normality. The Captain however, continued to spew vitriol, adding Nooney as a recipient to the list of punishments to come. It was left to Sergeant Wirrall to stand the men down, after which he looked at Laurie and shook his head.

"You know where to report."

"Yes, Sergeant."

"You as well, Nooney: soon as you've sorted the charges out for that lot." He pointed to the group the two men had arrested, shook his head again, and followed the Company back to the barracks.

The injured Arab struggled back to his feet, with gentle help from the two boys.

"*Shukran, shukran.*"

"What does he want?" asked Laurie.

"He said, thank you."

Late the next afternoon, Laurie was waiting in the ante-room outside the Captain's office. He'd expected to attend along with Nooney, but there was no sight of him. Indeed, since the events of the previous afternoon, he'd been largely elusive.

"No problem, mate," he'd replied when Laurie had apologised. "I'd do the same thing again. What you did was right." But after that, he was gone, seemingly unwilling to talk more.

The door to the office opened, and Sergeant Wirrall appeared.

"Private Laurie. Here, now." Wirrall's gentle side had taken a break.

Laurie marched into the room as bid, standing to attention in front of the desk, behind which centre-stage was Captain Hillary. To Hillary's right was an officer Laurie didn't immediately recognise, not least because of the utter distraction that seated to his other side was none other than Brigadier Regis-Templeton.

The Captain began to address Laurie, but the gravity of his impending doom signalled by the presence of his Commanding Officer temporarily overwhelmed. He was to be shot at dawn by his own side for protecting innocent Arabs. And all because of manure.

"Well?"

"Sir?"

Laurie's obdurate madness interceded once more as he played for time to gather his thoughts.

"Well, man?" repeated Hillary, though to similar effect.

"Laurie. Speak up man, damn you." He banged the desk with his stick.

Everyone jumped, even Sergeant Wirrall who'd been so conditioned to the Captain's behaviour.

The Brigadier though, was less amused and gave Hillary a disapproving look.

"Captain Hillary, if you don't mind…"

"Of course, sir…" Hillary hesitated, adjusted his cap, and continued.

"The actions you took in the square yesterday endangered the life of my men. They were foolhardy and potentially disastrous. What's more, you disobeyed my order."

His face was reddening as he warmed to the task.

"Put simply, you are an insolent troublemaker, a renegade, the sort we can well do without." *Bloody hell*, thought Laurie, he really was going to be shot.

"In your short time here, you've already undertaken a week's punishment detail, but all that seems to have done is to bring you closer to the enemy." There was a pause, and then the repeated invite from the Captain.

"Well? Speak, man."

"Sir… closer to the enemy, sir?" *What on earth did he mean?*

"Yes, Laurie, the enemy, your bloody Arab friends, the ones you stood in front of our rifles for, the ones who now think that they can have a friendly chat the next time we order them to do something."

Unhinged though Laurie now viewed the Captain to be, a continuing life remained distinctly preferable to an untimely death. He would need careful words.

"Sir, the Commanding Officer," and he nodded respectfully towards Regis-Templeton, "reminded us when we first arrived that the Ottoman, not the Hun, would be our prime foe here in Egypt."

"The Ottoman?" raged Hillary.

"Yes, sir, and I'm looking forward to facing them in battle. But…"

"But what, man?"

"But no one said anything about the Arabs, sir." There was a silence.

"I'm guessing that harming Arabs on their own patch, sir, in a country where as you've said, we're here to help, well that might be just be counter-productive."

This was too much for the Captain.

"You arrogant little toerag. A few months in uniform and you think you know it do you? You've been told time and time again; never trust an Arab. If in doubt, shoot first and then consider. Any other way will cost us lives. Don't you understand that, man?"

"We lost no lives yesterday, sir, neither us nor the Arabs."

Captain Hillary stared at him, the exertions of his fury reflected by the tell-tale moistening of his upper lip.

"Well, consider this Laurie. In the month before you arrived on this continent and settled into your spacious quarters, three men from the Regiment were killed in cold blood by Arabs they thought they were helping, and not so very far from where your little affair was happening yesterday. So had we not had the sense to see what was going on, do you really think that you and Nooney, let alone those pathetic low lives you were guarding, would have made it back to barracks?"

He had a point, thought Laurie, and clearly this showed.

"Exactly," shouted the Captain, now standing and prodding his stick into Laurie's chest.

"You're a disgrace, Laurie, that's what you are, a self-opinionated, unreliable, contemptible halfwit. Why I've half a mind to horse-whip you, here and now."

Suddenly, Regis-Templeton started to cough uncontrollably and Hillary's tirade abruptly ceased, as both he and Sergeant Wirrall scrambled to find a glass of water. After a moment or so, the Brigadier regained his composure and apologised for the interruption. He made no reference to the cause, but everyone recognised the effects of the gas he'd suffered on the Western Front.

"I'm so sorry, this cough seems to be no respecter of territory."

Despite his own troubling circumstances, Laurie found it impossible not to admire him. Not an ounce of self-pity. No pomposity. No apparent desire in the way he spoke to elevate himself from those around him.

"...but at least the interruption it caused gives me and Colonel Lowthian," he motioned to his fellow officer, "the opportunity to bring some clarity to this situation."

Laurie glanced at the officer again; there was still something he couldn't quite place.

"These are indeed difficult times, and in some ways, Private Laurie, you saw that for yourself yesterday. If we are to defend Egypt against the Ottoman, then you are right in your inference that we need our Arab hosts on board." Captain Hillary made a gentle though involuntary movement in his chair.

"As you will have realised by now, knowing whom we can trust, even amongst our own, is a devilish game, for which we currently seem pretty poorly equipped. Colonel Lowthian, will you please explain."

"Thank you, sir."

They were three simple words, but they hit Laurie like a shovel to the face. The things that had troubled that he couldn't quite place, well now he'd heard the voice of course he understood. Contradictory though this was to his internalised order of the world, the officer wearing the Colonel's uniform was in fact audibly, physically even, most definitely a woman.

She fixed Laurie directly with eyes that betrayed any predictive intent. Her hair was pulled back, tied tightly below the cap, her face fine featured and porcelain-like despite the rigours of the Egyptian heat. She spoke with a crisp assurance.

"I'll be brief, Laurie, you're a policeman back home?" Laurie blinked, still confused.

"Yes, sir."

"Yes, ma'am, you idiot," boomed a despairing Hillary.

She continued to look straight ahead at Laurie, though clearly irritated by the intervention.

"And from your records, a trustworthy one."

"Yes, ma'am."

"Good. We're in need of soldiers we can trust, who think on their feet and have a good brain. We need police here Laurie, not just for our own men and those from the Empire, but to help within Cairo and beyond." *Bloody hell*, thought Laurie, now paddling in deeper confusion.

"I've seen enough to think you can be a valuable asset."

Asset, seen enough… what…?

Then Laurie remembered the medic or administrator woman he'd seen amongst the officers at the men's first briefing in Cairo… this was, in fact, her. She was also the one standing quietly in the shadows and listening to his dressing down afterwards, by Captain Hillary.

"You are to be assigned to the MFP, the Military Foot Patrol. This means you will need a rank to reinforce your status, so you are to become a Lance Corporal."

What? A moment ago he was in fear of court martial, but now he faced promotion?

"You will report ultimately to me in the Arab Bureau section of the Cairo Intelligence Department. Much of your work will be in plain clothes and, to all intents and purposes, you will appear to be a British businessman. For official purposes only, you will remain a part of your Regiment, and will respect the command of Captain Hillary."

She maintained her gaze for a moment, searching for further insights into Laurie's mind, even though she was satisfied she'd already seen enough.

"Do you understand?" Laurie nodded, still stifled by the turn of events.

Captain Hillary, on the other hand, appeared far from convinced. It seemed that he hadn't been a party to the decision-making.

"Prepare the necessary paperwork, Captain, and have it together with Laurie at the Provost Marshall's GHQ at 2 pm tomorrow."

"With respect, ma'am, Laurie has shown himself to be both antagonistic and downright disobedient, and for the sake of the other men should be—"

"Punished severely?" she said, cutting him short.

"Enough, Captain Hillary." She turned to face him squarely, pinioning his eyes within their sockets.

"'With respect', you say. I've lost count of the times I've heard that said to me. It has invariably meant exactly the opposite. What will really count for 'the sake of the other men' as you put it, is that their talents are used to good effect. Tomorrow 2 pm, with no further word on what is now a secret matter. Do you understand?"

"Ma'am," replied the Captain, moving awkwardly around his seat.

With that, the dazed Laurie was marched out of the office and back through the ante-room by Sergeant Wirrall.

"Lucky boy, hey?"

"Sergeant?"

"MFP and now the Arab Bureau; not long been up and running have that lot. So you're pretty much in from the start, Laurie."

"I don't understand any of this, Sergeant."

"Neither do I, Laurie, nor do I want to. What I do know is that they've got a right bunch of odd types working for them; all sorts there are so I've heard." He smiled.

"So don't worry, you'll get along just fine."

CHAPTER 3

The Placa De L'Esglesia in the centre of the village of Es Migjorn Roca was well used to shows of power. Menorcans had been imperiously subjected since Phoenician times. Greeks, Romans, Turks, the French, the British, and now once more the Spanish, had marched across their lands, used their harbours, and built forts. Such invasive force was customarily accompanied by summary judgement, persecution and repressive taxation, exercised at will by the authoritative stamp of superior weaponry over the liberality of reason.

Llucia Quintana wielded her power differently. Today, this meant goats. On a beautiful Mediterranean spring morning and just before the heat, she stood on the small flight of steps that led to the church of Sant Cristofol, surveying one of her herds. She could have used her shepherds to bring them back from the plateau straddling the road to Alaior, but that wasn't for her. She needed the physical connection with the land and stock that had been so hard won. Neither did she need to lead them through the heart of the village. The drover track to the east would have been easier and connected with the lane to her farm at Turo Vell, a mile further south. But today of all days was one to engage with the land she adored, the animals she loved, and the people who owed.

"Good morning, *Señora* Quintana."

She turned her head to see the tall and haunted figure of the village padre. Although little more than thirty years of age he was stooped, fragile of frame, and visibly burdened. His dark robes dirtied by neglect and poor aim, hung off him as if attempting escape. Whilst the greeting was unusually bright, the tortured face of Alvaro Marin betrayed his inner self, and this pleased Llucia Quintana.

"Good morning, Alvaro, I am so pleased to see you."

She loved to ignore his title and to parry his insincerity.

The padre pointed towards her goats, now tightly corralled into the Placa by three sheepdogs guarding the only exits.

"Your flock…" he began, oblivious of any irony.

The nearest dog thinking his hand to be a threat, nosed towards him baring its teeth. Startled, he jumped backward.

"…they seem well trained."

"The dogs or the goats?"

"The dogs, of course."

He looked at her, already feeling half-exhausted by the encounter.

"Well, the goats may remind you of your congregation at Morning Mass."

"*Señora*, please…"

"But of course, there are well over a hundred goats in front of you here, at least twice as many as you normally cope with."

"*Señora*…"

"Though the dogs, well, I agree, like you they are trained."

His mouth started to dry.

"They threaten with their certainty," she continued, "but the real skill is in the way they affect the mind of each goat. If just ten of the goats thought for themselves, there would be anarchy. They might find greener pasture, freedom, a better life, the others might follow, and then where would we be?"

She was sure he understood but as ever in her company his face retained its muted expression.

"*Señora* Quintana, please, I am acquainted with your reticence in holy matters but I beg, do not damn us all."

He too knew how to pierce, and she smiled.

"Shall we...?"

He signalled to the doorway, and she followed him through it and into the cool, dark interior of the church. They paused for a while, allowing their eyes to accommodate to the change, ensuring an unwitting moment of shared and silent contemplation; he, troubled by the spiritual confrontation she unfailingly brought; she focussed solely upon the business.

"Would you like to take my confession?"

The padre looked at her blankly. This was the last thing she wanted.

"If you wish."

"Let's sit here awhile then, in the family pews rather than inside that filthy box of yours, and study the walls."

"The walls?"

By now, the darkness had lifted. The church was brightly whitewashed and airy, a welcoming space completely lacking the morbidity she associated with other traditional buildings. Four or five rows ahead of them and high in the chancel hung an imposing wooden crucifix. It framed a classical altar below, on which stood a large marble statue of St Cristofol, bearing the weight of a traveller upon his shoulders.

"These images on the walls," she said as she pointed towards the altar, "they speak to me every day. No matter where I am, what I do, I think of them."

"And what do they tell you?"

"That we all need something to trust beyond ourselves, beyond people."

The padre sensed where this was going. Normally, he welcomed personal revelation, but he knew too much about *Señora* Quintata, who she was, what had happened to her and the binds that held him, to be in the least sense comfortable.

"You know of a very powerful church man, now in Palma, who was influential in this very building thirty years ago."

"*Señora*, please..."

"He took me in when I was vulnerable, looked after me, helped provide for what was left of me and my family after the destruction of our farm."

"*Señora*, I understand that what proceeded was wrong..."

"Wrong?" she spat, "I came to think of that man as love. He was kind, he held me up, taught me to think for myself, to be confident."

There was a silence.

"And then I found out it was he who had witnessed the attack on my family, sat by as it happened, so that the church, this church, many others, might benefit from our lands."

"*Señora*, I know that…"

"…and that the love he had encouraged me to find, beyond all the hatred, just like his promises about justice, about righteousness, were no more than words that had been practiced upon others, their families, before me and no doubt since."

There was another moment of quietness, this time congealed in threat and rancour.

"*Señora*, he is one man. He is not the body of this church. He has confessed. He remains a man of holiness and serves his people faithfully."

Llucia stared into his eyes. She no longer felt rage at the evil that had happened, or at the apologetic blandishments made on its behalf. Such feelings had long passed, consigned less they possess her to a locked inner draw. No, her expectations of others were now limited by what she could control in them, and in the padre she therefore had the greatest of confidence.

"Those images…" and she motioned at the chancel, "…they give me strength to see beyond the words, the actions of others, towards an inner peace. They feed my soul, Alvaro."

He ignored her gaze and looked ahead.

"It was those that encouraged me to adorn this building with the objects that are hanging here, the treasures stored within its vaults that would otherwise be lost to civilisation for good."

"No, *Señora*, no…"

"…and I am here to tell you, Alvaro, to prepare in the months ahead for the acceptance of a work so ornate, so valuable, that once sold will enable your precious flock to double the size of this building. In fact, so precious that every church on the island will be able to ring out the joy on their new bells, build their schools, pay their clergy."

The padre held his head in his hands, and gently slumped forward.

"It is not a large painting but will need to be prominently hung and in plain sight, an asset for your congregation to admire, referred to even during your long sermons, something for which you have developed quite a reputation."

"This is further unworthiness…" replied the padre mumbling from behind his hands, "…I cannot… will not continue to allow this…"

"Of course you will. I pay for you. I pay you well. You are my very special little Alvaro Marin."

She patted his head.

"And you have been so helpful since you arrived, so… faithful to me, something I shall not forget."

"But this is stealing, yet again…"

"Of course not; this is repatriation. The war is unkind to us all and obeys no sovereign. Nevertheless, it provides opportunities, reminders of the need to be prudent, to hang on and plan for the good times. You, more than any of us, will know that the people need food in their belly and roofs above them. They need jobs. They clamour for forgiveness, for affirmation. Those images hanging from the wall, give them… give me, the strength to provide for that."

The padre shook his head. His position was hopeless.

"And there is the little matter of the episcopacy of Palma. Can you imagine what would happen if my suffering was to come to light? Imagine all the heads that would lop and fall, all the work of those many good people that would unravel, the destitution that would arise… it hardly bears thinking about."

She stood up gently, stretched her shoulders a little, and began to move away leaving the padre with his thoughts.

"Rest for a moment, why don't you?"

She rose and began to wander around the building, examining the artefacts, pictures and collections with the focussed absorption and affection of a concerned curator. When she returned some twenty minutes or so later, the padre was still flopped, but this time seemingly deep in prayer. She nudged his side and he slowly raised his head, troubled eyes revealing dried tears.

"Thank you, Alvaro, I am touched."

"*Señora?*"

"My son's poetry; you have it in your library."

He nodded his head. "It is a gift that he has, and which I am proud to hold here for all to see."

"Even so, that is generous of you."

"It is beautiful, sincere… and it is legitimate."

She moved down next to his ear, as if to confide. "Legitimate? You of all people talk to me of legitimate?"

She nodded her head and tutted.

"Please, Padre," she said, now staring intently at him and placing her hand upon his shoulder, "be more careful with yourself, with your thoughts, with what you say. Only you and the innocent of Palma know directly of our arrangements. In time, the church will come to see your talents for what they are, and reward you, too. But for now, you are useful here…"

She continued her gaze for a moment, her face now close enough to smell his pain.

"…though be assured that should anything happen to me, my suffering can never be lost, as its story is safely stored with others I can trust."

She began to move slowly away, smiling at the crumpled figure in the pew, before eventually reaching the door and out into the Placa. Her dogs leapt to their feet, and a few irate villagers bewildered by the herd, stopped their cackling and shouted their greetings, heads respectfully bowed.

Benevolence and obedience, she thought, the kindliest of bedfellows, and with one firm whistle the dogs and the herd were off along the Cami d'es Cementiri, away from Sant Cristofol and down towards the farm at Turo Vell. It was indeed a very beautiful day.

Oriol Quintana had a captive audience, not that the children sat around him needed containing. He was reading to them in the way that only he could, entrancing the oldest with the lilting lyricism of the verse, and becalming the youngest within the most beautiful repose as his voice rolled over the rhythm and allurement of the words:

"*Tears, idle tears, I know not what they mean,*
Tears from the depth of some divine despair
Rise in the heart and gather to the eyes,
In looking on the happy Autumn-fields,
And thinking of the days that are no more.

Fresh as the first beam glittering on a sail,
That brings our friends up from the underworld,
Sad as the last which reddens over one
That sinks with all we love below the verge;
So sad, so fresh, the days that are no more.

Ah, sad and strange as in dark summer dawns
The earliest pipe of half-awaken'd birds
To dying ears, when unto dying eyes
The casement slowly grows a glimmering square;
So sad, so strange, the days that are no more.

Dear as remember'd kisses after death,
And sweet as those by hopeless fancy feign'd
On lips that are for others; deep as love,
Deep as first love, and wild with all regret;
O Death in Life, the days that are no more!"

As he finished, he looked up at the eyes focussed so intently upon him. The oldest and only boy was his son Ignacio, just twelve but already the coming man. The youngest, four-year-old Marta, the child of Sofia, one of nine step-sisters, was fast asleep on a cushion next to him. Beyond the large terrace where a goodly number of the children of the family were gathered, and a distance on from the dry stone walls of the lower fields, he could make out the pale blue of the Mediterranean lapping the shoreline at Cova De Santo Tomas. The very faintest trace of brine confirmed that today, it was at rest.

On the spring air were smells of primrose and japonica, infused with aromatic bites of lavender and thyme. The stunted pines and cedars along the valley down to the Cava des Coloms swayed in gentle balletic unison, their roosting occupants at one for once in their contented perch, save for the odd occurrence of a deterrent cackle.

These were golden times, alone with his family's future, as sweetly precious as the natural world and the land he loved.

"Ah! I hate all that love and kisses thing."

Aina, Oriol's youngest daughter, was the comedian of the tribe, and the children burst into laughter. Oriol laughed too. Seriousness punctured was always welcomed in his world.

"Thank you, Aina, you are right, there's lots of that in this poem."

"It doesn't rhyme either," she said, to further smiles.

"Yes, Aina," said Oriol slowly, "I'm grateful also for that observation."

"Can't we hear one of yours, Uncle?" inquired Julia, thinking perhaps that despite the laughter Aina may have overstepped the mark.

"Next time, Julia, but kind of you to ask. If I could write anything so beautiful, then I promise I would read you nothing else."

There were muffled protests of disappointment. Young as they were, they were proud that the Quintana name was known for its art, as well as for its control.

"The reason I chose this for our poem today was almost exactly for the reason that Aina mentioned: love. But not just the love for each other… and yes perhaps some of that kissing, Aina…" the sniggers and laughter rose gently once more, "…but for the love of this beautiful world that surrounds us."

He pointed to the scene beyond them he'd been viewing, and they turned to look.

"Never ever forget that. Keep it with you always wherever you are. There may be great powers around us destroying each other, but always, always, look beyond the strife, the loss, the grief. There is a great peace in the lives we lead now, and in our marvellous world. Children, be strong in this faith; it is the one thing that can never be lost to thieves. The truth that rests in your heart can never be stolen."

"Uncle."

It was Abril, one of the oldest yet most hesitant of his nieces, and already the subject of various suitors.

"Yes, Abril, please, go ahead."

"I adore this poetry. It speaks to me too, but…" and he waited for her to gather strength, smiling encouragement, "…the padre tells us to find love through the Psalms, and through prayer and obedience."

Oriol nodded.

"But even he reads my poetry." Abril cheered; some of the older ones chuckled. "And what is poetry save a prayer for goodness, thrown onto the page from deep in the soul?"

He lowered his voice to a conspiratorial whisper.

"Here's a secret name for you. Don't tell anyone."

The children craned toward him, determined not to miss the information he was about to entrust them with.

"The poem I have read is by a man called…" he contorted his face, pausing theatrically before bellowing, "Alfred Lord Tennyson."

They burst out laughing.

"Yes, I know, it is a strange name I'll grant you, but remember he was, poor fellow… an Englishman."

There was more giggling.

"But his words are beautiful, are they not? They entice you to hang onto your dream, to value the splendour of the days that you have, to remember always that freshness, that beauty in your birthright, and the simple joys of the world that God has provided, both for us…" he put his hand across his mouth and whispered, "…and of course… for the padre."

There were more smiles. Oriol's irreverence was always infectious.

He leant back behind his chair and pulled out a painting that had previously gone unnoticed. He stood and held it more closely so that they could all see, and motioned to them to stand and examine it if they wished. They moved forward, eagerly jostling for a view. How they loved these adventure's; the farm was the only place where they ever really encountered such learning.

"Now tell me, in this painting, look carefully. What do you see?"

There was a momentary pause followed by a flurry of hands from the younger ones. By now Marta was fully awake, and Oriol pointed to her encouragingly.

"It's very... very... beautiful."

There were a few groans.

"No, no, she is right; that is the first thing I noticed too. Well done, Marta. Why do you say this?"

"Well, it reminds me of the river... with the cows drinking from the water. I like cows, Uncle."

There were chuckles.

"That is brilliant, Marta, anyone else?"

Jana, one of the older girls, spoke up. "I see the large city in the background, Uncle, across the river and beyond the bridge. It looks larger than Ciutadella or Mao even. But the dome of the church...I don't recognise it."

"You are very observant, Jana, and I can confirm your ideas. This is not a Menorcan city. In fact, it is Spanish, most likely Madrid, as this was painted on the banks of the Manzanares River. It's by Casimiro Sainz, one of Spain's finest landscape artists."

There were a few gasps from the youngest amongst the group, thinking this appropriate to such an announcement even though they had no idea why.

"But I do love the colours in the moody spring sky, the deep ochre of the houses on the river bank..." continued Jana. Oriol's heart leapt. "...the baked browns of the grassy bank, the reflection of the sun on water..."

Oriol gestured to others to join in, but after a brief pause it became apparent that the waters had run dry.

"So, from the lack of further response, it's clear we have much to understand, whatever our age."

They looked at each other, fearing a rebuke, something they rarely associated with him.

"Can you not see?"

They craned forward, and stared hopefully, emphasising if nothing else their intent to please.

"Look, it is there, right in front of your eyes."

He pointed to the figures along the bank in the near distance.

"Washer Women," he exclaimed.

There was a muted gasp. Of course, they'd all seen the women in the foreground of the picture, but hadn't thought to comment upon the ordinariness of something they all saw on a daily basis.

"In this room, apart from myself and Ignacio, you are all girls, young women," he said, and they all looked around, "is this what you want to become? Is this really the role fit just for a woman? Is not the beauty of the natural world in this painting defiled by such intrusion and wrong?"

There was a further, more awkward silence, though even the youngest was confident that Oriol was trying to lead them to something important.

Aina felt the accompanying stillness needed piercing and piped up.

"Pappa, do you help Mamma with the washing, then?"

Oriol rolled his eyes and forced his arms onto his hips in mock fury, and the group once more convulsed in laughter.

"Of course I do, and well done for asking, though perhaps my help is not enough if you are so unaware of it."

He gestured to the broader group

"I am sure all of your fathers help as well."

A huge din ensued, with hoots of derision and denial. Aina started waving her hands and shouting for quiet.

"So, Pappa, you are a washer woman," she shrieked above the noise, "is that why we have the only boy in the family and all the others' uncles can only make girls?"

The terrace erupted with joy, only ceasing once Oriol raised his arm.

"I think there may be more to it than that, Aina, though tonight girls..." he dropped his voice again... "don't tell them I said this but you should go home and ask your fathers to start helping with the washing... and see what happens."

For the next few minutes, there was happy pandemonium as the children compared the possibilities of family growth that might result, particularly the relative desirability of the arrival of a brother. Having enjoyed the moment, Oriol shushed them once more.

"So, through all its great beauty, what this painting shouts to me is that for women, as well as for men, the opportunities in life should be the same. Where is the painting entitled 'Washer Men'?"

He looked around the group.

"Exactly, there isn't one. Please, think about that when you start to make choices with your life. What is good for a man is also good for a woman."

"And the other way around," shouted Aina to the merriment of all.

"Pappa."

"Yes, Ignacio."

"Is this painting real?"

Oriol understood the trajectory of his son's enquiry. He was a sensitive, deeply thoughtful young man.

"Well, Ignacio, do you regard it as beautiful, does it mean something to you, too?"

"It does, Pappa."

"So does it matter, my son? What if it is a likeness that's been painted by someone else?"

"Well, only so much in that if it is real, it will be worth a lot of money."

"To whom? The artist? I can tell you that the man who painted this was unwell for much of his life. His work was bought cheaply by those who perhaps took advantage, selling it on for great profit."

"It looks real to me, Pappa."

"To me too, my son. And if this is also the painting that was stolen first by the French army and then by other thieves, we shall have great joy in restoring it to its rightful place in the greatest gallery in Madrid."

"And will we be paid?"

Oriol smiled.

"We shall indeed, handsomely, in fact. And the money will help Sant Cristofol and also, I hope, our Menorcan renaissance and the return of our island's independence."

The group had become hushed; a seriousness had entered the discussion that spoke to any age.

"You see, children, what a poem and a painting can do? The power of beauty? Come, time to get back to your houses." And he held up his arms.

"By the way, the poem and perhaps even the painting, are in what is called the 'Romantic style.'"

He started shooing them off, waving goodbye.

"So, maybe tell your parents about the 'Romantics' when you get back, and what with that and papa washing the clothes, maybe you can help the Quintana's make more boys."

"Urgh," screamed Aina.

Later that same evening, with the farmhouse now settled, Oriol walked to one of his favourite places and sat down. The elevated well in the centre of Turo Vell's courtyard was an imposing construction, composed of four roughly hewn limestone walls the height of two tall men, in the south wall of which was set an access door. This, in turn, was reached by a number of limestone steps, made necessary by denudation around the well's base from years of hard-worked water-raising. It created a shrine-like impression to the completed form, confirmed all the more, both by its dome-shaped roof and, in keeping with the surrounding farm buildings, its whitewashed interior walls. For Oriol, it was a place of sanctuary.

Directly south of him and below the field walls now obscured in semi-darkness, the distant waves in Cova De Santo Tomas were angrier than earlier in the day, the portent of a storm. Behind him and to both sides were the farm buildings of the extended family, lit by dimmed hearth fires and flickering candle lamps. Twelve Quintanas lived here, including his mother Llucia, her eldest offspring and their children. Over twenty others, direct progeny and their issue, occupied Quintana family farms to the east of Es Migjorn Roca, in Alaior and Ferreries. Very little happened in this part of Menorca without Quintana knowledge or say so.

Oriol pulled out a notepad from his back pocket, balanced it on his knee and began to write. A small grubby pencil he carried everywhere and good enough with which to legibly scribble a first draft, was fixed in his left hand. The half-light from the farm provided the barest sufficiency of illumination, its maudlin entrancement matching his mood. The first lines came easily:

"*I met a man today.*
Angered, razored, kettled by the certainties of others.
Battered on the blasted heath of his business,
His life a fishnet of uncertainty."

But then… nothing.

He sat gazing at the darkened sky as around him legions of Cicadas hissed and clicked. In the gorge a mile or so away, the piercing shriek-hoot of the hunting Scop Owl added its signal of derision. His poetry was at its most effortless when he was at his lowest, so on this evening, he too should have been flying, but the coming storm he'd presaged felt suddenly very personal.

"Oriol."

It was his mother, Llucia, shouting across in his direction from the farmhouse. They would often meet in the evenings, sat on the well steps, to check both on each other and the business. On occasions when he was particularly low, he would stay motionless and unresponsive, hidden within the shadow of the well, knowing she would not walk across without his reply. But he knew that on this night there were pressing matters, and he was now the responsible Quintana.

"Yes, Mamà, I'm here."

She quickly crossed the courtyard swatting furiously at the mosquitoes that she insisted preferred her company to his, and sat down next to him.

"Damn these insects," she spluttered, though the increased darkness would soon give respite.

"I heard that you spoke to our padre this morning," said Oriol, his eyes arching in expectation.

"He's a fool," Llucia hissed, "but he's our fool. He will make the necessary arrangements for our next artwork."

Oriol smiled.

"And that you showed our herd off to the village?"

"Word gets around I'm glad to see. And if that word is that I'm also still around, then I'm very content."

Oriol shook his head gently; she was indeed a force of nature. He waited for a moment for her breathing to steady. She was still in good health, given the rigours of her life, but he treated this good fortune with loving caution. There were important things he had to say.

"I have spoken with my contacts. We shall be ready to sail from Mao in a few weeks, the weather and our German friends permitting."

"German friends?" replied Llucia.

Hard-won experience had bestowed upon her an acute awareness of the need to plan for every eventuality, which in turn demanded accuracy and detail from those upon whom she relied.

"The Andreassen family in Mao will supply the boat. But they need the certainty that it will be the winds rather than a submarine that will challenge our success."

They were both aware of the grave risks the Mediterranean posed for unidentified shipping. The Andreassens owned a large fleet of fishing vessels based in the imposing deep-water harbour at Mao, but increasingly, such boats risked the assumption they were supplying the allies and therefore fair prey to this new form of warfare. Initially, the Germans had given warnings before attacks, surfacing before any sinking to offer evacuation and rescue to those aboard the doomed vessel. But times were changing, and the British navy had recently suffered significant loss of life, for which it seemed to have little response. The Andreassens had already had their scares, and were wary.

"They have trusted contacts with German naval officials, and insist they will know when we have a clear passage to Port Alexandria."

Llucia was silent for a moment, considering her son's information.

"And for the route back as well?"

"I shall pick up the works from the supplier in Cairo and then make my way back to the coast, awaiting the Andreassens' signal. They have further trade in Palestine to complete before returning for me, but we have a well-worked arrangement of which I am confident. As you know, we make it well worth their time to prioritise our business."

Llucia appeared unsettled and frowned slightly.

"Are you still sure about them?"

"As sure as they are about me, Mamà."

He could see that she was unconvinced.

"They were bankrolled by Arnao Reus and as such, still owe us. We continue to help them with the British permissions they need to trade in Egypt, and we give protection when their fleet is in Mao storing our special items."

He knew that mention of Reus would reassure. He'd been Mao's major banker, with very deep pockets and an extensive reach. He was an extraordinary broker for the port and its businesses, and had bailed the Andreassens out on several occasions. More significantly, Reus was his mother's late and very last husband. The Andreassens' debts to him were now debts to her and the Quintanas. From this estate were also houses in Mao, quarries near Ciutadella, and farmland with extended vineyards in the nearby Binifadet. But his most important legacy was the extensive and manipulative manifest of contacts with the Spanish authorities on the island, and the subsequent trading operations this enabled with the British, the Ottomans and Germans, links the family used well. The war had advanced an ongoing opportunity for the Quintanas to provide for Menorca, and for Menorcans, in turn, to show them their gratitude.

"Arnao was a difficult man in many ways, but I put some of that down to his age. I may have worn him out before his time, but he was generous in his passing."

Oriol smiled. His mother had experienced many adventures with her partners, some acceptable, others damaging, but all had one thing in common: with their expiration, she prevailed.

Her family had been driven from their landholding during her teenage years, her parents killed, her brothers sent to the colonies. They were Catalan speakers, interested only in the challenge of everyday survival that afflicted every poor farming family. This meant little to the Spanish incomers, who used this language pretext and the illusory threat it posed to the established church to drive them away from what was rightfully theirs. Llucia escaped their murderous assault by hiding in the well, and for the subsequent three years was cared for by the catholic mission in Alaior. For the first of those traumatised years, she was unable to speak and barely able to walk. For the second, she cared for her baby and mourned. For the third, she plotted revenge.

"You are safe now, Mamà. You have saved these lands for the Quintanas, and are loved and respected."

"By the family I know, but the others?" She nodded her head. "It is a simple fact that the more we help to improve their lives, the more they will continue to despise."

She stretched her hand across to Oriol's.

"My precious son, now you are head of the family, things will change, I know. But do not expect reward from those you are driven to help. Prepare yourself too, and those who follow you, for the shackles that such responsibility brings."

There was another silence. Then Oriol asked the question he so needed answering.

"Mamà, the man you met in those terrible times… was he a good man?"

He had long since given up hope of acquiring detailed information about his father, what he looked like, how he behaved. His mother's nightmares about her past were hard to witness once they kicked in, and he did all he could to avoid triggering them. She thought for a moment.

"As I remember, a noble man, kind, generous… exactly the sort who would tell his daughters never to be washer-women."

He grinned.

"Yes, I heard from the children that you have an ingenious solution to our lack of male heirs?"

This time they both burst into laughter before returning again to the question.

"Of the men I have known, he was my greatest love. He was a good man."

She squeezed his hand more tightly.

"Then one morning, just a few weeks before your birth, he left for his work, and both he and his goodness died. I was told he had drowned. Fell into the harbour at Mao, trying to help steady a small sailing lug to the harbour wall in the rising tide; his body washed out to sea. But this I think you already know."

Oriol placed his arm around his mother's shoulders, and for a while they remained perfectly still, consoled by each other's love. He knew that between his father and the old man Arnao Reus, four other men had dominated her life, or so they had thought. Biel Alexander, the Alaior farmer who had conspired with the Spanish to take Quintana lands, had died within two years of marrying her. Her next husband Pau Carles, the brutaliser of Ferreries, killed himself with alcohol after seven years of aggressive marriage, freeing both Llucia and the village from his torments. Neither man had male heirs, so their estates passed to Llucia.

Then Hugo Barrera, an old farmer from Es Migjorn Roca, tried his best in love, but what he most desired was care and tenderness in his final years, and this she gave. Upon his death, she formally regained her family lands at Turo Vell that he'd managed for Biel Alexander, together with the increased influence this gave over the church.

That left Eric Farregy, a man strong on acreage but weak on breath. His death was not a surprise, as neither by now was the transference of his lands and fortune to Llucia.

In every case she had genuinely tried love, but the presiding assumptive arrogance each man held towards her perceived feminine fragility ultimately enabled her predominance, and the extension of the Quintana domains.

But now, at nearly fifty years of age, she no longer needed or desired anything from a man, save that her own family was properly respected. And in this desire she had been fiercely successful.

"I shall be safe, Mamà. You are with me, and my father is always in my heart."

Llucia though, found little comfort in his words. Oriol was special. The family, the villages, even she, had come to depend upon him. He hadn't experienced her terrors, but they both held a shared passion for their lands. She hated not being able to be truthful with him.

"There is something else I need to ask."

She looked at his eyes and saw the kindness and beauty of his father.

"This will be my last journey to Cairo."

Inwardly, she gasped with joy, but dared not show it.

"There are things happening there that make our business less fruitful. The British are reorganising their operations. I have heard they are planning a new leadership for the city and the Andreassens' contacts insist this will make our ventures far less worthy."

He paused.

"I need to know that this decision meets with your approval."

This was so typical of Oriol. He no longer needed her approbation, as he'd shown himself to be both masterful and confident in the leadership she'd passed to him. Yet his underlying compassion for the well-being of others, particularly her, remained undimmed.

"Of course it does, Oriol. None of us rest when you are away."

He was relieved. His journeys were becoming more perilous, though their dividend provided lucrative remuneration for the family.

"This acquisition is of extreme value, more so I suspect than any other we have dealt with. It's for the British. I'm told that after we pass it on, it will hang in a museum in London, for safety."

They exchanged a knowing look. Theft had many names.

"So, the loss of these items will mean we shall need to reorganise and adapt the way we work."

"Putting extra bread on the villagers' tables may therefore not be so easy," replied Llucia.

"But that we must do, Mamà, and more. We are in a position to help the people liberate themselves, to live as Menorcans rather than Spanish chattels. Whilst the eyes of the wolves are elsewhere, we must act."

Such talk worried Llucia. She respected her son for the idealistic aesthete he'd become. Noble though his intentions were, she knew better than he that what Menorcans desired most was food, shelter and certainty. For now though, such thoughts could wait.

"Tell me, what is it that the good padre will need to hang on his church wall when you return? I have already been generous in my description of it to him."

Oriol smiled.

"A painted limestone relief figure of a woman by the name of Hatshepsut. She was a commoner who became the Pharaoh."

He fixed her with his eyes, furrowed his brown and leant her way.
"Does that remind you of anyone?"
"Surely not?" she replied.
"Oh, and she's about three and a half thousand years old."
They laughed.
"Ah… yes, now that's starting to sound familiar."

CHAPTER 4

"Keep your mouth shut and look straight ahead."
Sergeant Wirrall's head was in a pyretic gallop. He needed to get Laurie to the tram stop on Sidi El Madbuli Street, across from the barracks. It would take forty-five minutes to make it to the meeting arranged by Colonel Lowthian at the Provost Marshal's office. Lateness wasn't an option.

At the gate awaiting them stood an escort party of four men from the ranks. To Laurie's significant perturbation, they were accompanied by an irate Captain Hillary. No pleasantries were exchanged, and upon sighting his recent affliction, Hillary sped off over the road, with Laurie and the group closely in tow. Sergeant Wirrall brought up the rear. It wasn't a guard party, but Laurie felt in every sense the felon.

Within a few minutes, a tram arrived with its hand-painted number and *'Museum'* destination prominently displayed in Arabic and English. It screeched to a halt with the noise and contorted gracelessness of a large metal rack being dragged across an abattoir floor. Hillary jumped purposefully aboard the first car, pushing aside those attempting to disembark, and with a flash of his stick, ordered the remaining and now disgruntled passengers to the back. He sat down, protectively cocooned by his men, though Laurie remained standing. Within five minutes and just a few stops later, the cool from the breeze through the open carriage gave way to an oppressive swelter, as they jumped off at Bulaq Street, turning right down Suliman Pasha towards the British Army General Headquarters. In no time at all, they were sweating heavily and swatting flies. Captain Hillary, keen as ever to maintain appearances, pulled the men across to the shade provided by the Edwardian frontage of The National Hotel.

"We're going to be a few minutes early with our parcel," he said, pointing with his stick in the general direction of Laurie whilst simultaneously affecting the expression of examining a dead rat, "so stand for a moment and maintain formation. Keep your eyes peeled. Never let the Arab out of your sight."

As Laurie surveyed the street scene around him, the only people who looked remotely interested in the escort party were the be-suited management team, now gathered nervously behind them at the main entrance to the hotel, doubtless concerned they were about to be the object of a military inspection.

"When we get to GHQ, present yourselves at your best. Stand in guard order inside the main atrium whilst I deal with the matters of the day. Remember, you are representing the Regiment, so put on a good show," and then, as if to emphasise the significance of the moment he added, "this might take several hours as there's a lot I need to let the people there know."

There was a look of resignation from the men; even Sergeant Wirrall seemed wearied. He knew from experience that the Captain's interests were entirely personal, and that no opportunity however small would be missed in self-promotion.

After a few moments the party set off, but more slowly now given they were ahead of time and under pressure, for the sake of appearances, to sweat less profusely. As they drew level with the elegant four-storey façade of the Belgian Diplomatic Agency alongside the roundabout on Suliman Pasha, the wealth differential between this area and that next to their barracks became even clearer. There was a statue of sorts at its centre that Laurie couldn't quite make out, surrounded by majestic palm trees, bowing as if in adulation. Around this trotted dozens of well fed and immaculately groomed horses, each drawing a polished open black carriage and intersecting with each other as if in some subtle, unannounced waltz. They were laden entirely with cargoes of a business or military essence, all earnestly engaged in decision-making.

There were no donkeys, traders, or street hawkers. The dominant tribe on display here was European. Unlike the manic trading scenes in Midan Bab El Hadid, there was an air of country gentility about the place, the sort that accompanied those who could most afford to pay for others' time. The whole scene was benignly managed by a single Egyptian policeman in a dark formal uniform and prominent military fez.

The buildings themselves struck Laurie as grand. Over the roundabout to the south was a four-storey building coated in polished limestone, advertising itself as the Italian Club. Others like the Danish Diplomatic Agency and the British Consulate seemed assuredly gilded, regal even. He'd seen cathedrals in Lichfield where he grew up in and Worcester close to his village, but beyond those and a few other municipal buildings, nothing in his experience quite compared.

Dominating in every sense though, was the spectacular five-storey edifice of The Savoy Hotel with its sumptuous dome-topped basilica. The chandeliers visible through its huge windows threw sunlight back onto the street, glinting like the moonlight off a calm Mediterranean Sea. It was as if a huge and dignified ocean liner had rested its sophisticated prow alongside the square, its' exquisite beam flowing behind along Quasr El Nil and Suliman Pasha Street.

"Follow me, men, remember your instructions."

Only now, as Laurie and the escort crossed towards The Savoy, did the Union Jacks that hung off the canopy above the entrance and the sentries stationed outside signal the real significance of this building. So this was the British Army Headquarters?

Inside and, as instructed, Sergeant Wirrall and the troop stood dutifully to one side of the atrium, parked for maximum visibility just below the main staircase. They were far from out of place though, as military groups were gathered in pockets across the concourse, and not just the British. Captain Hillary pushed through them and up the stairs heading to a first floor reception area, with Laurie following obediently in his trail.

The Captain introduced himself to a civilian official sitting at a large oak desk positioned just outside the guarded door to the Provost Marshal's Office. Hillary passed him some papers and muttered something inaudible, though clearly with regard to Laurie. After what felt like an interminable due diligence, the papers were stamped and the official signalled to the soldiers behind him to allow the Captain and Laurie through. Once inside they were led across a huge floor space covered by dozens of desks at which were gathered huddles of men, for the most part military, noisily engrossed in frenzied activity, and eventually ushered into a quieter side room.

For a moment, there was an intense awkwardness as the two sat side by side in repulsed silence. Then the door flung open, and in strode a very tall, pencil-thin man, impeccably dressed in a Major's uniform, save for a cap, which he carried neatly under his arm. He wore thin, rounded spectacles, which perched upon a small nose, and his black hair was unfashionably slapped and greased to one side of his head. He was immaculately manicured, though remarkably pale and gaunt for someone who had presumably been exposed to the Egyptian heat. Both men immediately stood to attention.

"Stand down, men, please. Major Fogge, Army Intelligence, two 'g's' one 'e.'"

He beckoned to them to sit, and collapsed his own pipe cleaner framework into a wicker chair strategically placed for him, or so it seemed, given that his fully extended legs covered the remaining floor space.

"Captain Hillary, I see from your papers you were at Oxford."

"Yes, sir, Balliol College."

Major Fogge smiled reassuringly, though to Laurie there was something of the eel about him.

"Ah, established in 1263 perchance?"

Captain Hillary looked surprised, though the certainty of Fogge's comment indicated that this was a statement of fact rather than a question.

"Sir?"

The Poet Laurie Ate

Fogge nodded and smiled.

"Same college as myself, you see, Hillary. Jolly well done."

He leant across and shook the Captain's hand.

"As another esteemed fellow, our much maligned and recent former Prime Minister Herbert Asquith reminded, and I quote, *'we Balliol men are indeed blessed by the tranquil consciousness of an effortless superiority'*."

There was a moment of quietude and cerebral calm, as the pair settled into meditative reflection and shared affection for those former glorious days. Then, and with a start, Fogge turned to Laurie.

"What about you, Laurie? I read that you were at St Mark's."

"Yes, sir."

"Ah, so you were a college man as well, then?"

"No, sir, Free School, St Mark's Church, Lichfield."

Fogge seemed slightly disappointed.

"Free School?" he inquired.

"Well, that's what they called it, sir, even though we had to pay."

"Ah, my parents too, Laurie, paid hugely on my behalf, a noble sacrifice indeed."

"Yes, sir," continued Laurie, "penny a week until I was eight, then after that, nothing."

"Nothing?"

"Well, it would have risen to tuppence a week, but I was asked to leave."

Fogge looked confused.

"That sounds bad form, Laurie."

"Not really, sir. My parents hadn't the money and I hadn't the temperament."

Captain Hillary began to shuffle, and his nervous head tap reappeared. Fogge rearranged his legs.

"So, how on earth did you get by?"

"Bird Street, sir."

Fogge gave him a blank look.

"The Library there had everything I needed. Travelled the world on its shelves."

There was a pause whilst Fogge took stock.

"Yes, indeed… well… thank you, Laurie, yes, thank you so much."

He looked at Captain Hillary for some insight into a situation he'd perhaps misunderstood, but the Captain stared straight ahead. So he turned to the business of the meeting.

"It appears, Laurie that you have made a very favourable impression in your short time here."

Hillary's eyes momentarily closed.

"Colonel Lowthian has instructed me to sign off your papers so that you can join us here as a Lance Corporal, pick up your kit, and so on."

Laurie's continuing amazement at the turn of events must have shown.

"Oh yes, quite something for you I'm guessing, all of this?" said Fogge.

"Yes, sir, thank you, sir."

"Don't worry, it will all become quite clear, and Colonel Lowthian herself will fill you in with the details presently. I'm sure Captain Hillary is very proud of you."

He looked at Hillary, who despite the tightening blood vessels in his neck, forced a confirmatory nod.

"In a moment, one of the staff will take you to the Arab Bureau people along the corridor. On the way you'll be fitted out, documented, dispatched; come to think of it the very sort of thing that happens prior to the coffin lid closing."

He laughed, impressed by his own cleverness, and Laurie thought it impolite to at least not smile.

"But don't worry, whilst you're with us you'll be safe as houses."

He cracked his knuckles, not just once but three times, as if part of some ritual.

"By the way, Laurie, just so you know, Colonel Lowthian relies upon me to be her 'go-to man', so to speak. Do you understand what I'm saying?"

There was a thinness of the mouth that belayed the confidence with which Fogge spoke, and though Laurie nodded, he was aware of the need for caution.

"Yes, back at the barracks I'm the oil, if you like, between the Bureau,

Military Intelligence and the regular army; Captain Hillary will be my man there."

He straightened himself in the chair and moved conspiratorially forward towards Laurie.

"Anything that you hear or learn therefore, or any tasks required of you that the Bureau directs, no matter how small they may appear, you must let me know. I want to be very clear about this matter."

This was an order, and Laurie wasn't about to desist.

"Yes, sir."

"Jolly good, I'm glad we understand each other. I'm looking forward to seeing what you can do for us, Laurie."

He settled down once more into a horizontal repose, and then proceeded into small talk with Hillary, almost as if Laurie was no longer in the room. Their conversation mostly seemed to focus upon jolly japes at Balliol, but Laurie didn't take much notice. Their world was very different from his, and he was fervently trying to keep pace with the turn of events.

Eventually, Fogge picked up a small hand bell that was below his chair and was about to ring it when Hillary protested.

"But, Major, there are also things I need to tell you about Private Laurie."

"That's Lance Corporal Laurie from now on," corrected Fogge.

Hillary's eyeballs extruded, pupils on pikes.

"Sir," he blurted, a slight dribble about his lip, "this man disobeys orders."

Blimey, thought Laurie, *he still wants me shot.*

Major Fogge paused for a while and then smiled in that slightly worrisome way.

"Captain Hillary," he said slowly, "this is the Arab Bureau. The more off the wall the people here are, the more they seem to get on. Remember Balliol? There were some very odd sorts there, too."

You're right there, thought Laurie.

"But, sir…"

Fogge turned his head and cut him short.

"That's enough, Hillary. Forget about all the cranks and the low-lifes. For heaven's sake man, we even have a women officer working here."

That and the bell summoning a secretary seemed to do the trick. The three men stood and saluted, Laurie was passed to the secretary for his next appointment, whilst Hillary was reminded of the way out down the stairs. As he reached the bottom, a cheery Sergeant Wirrall greeted him.

"Welcome back, sir, and well done. That didn't take half as long as you said."

The Captain could not contain himself.

"Fuck off, Wirrall."

And that's exactly what they all did, back to the barracks: but without their package.

"They'll be ready in an hour, Lance Corporal."

Laurie blinked; this was the first time his rank had been used to address him, and it was freely extended, without baggage. The photographer had told him to say "cheeky" as she pressed the shutter on her box camera, and for some reason, this had cheered him.

"Thank you," he replied, "if ever my family sees this they'll be even more convinced that I'm on a holiday."

She smiled.

"Well, once it's been printed and fixed to your passes, we'll run some extras off as post cards if you like, a perk of the job. You'll have some explaining to do."

She was right. What was he to say to them in a few short sentences that would explain his new circumstances?

Following the meeting with Fogge, he'd been led down a series of increasingly dingy stairs and through service corridors to a complex of store rooms in the hotel basement. It wasn't brilliantly lit, though huge fans on the ceiling did at least create a cooler environment than elsewhere in the building.

Each room appeared to have been kitted out for different purposes. Some had shelves full of files and maps, others held what seemed to be technical equipment piled up in an ad hoc fashion against the walls. In one of the more illuminated areas he'd been issued with a small revolver, a British Webley .455, for which he'd signed, plus a multipurpose knife, for which he didn't. The former was to be strapped below his jacket, the latter fixed to an inside pocket. Both were to be kept out of sight. He was also issued a whistle, with *J Hudson and Co,1916 Birmingham* inscribed upon it, and a compass. The box it was in read *Night-Marching Compass Army Issue* with the wording, *Invaluable to the military man, tourists and explorers.* As requested, he signed separately for these, doing his best to stifle a grin.

"Couldn't I just sign once for the lot?" he'd asked.

"Different departments," came the reply.

The military types who served him were assisted by smartly dressed locals, all of whom spoke impeccable English. They were courteous, efficient and likeable.

"Please, sir, it's important," one of them insisted, as he helped Laurie choose a lightweight white suit from the long racks of civilian clothing, arranged carefully according to size and style, "you must check the fit in the mirror."

Despite Laurie's protests that all of this was completely inappropriate for a soldier, he was gently informed that it would be necessary to his role.

"And these?" Laurie squirmed, as he struggled into the white straw boater, leather shoes, shirt and tie that completed the outfit. His assistant smiled reassuringly.

By the time he found himself standing for his photograph, posing stiffly as instructed, the unexpected was becoming the norm.

"And this?"

He looked at the photographer who'd positioned him directly in front of a large backdrop of the Great Pyramid at Giza.

"Wouldn't the army prefer me to be photographed in the barracks?"

"Well, look at you now," she said, "you're very dapper in your new suit and hat. You look like an important figure and a civilian, not an army man at all. Just what the Bureau needs."

She could sense his next question.

"Everyone who comes from Europe to work in Cairo has a photo taken there, over in Giza. It's just that we've brought the pyramid to

GHQ. To our Arab friends and with a picture like that, you won't appear as a military man, well, initially at least. And to our own lot, you'll mostly just pass as a business type."

Laurie shook his head, increasingly accustomed to the bewilderment of his position.

"Anyhow," she said, extending her hand, "welcome aboard."

The informality threw him. Shaking hands?

"Go on," she said, "it's OK." He obliged.

"We're just the 'downstairs lot' by the way, but anything you run out of, please shout."

At that she waved to the official who'd accompanied Laurie from his meeting with Fogge, to come over.

"Think you'll be needed presently by the top brass upstairs, so… tally ho."

He turned and started to follow his silent guide through the warren in the underbelly of The Savoy, but stopped suddenly: the photographer had shouted after him.

"Oh, almost forgot," she said, "and your new army kit, Lance Corporal stripe and all, will follow with your photos. There might be times when you still need to wear it."

She waved cheerfully and went back to her duties.

It must have taken a good five minutes to make their way back to the office where he, Hillary and Fogge had met earlier, but they didn't stop; walking on past room after room, all numbered in The Savoy's elegant styling. Occasionally, a door would open and a face appear, or a half-conversation from between the room's invisible occupants would reveal itself. Sometimes officers would brush past them along the corridor, mildly confused by the civilian dressed in a white suit and boater, stopping to salute them.

Eventually, they came to a sharp turn directly ahead of them straddled by a pair of doors, one of which was hanging off its hinges, its number at an angle. His guide ushered him inside, taking care not to further dislodge the door, and indicated to Laurie to sit on one of the three upright seats squeezed into the narrow entrance. He then disappeared beyond, into the room, returning after a few minutes.

"Wait here," he said firmly, before departing once more. But this time back down the corridor from where they had come, leaving Laurie sat upright on his chair, knees close to the opposite wall.

There were low mumbles coming from somewhere inside the room, but the thing that struck him most was the run-down nature of the space in which he was seated, not at all what he'd expected of The Savoy. It stank of cigarettes and the ceiling was yellowing. The wallpaper was dirty, worn away completely in places where it had been leant against, and the carpet threadbare. Whatever went on here either involved lots of people or those with a scant interest in their surroundings.

He began to attune to the conversation emanating from further inside. There was laughter, as well as pointed discourse. He strained to listen, but then things suddenly became audible, as if a door somewhere had opened, so much so that the proponents in the discussion might just as well have been sitting a few feet away.

"So, why would you assume that the ineffability of existence is a truism? Once you do that, you prejudice any attempt at rational understanding, let alone debate?"

Laurie thought he recognised the voice, but the context within which it was framed threw him.

"Because, John, there is no other way to approach my philosophy in life, and more importantly, my faith."

"And so by virtue of your self-distinction and birthright you condemn others who dare to question?"

There was a pause… *hell*, thought Laurie… *surely… that voice… that's Nooney?*

"Come on, John, you're being both antagonistic and obdurate. We should all be working for one another as good Christians."

"I am."

"What? Come off it, old boy, you tell me frequently that you're a confirmed dissenter type."

"Ah, there we have it, so now you have to sink to using a label to hang your well-educated brain on."

"No, John, but if you are telling me that my familiarity with St Thomas

Aquinas and the example he set for a life well led is indeed a crime, then yes, I'm a condemned man."

"There you go again, if in doubt, rely upon someone else to tell you what to think, someone who, let's face it, parodied Aristotle for all it was worth… and then you ignore the entire wisdoms and teachings of the east for example, as if their traditions count for nothing."

It was definitely Nooney, thought Laurie. *This was Nooney. Who was John? What was going on?*

"I don't doubt the ineffability of God," said the now exercised voice from the beyond.

"Nor me, necessarily, it's just… well…" said the raised reply from John.

"Well what? Come on, spit it out…"

"…I'd still like to test the concept."

At which point the owners of the voices broke into uproarious laughter, mutual light-hearted abuse, and self ridicule.

"Noah, don't get me going again."

"Sorry, John, old chap, but it does help to share." Both men guffawed again, absorbed by the incredulity of such an argument at such a time, in such a place.

They rose from the battered armchairs in which they were slouched, and moved into the next room on their way to leave the Bureau by the main door. Upon seeing Laurie sat in the corridor, looking bemused, John gasped…

"Laurie…" he yelped, "it's you."

"Nooney?"

There was a momentary lull as both men registered their shock.

"Don't you mean John, old boy?" said his colleague, Noah, who to Laurie's eye, though clearly an officer, appeared somewhat dishevelled. He had most of the khaki uniform expected of such a man, but not necessarily in the right alignment. Nooney, on the other hand, was smartly dressed in a light brown suit similar in cut if not in colour to the one Laurie was now wearing.

"John?" inquired Laurie, still confused.

"That's me, Laurie. It's my Christian name."

This was the first time since leaving home that Laurie had heard such informality used between soldiers. Not only that, but Nooney appeared to be on first-name terms with an officer.

"Tell you what, John," said Noah, recognising the awkwardness, "I'll leave you to get on with things here and we'll catch up later. It was great to talk."

With that, he shuffled out into the corridor, leaving the pair alone.

"What the—" began Laurie, before he was interrupted.

"I know," said Nooney, "strange way to go about things, but it'll soon start to make sense."

"After the incident in the square, you seemed to disappear," said Laurie, "thought maybe I'd dropped you in it or worse?"

"No, no, nothing like that at all: it was my teeth."

"What?"

"Yep, I fell over when Hillary tried to kill us and bashed my mincers, needed the ivory quack to patch up the breaks." He theatrically pointed to a molar, pushing his head at Laurie for inspection.

"Bugger off, Nooney."

"Exactly what the dentist said, Laurie, but I gave him my gin ration and he sort of fixed it."

"What?"

"Well, he said… 'Lance Corporal Nooney, I'm going to have to extract them', and I said to him, 'look, Doc, these are my teeth and I'm quite attached to them. What's more, they seem to be on speaking terms with me as well, so if it's OK with you just buff 'em up a bit, stick a plaster on 'em or whatever, and let's all get along just fine.'"

Laurie puffed his cheeks and blew out some air.

"Nooney… what the hell are you rambling on about?"

"Nerves, mate, you always make me nervous."

"Give over, Nooney, all this mate stuff and larking about. Yet here you are, talking on first-name terms with some officer as if you were his equal, about stuff I've never heard of, and dressed to the nines as well. I mean look at us, we could be…"

"Twins?"

"Shop dummies more like," said Laurie.

"Anyway, Noah and I are equals."

"What?"

"We both did philosophy."

"You went to a University? But you're from New Zealand."

"Thanks for the compliment," said Nooney, chuckling.

"Hard to grasp, but yep, University College Auckland, my home town. Miles bigger place than your piffling Worcester by the way. And as for Noah, or Colonel Grice-Farquharason to give him his full rank…"

"A Colonel…?" Laurie was truly stumped.

"…well, he did the same course at Cambridge, even sat the same papers, though we had to wait six months for them to arrive by boat in Auckland. We were sort of an off-shoot of his mob, if you get my drift."

Laurie realised he'd significantly misjudged Nooney. Their friendship, based upon mutual respect, humour and survival, had obscured the normal courtesies of enquiry.

"So you see," he continued, "Colonel or Lance Corporal, we're cut from the same cloth."

Laurie began to connect the pieces. The various meetings, his own apparent promotion, Captain Hillary's antipathy, the mania he'd just experienced in The Savoy basement, and now this, his friend Nooney, dressed almost identically as himself, parlaying academically with a British officer.

"So the Arabic you used in the square?" Laurie asked, now calmer.

"Yes, mate," Nooney nodded, "gained a basic fluency when I studied Islam, and it sort of went on from there."

Laurie raised his eyebrows, though little was surprising him by now.

"I even taught it for a while to the merchants who sailed from Manukau Harbour in Onehunga, back home. They found it useful to have some understanding of the worlds they were trading with by learning the local lingo. Not a bad idea is it, Laurie? Pity the British haven't discovered that yet?"

He laughed, and Laurie, now more relaxed, grinned. It was hard not to like Nooney.

"That's why you're here, then?"

"What, the Bureau? Blimey, I bet you're good at crosswords, Laurie... six letters across, *useful language to know if you join the Arab Bureau...*"

There was another lull, and then...

"The way you spoke to that Colonel... well, it was very different to the way you speak to me."

"They're both me speaking. Nooney, the same bloke, just temporising."

Laurie went quiet.

"It means..."

"...I know what it means, Nooney."

"Of course you do, mate. We're cut from the same cloth you and me." He tugged at his jacket for emphasis. "You're the equal of anybody I've ever met."

He shoved Laurie on the shoulder.

"Thanks, but if only..."

"...sincerely, Laurie, and stop the horseshit."

This brought Laurie up with a start.

"I talk as I need to, as do you. I deal with people as I find them, as do you."

This was a serious Nooney, one he hadn't previously encountered.

"We both know there's those born with opportunities that promoted them beyond their talents. But in this place," he signalled about him with his arms, "the likes of us are freed."

"Nooney."

There was a shouted command from within the room.

"Lowthian," mouthed Nooney.

"If you'd accompany Laurie I'd be grateful."

Nooney pointed at Laurie and smiled. She already knew he was there.

"You're in demand," he whispered.

Laurie stood and the two men moved further inside the Arab Bureau.

As Laurie had concluded, there was indeed a sequence of interconnecting rooms, seemingly stretching along the lines of the adjoining corridors. In the first room were the armchairs Nooney and Colonel Grice-Farquharason had been occupying a few minutes earlier, plus a whole sequence of cane chairs lined up against a wall. There was a low desk at one end, and a large plain board nailed to a wall. Other than that and scattered newspapers, it appeared quite spartan.

"Briefing room," muttered Nooney, though to Laurie it looked and smelt like a small, distempered church hall. The only things that seemed to have worked in it for quite a while were the fans slowly rotating on the ceiling.

They moved on and through a gap in the wall opposite, where once there had been a door, and into the next room. Colonel Lowthian was standing with her back to them, engaged in a conversation with a civilian, a man of good height, dressed smartly in a dark suit. They turned around and Laurie went to salute.

"No," said Colonel Lowthian sharply, "not whilst we're in the Bureau."

"Yes, ma'am," replied Laurie, keen not to show surprise. He was beginning to understand.

"And none of that 'ma'am' stuff either."

She fastened him with that stare, and beckoned them both to a chaise longue stretched in front of the large, inelegantly curtained French windows. It seemed an odd place from which he and Nooney should try to appear at ease.

"We put all our new people there, right in front of the window."

She paused, just enough to cause mild consternation.

"That way if there is a sniper over the road, you take the hit."

She laughed.

"Joking, of course, welcome aboard," she said, and to Laurie's consternation she shook him firmly by the hand, the same too with Nooney, though clearly this wasn't their first meeting.

"Let me introduce my colleague." She turned and motioned.

"Peter Moussabey," said the Arab-looking man to her left, "very pleased to make your acquaintance."

He smiled and bowed gently toward them. His English seemed perfect.

"Peter is a manager from The Agricultural Bank of Cairo. His family have lived here for two generations. He will be working with you."

She pulled up a chair for Moussabey, then for herself, and sat down quite informally opposite the two men. The hair that had been so neatly tied in their last meeting now hung loosely, the top few buttons of her khaki shirt were missing, and the collar was unpressed.

"Smoke?"

She pulled out a packet of cigarettes and offered them around. Nooney accepted, Laurie and Moussabey politely declined.

"I'd offer you a whisky, but it's probably too early in the day and I know that Peter here doesn't imbibe, so let's press on?"

She was already quite the most unusual woman Laurie had ever met.

"You were recommended to us by Nooney as someone we could rely upon."

She noted Laurie's quizzical expression and glance towards his friend.

"Yes, I know, more of the unexpected, but hopefully, things are falling into place. Nooney has been an important asset for the Bureau. He's trusted by the ranks and respected by our Arab friends."

Moussabey nodded affirmatively.

"He's been able to keep an eye out at ground level, form allegiances, gain information, keep us ahead of things. Indeed, so successfully that we need to increase our manpower on this side of our work. He mentioned you to us, and from our own observations of your behaviour, we believe him to have made an excellent recommendation."

Behaviour? Laurie could only think of the scrapes that had thus far dominated his time in Cairo.

"You are an independently minded pain in the arse, Laurie," confirmed Lowthian, as if clarity was somehow needed.

He feared the next uttering.

"…and that's just what we need in the Bureau. We don't want those who blindly follow orders or spout the obvious. Nor do we want those who tell us what we want to hear. That's for the regular army. We need people on our team who can see an issue before it arises, people that can think on their feet, spot the danger, find a solution."

She lit her cigarette and then passed it across to Nooney so that he could do the same.

"The people we use here are smart. You'll fit in well."

Bloody hell, thought Laurie.

"We've got mathematicians, philosophers, medical men, engineers, teachers such as Nooney, and the odd crook. Talking of which, I'm an archaeologist, just so you know. We all bring our differing forensic skills to the tasks here. And now we have an expert on the criminal mind."

Laurie was beginning to doubt she had the right man.

"Your record from the Worcestershire Constabulary confirms this, both as a dedicated and effective policeman and an irritant to authority."

She smiled, and Laurie relaxed a little. He could agree at least on one of those descriptions.

"And I have seen some of that with my own eyes in the way you've operated here. Together with Nooney and Moussabey, you must now bring those talents to the Bureau."

There was a brief pause whilst she shuffled through some papers. The course set by his enlistment had now distinctly altered, but he felt curiously enlivened by the turn of events. He'd become used to challenge. It was dishonesty to the soul that he detested.

"Nooney, can you give a brief synopsis?"

"You rightly said, Laurie, that I went missing on a few occasions in barracks. Well, with Peter's help, we've been gaining information on the workings of enemy intelligence here in and around Cairo. We've packed a few hits in the field recently, and some of this may well have been down to information that's making its way to the Ottomans."

"You're very modest, Nooney," interrupted Lowthian.

"You and Peter have already probably saved British lives and not an inconsiderable amount of possessions. It's just a pity that our leaders at home and in the field have been less competent."

Laurie was pleasantly surprised by the criticism.

"We're hearing so much about our undaunted perseverance in the face of overwhelming odds and the bulldog spirit amongst our troops," she continued, " but the real problems are with the incompetents that lead them."

He was warming to the straight talk.

The Poet Laurie Ate

"This year has gone very badly. Shortages of munitions and supplies, blinkered vision, unfulfilled promises, followed by lies, deceit, and then the heaping of blame for the subsequent calamities upon the smaller people sat further down the tree. Gallipoli was a nightmare. That and the disastrous losses at Gaza, have belatedly alerted London to the realisation we might actually hold the key to this war, here in Cairo. If we lose all of Palestine and the Sinai, Egypt will follow and the war will be as good as lost. If though, we sweep through and on toward Turkey, the Central Powers will be paralysed. Thank God Allenby will soon to be in charge, a man with actual balls."

Laurie coughed and Nooney almost spat out his cigarette.

"My apologies, gentlemen… Nooney, please continue."

"We're here, Laurie to collect information from whatever source we can, and bring that back to the Bureau. We're not alone. We've got good local people here whom we can trust."

This was the first time Laurie had heard the word trust used affirmatively about an Arab.

"They're at every level. They believe for the most part, that the British will be faithful to the Arab cause. Some, of course, just like the extra money they can earn, so we've always got to use caution."

This rang a bell.

"Ah, that's what you meant by 'our people' that day we were in the square," said Laurie.

Nooney nodded.

"And… Manoli and his performing donkey… they're with us too…?"

"Just Manoli, not the donkey, though come to think of it, we should keep a closer eye on his monkey."

Everyone broke into laughter.

"Must admit," said Laurie, now growing in confidence, "that some of the blokes have been complaining that back home they think we're having it easy here. Be good to set that record straight."

"Too right, Laurie. It's not just your lot," said Nooney, "we're known as 'Massey's tourists' by our mob."

He looked at Laurie's blank expression.

"Bill Massey, our Prime Minister. We do have them as well you know in New Zealand."

He raised an admonishing eyebrow towards his friend.

"You're gaining a rapid education in the broadening of horizons," said Lowthian.

He grinned in acknowledgement.

"Our work and sacrifice here needs to be properly understood to ensure we get the support we need to finish the job."

She left the sentiment to hang for a little before continuing.

"You're a married man, Laurie. How is your wife coping?"

The words landed like an exploding shell. His darkest place, his betrayal, bolted down, deep within the hippocampus, exposed and writhing once more.

"It's very hard for her and the children," he replied, faltering.

"Can she rely upon others to help her, what with you a policeman?"

"It's a struggle. We live in a village, but we can never really feel we belong there."

He looked away from Lowthian's unnerving glare.

"There's an unmarried sister who has moved in to give a hand, though she has to go back and forth to Birmingham when she has the money, to support her parents."

"Can't be easy for either of them," continued Lowthian. "The story of womanhood the world over."

This was an uncomfortable line of questioning.

"Good God Laurie, they still won't let us vote."

Laurie recalled the suffragette meeting he'd policed in Worcester. Bolshie bunch, he'd thought at the time.

"They do where I come from," said Nooney, attempting to alleviate the atmosphere, though from Lowthian's expression, it wasn't helping.

"So, sacrifices come in all shapes and sexes," said Lowthian. "Peter here has quite a family of young women whom I hope one day will have the chance to rule Egypt."

Laurie had quite forgotten for the moment that Moussabey was present.

"Ah, that would indeed be quite something," Moussabey replied.

Laurie looked across at him and noticed there were kind eyes and a gentle smile.

"Peter is the paymaster for our local supporters, and of course, so much more. He knows everyone. I will tell you, as Peter wouldn't, that when we talk of sacrifice, he and therefore his family are taking the greatest risks of all."

Laurie studied Moussabey's face for a reaction though he remained inscrutable.

"Peter's full name," continued Lowthian, "is Hisham bin Moussa. But because most of his work at the bank has been with Europeans, particularly the British, he's adopted the name of Peter Moussabey for ease and familiarity…"

"I do not really mind this…" interrupted Moussabey gently, "I have found that many British businessmen and officers would prefer to think of me as a fellow countryman, than a man with a real Arabic name. Besides, Peter Moussabey is such a pleasant name." He beamed.

"…and because he is serving us in support of his country, this threatens his safety, and that of his family. There are many here who see things very differently from us."

She looked at Laurie.

"Germans, Ottomans?" he suggested, seeing that a response was required.

"Yes, plus the local nationalists who hate British rule," she replied, "and groups who detest Coptic families such as the Moussabeys."

That, thought Laurie, *was a lot for one good-hearted man and his family to bear.*

"Why such religious hate?" he asked.

"Why indeed?" said Moussabey. "It is a very complicated thing, but yes, why oh why?"

"So, his skills," continued Lowthian, "are essential to us, as therefore is his safety. His role on our behalf must remain secure."

She passed a form to Laurie and pointed to him the signature it contained. It was his own.

"You signed for your kit. You also signed up at the same time to absolute secrecy with regard to your work here at the Bureau."

Laurie blinked; he hadn't really recognised that the process in the basement had contained such an oath, but there it was in his own hand.

"So, one wrong word from you or Nooney and Moussabey, and almost certainly many others, will be placed in great danger."

Laurie had no intention that this notion should linger, or that the service to which he was now committed was anything other than of grave significance.

"I understand," he said.

"That's good," replied Lowthian, "as failure to follow such orders will indeed result in you being shot."

CHAPTER 5

"Well, that was a most splendid meal. As always, quite the best there could possibly be in the whole of Cairo. And such wonderful company, too."

Brigadier Berrington Regis-Templeton raised his wine glass in a toast.

"To the Moussabeys, and their beautiful daughters. May they have health, happiness, and fulfilled lives."

"And to Egypt," added Colonel Lowthian, "may it prosper in peace and harmony."

"Hear, hear," shouted Peter and his wife Hanna in perfect celebratory English, smiling graciously towards their friends.

"Hear, hear," said Germaine, the oldest of the Moussabeys' daughters, thrusting her glass of water high into the air, and causing great amusement.

Much to the delight of their two British guests, she'd been allowed to stay up late to join in the evening's gathering. But now it was time for bed, and Peter Moussabey made his temporary apologies, too.

"I know she is nearly fifteen," said Hanna, "but she likes to read with her father before sleeping, and despite his protests to the contrary, Peter loves that she still feels this way."

"The Classics?" asked Lowthian.

"Well, she has read Homer and is interested in most things the ancient world has to offer."

"*Nonnus of Panopulis?*"

Hanna frowned.

"Germaine described him as 'an old degenerate'. In fact, she only made it part way through Dionysiaca. She said that if that was the best poetry an old Greek living in Egypt could manage, he would have been better advised to allow his wife the quill."

There were more smiles.

"She can be fiery at times," continued Hanna, "and seems more interested in questioning Peter about what's in the newspaper, when we can get one that is."

"Good for her," said Regis-Templeton, "though I suspect perhaps she has to read far too much about our British interests."

"Well, yes, you do write what you want us to know rather than that we would wish to read; and this from the country of freedom. Imagine instead though, it was the Ottoman who still ruled us. We hear from Damascus that journalists have been rounded up on Djemal Pasha's orders to prevent them spreading rumours of attacks upon Armenians. Their newspapers say nothing of this. Compared to such repression, your influence over Cairo is, shall we say, far easier to tolerate."

"I'm afraid," cut in Lowthian, "those stories aren't simply rumour. I've seen the slaughter to which they refer for myself."

There was a brief moment of stillness, as if she was preparing an inner protective wall to enable what was to follow.

"My background has enabled me the excuse to travel throughout your country as someone who loves Egypt, rather than as a woman attached to the British. On some of the earlier trips, I was accompanied, thanks to Peter's contacts, by a guide; a priest as it happened. He seemed trusted by the people we met, whoever they were, and his knowledge of the routes and water supplies was critical. It gave me some status when meeting tribal leaders; after all, how could a woman be of relevance unless substantiated by a man?"

Hanna grinned. She recalled the spin that Peter had used to describe his early work with the Colonel, "I am nothing more than her camel guide and apologist."

"The priest always made the introductions. Then the male officer of our party would speak. Generally, I bided my time, though I rarely had long to wait. I understood most of what was said, so when I heard them talk privately about me, often scurrilously so, I would interrupt, speaking directly in Arabic. I would show my understanding of their situation and suggest they take my presence and that of the British seriously. They were generally speechless for a few moments. But gradually the barriers came down, and we began to see the beginnings of the alliances we have today."

She paused and sipped at a glass of water.

"As London started to understand the value of such work… far too slowly, I would add… I was given broader rein and greater support. We became trusted, valuable. We were able to map the terrain, plan the routes that the military would need for the advance into Palestine."

She stopped for a moment and looked at Hanna. She deserved to know.

"It was then I saw first hand how the Armenian quarters of towns taken by the Ottomans were razed to the ground, bodies mutilated, used for target practice. The dead were left where they fell. The smell was unbearable. The wells, the wadis, were filled with corpses, the women taken away. It was a horror like no other. But any references to it were blamed upon ethnic rivalry. The very last people it seemed who were to have blood on their hands, were the Ottoman themselves."

She shook her head in disbelief.

"How on earth can such things still be happening? This is 1917, for heaven's sake."

Lowthian's words punctured the earlier veneer of cheerfulness, and there was a darkness in her voice. Such things would normally remain unsaid. But there was a grotesque brutality in their here and now. She knew whatever righteousness they craved, whatever morality, inhumanity would not abate whilst they simply talked.

"I should say," continued Lowthian, trying to balance the desperation with something positive, "that if anything good is to come out of this, it's that we now have an extensive Arab network working with us across Egypt, Sinai and into Palestine, to defeat the enemy. The attack last year on Mecca signalled how such cooperation can work to our mutual advantage."

"All this brutality…" sighed Hanna, unable momentarily to continue.

"And what about afterwards?" she asked eventually, now bristling with emotion. "When all of this is over, what will become of Egypt?"

There was a moment's hesitancy; how to answer such a question? Lowthian looked across to the Brigadier.

"I hope the British Protectorate will be a first step," he said.

"There is at long last a realisation in London that the critical axis in this war lies between where we now sit and Syria. We need Egypt as much as it needs us. Arab support is essential."

"Yes, but do you know which Arabs you can trust?"

The Brigadier was surprised by her response. He was far less expert than Colonel Lowthian on the intricacies and familial loyalties that bound the Arab cause, but assumed that Hanna, the most intelligent and erudite of Arabic women, would be more concerned about the threat from the Ottomans.

"We are fortunate," he replied, "to have a government in power here that's happy to work with us."

"Puppets, some would say?" retorted Hanna. "This government did as it was told, every Egyptian knew that, and only those who benefitted really rejoiced."

"Perhaps," said the Brigadier, "but they help us control the dissidents who would otherwise destabilise your country, a circumstance in which we would all be losers."

"It must be difficult," she said, recognising the slight she may inadvertently have offered, "to be fighting here, protecting a country that doesn't value you?" She and her husband had become close and trusted friends, as well as the most reliable of helpers to the British, and she'd meant no offence.

"It's quite understandable," he replied, acknowledging her unerring ability to touch a nerve, "though I hope that we are regarded more preferably than our predecessors." He knew few Egyptians pined over the collapse of three centuries of Ottoman control.

"I can understand your trepidation," interrupted Lowthian. She was more acutely aware of the fears Hanna faced; the Moussabeys were members of a significant minority within the city.

"Your faith must also be threatened?"

"I have no faith as such," replied Hanna firmly, "apart from that in love and human kindness. But Peter is more persuaded than I. He's an important part of the Coptic community here and therefore well known. Possibly far too well known by some of those murderers you politely call dissidents."

The Brigadier nodded. He understood.

"Our children attend the Coptic school just along the road. They see the graffiti on their school wall, the threats. You congratulate us upon our English, but let me assure you, it's a necessary response to our circumstances; an escape mechanism should we need it. Try as we might, we seem unable to avoid the consequences of the historical accidents that placed us here."

At that point, Peter Moussabey reappeared, apologising for his absence.

"I've left her to read alone," he said, smiling, and the mood lightened. "I think she's reaching the age where I am in the way."

"Hanna, what's gone wrong?" She gave him a startled look.

"Our guests, their glasses are empty; we shall be damned."

They all laughed, partly in relief, and the wine flowed once again.

Later in the evening following the meal, they moved to what Hanna described as her 'European Parlour' at the back of the house, overlooking the enclosed courtyard they shared with neighbours.

The Moussabeys made no denial of the fortuitous circumstances they enjoyed within the Cairo economic order. Their heritage had built wealth, and they lived comfortably from the resources this provided within an apartment block on Shari El Saqqay, in the elegant quarter of El Nasriya. A few hundred yards away to the west, stood the major ministry buildings of state, and even closer to the north, the magnificent Abdin Palace, home to the Khedive, leader of the former Ottoman protectorate. Since 1914, and under British tutelage, this had become the seat of the Sultanate of Egypt.

The traders and livestock that accompanied other parts of the district were absent. Instead of the generic vapours of waste and decay their street threw powerful spring scents high into the air. Shari El Saqqay was tree-lined with botanic escapees from the nearby Palace gardens, and mimosa, frangipani and flame trees, protected by decorative iron railings, adorned the pavements. It was impossible not to be consumed within the allure this conveyed and to assume that all was well.

Their house was one of four within the block, with balconies backing onto an inner courtyard adorned with sculpted palms, flowering poinciana and pomegranate, all set around a large central water garden. Under the shade of each terrace lay seats, separated by Roman columns and statuettes, creating the appearance of an undiscovered oasis of charm and tranquillity. None of this could be imagined from the street, as the block appeared quite plain and shuttered, save for the pleasantry of a single Juliet balcony and the paved steps up to the door.

The inside of the house was spacious, but most startling was the parlour where they were sitting. Whilst the other rooms were pleasantly arranged and functional, it was this that gave the fullest insight into the desires the Moussabeys held for the future.

The high ceilings were corniced, the walls papered plainly or painted white, draped with expensive coverings of decorative rugs. There was a four-seat settee, large individual sliding chairs, and sideboards in mahogany, on top of which were photographs of the family. The illumination was provided by elegant glass-domed candle lights affixed to the walls or standing on side tables. On the main wall above the fireplace hung a large French mirror, and greenery of all sorts filled the large, upright vases guarding the corners of the room. On the floor lay an expensive woollen carpet and the whole room conveyed an appearance of middle-class Victoriana.

In such surroundings, close friendships were easy to develop, and for the remaining hour of the evening the war remained a long way off, save for the ever-present legacy of uncertainty.

"We love Cairo," said Peter, "this is our home. But we remain outsiders. We are still not trusted to have the same rights as other Arabs. Yes, we have our school and faith, our own cemetery; but we worry what will happen when the British leave."

"Have you personally suffered attack?" asked Regis-Templeton.

"No, though there are shops who won't serve us, traders who spit when they see us. We are sometimes charged more than others."

Regis-Templeton grimaced.

"If there are shortages, we are most likely to be the first to suffer. So you see," he pointed to the surroundings, "all this is superficial. There is no certainty for us, only the reliance that we are forced to place upon our Coptic community, further ensuring our isolation. Even our church was invaded by criminals last Easter."

"Religion," said Hanna, "used as a means by our leaders to court popularity. But in times of hardship, blame the outsiders, the ones who have helped build this country for the last two hundred years."

"What we desire most when all this is over," continued Peter, "is an Egypt full of Egyptians, rather than those who call themselves Muslims or Copts."

"So you see, your talk of 'all Arabs,'" interrupted Hanna, looking towards the Brigadier, " is a fine ambition, but I'm not sure 'all Arabs' have Egypt's best interests at heart."

She continued to look intently at Regis-Templeton, but held back from the many other thoughts on her mind. He was now struggling with pain from the leg wound suffered on the Western Front, and the dry cough that had plagued him all night was worsening.

"But come," she said, "let's not dwell on these matters. We are all pleasantly tired, I can tell. Maybe we should save some things for another day?"

She smiled engagingly, and with gracious ease helped her guests to their feet and then to the overcoats necessary against the cool of the Cairo night. They embraced, exchanged thanks, and said their goodnights.

Peter walked them both down the stairs, through the courtyard, and across to the front door.

"There is just one thing that I must ask before you go," his voice lowered less Hanna overhear.

He looked directly at Regis-Templeton.

"When you said that the British are committed to supporting all Arabs, do you believe that London really feels that way?"

His British friends exchanged glances. Much as they desired to give the assurance he sought, there were some questions for which they had no truthful answers.

For the first few months of their new deployment, Laurie and Nooney did exactly as bade by their superiors at the Bureau. They became a familiar sight in the crowded squares, streets and alleys of central Cairo, as they led a small troop from the Bab El Hadid barracks searching for contraband, checking traders' passes, examining the registration documents of shops and café houses. On the dignified broader boulevards where the pace of life was slower, these duties were undertaken in a way Laurie was familiar with back home. But walk a hundred yards or so and they entered a distant century. Every step risked menace from the demands of beggars; filth and decrepitude predominated. Worse still, in amongst the hordes of legitimate traders peddling water, fruits, cigarettes and every imaginable item, were those bent on petty crime. To interfere invited a free-for-all, something they quickly learnt to avoid.

In these early operations, they wore their regular Military Police uniform rather than the civilian suits issued by the Bureau, and were accompanied by an Egyptian Police colleague to help smooth proceedings. They remained based at the barracks but were spared interaction with Captain Hillary. On occasions though, Laurie bumped into Sergeant Wirrall. He would wince mockingly, followed by a smile, once even uttering, "you lucky boy."

Other than that, time passed uneventfully, and the pair began to run an effective routine that embedded them within the working ways of the locals. In wishing to minimise confrontation, they frequently overlooked minor offences, gave warnings rather than sanction, and so began to be regarded as fair-minded.

This also brought them leads. Laurie's team of nightly helpers during his punishment detail had indeed been doing their best to illicitly recycle the contents of the barracks cesspit for pecuniary gain. But as the consequences of such revelation may have been disastrous for the individuals involved, largesse was applied to the strict requirement of the law. Arrests were avoided, whilst at the same time ensuring the respect of what in time might become an admittedly unreliable group of informants.

An unannounced raid led by Laurie and Nooney on a brothel in the El Quolali district, just west of the barracks, had unearthed a number of men of substance, both Arab and European. Their presence and exposure in this unregulated activity at a time when the 'Purification Society' movement in Egypt was becoming voluble was a huge embarrassment to the authorities.

One of those apprehended had been masquerading as a Swiss Banker, but in reality, was a German national. He'd agreed to work for the British as the price of anonymity, though the usefulness of his contacts was judged as limited. But it nevertheless sent a message; the British had indeed ramped up their own powers of surveillance.

"Reminded me of Wazzir, that one, mate," said Nooney, as they'd returned from a debriefing with Moussabey and Lowthian.

Laurie looked askance, awaiting further revelation.

"Yeah, first bloody battle of the war I was involved with, and it happened to be against my own lot."

"What do you mean?"

"Over by Clot Bey Square, Haret El Wasser Street, some parts were quite smart, cafés and the like, but down by the fish market, well, it wasn't so good back then, a big red-light area. Aussies got a bit carried away, bashed up the place, burnt down some buildings. We were there politely requesting the antagonists to desist, go back to the barracks, but in the end we had to call in the mounted blokes. And then when that failed, we progressed to the regular army. Two days it took to calm things down. Can you believe it?"

Laurie was less accustomed to the workings of a brothel.

"What caused it? Had the blokes been upset somehow?"

Nooney burst out laughing.

"Heard it all now, Laurie, what are you like?"

Laurie was still bemused.

"Of course not, you pommie dope, they were all being forced to pay more for their partying by the taxes your lot began imposing…" and he winked, "…for the services being rendered."

"What? How could that be possible? Even I know what they were doing's not allowed. You were breaking up an illegal gathering. You can't tax something like that, even the Egyptians want it banned."

"Might be illegal, mate, but does that make it wrong? You'd have more luck trying to sell that idea to a mummy."

Nooney knew his friend was clueless in such matters and over-optimistically moralistic about the fighting soldier.

"So, for me and you to come out of that place in El Quolali with our new German friend and the building still intact, well, that was a bonus in comparison."

They'd also uncovered a small-time ticket racket on one of the tram routes run by the Belgian *Societe Anonyme des Tramways Du Caire*. A group of locals were selling pre-printed tickets for the line across the Bulaq Bridge that crossed the Nile out to El Gezira. The greater presence on this route of Europeans, gullible enough to believe they'd bought a cheaper passage, gave a delicacy to the exposure. More significantly, it led Nooney and Laurie to a clandestine printing press east of Cairo, towards Heliopolis, that was circulating anti-British propaganda, which in turn was now being usefully manipulated by the team at the Bureau.

Contrasting with this, was the work they were beginning to undertake in their civilian disguise. For this they were billeted at the opulent Grand Continental Hotel, along with the rest of the Arab Bureau and officers of the regular army GHQ. Their rooms were small and subterranean, but pleasanter by far than the barracks. Once above ground, they were able to set foot in the freshness of an early Cairo sunrise, to be greeted by the tonic of Opera Square and the Ezbikya Gardens.

They operated alone, receiving their directives at morning briefings in the Bureau, the general thrust of which was that they use their talents as naive business types to unearth the illegal workings of the more formal Cairo economy. They took it in turns to lead on their alleged commercial interests in the city, slowly winding in the medium-sized operators with whom there had been some suspicion, employing their charm and sincere innocence.

Initial introductions were generally made by Peter Moussabey, acting as their local financier, thereby confirming the serious intention behind their offer. Then the sharply suited Messrs Nooney and Laurie would concoct a plausible story about an export business they wished to establish, pay a retainer, and extend their network. This was purely information gathering at first, with the Bureau needing to establish the degree of confidence and security that existed in British-controlled trading operations and regulation. Gradually though, the pair extended their reporting to the investigation of rumours about the ways to subvert restrictions; ways which might need controlling as the war effort developed.

But the more they collected information, the clearer it became that food shortages, so unpopular with the local population, had a cause far deeper than could be explained by either market forces or environmental constraint.

Egyptian consumption of sugar was huge, and sweetness appeared to be a constant requirement in Arabic food and drink. Over the course of the last year, supplies had declined, causing prices to rise, further reducing access for the majority urban poor. The British occupation had been blamed, though many local entrepreneurs had also applied their hardest efforts to encouraging this belief, in order to inflate their own charges.

Nooney and Laurie had unwittingly stumbled upon a potential source of the shortage. They had developed contacts with a sugar refinery, initially built for Khedive Ismail by the French but now in the hands of a local Arab family. Having promised moderate investment and exchanging a retainer, they'd been taken on a tour of the facility on the bank of the Nile, just south of Cairo. Whilst they'd judged the visit to be necessary for the purpose of good relationships, it had proven drearily dull and very uncomfortable in the stifling heat, made all the worse by the noise and smell of the processing. However, one throwaway comment had caught their attention as they'd passed the steam clarifiers that received the raw cane-juice.

"This," said the owner, pointing at the boiler and using broken English, "for Cairo." He then pointed outside to the railway sidings where the finished refined products were being loaded.

Then, turning back to the boiler area he indicated a separate channel leading from it that ran into a different vacuum evaporator.

"Also, for Cairo," he said, "or for you… your King?

They reported this snippet back to Lowthian, who immediately recognised its potential.

"I want you to travel to Alexandria tomorrow. It may be nothing, but we've had information that vessels berthing there are finding new ways to avoid their manifests being obvious to the authorities. Most are Arabic, so I will ask Peter to go with you. If this sugar company has outlets there we're unaware of, then it could prove most useful."

There was a slow train at first light from the main station next to Midan Bab El Hadid. Whilst this added a couple of hours onto the journey, it was also far too early for the mob of soldiers who'd be returning on the later express to Alexandria from their leave in Cairo. So, the three men were left to travel in relative peace, save for the loud conversation of the locals and, in some cases, the cackle from their means of trade.

"I think it's a chicken," said Nooney, who'd been studying an elderly man with very thin legs, holding a cage containing a bedraggled creature.

He was trying to keep up spirits, though neither Laurie nor Moussabey had seemed amused.

The carriages in the local trains were windowless, so on occasions during strong side winds, particles of discarded food tossed out of the window up-train re-entered with bullet-like force further down. A random pip or two from a tomato suddenly struck Nooney on the forehead, and he screamed theatrically, as if floored by a terminal blow.

That at least amused the pair, as well as their startled fellow travellers, so unused were they to seeing a European with a sense of humour.

"Now that is funny," said Moussabey, "but be careful, worse may be to follow."

He nodded to the squat that passed as the toilet ahead of them in the carriage.

"Strategy, you see, gentlemen. I said to you earlier that we should sit upwind of the commode, but did you listen?"

They smiled.

"Mind you," said Laurie, "I've heard that some of the first deaths amongst our men over here occurred when they hung through the windows to get some air, and the express coming the other way hit them."

"Blimey, mate, that's terrible," said Nooney, his face creased in horror.

"It's true," said Moussabey, "there are times when it is astute to keep one's head down."

"Try telling that to Laurie," said Nooney, and he and Moussabey chuckled.

They arrived in Alexandria at midday, pulling into the station near the Western Harbour. Laurie recognised the view along the quayside, now crammed with small boats and steam tugs, as the one he'd first spied upon arrival from France. The only marine traffic that day had been naval, and any excitement or curiosity had been quickly trampled as they rapidly disembarked onto railway freight waggons for the journey to their camp at Sidi Bishr, east of the town.

Today the high sun was at its fiercest, though the lighter cotton in their suits gave Nooney and Laurie some relief. Moussabey, on the other hand, seemed quite unaffected. He signalled for a carriage from the square outside the station concourse, instructing the driver to take them to Raas al Tien.

"Our customer is, should I say, a long-time contact," said Moussabey with his customary understatement.

"He knows me both as a financier and an opportunity; someone with contacts who might be useful to him. He doesn't like me of course."

"Well, he's not alone there then," said Nooney, smiling.

As the horse suddenly pulled away, he was caught unawares, and fell forward onto Moussabey's lap.

"You were saying?" said Laurie, giving Nooney a sideways look.

"I shall make the introductions," continued Moussabey, brushing away both Nooney and the humour, "then leave for an hour or so as if to establish the legalities, and return for you later in the afternoon. He speaks English, though don't let on you know this, and for today Nooney, please, no pigeon-Arabic."

Nooney nodded.

"Should we need more time, then we shall stay in town tonight. If not, then we might just make the last train back to Cairo."

Much as the pair admired Moussabey's efficiency and stoicism, they were already hungry and tired, so an overnight delay would not be unwelcome.

Laurie had seen little of Alexandria during his training there. The desert camp had offered slim relief from the monotony of marching, sand and flies, save for its YMCA, and mess tent. There was also the fortnightly treat offered by the dip in the Mediterranean Sea, but any thoughts of passes into town at this early stage were frustrated by the army's need to produce zealously drilled professionals.

So, he was pleasantly surprised to see the centre of town had scenes of splendour and elegance not unlike those of Cairo. But there was much less of it, and they were soon into squalor as they passed through the fish markets of the Mohammed Quarter on the promontory that separated Alexandria's two main harbours.

This poverty, far beyond anything Laurie had seen at home, worse even than in Cairo, continued to affront. How did people survive in such conditions? Why were they seemingly so pliant?

The carriage pulled up outside the offices of the boldly signed, *Alexandria West Bay Shipping Company*. It wasn't just the frontage that impressed, as once inside, the modern furniture, expensively decorated walls and huge fans pointed to a business that was suspiciously more successful than anything else on the street.

They had been greeted by a smartly attired young man, with Moussabey doing the introductions and explanations. The three men were then led through to the owner's office in the inner sanctum where a large Arab gentleman, wide as he seemed tall, and who called himself 'Smith' but clearly wasn't, greeted them all, particularly Moussabey, as if they were long-lost friends.

After the informalities and cups of tea, the business began, and in no short time Moussabey and Smith were engaged in heated confrontation.

Nooney had an idea of the exchanges, but both he and Laurie played dumb as instructed. After a lull in the proceedings, Moussabey turned, eyebrows raised, and in slow and pedantically exaggerated phrases developed the plot.

"Mr Smith is interested in your investment."

Both men nodded agreeably and smiled at the owner. From the discussions, this had seemed most unlikely, but Moussabey knew what he was doing, and all three knew that Mr Smith understood every word they said. They wished the illusion of their innocence to this fact to be quite clear.

"Oh, that's excellent," replied Laurie, "please affirm our determination to work with such a trusted partner."

Don't overdo it, thought Nooney.

"He could see a way to your proposals to ship the tonnage of sugar you wish to invest in across to Spain," continued Moussabey, "but insists that the risks are ever increasing, as therefore is the price."

Nooney and Laurie looked at each other in the mature way that businessmen with an exaggerated sense of self-confidence had always done. Then they briefly consulted a page of figures Nooney had open in his pocket diary. Laurie pointed to a spurious number or two on the page. Nooney then turned over and ruminated upon a note about writing home to his mother, asking her to knit him some lightweight socks. This completed, they nodded together in confirmation of both their agreement and shared acumen.

"Please tell Mr Smith," said Laurie, "that we understand his dilemma, and that we are interested, fair-minded and honourable."

Blimey, that'll cost Moussabey and the Bureau even more up front, thought Nooney.

Mr Smith appeared to smile, even before Moussabey had finished conveying the message, but the temperature of the debate between them soon rose again, and this time matters seemed terminal. Short of throwing things at each other, the disagreement between Smith and Moussabey could not have been more pronounced. Then, as suddenly as it blew up, the aggression fell away.

"Well, that seemed to go very well," said Moussabey, much to their amazement, "so if it is alright with you two gentlemen I will leave you for a while in Mr Smith's good hands. I shall go into town to set up the securities he will need and meet with the legal people. I believe that there is a basis for a deal that can be agreed upon."

Nooney and Laurie smiled in gentle yet understated triumph, and so too it seemed did Mr Smith, though his expression quickly changed when Laurie caught his eye.

"One thing still to establish is that as Mr Smith knows you are the legal owners of your company, he, in effect, will merely act as the lessor of the boat, and thereby the transactions will be under your names; his vessel, your risk, so to speak. He will therefore be able to legitimately assume you are simply transporting sugar. Whatever other cargo you may wish to… shall we say… include within the load, will be entirely your responsibility."

Moussabey paused, before uttering his benign reassurance, that "as you will understand gentlemen, this is purely in case of any misunderstanding with Egyptian and other foreign national authorities."

They nodded.

All three sensed that, indeed, they might be on to something.

"And he knows your interests, particularly in trade through neutral Spain, and confirms you can rely upon his absolute discretion at all times."

At that, Moussabey made his apologies and left, and Mr Smith sensing their underfed status, arranged with his assistant for food and more tea, which was dutifully brought in from the café next door.

They were both very hungry, and snaffled down the array of fruits, hard breads and nuts on offer, whilst gratefully confirming their enjoyment, indicating through every action that they really were men of honour. He, on the other hand, placed great emphasis upon ladling sugar into their cups.

"Sugar… good, yes?" he said with some difficulty, and they nodded. He reached into his pocket and pulled out some bank notes.

"Sugar is money…?"

They perfectly understood the equation and made encouraging signs of recognition.

He beckoned them to a very large map that was placed on the far wall of his office. It showed the Mediterranean from Gibraltar eastwards to Palestine, with Alexandria prominently indicated to the south-eastern quarter. The Red Sea and its interconnection to the Mediterranean via the Isthmus of Suez and Port Said, was also clearly visible. Attached by pins were small models of boats, many grouped together near to ports across the map. There must have been over a hundred such models, mostly small and similarly scaled, though a few were significantly larger.

The majority were positioned along the North African coastline in places such as Algiers, Tunis and Port Said, with a cluster near to Alexandria itself. Italian and Spanish locations seemed the next most popular, with a few scattered vessels to be found in the Red Sea. Maybe less than a dozen were in the middle of the sea, distant from land.

Mr Smith pointed to them to look more closely at the models, indicating markings on their stern which under such scrutiny were now clearly visible.

"Number," he said, repeating it again to ensure comprehension.

"Number… look."

As they focussed, they saw that the markings were Arabic numerals, inscribed by hand. The boat he'd pointed to had what appeared was a '7' written backwards.

"Six," he said, and they confirmed their understanding, though in Nooney's case somewhat quizzically.

Mr Smith thought that further instruction was needed, and pointed out a boat with a large letter 'E'

"Maybe three," said Laurie, cheerfully, holding up his fingers to confirm.

"Four," exclaimed Mr Smith.

He then stretched his hand across to a boat mid-Mediterranean. This had a number '9' on its stern. Eager to impress, Laurie pursued the logic. Semiotics had never been a skill, but he would give it a go.

"Ah, eight… or ten," he suggested, with a slightly triumphant grin.

"Nine," shouted Mr Smith.

"Good, yes?"

What was also apparent from the map though, was the scale of Smith's company, and the potential that any unregulated trade may therefore be having on supplies to Egypt. After all, this was just one of many such companies operating from Alexandria.

Mr Smith moved across to a lectern, which was standing beside the wall to one side of the map. Resting upon it, rather as would a King James Bible in a side chapel, was a large and impressively bound ledger. The numerals of each vessel were matched by an Arabic name, presumably that of the boat, and there were dates and lists seemingly set against each sea journey, accompanied by sketch maps and notes. As they looked further along the wall, there were other ledgers on shelving, further confirming the size of the operations involved.

He pointed on one of the pages to boat '31' where there were details of tides and ports along the Spanish coast.

"For you… this good?"

They made a reasonable effort at affecting interest in both the manifest and then returning to the map the current position of this, their potential boat, in any future arrangement. They refrained though from firm commitment. It seemed enough for the time being, to nod considerately, and for the next few hours Mr Smith engaged the pair with his well-constructed broken English and new-found passion for the sugar trade. They, in turn, responded with polite gratitude deemed sufficient to cement the relationship.

And despite the pretence at their separation by an uncommon language and the slowness apparent in their understanding of the rudimentary rules of engagement, the trio nevertheless found unexpected enjoyment in each other's company.

By the time Moussabey reappeared therefore, the chances of an investment hadn't been damaged, and he was pleased, surprised even, to see the bonhomie that had developed in his absence.

He presented a number of papers to Mr Smith, and the Arabic conversations that followed were this time quieter, if still not particularly amiable.

Yet the potential for their good work to be undone by Moussabey's frostiness with Smith was becoming troubling.

"Well, Moussabey," said Laurie, quite sternly, anticipating an opportunity to circumvent any potential antagonism, "perhaps we should call it a day for now and arrange to meet at a later date. Can you make that suggestion to our colleague?"

Moussabey bowed in agreement, and for a few minutes returned to further discussion with Smith about this prospect.

"Two weeks today," he said to them eventually, "and maybe if you two gentlemen would oblige, you could perhaps entertain Mr Smith in your offices in Cairo?"

Blimey, thought Nooney, who, up until this point, had kept a low profile but was now concerned this might throw Laurie. After all, he was newer to this and hadn't experienced how effectively Moussabey and the Cairo team could set things up.

"Of course," replied Laurie, "that would be our pleasure."

Nooney was relieved. He really needn't have worried. Laurie had understood the nuances, and played a blinder.

After a further few minutes of agreeable small talk, they made their excuses, exchanged the friendliest of goodbyes, and alighted a carriage that had been called for them to make their way back to the station.

"So far so good, gentlemen," said Moussabey quietly, "but remain cautious." He indicated towards the driver ahead of him; a reminder that the ears of others could hold perils.

The rest of the journey passed in silence, but once they'd been dropped off and were alone, Moussabey congratulated them upon the day's activities.

"We have a bite, as I believe fishermen say, though landing the catch will be harder."

"Particularly given its size," said Nooney, alluding more to Mr Smith's person than the scale of duplicity they'd undertaken.

"Better to return to Cairo tonight," said Moussabey, "too many interested parties here." And tired though they all were, this seemed the sensible option.

"Tell me," said Laurie, "what is it about you that he found so unpalatable?"

"Well, mostly I suspect that I appear to be doing very nicely from my attachment to British businessmen."

"But he's doing alright himself with that, isn't he?" replied Laurie.

Moussabey grinned and shook his head.

"There may also be something else… he is a Muslim."

Laurie was confused.

"…whereas I am a Coptic," said Moussabey.

Laurie's puzzlement continued.

"We occasionally struggle with each other."

There was a prolonged silence. Despite his ignorance about such matters, Laurie was aware of the sensitivity, and anyway, the day had presented stresses for them all. What they needed most for the journey back to Cairo and the Continental Hotel, was peace.

As they moved through the booking office to catch the last express train of the evening, a growing wailing noise arose from the platform. "Waltzing Matilda, Waltzing Matilda, we'll come a Waltzing Matilda with you…"

The untrained massed choir of intoxicated, sweating Australian troops travelling to Cairo for three days' leave, were chorusing their shared heritage. The three men wearily made their way as far as they could, away from the noise and towards the front of the train, squashing in alongside a wary group of locals. There would at least be some small solace in being upwind for the return.

The journey back on the express was mercifully quicker than that of the early morning, and they even managed to sleep for part of it. As they disembarked in Cairo, both Nooney and Laurie found their lightweight business suits of little protection in the cold of the late evening. Moussabey seemed immune but sympathetic.

"I will see that you get some heavier overcoats," he said, and they nodded. Neither would have asked for this; he was indeed a kindly man.

Very little was happening as they wandered across Midan Bab El Hadid, though the cafés and night-life of the surrounding streets were still very much alive. They'd resigned themselves to a significant walk at the end of what had been a very long day, so felt fortunate to make the last Munira tram.

The Poet Laurie Ate

As it rumbled into Opera Square, Moussabey shook their hands warmly, and the two men alighted to leave for their quarters at The Grand Continental Hotel.

"Thank you," he said. "I believe today's business will prove very fruitful."

He waved to them from the tram as it departed, and they both felt touched by his warmth.

"He's a good sort," said Laurie, as they strolled across the Square, "he's got a lot on his plate working with us."

"What do you mean?" replied Nooney. "He knows we're a decent team, that we can get results."

"Not that, Nooney. It's just that now he's relying upon us more than we are upon him."

"Meaning?"

"Well, without him, our work here would be very difficult, but without us, our troops, his future and that of his family would be unbearable. You saw how Smith spoke to him."

They were just entering the hotel foyer and were greeted royally by the doorman.

"You're right, mate. Must admit, though, for a while today I thought he almost got in our way."

"That said," replied Laurie, nodding in agreement, "I can't imagine what's really playing through his mind. If Smith and his mates were given free rein, I'd hate to be in Moussabey's shoes."

They were just about to descend the stairs to their basement rooms when a concierge called Laurie across.

"See you in the morning, then" said Nooney. "It's been good one, today."

Laurie walked to the hotel desk and was passed a letter. His wife's handwriting was instantly recognisable from the address and he could barely hide his elation. He skipped down the steps to his room.

He was justifying the trust placed in him by the Bureau; his talents were at last being recognised. He could hold his own with Nooney and Moussabey, men he'd normally feel more capable, more elevated than he. On top of that, they depended upon him at times; the insignificant boy who'd run away from school, from the life sentence of an apprenticeship, whose superiors had threatened he would never make anything of himself. But here he was, on another continent, relied upon as an equal, with a purpose to his life, a status. His decision to enlist had been justified.

He unlocked the door and entered, lighting a candle in the globe on the tiny cupboard by his bed. There was barely space to turn around, yet it was private and beyond anything the barracks could offer. Sitting close to the flickering light, he carefully unpicked the envelope and pulled out the letter. He could feel his wife's hand on the page as he gently caressed the paper. He held it to his lips, then pressed it against his cheeks.

He began to read;

My dearest Thomas,

How are you my darling? Every night we pray for your safety. It seems so long since we parted. The children constantly ask about you. They were excited to receive your news. Are you still in Alexandria? We worry you may be sent to the trenches.

My sister has gone home to nurse, as momma is seriously ill. I fear it will not be long now. We are getting help from St Mary's Relief, I am sewing, and the boys will be working for Mr Sprosson in the summer with the fruit harvest, so that will help.

We all cry for you and miss you dearest. We pray for your return to us.

Loving affection,

Eve

The edifice of joyous self-justification crumbled. His wife's words were far braver than anything he'd achieved. They'd all been burdened by his desertion. But still they loved him.

He fell to the cold stone floor and wept.

CHAPTER 6

"Good morning my beautiful grandchild."
Llucia beamed as little Aina came running across the field that fronted the Cava des Coloms.

"Why, you are in such a rush."

Aina smiled, her face flushed by the scramble down the path from the Quintana farm at Turo Vell. The exertion and excitement left her struggling for her words.

"Steady yourself, my lovely one; what have I told you about running around like a young spring hare? Here, catch your breath; let me get you some fruit."

But what Aina had to say couldn't wait. She adored her grandmother and wished more than anything to obey, but this was too important. As Llucia took her hand to walk towards the cave, she pulled back hard.

"No, Nana… the padre…"

Llucia could see that she would have to listen. The precious younger daughter of her beloved son was insistent, just as he would have been at her age. She knelt down and put her arms around Aina's waist.

"Tell me then, Aina, it must be important for you to turn down that fruit."

Aina smiled, her breathing slowing.

"The padre, Nana; he's at the farm."

Aina's face was full of the wonderful innocence of her young years, and how Llucia adored her for it.

"He wants to see you, so as the fastest, I said I would come to the Cova to tell you."

Llucia hugged and then kissed her granddaughter and held her tightly for a few moments.

"You are such a wonderful girl to find me so quickly, and with such an important message. You're the best granddaughter a nana could ever have."

Aina's face lit up.

"Come, sit awhile so that you can get all of your breath back, and then we'll make our way back to the farm."

But something was still troubling Aina; rest seemed the last thing she desired.

"What, you're still not happy I can see," said Llucia, smiling reassuringly.

"The padre, Nana, will he think we are not going back?"

Llucia knew exactly what the padre was thinking and why he was visiting, but it would be very many years before Aina needed to be concerned by such insight.

"Ah, you know how the padre likes to talk, I am sure he will be so happy in the company of the Quintana children, perhaps he will read some of your father's poems to them?"

Aina seemed delighted with that thought, and quickly settled.

"Come then, there are a few things to finish here. Perhaps you can help me?"

She took Aina by the hand and they walked towards the huge entrance to the cave, greeted as they did so by the farmhands who were loading a line of carts. The huge dome of the interior was only partly lit by the sunlight, the darker beyond relying upon dozens of very tall candles, and there was an odour not unlike the inside of Sant Cristofol at Mass.

"Nana, it smells like the church. Padre would love it here."

Llucia grinned and squeezed Aina's hand. She very much doubted he would, though his candles had come in useful.

"We keep all our gifts here, Aina."

She pointed to the ledges crammed with wine bottles, cheeses, pickles, preserved fruits, and then beyond to a hewn-out chasm near the back of the cave, where hundreds of sacks of grain and other foodstuffs were stored.

"It is important we give back to those who are most in need. We try our best to use the advantages we have been given to support others."

"That is beautiful, Nana. It is what the padre would want."

There were more labourers visible now, sorting produce to be stored or stacking crates to be carried out to the waggons. There was also some building work going on to complete a mostly constructed storehouse, next to which stood a group of small huts. Aina asked what they were used for.

"Sometimes, Aina, our workers are too tired to go home, and so we have these little homes to help them sleep if they wish."

She omitted to mention that they would also be armed, patrolling the entrance to the Cava des Coloms with strict military precision.

"Aina, just over there are some fresh oranges, perhaps you would like one whilst I quickly finish my work here?"

Aina nodded and skipped away.

"Go and pick one up and then wait for me for a while. I'm just going to talk with your Uncle Gil." She pointed to her eldest daughter's husband across the cave who was deep in conversation with several of the workers.

"Ah, Llucia," shouted Gil as she approached, "I saw you come in, but forgive me, we are trying to load the wine and fruit as quickly as possible, and then cover it from the sun."

Gil was in effect the second-in-command to Oriol within the family network. He shared this honour with his wife Isla, Llucia's third daughter, and the strongest leader amongst her girls. They were a formidable coupling, and Llucia trusted them.

"I understand, Gil," she replied, "I just wanted to check that we are delivering as normal these next few days, though I can see from the industry here that everything is in hand."

"As you had asked, Llucia," he replied, "by Sunday morning we shall have supplied all our needy with gifts. They will attend church with a smile."

Llucia had earned her status as the largest landowner on the island by hard fought right. Her patronage though, and with it the Quintana future, was bought. The products of her lands, the rents from her properties and the incomes from her trades provided huge surplus. But significant donations from this resource also filled the larders of her people, whilst her farms offered labour and her men guaranteed protection. Even the church had submitted to her landed superiority. In a time of great uncertainty, the Quintana family had come to represent security for the many… the far too many, that surrounded her and her family.

"Gil, I must ask, have you discussed with Oriol the arrangements during his next absence?"

Gil was surprised by her question. She rarely interfered these days, but was always consulted with, and he was grateful of her confidence in him. This though, was very unusual.

"We've spoken at length, Llucia, about the time he should be away, the way we'll move the artwork onto its new owner, and the things that need to be maintained whilst he is journeying."

She still appeared troubled.

"Gil, I need to ask you this but please, do not mention it to Oriol."

This really was unlike Llucia.

"Do you think it will be safe for him to make this journey?"

Gil hesitated for a while before replying.

"I tell you honestly, Llucia, these trades are becoming harder. This needs to be the last. There is never certainty but this I can say: Oriol is the most gifted person I know, he is meticulous and astute. Nothing will be left to chance I assure you. Whatever is thrown his way he will deal with."

Llucia squeezed Gil's arm.

"Thank you, Gil. Above everything, you can see that I am still a mother."

Aina had talked nonstop to her nana as they walked up the track back to Turo Vell. Nothing was beyond her attention, and Llucia loved every precious moment. Why was it that the field walls were made out of odd-shaped stone? Couldn't they afford straight ones? Who said animals didn't smile? What makes a chicken? How did waves break and then get back together again? Where exactly is the end of the world the padre talks about?

"*Señora*... as I was saying."

Llucia had strayed from Alvaro Marin's monotonous monologue about the health of Sant Cristofol and its congregation, and back to little Aina and her beautiful questions.

They were sitting on a hay bale across the farm courtyard from the well. A band of rogue crows flailed noisily across the sky above them, and she found the noise remarkably uplifting, their tones enchanting compared to the whine proffered by the padre. She began to regain something of the thread and nodded towards him.

"...and to continue..."

Yes, you just do that, thought Llucia; see where it gets you.

"...it would be very helpful if the church could use that old barn of yours for a reading room for the children on a Sunday after the service."

"Old barn?"

"Yes, the one on Cami d'es Cementiri; you know, the door is missing, and inside it is empty."

Yes, of course she knew, but how could he not?

"Ah, that barn," she replied. "Well, what an interesting proposition. You are aware that the Quintana's will always help."

He tried to smile, but instead a wispy sneer slicked down the sides of his mouth.

"But first, why a room for reading, have you not space enough already?"

Just what he'd been waiting for, as she knew.

"But, *Señora*, there are already so many precious items that Sant Cristofol hosts for the Quintana family, and I fear we shall run out of places for our gentler flock."

Llucia looked him straight in the eye, withholding for a moment what she needed to say. It wasn't that she took any pleasure in the act, rather that she wondered where actually was the man within the vestments?

"Why can't the children sit and read inside the church? There are many pews."

"But they are family pews, *Señora*; this would be unpopular. And the church is a sacred place."

"Perhaps if the children sat there and read that Jesus said, '*suffer little children and forbid them not to come unto me, for such is the Kingdom of Heaven*' they would understand more clearly this 'sacred' that you talk of? Though maybe you fear their noise? Or is it that you have simply misplaced the notion that the sacred might think that they, too, should be listened to?"

The padre's face shrank inwards. Until now, he'd hoped to deflect any matters of mutual dislike through their common interest, but such confidence had been foolhardy.

"And anyway, would it not be better for the children to find the sacred by, shall we say, running around in the field next to the barn enjoying themselves as children should? After all, they would need it after your service wouldn't they?"

His eyes widened, as any words that may have been forthcoming were now so depressingly harnessed.

"The barn?" she continued, her voice rising though still containing the anger bursting within.

"The door? Empty you say? You really have no idea do you?"

"*Señora?*"

She paused again. Was he really so very stupid, an innocent without measure perhaps, or was it rather he was knowingly noxious towards her?

"My parents, my family, were butchered in that barn."

The padre gasped, shocked and revolted by her words. He lurched backward as if recoiling from the appalling imagery.

"The door is off, left exactly as it was when the murderers left. The barn is empty… now… but that day it was filled with the smell of death, and the anguish of the dying."

She waited for a moment for the words to find their worth. The padre avoided her gaze, his discomfort intense. It was pity, she decided; yes that was it, the overriding emotion she had for this man. He was, in every sense, pitiable.

"You talk of the sacred. That empty barn, as you put it, truly is sacred. It is, and always will be, a memorial to the innocents of my family. I lived that day, but my innocence died."

"*Señora*, I had no idea..." whispered the padre, now gaunt, eyes searching the floor.

"Of course you didn't, though you have been here for how many years? Do you not look up beyond that world prescribed for you?"

"*Señora*..."

"Do you not deal with actual injustices in the same way that you preach about them?"

"*Señora*, I never for once realised that..."

"That what? That the holiness now residing in Palma should possibly be accountable for his sins?"

The padre was now in need of his own absolution.

"*Señora*, we have discussed this many times; he would not have known of the full transgressions; he is a good..."

"A good man?" she interrupted, sizing him as a predator about to engulf its prey.

"You tell me this, even though the story of his evil has yet to be heard within the episcopacy over which he presides."

They sat silent together for a brief moment, the burden of pain lying heavily upon time. And then she pounced.

"Which is why you are here."

The padre lifted his head.

"You are shortly to travel to Palma for your annual meeting with those very many colleagues, and of course with the 'Innocent of Palma' himself. Whilst you are there you, will carry out a small favour for me."

He closed his eyes.

"I have a letter that you should pass to him. You see, something really quite straight forward."

There was another pause, a silence that aggravated his already visible discomfort, but she let it continue until its flow overwhelmed.

"I cannot," he muttered.

She remained silent, long enough for his exhaustion to be complete, for his downing to be a formality. By the time he spoke again, it was hard to hear him above the army of early-afternoon Cicadas.

"I cannot be involved with your scheming," he whispered.

She laughed dismissively. He was even beneath pity.

"You are a woman alone, you do not know of the forces you will unearth if this malady persists."

"What do you know of a woman alone?" She spat. "You think that I need a man for my approbation? You are despicable. Look around you. These buildings, the land, they are the work of a woman; the love within my family, the work of a woman. And the health and livelihood of the people and your church; also the work of a woman."

He went to speak again but she hadn't finished.

"As for the forces of this world, I am well aware of them. But if it is the next world you refer to, then I don't expect to see you there, a mercy for which I am grateful."

With such talk of the spiritual the padre seemed to rally, momentarily.

"I warn you," he said, now looking her in the eye and more audible, "persist with these actions at your peril."

Llucia felt pleasure that at last she has elicited something of the man within the weakling frame that faced her. But the moment quickly passed.

"You threaten me?" she asked.

"I have control of the things you need."

"Such as?"

"The walls and store spaces of Sant Cristofol."

She slowly moved her face so that it positioned uncomfortably close to his and examined his features, as if searching for a mole. He tried to back away, but there was nowhere to go.

"I have no need of that which I already own," she hissed, "indeed one wrong word from me and your reputation, for what it is worth, and all those ordained benefits you enjoy, the huge Manse, the bowing patronage of the faithful, your 'living' if that's what you think it is, would be at an end, and you would be pleading with me to protect you in your escape."

"I have nothing to be forgiven about," he responded.

"Maybe not," she replied, "but that can be arranged."

For five minutes or so, the pair sat together, and from the farm house would have appeared as friendly acquaintances, contented in each other's company. The blood that drained from the padre's face though would have filled the well.

Llucia decided to put an end to the numbness, and passed him the letter. It was addressed to *His Excellency Paulinus, The Bishop of Es Gara, Seminari, Palma Balears.*

"You will pass this to him. If there is one moment's hesitation, tell him it is from Llucia from Es Migjorn Roca, whom he will remember from the troubles during his time at Sant Cristofol."

The padre barely had the strength to shake his head.

"I have no words…" he whispered, and Llucia looked at him and then smiled.

"At last, we have established the perfect relationship."

They stood, and the padre shuffled off, heading for the gate. Llucia's eyes followed him. For the briefest moment, she regretted the dialogue she'd inflicted. But then she remembered the barn and the world now available to her beautiful granddaughter, Aina, and her many questions.

"Oh, and, Alvaro," she shouted, "maybe next time we meet you will be able to tell me where exactly to find the 'end of the world'?"

"We must cast our nets."

Elisheba Andreassen stood at the wheel on the tiny bridge of *The Adelphi*, calmness personified within the storm that surrounded them. For the last three days of high seas, Oriol had gazed with increasing admiration and respect as she and her younger brother, Mattityahu, had mastered the challenges of an ungrateful Mediterranean and brought him safely to this point, thirty miles from the Sicilian coast. Oriol had planned to be of some help to the crew even though he himself was the valuable cargo, but severe seasickness had dogged both this intention and his pride.

Elisheba's instruction had led to urgent action from the three deck hands aboard, and with practiced efficiency, and despite the conditions, they winched the fishing nets from below and over the stern into the waters. Oriol had made these journeys with the Andreassens for many years, and the one thing he knew was that in weather like this, it was unwise to risk the stability of the vessel by trawling.

Elisheba could tell what he was thinking and handed him binoculars, pointing at a distant dot visible as they peaked the crest of each wave. He tried to focus but, even though he had nothing left to vomit, the nausea was overpowering. He passed them back, apologetically.

"U-boat," said Elisheba.

No further words were needed. Even though the risks were great, to appear as a functioning fishing boat trawling in such rough weather might spare them unwanted attention. With the sinking of British vessels in the Dardanelles, U-boat operations had become increasingly incisive; *The Adelphi*'s registration as a Spanish neutral wouldn't necessarily protect it from attack.

"Do we need to signal?" shouted Oriol, trying to be heard above the noise of the storm. He knew that the Andreassens' German contacts were reliable and that perhaps this would alert as to their identity.

"Not yet," she replied.

"We knew we should keep clear of the waters around the Straits of Otranto, the Ionian Sea even, but this isn't normal. We must keep a direct approach hoping that in these seas they see us dropping our nets and therefore judge we are nothing to fear."

The Adelphi was one of the Andreassen's more reliable boats. It was neither large nor small, a 'Drifter' some ninety feet long that on a good day and in a calm sea could journey at an unremarkable nine knots per hour. British-built, it was now in fourth-hand ownership, berthed in Mao and Spanish flagged. It was to all intents a low grade chugger, and this was its greatest strength. From a distance, and particularly in heavy seas, its low wooden hull lay so close to the water that it often passed undiscovered, or simply as the irrelevant trawler that for part of the time it was. But today could be different; the sail may have been down and secured, but the smoke from the coal burner powering the engine was leaving a filthy black trailing flag of recognition.

"Why has it surfaced?" asked Oriol. Elisheba hunched her shoulders.

"Could be they are releasing waste gases, taking in fresh oxygen… it's unusual in such conditions."

"Or to use us as target practice," laughed Mattityahu, who had crammed in alongside them on the bridge and was trying to focus on the U-boat's movements.

By now the three deck hands would be clearly visible from a distance, dressed as they were in yellow oil-skins and working the nets. Oriol marvelled at their synchronicity, making light work of both the boat's movement and the physicality required. For a further ten minutes, Elisheba kept the vessel at maximum speed, but once the trawl was fully active, she slowed and this, together with the dragging action of the nets, made the boat roll even more. She was a skilful skipper, but this was testing.

All eyes now fixed on the distant dot. Were it to accelerate towards them, they would know within the quarter whether they were to be considered friend or foe. On the other hand, should they themselves deviate to avoid confrontation, they would risk be hunted down by a boat that on the surface, even in these waters, could travel at twice their top speed.

There were two options. Either they could risk that they'd remained unseen and attempt to change bearings, or they could continue their course and thereby confirm their innocent intent, as their approach and wide berth would provide no serious opposition for the U-boat.

"Be ready to move to the gun."

Mattityahu nodded his understanding, though both he and his sister knew that the six-pounder hidden below the tarpaulin at the bow would be no match for any enemy firepower.

For the next half an hour, *The Adelphi* inched toward the dot. For the crew, there was no question of bravery, nor time to dwell upon the horror that could consume them; they were transfixed by their duties to each other, grimly determined, sailing toward the jaws they feared yet praying they cheat it of quarry.

Oriol, on the other hand, remained too nauseous to be of any use, though in truth there was little he could have usefully contributed. The

Andreassens and their crew appeared fearless, and he'd been right to trust them with his life.

"They don't seem to be closing," shouted Mattityahu, who by now had slithered his way to the fore, roping himself precariously to the davit.

He raised the binoculars to his eyes again for what seemed an age, before flinging out an arm and signalling his confusion. He crawled slowly back to the bridge, stopping for balance each time the boat crested another huge wave, holding on for life as the waters briefly submerged him.

"I can only see their stern. It's definitely a U-boat, but it's impossible to make out any markings or activity on the deck."

"Are we out of range?" asked Oriol.

"For us, yes," replied Mattityahu, "for them, probably not."

"Is it possible they still haven't seen us?"

Just then, a distant boom distinctly audible despite the noise of the storm, stopped the conversation dead. Within a few seconds the deathly whine of successive shells fizzed above them and into the sea a hundred yards beyond to starboard. There was pandemonium on board.

"Cut the nets," screamed Elisheba, "cut the nets."

The deck hands worked with a new fury despite the impossibilities of the heaving sea, hacking frantically at the ropes that tethered the precious means of their labour to the winches.

Another eruptive punch of evil broke through the rage, and a second volley of shells whooshed towards them, this time landing well short port side but exploding with the force of four or five sea mines, shaking the boat brutishly to one side. Mattityahu scrambled as best he could to help with the nets, and Oriol went to follow but Elisheba shouted at him to stay.

"Cut the nets," she screamed again, raging almost uncontrollably, as another huge wave passed over the boat and a further volley of shells exploded in the distance ahead of them.

The boat shuddered and Oriol feared the worst as he clung on to a guard rail. Elisheba fell, ramming heavily against him, but her left hand remained clutched to the wheel, and somehow the boat righted.

The terror was all consuming. Proud though each was of their strength to survive, they were beyond anything that rational thought could assist.

There were many ways to die but to do so in such isolation, in dread and insignificance and engulfed by raging waters, was beyond imagination.

"Mamà, my father, the man you met in those terrible times… was he a good man?"

Oriol could see the pain in his mother's face as she struggled for a way to explain.

"He was my greatest love. He was a good man."

There was shouting from the stern, and Oriol hove to from his momentary imagining to the nightmare that surrounded him.

"Nets away," they bellowed, and now free of the restrictive burden of the trawl, the boat lurched forward, causing him to bang his head against a window of the bridge. He registered there should be pain, but felt nothing but numbness.

The deck hands now edged towards the hold. As the boat rolled, one of them fell down the steps that led into it, followed by a huge deluge of water. The other two clung to the hatch cover as if awaiting his return, and remarkably a few moments later, a head reappeared, followed by two rifles. They helped pull him back on deck and all three crawled to a gap between the hatch and the single lifeboat, propping themselves in the void, forcing their legs against a winch jack and their arms under a rope that tied down the tarpaulin. With two rifles between the three of them, they were at least assured of a pointless means to cope with the enemy, or more likely, their own mortal end.

Mattityahu, seeing this glorious futility, made to return to the gun on the bow, but Elisheba, visibly shocked but fighting for self-control, shouted to him and waved for him to get back to the tiny bridge.

"No point," she wailed.

"But I must…"

"No, no, no," she screamed, now almost manic, stay in here."

She pushed the boat back to full-speed and changed bearing.

"We have nothing to lose," she shouted, and Oriol and her brother both grimly nodded their assent.

Another dull thud, lighter this time, sounded from the direction of the dot, and they waited in collective terror for the fizzing whine to get louder and impact, but this too fell short to the port side, though still close enough to heave the boat uncomfortably to its side.

Everyone aboard dared hope, but no one spoke, and this was how things remained for the next hour. Even though the firing became infrequent, ultimately ceasing, there was no certainty that the U-boat hadn't submerged and would eventually finish the job. The high seas prevented any confirmations, and the intensity and strain prevented further conversation.

After a further hour, the seas began to settle, and with it an intense fatigue borne out of the immense stress and effort becalmed them all. Elisheba was just about awake, hanging across the wheel. Mattityahu was hunched asleep against Oriol, and the exhausted crew spread limply across each other cocooned within their void, still clutching the two rifles.

"Then one morning just a few weeks before your birth, he left for his work, and both he and his goodness died… drowned… fell into the harbour at Mao, trying to help steady a small sailing lug to the harbour wall in the rising tide; his body washed out to sea… but this I think you already know."

"Oriol my son, Oriol…"

"Father…?"

"Oriol… I'm here. I'm here with you in the water."

Frantically, Oriol tried to swim to his father but the seas were too high, and the weight of his clothing was burdening his efforts.

"Father, I will soon be with you. Stay; I am coming. Father, father…"

But the chasm between them was widening, and despite his enormous efforts, his father was drifting further away, slipping beneath the waves.

"Father… father, stay…"

Oriol awoke with a jolt, his dreaming physically manifested in screams that brought him back to his senses. Mattityahu roused from next to him but quickly returned to slumber. Elisheba remained too exhausted to notice, prostrated across the wheel. Surrounded as he was by chaos and despair, his personal madness remained unwitnessed.

The boat was bobbing more gently now, the hum of its engine giving assuredness to the fact he was still alive. He gently shoved Mattityahu to one side and struggled to his feet. There was blood on his clothing and hands and he examined his slumbering partner for signs of injury, though he seemed perfectly fine. He steadied himself against the bridge rail, and focussed on the sea about him, straining towards the horizon in all directions. Nothing. He lifted the binoculars that were lying below Mattityahu's hands and placed them to his eyes. Again, he examined the waters, squinting as best he could through shaking hands. Nothing.

His nausea had completely passed, though there was what felt like a bruise to his forehead. All that surrounded them now was the calming azure beauty of the Mediterranean Sea and the alluring smell of a gentle sea-breeze.

"That's quite a gash," said Elisheba as she watched Oriol absent-mindedly prodding the wound to his head. He smiled, though somewhat through gritted teeth, as the pain was now quite sharp. As to how this wound had come about, he had no idea.

They were berthed for the day in Syracuse, a welcome shelter on the south-east coast of Sicily, entirely unplanned until the events of the previous day. Their sailing routine when crossing the Mediterranean was generally reliant upon the use of Andreassen facilities on the island of Malta, then setting south for the relative safety of Italian dominated Tripoli. From there, they would hug the protection offered by the North African coastline and their extensive network, to protect them from suspicion. But the heavy seas and the attention of the U-boat had thwarted that expectation.

"My conclusion for what it's worth," said Elisheba, "is that they'd had difficulties and been forced to surface. So they'd problems enough of their own without the unwelcome attentions of ourselves."

"Fortunately, they were poor shots," replied Oriol.

"Exactly so. They wouldn't normally fire like that, surfaced and in a rolling sea. It was impossible for them to accurately target us. I believe they were frightening us away."

"Did a good job as well," laughed Oriol.

The boat was roped against substantial limestone walls on the Ortigia

Island side of the town's ancient outer harbour, with just the briefest of motion to indicate that they were on water. Mattityahu and the crew were ashore, attempting to replace the abandoned nets. Given their shared experience of the increasing hazards these trips presented, a fishing vessel without nets would be awkward to explain if challenged. Oriol had offered payment, feeling somehow responsible for their loss, even though he was not the sole reason for the journey.

"These are our risks," Elisheba had pointedly replied, "you are merely part of the necessary excuse."

And sharp though those remarks at first had appeared, Oriol reflected she was indeed correct. All being well, the hold of the boat would soon be filled, and returning to Mao with the products of the everyday trades that continued in spite of the war. A significant and mostly legitimised part of that would be for the Quintana coffers, though these, together with the other goods aboard, would also represent a healthy return for the Andreassens.

There was more though to this family than Oriol could quite place. The boat would move on to Palestine once he was ashore in North Africa, to trade with the Turks, he suspected, though any attempt to seek anything other than the most general information about this was rebuffed. The Quintanas prided themselves on their forensic knowledge of those with whom they engaged, so he found this frustrating. Any trades in Ottoman dominated Palestine were perilous.

"We owe your family a debt of gratitude and the honesty of our word," Elisheba had said on the distant occasion Oriol had chosen to pursue the matter, "and the independence to maintain our and your businesses without the conflict of unnecessarily shared knowledge."

They were stretched out on the benches of the mess deck, which lay amidships occupying a part of the original hold. Around them lay debris from the previous day's encounter, though the crew's rifles were now stored back in the secure magazine and out of sight, and the bunks in the small wardroom were drying out.

"So," she suddenly said, changing the tone, "it took a German U-boat to bring the poet to his *Odyssey*."

Oriol was quite startled.

"Behold, I bring you Syracuse." She waved her arms about her towards the outside world, requiring his recognition.

This didn't immediately happen, so she set upon a more direct and literary route.

"Why so one-eyed?" she implored.

He smiled. First she'd called him a poet, when few had ever done so before, and now her allusion to Cyclopes was both unexpected and comical, though he doubted few of those who knew him would have laughed. The head of a poet was indeed quite solitary.

"It is unusual to meet someone who remembers the literature drilled into them when young," he said eventually, and she gave him a discouraging look.

"Or someone who has also since those days read and re-read Homer's works?" she said dismissively.

He recognised the rebuke and, in it, an underestimation of her that he would not tolerate for his daughters.

"There is majesty in his words," she continued, "and a challenge."

He went to interrupt, but then felt the better of it.

"His words brought us civilisation, but where are we today? The world is tearing itself apart because of leaders who value themselves above all others. Where is nobility? Does the evidence of past folly go ignored? Do beautiful words not matter?"

She shook her head in gentle despair.

"No matter how glorious the prose, without the means to effect its intent, we remain as the Cyclopes, ignorant, barbaric, myopic."

Oriol was beginning to regret his own misjudgement of Elisheba. He had admired her courage and skill as a leader, but had not considered a capacity beyond such usefulness. Perhaps he too valued himself above all others?

"I cannot claim any merit in my own writing, save that it describes a kinder world and reminds me of the man I would hope to be."

"And what is that?" she replied. "You, me, we are trapped by a tyranny that crushes ideals, that demands we should respond. Yet still we dither, consumed, challenged."

Oriol was confused.

"Challenged?"

"By Homer, by righteous action, by words beautiful or blind, that, as you might say, direct us."

"I still don't…"

"You write beautifully; I have your poetry." He smiled, amazed and delighted by her compliment. "But to achieve that world have you become a mercenary?"

Oriol was pole-axed by the assertion. She had invaded a personal nightmare. Good man though he strove to be in a world of fiends, he led a family who dominated, and made the many depend upon their magnanimity. As for the war raging about him, he saw neither friend nor foe, simply opportunity. How indeed did his words, his virtue, match with such self-enhancing pursuits? How would such contradictions enable the enlightened legacy of which he wrote?

"My family had to fight hard for its rights," he mumbled, "…rights which I now fight to extend on behalf of the many."

Elisheba could tell her words had hurt. The Quintanas had been benefactors to her family business and sensibility determined caution. But her free spirit also recognised in him the willingness for introspection that accorded with her own. And besides, she had bigger fish to fry.

"A Menorca that rules itself, if I am not mistaken?" she suggested.

He fixed her gaze directly, determined to resist the invitation to elaborate. She waited for him to speak, visibly impatient that the question remained hanging.

"So what about me you are doubtless thinking?"

Again, he remained silent.

"Do I too have ambitions that conflict?"

"I have always tried to respect your family's request for privacy with regard to your business," replied Oriol. "I wouldn't dream to inquire beyond the direct trades that affect me."

"There you go. Have you not looked beyond?"

The interaction had already unsettled him, but now there was a passion in her voice that portended menacingly.

"You are not alone in suffering for freedom. For a Jewish family in search of a homeland, such suffering also has huge meaning."

He had no idea she was Jewish, nor that it held such significance for her.

"Our voyages include trade in Palestine. Not the easiest place you might think in which to engage. That's because our business is dominated by a burning passion to right the wrongs inflicted upon us over centuries, to return to the land of our forebears."

There was a silence. Oriol had his own view of the complicated history involved, some of it learnt at first-hand. The British were now massing their army of conquest in Egypt, ready to cross into Palestine and replace centuries of Ottoman rule. Only the unwise, or someone so heavily convicted as Elisheba, would continue to trade there. And only a fool would place their faith in the British should they replace that old order.

"So your trades," inquired Oriol, sensing the obvious but wishing to deflect, "they are much more than just commercial?"

Elisheba hesitated.

"Let us say, they are just trades, that we receive support to enable them, and that one day when this war is finished, we shall return to the land we were promised, that is rightfully ours."

Oriol's head was now full of dangerous questions he knew she wouldn't answer; any incaution by her risked jeopardy. There would be no mercy for a Jewish crew with neither purpose nor explanation, in Ottoman waters. So either the gains from the trade were so great as not to be denied, or she could rely completely upon the support she mentioned.

But those waters were dominated by Turkish and German boats. Why would Germans help her against their ally? Hadn't they tried to sink her boat? And the British? His contacts with them showed they too were cautious of the calamity that could befall any expedition off the Palestinian coast that wasn't assured of success. Why on earth would she therefore expect their support, let alone reply upon it? She was engaged, he therefore concluded, in trades that he would never condone or sanction.

Yet, there was something wonderfully and irrationally admirable in her fervid madness, whether or not the destruction this would cause left him without a means for his return home.

"Are you sure that what is rightfully yours is a passion worth dying for?" he asked finally.

She smiled, now more relaxed and at ease, touched by his genuine concern.

"Is it really a life," she replied, "without passion?"

CHAPTER 7

"Ah, thank you for responding so promptly to my request, Lance Corporal Laurie."

Major Fogge slowly unfurled his legs from around his desk. His oleaginous smile and transparently insincere politeness only served to heighten Laurie's indifference towards him. Unlike the rest of the Bureau, Fogge had retained a formal civility in their few interactions, and Laurie remained uncertain as to the Major's intentions. He'd shared this concern with Colonel Lowthian, particularly that Fogge might try to involve himself in the work that he, Nooney and Moussabey were undertaking, and she'd sought to reassure him.

"I believe he's known by the other officers as 'Thick-Fogge,'" she'd said. "He's always saying to them, 'I am very clear' and it grates, particularly as it's so obviously the case that he rarely is."

"What if he orders our assistance?" Laurie had asked, knowing he'd already been saddled with an implicit command by Fogge to inform upon his activities.

"His father was a General," replied Lowthian, "opened so many doors."

This had shocked. Laurie still preferred to believe that it was talent that rose to the top and that the days of the establishment and the old chum's networks were diminished. Maybe though, in reality, Cairo was full of such 'British Fogge'?

Then, as he pondered, he began to think of Captain Hillary and the incompetence of his ways. And there were those same officers who, on most nights when he and Nooney returned to The Grand Continental Hotel, were happily dining, sipping wine, relaxing, reading the newspaper. None seemed overly eager or taxed by their responsibilities.

"He might appear to be an idiot, therefore," continued Lowthian, "but take care. It's useful just to feed him scraps, play to his self-importance. But he has no operational involvement whatsoever in our activities. Inform me if you have any real difficulty with him."

So, as he stood to attention in the small space that purported to be an office, Laurie at least felt the confidence that his judgement of the man was shared by his superior.

"How are things?" inquired Fogge.

"Very good, thank you, sir."

Laurie too could give great value to inner disdain.

"Jolly good, yes indeed. I thought it would be useful to catch up on events."

He removed his flimsy ringed spectacles, took what looked like a linen handkerchief from his trouser pocket, and started to wipe the lenses.

"Damn sand, plasters everything, makes it difficult to keep an eye on things, you know."

For a moment, Laurie expected Fogge to laugh at what may have been an attempted joke, but it was quickly apparent he'd no idea of the potential comedy in his words.

"I've been hearing excellent things about you, Lance Corporal Laurie."

"Sir?"

Laurie returned a practiced look of gentle bafflement. He'd learnt to be wary of praise from a viper.

"I have my contacts, you know," he said, perching the glasses back on his thin nose.

"Seems you had a jolly good trip to the seaside yesterday?"

Laurie froze. Only Nooney, Moussabey and Lowthian knew of their activities in Alexandria. Fogge was watching closely for a response.

"Lance Corporal Laurie?"

Fogge was waiting.

"Lance Corporal Laurie...?"

"Seaside, sir?"

"Yes, you know, the day out to Alexandria... beautiful beaches up there I believe?"

"Wouldn't know, sir."

Fogge squinted and creased his face a little, a thin tongue making a brief appearance, lubricating his lower lip.

"Wouldn't know?" he asked, his educated voice slightly raised.

"About the beaches, sir," replied Laurie, parodying a sweet yet discourteous innocence.

"I'm not on about the beaches, Laurie," said Fogge, this time more affirmatively and with a hint of menace.

He was becoming agitated. Laurie had this effect upon people he didn't trust or respect. He may not have possessed power, but he knew how to prick an inflated sense of self-assurance and entitlement. Fogge cleared his throat and tried again.

"I shall be more precise then, Laurie. You were on the early train yesterday from Bab El Hadid. Must have been a long day as you were back very late."

He stared at Laurie, who in turn stared back with that neutral gaze that said nothing yet infuriated.

"So, you were in Alexandria, and to be precise, you visited the town, not the beach."

Again Laurie stayed silent, though he could judge the growing anger this was causing.

"Did you have a good look around? Perhaps you went to the harbour, fished from the wall?"

Laurie stared directly ahead, scrambling to gather his thoughts. How much did Fogge know? Why these questions if he already knew the answers? What response would avoid the debasement of those relationships he'd determined to protect?

"Did you catch anything?" *Be careful*, thought Laurie.

"Not really, sir."

Fogge's eyebrows pyramided towards the scrupulously greased and parted hair. He turned his head to one side, hoping to encourage Laurie in further revelation.

"Well… just a touch of dysentery."

"What?"

"Yes, sir, I'm hoping it's just the gentler version but spent the night sitting on the chunderer."

Fogge's fuse shortened and his face drained of any unlikely blood. His elongated body unravelled upward in a series of uncontrolled lollops, rising from its seated position to full standing height, leaning towards Laurie like a dessicated tree fern.

"Obfuscation gets us nowhere," he said, raising his voice, "I am very clear about that."

"Sir?"

"Obfuscation, Laurie, do you understand?"

Laurie pondered the irony for a moment. Here was Fogge, a man from Balliol College asking him, a man from a church Free School in Lichfield, about meaning.

"Sorry, sir," replied Laurie, "if my words lack the clarity you require."

He noticed an involuntary twitch in Fogge's cheek.

"Ah, yes, very good, Laurie," replied Fogge, trying to maintain his inner assurance, "you get the meaning precisely, I see."

There was just a hint of the sinister attached to his sarcasm.

"Let me put it this way then, shall I? You were instructed to let me know everything required of you by the Bureau."

"Sir?"

"Maybe I need to spell things out again. Your smart-arse shenanigans might play well to those types you've found yourself hanging around with, but they don't pass muster here."

He moved backward away from Laurie, though awkwardly so, as there was very little space in the room. It was almost as if his mind had suddenly engaged with the imagery Laurie had presented of the consequences of dysentery; that belatedly he was attempting safe distancing on the grounds of health.

"I have a major role in liaison between the Bureau and Army HQ." He looked down at Laurie for a reply.

"Yes, sir, a major role, I understand."

Fogge paused for a moment, thrown by what, after all, might be an acknowledgement of a shared understanding.

"Ah, that's better form, Laurie. Much easier isn't it when things start to fall into place?"

Laurie remained silent, and Fogge took this for the affirmative.

"So, I shall need to know everything about your work if I am to keep the various parties informed. You were probably thinking that Colonel Lowthian would brief me on all matters of importance, and that therefore I shouldn't need to rely upon you as a source, especially what with you being a Lance Corporal."

Laurie could almost smell the pheromone within the gloat.

"Well, the thing is, Laurie, there are important matters abroad here that are way beyond your rank, but with which you can nevertheless be very helpful. For someone like yourself, I can appreciate it's quite difficult to see the bigger picture, to know how to respond in a way that avoids confliction and yet serves the bigger purpose."

Fogge edged his frame sideways to a corner of the wall above which the roof sloped, craning forward slightly to accommodate his head.

"I will be candid, as I can see you're a clever fellow. HQ needs to keep abreast of the goings on in the Bureau. There's a lot of types in there who are wild cards, the sort who don't salute or recognise ranks, become much too matey, prefer the natives. You'll know all this for yourself by now, of course. It's a great worry for HQ and therefore for the course of the war here in Egypt. We need to have people there we can trust, good people, those who enlisted to serve their country, those who have made great sacrifice to be here: people like you, Laurie."

Fogge paused for breath, the void filled by the challenges now seeding in Laurie's head.

"I know all about your trip yesterday, because it is critical for the future of our activities here that I do."

The directness stumped Laurie, and this was spotted.

"I thought that might encourage a more sincere pause for reflection," he said. "Eventually, we all have to engage with the reality of war. It must seem so far away for you as you keep the peace amongst the traders, ignore orders from the likes of Captain Hillary, travel the Nile on factory inspections, and bring good order to our brothels."

Laurie was staggered. How did he know all this?

"But for those of us who are required to prepare for the push into Palestine, information is power, and some of that information is more powerful than can ever be understood by those whom we depend upon to secure it; worse still if they cannot also be trusted."

Who was giving Fogge this information on their movements? Who was it that wasn't trusted? Laurie's mind was racing.

"I report everything to Colonel Lowthian, sir," he said, causing Fogge to look mockingly beyond him, as if to an invisible accomplice.

"Of course you do, Laurie, of course you do, dear chap. But what is it she does with it?"

"And to Brigadier Regis-Templeton."

He'd hoped that would impress upon Fogge the sense of desisting from further compromising inferences, but if anything he seemed further encouraged.

"Ah, the good Brigadier, the very same man who was invalided out here to receive the recuperative attentions of his mistress."

"Sir?"

"Very close to Colonel Lowthian, isn't he? I guess you can't fail to have noticed?"

Laurie was outraged by the suggestion.

"I've noticed no such thing, sir."

But Fogge wasn't deterred. He could see that he'd struck a rich seam.

"Why on earth they didn't just send him back to his country house in the Worcestershire countryside I really don't know? Just the sort of chap for your types out in the sticks, someone I would imagine you could rely upon when the chips were down. Everybody's favourite viscount back home, by all accounts."

Fogge was warming to his task and Laurie's suppressed rage at his surmising was now obvious.

"Yes, I can see that you're the sort to admire a man born with such entitlement. Why, perhaps you're round his place all the time?"

Laurie made his best to look disinterested.

"What, with his 'Viscount Littleworth' title and all; I believe he's quite something in your part of the world."

Laurie swayed forward and for the briefest of moments felt he might stumble. No wonder he'd recognised the Brigadier during that first briefing in Cairo. He was the very same man whose gamekeeper had attempted to shoot his eldest son when he strayed onto the Littleworth Estate, snaring rabbits. Laurie had been incandescent with rage. His son had made a mistake, but for someone with so much unearned authority to wield it in a way that mortally endangered his child, was immoral and unforgiveable.

All sense of perspective had departed him and, policeman or not, he was off to the Hall, cosh below his coat, determined to sort the matter directly. Had it not been for the physical intervention of his wife and son, his career and their paid-for living in the village police house would have been over.

Fogge had continued to speak but the words were lost, swamped in Laurie's head by the addle and inner damnation that had momentarily reclaimed him. The growing certainties of the last few months, upon which he'd become joyously reliant, lay mangled, the unspoken loyalties maligned. Worse still, Fogge, the source of the spike, was a man for whom he had little respect, and who possessed none of the talent, probity or humility of his closest colleagues in the Bureau.

But despite this, it was inescapable to conclude that this awful man knew these things… he damn well knew these things. How?

And that the Brigadier, who he'd admired, a decent and good man with a common touch, was also the very same man he'd hated so, who'd threatened his son's life. How could this be?

"Laurie? Laurie… answer man."

Fogge was still talking, and Laurie's ability to respond was diminishing. Feed him scraps, Colonel Lowthian had said… but be careful."

"Sir?"

"The Sugar Case, how far have you got?"

What? What's he on about? Feed him scraps.

"Early days yet, sir."

"So that's why you were in Alexandria."

"Yes, sir. Checking out the territory."

So, he doesn't actually know anything.

"Where did you go?"

"Traders in the square, sir, tip off that if we pressed enough about illegal passes, we'd eventually find some 'give' on the sugar situation."

"Good thinking, Laurie. Any news on the boat?"

"Not yet, sir."

What boat? The conversation with Mr Smith… surely not?

"Come on, Laurie, you must have sourced the berth."

"No, sir, whatever it is, it remains concealed, but we're working on it."

"Any leads?"

"None at all, sir, yet, you know that dealing with Arabs can be damned difficult."

He knew that would work.

"Absolutely true, Laurie, you're learning I see."

A lot more from them than from you, he thought.

"And watch that one who works with you, slippery fellow, untrustworthy."

Moussabey? Could he be the one passing this information on? Impossible.

"Let me know the moment you have confirmation, do you understand?"

"Yes, sir."

In truth, Laurie could tell that the Major didn't seem to have specific detail about their whereabouts the day before, other than their train journeys and the general subterfuge regarding sugar. He may just have been blustering. Whatever, it was very concerning. The information Fogge did have must have come from a mutually trusted source.

"One other thing, Laurie, did you hear anything about the art?"

This was too big a curve to follow.

"No, sir, nothing."

Art, what on earth was he on about now?

"Jolly good... or should I say," he stuttered as if correcting himself, "... to keep your ear to the ground on that one as well."

Laurie nodded. He needed so desperately to free himself from Fogge's attentions.

"Are you alright, Laurie?" Fogge inquired, as Laurie started to contort his face.

"Sorry, sir... the dysentery."

Fogge jumped with concern, though for himself rather than Laurie, this time banging his head on the low ceiling.

"Why yes, of course, jolly good, best you be off, make yourself... comfortable, shall we say. Remember, keep me updated at all times."

"Sir."

And with that, Laurie was dismissed. He walked with great urgency from Fogge's office, down the stairs and across the foyer at The Savoy Hotel, out onto the noisy Shari Qasr El Nil. It was mid-morning; the street was bustling with the wealthier of Cairo and the carriages of the Europeans, and the sun was already high in the sky, but still it felt less stifling than in Fogge's office. He needed to clear his head, talk with Nooney, get back to The Grand Continental and make sense of the conversation he'd just escaped.

But then he remembered that other eyes may be observing him, and that his pretence for leaving the meeting had consequences that required the necessary reactions. He sat on a wall for a moment, slowly bending double as if in pain, then leapt up and ran back into The Savoy at speed, heading straight for the lavatory on the ground floor.

He had his choice of cubicles and settled on an end perch. There he remained, moaning quietly for the next thirty minutes, leant against the lavatory door and desperate to make sense; a prisoner of his own agility, alone, yet still trying to do his duty.

For six days, Laurie sat on his troubles. He'd been far too busy anyway to find the space to discuss them, as he and Nooney were immersed in the business of entrapment. The office they were to use for Mr Smith's visit was on Shari El Madabigh, just across the road from Moussabey's formal place of work at The Agricultural Bank of Egypt, right in the heart of Cairo's business centre.

This was convenient for their task, both in its ease of access to the bank for any financial arrangement, and as the base for the efficiently functioning and generally reputable Cairo sugar trade. Those who worked there on a daily basis were used to Moussabey's presence as the banking arm for many of the overseas contacts, so there were frequently Europeans in his office. Nooney and Laurie had been regular visitors in the last few months, and so by now were almost part of the furniture. Their office, therefore, located within The Cairo Sugar Association, the very centre of the trade they were about to plunder, would, it was agreed, very much appeal to a man such as Smith.

The formalities of the agreement with the sugar refinery on the Nile had needed to be confirmed, and this had taken longer than they'd wished due to the demands of the owner. He had a better nose for deceit than for the aroma of his cane-juice, so had they appeared too eager to close a deal, he would have smelt a trap. They must have proven credible, as he accepted a price far lower than his opening gambit; doubtless though, it was still very profitable.

None of the documentation held any mention of his name or that of his company. In the unlikely event of scrutiny, the deal would appear to have been constructed through an unrelated Anglo-Egyptian Sudan company and therefore confirmed by the good offices of the British Protectorate, with paperwork so prodigious and opaque as to be both impressive and yet exhaustingly untraceable.

The protocols for Smith's visit were more predictable. This time Nooney would take the lead, confirming thereby the professional maturity of the relationship with Laurie, and Moussabey as before, would act as their Arab fixer. Lowthian would also attend, at her own direction, as she had insisted that a man such as Smith would expect the presence of a female secretary.

A smart carriage was dispatched to Midan Bab El Hadid to pick up Smith, together with the same young colleague who had greeted them the week before at the 'Alexandria West Bay Shipping Company' in

Alexandria. They were met at the station by Lowthian, who introduced herself in fluent Arabic, at once both bewitching Smith and neutralising the linguistic role of his assistant. Elegantly dressed in civilian attire, she bore little similarity to that of her more routine uniformed appearance, so the chance of even a coincidental recognition of her true self was minimal.

By the time the carriage was travelling south along Shari Nobar Pasha, her gentle yet precise commentary had deflated any tension, suspicion even, that Smith may naturally have held about the day's events.

"You may remember this building Mr Smith, as the site of the Khedivial Hotel," she had said as they passed the handsome Moorish-influenced building on their right in Khazindar Square, "a former home of Nubar Pasha, your first Prime Minister."

"A British puppet," Smith playfully interrupted.

"Indeed," she had replied, somewhat surprising him.

She was bright, he could see that, and by all appearances understood something of the Arab position in a way that seemed to have passed by the Europeans he generally dealt with. But she was a woman.

"You may not be aware that it has been bought by the Sednaoui family and is now a magnificent department store. For someone like me; it's far too expensive, but perhaps if you have time later you may like to stop off to buy a garment for your wife?"

Smith smiled, beguiled by her fluency, confidence, and British sense of organisation.

"They will, I am told, be opening such a store in Alexandria next year, with plans to ship their garments to Paris and London once the war permits." His ears pricked up.

This trip to Cairo may prove even more beneficial than he'd thought.

The journey progressed in a similar convivial manner along Shari Kamil, past the opulent European enclave that was The Shepheards Hotel, to which Mr Smith comically proffered a single finger salute. Lowthian chuckled; she was really enjoying this role, and Smith in turn seemed quite comfortable. They moved on beyond the elegant Ezbekiya Gardens where a small ensemble was playing from the bandstand to a mixed crowd of wealthy regulars, circled around Opera Square, before turning right into the commercial district along Shari Qasrel, eventually disembarking just a short walk away from the offices where they were to meet.

"What? This must be a high-level organisation. You are taking me to the French Consulate." Smith gestured, pointing to the building appearing ahead, garlanded without subtlety in an army of tricolours.

"Ah, it may look that way, but no, not at all," she had replied in faultless Arabic, smiling at the inference.

"We are less glamorous than they, but many times more efficient."

Smith laughed.

They entered through the impressive archway and large glass doors of 'The Cairo Sugar Association' building next door to the consulate, past a huge wall map showing the distribution routes of Egyptian sugar to all parts of the world, and on into the commercial atrium. The floor was packed with traders both local and foreign, but the predominant dress style was western with English and French the dominant languages.

Smith smiled approvingly.

"I hear money talking," he said, "though little of it in Arabic."

Lowthian got the drift and nodded.

"We hope for a mutually beneficial agreement," she replied. "Our money has no interest in national boundaries."

At the end of the floor was an entrance that led to a quieter corridor, along which were quite regularly placed offices. Each was identified by an imposing wooden door and attendant brass name plate. It was a haven of musty peace, a world away from the frenzy of the trading floor.

Lowthian stopped outside a door on which the small plaque read, *Trading Assurance Cairo*. It was the only office that also carried the company name in Arabic, and Smith noticed. They were welcomed effusively by Laurie, who led the initial small talk. As they were all eager to make the most of the day, Laurie quickly gave way to Nooney, explaining that here in Cairo, Nooney would lead the proceedings. Smith nodded his understanding.

Given the intense preparation and the additional layer of surety that Lowthian brought to the affairs, it was not so surprising that the meeting went well. Even the discussions between Moussabey and Smith proceeded with a level of dignity unrecognisable from the initial contact in Alexandria. Smith had no excuse to demonstrate his unnecessary hackneyed English or offer pretence at misunderstanding, and Lowthian's skill helped remove the burden from Moussabey to interpret as well as gather his thoughts. Indeed, Lowthian's translation proceeded almost as quickly as the words from his and Smith's mouths, and within the hour the outline of a deal had been agreed.

"Every two weeks, therefore, a shipment of sugar, generally two tonnes, will arrive at your warehouse in Alexandria for shipment."

Nooney was confirming what he believed were the mutually understood outcomes of their discussions.

"We shall transport this directly from our refinery, using the regular train routes. Occasionally, to vary and protect our options, we shall use the Nile and the canals. Our two companies' records will describe the produce as 'goods in transit', with the appropriate signatures and official stamp of His Majesties Protectorate of Anglo-Egyptian Sudan, plus a signed affirmation from The Cairo Sugar Association confirming this. Your fees will be arranged by Mr Moussabey, and will confirm they are simply for your transportation services."

Smith signalled his approval.

"You have friends in high places," he had said, Lowthian translating.

"Friends whom we love less dearly than they cost us," said Nooney, smiling.

"This problem I, too, understand," replied Smith, "officials who assist my business demand loyalty."

Nooney paused, hoping for a caveat about those officials that might prove useful to their eventual exposure of his subterfuge. But Smith seemed hesitant to say more. Nooney pressed him.

"Officials? Egyptian, British?"

Again, Smith seemed unduly reticent, but Nooney persisted.

"We cannot have barriers within our agreement, Mr Smith; we must be open with each other."

Smith burst out laughing, much to the consternation of those from 'Trading Assurance Cairo', and for a moment or two there was an uncomfortable feeling that their work was about to unravel. Eventually, Smith spoke.

"I asked you where your refinery was; you failed to reveal this. I asked you for the name of your company in Egyptian Sudan; you were unable to enlighten me. Yet, when I add the realities I face in these difficult times, you require answers and chastise me with talk about barriers?"

This was an unsettling change to both the mood and direction of proceedings. Nooney was fronting the operation. The one thing he was convinced of was that Smith would not respect dithering. Had he engaged with the stony faces of his team, he would have seen that they also were of the same mind. Do not give an inch.

"I ask simply that we might gauge a response," said Nooney. "I have no interest in the individuals, just their cost."

"Ah, the British and costs. Well, what about the cost of the forced employment of a million Egyptians in your army of occupation? What about your control of everyday Egyptian life, your censorship of the press, the charging of our government for your colonisation of our Sudan? Where is the equation you used to cost all of that?"

Nooney could not imagine that Smith was truly a patriot. The only certainty in his mind about the man opposite him, now suddenly protesting about the morality of empire and warfare, was that he was a very clever crook. This was, therefore, either a test for him and his colleagues, or they had significantly misjudged the man. He looked at Smith and attempted to speak with as much sincerely as would be credible.

"You speak of political matters," he said, "but we are interested only in business."

"There is no difference," replied Smith, "I, like you, will have to pay for both." He gazed at them with the seasoned look of a juggler assessing incertitude.

"For my business to flourish, I have to pay for the actions of the corrupt. Whilst you might think that 'oh, this is so typical of the Arabs', consider for a moment is it also possible that the British share with us the repressive excesses of leaders who are also corrupt, who benefit from their position, who ask the people to do one thing and then take advantage of the other? Perhaps for you too, there are just the smallest chances of there being one rule for those who legislate over you, and another rule for the rest?"

He paused.

"Maybe silken tongues flap and profit, wherever they are, be it Cairo or London?"

He reflected for a moment, pleased with himself, somewhat theatrically rubbing his chin.

"Come to think of it," he continued, "maybe wherever we are in the world, we are all just… Arabs?"

For a moment, no one spoke, with just the low buzz of noise from the nearby trading floor and the whirr of the gently gyrating ceiling fan for company. Smith had spoken with a sincerity that would have been convincing, were it not for the presumption of his utter conceit. Nooney decided to test this.

"How much?"

"Twenty per cent of your shipment is passed to me for the purposes of supporting my contacts."

"Two per cent," retorted Nooney.

"Ten," responded Smith.

"Three," replied Nooney. Even Lowthian was struggling to keep pace with translation.

"Five, and no less," said Smith.

"Agreed," said Nooney.

"Plus an account at the new Khedivial Hotel."

"What?"

Up to this point, Nooney had played a blinder, but the poker face crumpled.

"My wife," said Mr Smith, grinning, "has expensive tastes."

Nooney was still perplexed.

"The new department store on Khazindar Square," interjected Lowthian, briefly alluding to the morning's carriage trip from the station.

"Yes, alright, an account at the hotel-cum-Sednaoui store, but a limit—"

Smith interrupted, nodding his assent, but forgetting the need to wait for the translation.

"Yes, yes…" he said in broken English, avoiding Lowthian's services, trying to recapture some ground, "I believe… trust… you are… fairplay."

With that, the tension subsided and there were handshakes and smiles all round. Lowthian left the meeting, returning quickly with drinks to toast to their mutual success, and food to fill their empty bellies. She had also prepared an array of lavishly parcelled gifts to cement the relationship, and these were passed to Mr Smith and his assistant. The largest box was wrapped in the distinctive paper of the Sednaoui Department Store, and he beamed and bowed graciously as he received it.

After a further hour of convivial conversation, and with the day's deal done, the time arrived for Smith and his colleague to travel back to the station. Now lubricated and fully relaxed, he leant across towards Nooney and nudged him in an almost exaggerated spirit of conspiratorial chumminess.

"When we spoke in Alexandria, you said you wanted to commence shipping next month," he said, but this time allowing an almost exaggerated space for Lowthian's full translation.

Nooney nodded.

"We shall have a very good boat for you, I assure, with a crew who are amongst the most professional we use."

Nooney remembered the map Smith had shown them back in Alexandria, with vessels listed by their current location.

"Ah, would that be number 31?"

Smith's eyes widened.

"Indeed," he replied, motioning his respect, "She's called *The Adelphi*."

As his train pulled out of Midan Bab El Hadid station an hour later, Smith looked out of the window and allowed himself a contented smile; *what an excellent day*, he thought, *they must think me such a fool*.

"Unusual to see you here, mate."

Nooney had been at the bar with Colonel Noah Grice-Farquharason

The Poet Laurie Ate

and a few other of his Bureau friends enjoying a convivial drink when he'd caught sight of Laurie sitting alone at an outside table.

"Gin, hey?" he said pointing to the glass.

"It's water I'm afraid," replied Laurie.

"Well, let's just hope it's not straight from the Nile, hey?"

Laurie smiled, but Nooney could see that something was troubling him.

"Bit of the Black Dog, by the looks of things?"

Laurie looked confused.

"Trouble back home or something? Not easy being this far away from your family, I guess. Wouldn't know, of course. As you've regularly reminded me, I'm a single bloke and that world's a different place."

Laurie grimaced at the thought his past words could have hurt his friend. He could be less subtle than was sometimes healthy.

"Yes, sorry, Nooney, I'm sometimes far too clumsy with what I'm trying to say."

"Give over, Laurie, no offence taken, we can't always live the life of a 'sin shifter'."

"What do you mean?"

"Hey?"

"…a 'sin shifter'?"

"You know, Laurie, a 'forgive me lots'."

"Nooney… what…?"

"An 'Altar Walter'."

"Nooney…?"

"Come on, Laurie, you know… a 'lurch sinister'."

Laurie was lost.

"Blimey, Laurie," he said, speaking more slowly and clearly for effect, "…you know… a 'church minister', mate."

They burst out laughing, Laurie at his own naivety and Nooney because he'd made his good friend smile. Laurie could be a stuffed shirt on occasions and too intense for his own good, but he liked and trusted him.

It was early evening, the decorative lights in Ezbekiya Gardens across the way were beginning to glow in the half-dusk, and with the fallen sun, there was a pleasant chill descending. The musicians Mr Smith would have heard earlier in the day had long gone, replaced with a free public concert by the orchestra from The Opera House. So popular was this with the Cairo glitterati that there wasn't an available seat anywhere near the bandstand.

Laurie's view was obscured, but it hardly mattered. The music they were playing seemed even more engaging, having made its way to him through the crowd, the food and drink stalls, and the incessant clop and grind of horse and carriage around Opera Square.

"Ah, very funny, Nooney, I'll remember that one."

"So, what's this we're listening to then?" He knew that Laurie was keen on his music.

"Elgar. Quite amazing."

"Well, it's nice, but I wouldn't go that far, mate. Could do with a bit more oomph in the middle bit don't you think?"

Laurie smiled; he knew he was being wound up.

"What I mean is that I didn't ever expect to be in Cairo, let alone listening to a piece written by a composer from my own neck of the woods."

"Oops sorry, Laurie, I had no idea. My turn to put my foot in it."

"*Enigma Variations*, mostly pieces written about his friends I think."

"Were you one of them then?"

"What?"

"One of his friends… you know, let's face it, bit of an enigma yourself."

There was warmth and humour in his comment, but he was right. Laurie was constantly aware of the competing challenges within his psyche, the battles to accommodate service and sacrifice. Doing the right thing had made him headstrong, but at a cost to himself and those he loved. Despite the confident outward persona, he was too frequently tethered in a darker place.

"Nooney, I need to ask you… I was called to see Major Fogge a few days back."

"Blimey, bad luck, mate."

Laurie hesitated, but if he couldn't trust Nooney, then who was there?

"What do you think of him?"

Nooney stared absent-mindedly across towards the gardens, and for a moment Laurie thought he may have said the wrong thing. Nooney, though, had gauged his friend was in some turmoil.

"I'll choose my words carefully, Laurie, as I can see you're in need of some well-constructed objectivity… he's an absolute shit."

Laurie smiled. It wasn't the answer he was expecting, but then Nooney rarely wasted words. He felt an immediate sense of relief.

"Major 'Thick-Fogge' to the chaps at the Bureau, as he's always saying—"

"I'm very clear…" Laurie interrupted, and they bawled with laughter.

"He's called a lot more things as well, Laurie, so you need to be careful with him."

Reassured, Laurie decided to press on with his concerns, something he'd normally never do. Generally, problems in life were there to be solved, not shared.

"He expects me to report to him on all our activities."

Nooney looked alarmed.

"Has he ever asked you to do this as well?"

"Of course not."

"So why me?" asked Laurie.

The question drifted but without response.

"Seems he has some sort of liaison between Army HQ and the Bureau, only I get the impression that, at the Bureau, no one really wants to chin-wag anything with him."

Nooney was still trying to process what he was hearing.

"To put it bluntly," Laurie continued, "he doesn't trust the Bureau, and in particular, Lowthian and Regis-Templeton. He actually mentioned their names."

"In what way doesn't he trust them?" asked Nooney.

"Well, that's the thing, he didn't say anything to incriminate them, but he did seem to know all about our trip to Alexandria. How?"

Nooney's mouth dropped.

"You say 'all about our trip'. Does that include Smith and the Sugar deal?"

"Well, no. Either he kept all that back, or he was waiting for me to tell him. Chance I guess he could have been fishing for the details, so I just told him a load of baloney to keep him happy, then made an excuse and left. But the point is, either somebody we know and trust has fed him with information, or we're being watched."

The joviality in Nooney's earlier demeanour had gone.

"And why is Fogge hanging around anyway in the Bureau if he's not being used?" continued Laurie.

"Well, that bit at least is easy… or so I'd thought," said Nooney.

"He's just following the doors that were opened by his old man, courtesy of the British establishment; a few strings pulled here, a favour or two there by way of return, then find somewhere his detailed but useless knowledge of ancient Greek will come in useful and the Bureau becomes the obvious place."

Nooney paused for a moment, continuing to process their changed circumstances.

"You see, Laurie, the regular army doesn't really want us. The Bureau seems to be troublesome to them. So, they will have asked him to be the Liaison Officer knowing that he will concoct a role out of it, nothing too serious, but just enough to make him feel and look important, thereby saving themselves the hassle of looking after him, whilst of course doing nothing whatsoever to help us."

"But he knew something, Nooney. He definitely knew something."

"That's true, Laurie. I can't explain that, other than a lucky sighting of us at the station."

"Neither does he trust Moussabey, called him 'an Arab'."

"Well, he is, mate, and hallelujah to that, hey? Fogge and his type will always struggle with the fact that we trust the locals more than him, that we work from the point of view that they are human, too. And anyway, let's be honest, he probably yearns for the glory days of the twelfth century."

For a moment, they both sat quietly in thought, perplexed by the turn of events. Laurie's unburdening had also dismantled some of the protective framework Nooney had also erected to convince himself of the surety of their work at the Bureau.

"Lowthian cannot abide Fogge, of that I am sure," he said eventually, "she has always advised me of caution when I'm around him."

"Me too," added Laurie.

"She is the most efficient and respected officer that I have come across since joining this whole damn mess," said Nooney, "and I trust her."

The orchestra had now completed their repertoire, and the crowds were starting to leave the gardens, flocking across Opera Square, though so engrossed were both men, that neither noticed.

"I agree," said Laurie, "but Fogge also mentioned about her and the Brigadier."

"What do you mean?"

"He didn't say as much, but he suggested that he and Lowthian were, you know…"

"What?"

"They were, well shall I say… acting like a married couple when they were in private."

Nooney looked at Laurie with an expression of bemused wonderment.

"On occasions, Laurie, you can be a complete puritan, you really can."

Laurie was taken aback.

"What do you mean?"

"Well, does it matter if they enjoy each other's company that way?"

"Well, yes it does actually," he replied, hanging on to his precious principles, "he's married for a start, and has children. If he's like this in these matters of trust and honesty, what's he like in other things? And what about the effect upon his wife?"

"Did you ever enjoy yourself that way?"

"Absolutely not."

"So, tell me, did you abstain before your marriage, then?"

"That's different," replied Laurie.

"Oh really? So you didn't."

"None of your business."

"No, but you're critical of the Brigadier not playing by the rules."

"No, I'm not."

"After all, who's making up these rules anyway, and more importantly, whose checking for heaven's sake?"

"Look stop it, Nooney."

"So you did then."

"What?"

"You did the right thing and got married."

Laurie was now getting more agitated and Nooney was struggling. The issues at hand were serious enough without adding to them with the complications of fidelity.

"Look," said Nooney, calming things, "you've had dealings with the Brigadier since arriving in Egypt. Tell me honestly, do you have any reason whatsoever to believe from what you know of him that he isn't a decent man?"

His silence in response to the question affirmed this. Nooney was right. Until the inference sown by Fogge, the Brigadier had behaved exactly as Nooney had described.

"You set a high bar sometimes, Laurie, you really do."

Much as he didn't want to hear this, Laurie knew it was probably true.

"And anyway, how do you know that he has a wife and children?"

Laurie hesitated, but probably better that everything was out. "When I first arrived in Cairo and saw the Brigadier, there was something about him I recognised but couldn't place. Fogge, of course, was happy to let me know when deriding his abilities, that he was the viscount of the huge estate just two miles from my village."

"So?"

"His gamekeeper tried to shoot my son."

"What?"

"It was a misunderstanding, but nevertheless, he actually tried to shoot my son."

Nooney buried his head in his hands.

"What a shambles," he muttered.

For a few minutes they sat looking at the gardens, and then across to Opera Square, searching abstractedly for a solution.

It was Nooney who broke the silence.

"It's complicated enough as it is to deal with all this lot here, without carrying all that burden."

Then, after another moment's pause he turned and faced Laurie squarely.

"Right. What's your feeling then?"

Laurie so admired the man. He knew Nooney would have a plan, but in the true spirit of consideration that epitomised him, he was asking him about his ideas, as always, putting the other first.

"My stomach tells me that for the moment we keep this between ourselves. Fogge's the one I don't trust, especially as his sidekick at HQ is Captain Hillary…"

Nooney nodded.

"…just keep our wits about us," he continued, "until things become clearer. All of this could simply be speculative, the imaginings of Fogge's mind. Once we have some detail, then we alert Lowthian. Her reaction will say it all. Like you, I've no doubts about her."

"Agreed Laurie; stay alert, sounds the best plan for now in the absence of anything else. We could do without it, but we are where we are."

There was a further silence, though this time calmer.

"And all this gamekeeper stuff with the Brigadier and your son," said Nooney, "you've got to let it go, it's not good for you."

"I'll try, Nooney, I really will. But if someone shot at your son, would you just move on?"

"Probably not, mate. But I'd try to rationalise where the greatest damage was; my son's fine but here am I, still consumed with all this anger. Not sure I could cope with that. Hate can bury the victim."

"It's the unfairness of it all though, Nooney. Sitting by and letting things pass never gets us anywhere, either."

"You're a well-read bloke, Laurie."

"Am I?"

"Well you're always telling me stuff that you couldn't have possibly dreamt up yourself."

Laurie smiled.

"Well, mate, I've done a bit of work back home in the library as well."

"Go on."

"I read something once that really stuck with me."

"What, that the earth isn't flat?"

"Even more profound," replied Nooney, ignoring the dig; "it said something like this: *'it's useless to attempt to reason a man out of a thing he was never reasoned into'*."

"Where is all this going?" asked Laurie, giving Nooney a sideways glance.

"So, what I'm saying is, that maybe when it comes to the likes of Fogge, Hillary, and all those others you come across who defy the logic of your thinking, even the Brigadier if you like, you should hold to those words. These people come differently prepared than you; they're from another place. Either that or they're simply not bothered beyond anything other than that which fits their self-interest."

Laurie, for once, remained silent.

"Put simply, Laurie, no matter what you might say, they just won't understand you; you might as well talk to a wall. Think about it, mate; might help take away some of the pressure you put yourself through."

It was now turning chilly and they were dressed in their day-fatigues. They got up to leave and Nooney slapped his friend on the shoulder.

Laurie smiled and thanked him. He was glad he'd confided, that there was a plan, and that things were not quite so bad after all.

"Time for a kip, I guess," said Nooney.

With that, they left for their beds, blissfully unaware of the impact that Mr Smith's boat number 31, two days north west of Alexandria, was about to have upon their lives.

CHAPTER 8

Llucia Quintana had survived by instinct and aggression, her soul entombed by a carapace of deceit; upon this foundation, she'd built an empire. Yet the diaphanous heart within was shredded. The greatest love of her life lay silent.

It had been a month since Oriol sailed from Mao bound for Alexandria, yet there was still no word. The Andreassens arranged sailings so that their company boats met mid-Mediterranean in Valletta, on the island of Malta. This maximised trading capabilities and the sharing of intelligence about the safety of the waters. Nothing exercised the minds of crews quite as much as the whereabouts of the German, British or Italian navies, their mines and submarines. It also meant that within seven or eight days of sailing, Llucia would receive confirmation from vessels returning to Mao that her adored son had reached Malta, and within a further week or so that he should be ashore in Egypt. The silence, therefore, was unbearable.

"May I get you something, *Señora?*"

Llucia had been deeply abstracted, and hadn't noticed the waiter.

"Oh, I'm sorry… nothing other than water. Thank you."

Gil had begged her not to leave the farm at Turo Vell.

"Llucia, the weather may have forced them to rest up elsewhere, they may be helping a stricken vessel, or they may simply have been missed at Valletta."

"They were not there though, Gil, and worse, no word that they made it to Egypt. Something has happened."

"Oriol leaves nothing to chance, Llucia, the Andreassens are the best there are. Whatever the delay, there will be a simple explanation. He would not want you to do this."

She was not to be deterred.

"I am going, Gil. You and Isla must not speak of this to anyone."

Gil had known her long enough to recognise she wouldn't be persuaded. And in truth, he too sensed something was wrong. So she'd set off on a journey she'd made frequently when building the family trading links, but which she hadn't undertaken for several years. Were it not for the circumstances, she would have enjoyed the challenge, a reminder of the old days, the excitements, the risks, the deals.

The newly instituted steamboat service from Mao to Palma on the island of Mallorca may have been faster, but it was noisier and less nimble than the sail version, so it was a far from comfortable passage. But in dangerous waters, speed was of the essence. Within twelve hours of boarding she had made the crossing, and was asleep in her room at The Gran Hotel on Placa de Weyler, in the heart of the town, just a short walk from the cathedral.

Despite the rigours of the journey and the burdens that haunted her, she'd awoken this new day, rested and with a clear head. She'd spent the morning preparing for her meeting, determined for the sake of her child to control the hatred that howled within her.

"Your water, *Señora*."

The waiter had returned, making the most impressive show of this the simplest of tasks.

Llucia thanked him and smiled to herself; this was, after all, one of Palma's most expensive places to stay, so there was an undoubted expectation upon the poor man to perform, something she neither desired nor felt comfortable with. But she could easily afford all the trappings, including the private lounge required for her meeting, and this superficial opulence was an essential backdrop to her task.

"My guests are due mid-morning. Will you please ensure they are greeted well and brought through to me?"

She passed him a five peseta note and gently brushed away his shock at her generosity.

For the next hour she sat alone, collecting her thoughts, rehearsing. She'd received confirmation from the Seminary that 'His Excellency Paulinus, Bishop Emeritus of the Diocese of Arage' would indeed meet her as she'd requested, to discuss her offer of a legacy. At least Padre Alvaro Marin, fool or otherwise, had done his job and passed her letter to his office.

Llucia had longed for this day. For almost three decades she'd imagined the retribution she would visit upon the man who'd nearly destroyed her, whom she'd thought of as love but instead had sat by and watched as her family was butchered. This was the moment she'd wanted most of all, and with it, to be lifted from the guilt of her survival, her weakness and her failure to protect those she adored.

Yet now, at the very hour of atonement, she needed this man, the creature she loathed, to help save her son.

There was a knock on the door and the waiter entered. He looked ashen.

"Excuse me, *Señora*, there are two gentlemen to see you. I had no idea…"

Llucia interrupted him.

"…Two?"

"Yes *Senora*, they are especially elevated men, holy even. Are you sure these are your guests?"

Why two? she thought.

"Yes, of course they are my guests. Did you think it not possible?"

Llucia had spent a lifetime assailing such jaundice.

"Oh, not at all, *Señora*, it's just that one of them is Paulinus."

She noted the informality in his choice of title.

"The greatest and most respected of any man amongst us…"

Llucia hadn't expected this.

"…a hero to the poor. He has done so much."

There was further hesitancy.

"Forgive me, *Señora*, I've said too much. I will bring them through."

For a moment she was back in Es Migjorn Roca at Sant Cristofol, being held and comforted by this most trusted of men. He was tall, awkwardly handsome with the kindest of eyes, and she loved him. His words, his embrace, everything about him lent her strength. She could just about imagine a new life if he was beside her. He'd promised he'd always be there, and she'd believed him.

Then the door opened. Two men appeared, both tall. One was accoutred in an outdoor cloak, full-length cassock and clerical-collar with a prominent crucifix displayed above his garments. He carried a small leather case at his side, to which he looked conjoined. The other was distinctly less formal in an untidy, dark suit and creased shirt, opened at the neck. She feverishly scanned them, heart pumping, desperate to identify the priest she'd loved, the man she now detested.

As they approached, she stood, expecting the bishop to require her gracious obedience. She'd determined in advance this would not happen; she would neither genuflect in recognition of his holy status nor kiss the proffered hand. That was what other subordinated women did. So she looked at the palm thrust her way by his elegance, grabbed it firmly and held on, staring directly into his eyes. For a moment, she could tell he expected her to be supplicant, but the continuous grip quickly confused, and the confidence of the man within the vestments quickly diminished. He began awkwardly to wrestle his hand free.

"Señora Quintana," he said, clearing his throat and attempting to restore some prestige to his office, "I am Padre Perez, Secretary to the Diocese of Arage."

Startled, she looked more closely at the features staring back towards her. They were very much younger than she'd expected, pallid, wearily vacant. This was not the man she'd imagined.

"Please," he said, stepping aside, "may I introduce to you to Bishop Paulinus."

And there he was.

For a moment, they stood quietly in their awkward triangle, Llucia temporarily mesmerised. She'd expected a grotesque figure, older than his years, unkempt, detestable. Yet to the contrary, there was youthfulness in his three score years and a peace and stillness around him. His face shone with a brightness undiminished by the distance from their last meeting. And those eyes, she could never forget the eyes. He was smiling.

"I see you like holding hands," he said.

She wanted to laugh, to hold his hand even, to be back with him at Sant Cristofol. But she just looked. He seemed to be trying to put her at her ease.

"The way you held Padre's hand just then, I recognise a strength of purpose."

He continued to smile, whilst Padre Perez rocked backward on his feet, starting to suspect an awkwardness for which they were unprepared. Still, she stared.

"Señora, I hope you are well; your letter and invitation here were greatly appreciated."

Much as she hated the thought, he seemed kindly and considerate. In every movement of his face, in the way he held his hands together before him, he was the loving man she'd known.

He tried again.

"My secretary tells me that your padre was most insistent. I believe he spoke very intently about you."

She knew that she must speak, bury those momentary glimpses of the past; her son needed her.

"Please," she said, beckoning them to choose armchairs.

She sat back down with the sun behind her, shining brightly through the hotel's elegant modernist window and directly upon them, exactly as she'd intended.

"I hope you had a good journey," continued the bishop. "It has been many years since I last had the privilege of leading Mass in Mao. Such a beautiful town and a glorious island."

He smiled again, and a simple dignity, a generosity of spirit, tumbled from within him.

"Señora?"

Her quietness wasn't something he was unused to. Those in his presence were frequently overpowered by his office, initially at least.

"Your letter. It mentioned that you wished to confer a great kindness upon the church."

He gestured towards her gently, and for a moment the rage fell away, wrong-footed by love.

"We are always blessed when such opportunities arise. There are so many in our midst who need our devotion to their needs, to bring them God's joy, and even the smallest gifts can do so much."

He did indeed appear to be a remarkable man. There was no side to him, no hint of pomposity in his words or grand statement in appearance. She would have paid him no attention had she passed him in the street, yet here he was, both 'hero to the poor' and the cause of all her grief, who seemingly had no knowledge or memory of her.

"Thank you for agreeing to meet with me," she said, trying to discern a way through this new reality.

His smile became broader.

"I do have a legacy I wish to discuss, though I'm not sure how it will help those poor to whom you refer?"

Padre Perez shuffled on his seat.

"You see, my business here is more direct than that, and of a personal nature."

She appeared to hesitate for a moment, and the bishop interceded.

"*Señora*, is it confession that you need from me? If so, then that is also my desire."

She nodded to the contrary.

"Or maybe you are concerned that any such direct gift would be used for general matters in the cathedral and not for a specific project that you may have in mind to help our people. I must assure you that I, too, detest the scattering of munificence upon a building, or upon relics to hang from a wall."

Padre Perez seemed perturbed by this and began to fidget with his beautifully manicured nails.

"I sent you a letter."

There was a moment's blankness. He turned to the padre, who in turn reached for his case. She realised the bishop hadn't seen it, relying, as she now saw, upon his secretary.

"Forgive me, *Señora*," he said, as Perez fumbled inside a large envelope and passed him the letter.

"It is there, your Excellency," the padre said, pointing on her letter to the bequest Llucia was offering.

The bishop seemed unimpressed with his aide, whose face now matched the colour of the ecclesiastical socks peeping from below his cassock.

"I do not always get to see the details I should." There was a moment's pause whilst he studied the letter. "You said your bequest is direct and personal. I can see the generous nature here about which you write, but you do not elaborate beyond the generality."

He waved his hand abstractedly.

"Perhaps you would be able to say a little more?"

She steeled herself.

"Inside that envelope there was also a smaller item."

They both looked towards Perez, who, sensing their instruction, fidgeted once more inside his case, though this time pointedly more laboured and with graceless ado, before retrieving a small photograph. He passed this to the bishop who studied it closely for a moment.

"*Señora*, is this the man you are really here about?"

She sat silently, staring at him.

"Does he need help?"

Again she paused, a tension inching between them.

"There are three of us that need help," she said, "two of whom are in this room."

Perez started to wring his hands, and a knee began bobbing up and down below his garment. The bishop though, sat perfectly still, compassion etched throughout him. He looked again at the photograph.

"I can see you need to tell me more. Would it help if I asked Padre Perez to wait outside?"

She nodded and the padre, visibly relieved, gathered himself and his leather case and made quickly for the door.

Once the latch closed, the bishop edged his chair to one side.

"The sun," he said, motioning to the window.

"Please... continue, be as direct as you like."

"That photograph," she said, "the man there is my son."

He looked again at the image.

"He looks a fine man, *Señora*."

"Indeed," she replied, "I am blessed to have him as my son. My family is now much extended, but Oriol is at its heart."

"A beautiful name for such a man," he said. Llucia raised her eyes.

"Oriol," continued the bishop, "Aureus in Latin, 'golden'. He has a golden heart."

"He lives his life in such a way that's true. He is the beloved head of the family and runs our many farms and businesses now that I am becoming too old. And he writes. He is the most beautiful poet."

The bishop smiled.

"Ah, that indeed is glorious. Many times, I am challenged by those who deny our faith. They say to me, 'scientists say this, scientists say that' and I chuckle and say to them, 'show me a scientist who can also write beautiful poetry and I will listen with even more intent.'"

He laughed again, encouraging her to feel comfortable in his presence.

"He is also a man whom the community revere," she continued, "his mother has too many enemies from her years of venture, but he brings an enlightenment that she could only dream of."

"*Señora*, even from our short time together I am sure his goodness is as much yours as his."

She smiled, and for the first time in their meeting, their eyes fully joined.

"No, I begin to see something I had always longed to believe. That it was from his father that this beauty flowed."

She pulled an old, neatly folded newspaper page from the bag that lay beside her chair and carefully opened it up.

"The community I talk of is Es Migjorn Roca. You may remember it."

He sat motionless.

"The church we serve and from whence that padre who conveyed my message to your secretary came, is Sant Cristofol."

Again, there was no hint of an emotion from him. She passed him the cutting.

"Please, that photograph below the headline… you may recognise it."

Indeed, he did. It was from the 'Mahon Catòlica' a broadsheet for the diocese of Mahon, from 1890. He studied it for a while.

"It is hard to remember that man," he said, "it seems so long ago now, but it was a happy day. To be called for my ordination had been a long-held dream. I had quite forgotten the obligatory photograph."

She waited for a moment as he perused the brief report that accompanied the photograph, shaking his head and tutting.

"A lot of unnecessary fuss wouldn't you say?"

"The photograph your secretary gave you," said Llucia, "please… place it next to your photograph in the newspaper. Those two men… they are not quite at the same age, but they are close enough to see."

He peered at them both, now arranged side by side.

"Close enough to see what, *Señora*? Your son?"

He looked up, his eyes suddenly full of seriousness.

"No, Bishop Paulinus, not my son."

She paused for a moment.

"Our son."

The shock was instant. He went to speak, but an oppressive compression rolled through his body rendering it impossible. He looked again at the images. They were so alike.

He closed his eyes and for a minute or so, nothing but the occasional distant conversation from the street beyond pierced the wretched silence within the room. He sat there in his darkness, the only wall behind which to hide from the two words that had eviscerated him; *our son*.

When at last the lids parted, those beautiful eyes were gone, submerged by thickening grief. This was the day she had dreamt of… and she hated it.

"…son," he managed to say.

His speech was weak. Gone was the warm and generous comfort he'd brought with him to the room. And gone, too, was the spark that belied his years. Now, suddenly, he resembled the crumpled figure she'd expected to meet. But still, there was an unmistakable sincerity. He hadn't questioned her assertion. Rather, it appeared, he was clinging to the word as it fell from his mouth. He had a son.

"Since the slaughter of my family, I have survived so that I might see this day."

She saw the tears begin to slide to the side of his face.

"You tended me, supported me, you enabled me to survive. More than that, you allowed me to love you, to find trust again."

He pulled an old rag from his coat and held it to his face.

"Then you left."

He continued to dab his face before her, speechless, pathetic. She could contain herself no longer; the years of suffering and darkness would not allow it.

"You left," she screamed, "after watching the massacre of my loved ones in that barn, you left."

She was close to his face now, as if the shouting and the spitting that accompanied would erase the horror. She began crying uncontrollably.

"You left... and then... Oriol."

She grabbed him by his shoulders and shook him fiercely, her face still in his, the force of her words, her breath, covering him like a fiery shroud. He made no effort to defend himself, save for the tears now soaking his collar.

"Golden?" she shrieked, "yes he is golden, but how would you know? You may see yourself as a hero to the poor, but you're evil and I hate you."

She slumped back in her chair, spent by the guilt and pain of nearly thirty years of regret and loathing, and the burden of fear she now held for the safety of her son.

For a moment or two they sat facing each other, uselessly exhausted, she weeping uncontrollably; he bowed with his head in hands. There was a knock at the door and both sat upright in pretence towards formality. After a moment, there was another knock and this time the door opened. Padre Perez stood at the threshold still clutching his case.

"Is everything alright, your Excellency?"

He must have overheard the commotion, and his speech and body were contorted in an exaggerated obsequiousness towards his master.

The bishop didn't turn or speak. He simply held up his hand and waved him away. This time the padre's rush to depart was less apparent, and he tarried, seemingly studying the scene, smelling the atmosphere, as if surveying for the evidence of a crime. The bishop waved again, and he left, closing the door behind him.

Once more they sat in silence, muted to the spot.

"Son," he repeated, this time more audibly.

Llucia's tears were now exhausted, and she wiped her face with her hand.

"I never dreamt…"

His words tailed off and he shook his head.

"Dreamt what?" she asked.

"That I would ever have a child."

She was startled. He hadn't rejected any notion of paternity, there had been no immediate denial or dismissal, both of which she'd been expecting.

"I didn't know. This will not help you, but I didn't know."

Since the day he'd left, she'd lived by her wits and intuition. Detestable though she'd imagined him to be, abhorrent though she found the notion of his sincerity, the evidence of her eyes told her otherwise.

But she persevered.

"The murder of my family, the destruction of our land, you didn't know of that either?"

His lips tightened and he shook his head in despair.

"I was there that horrific day," he replied, "it's scarred upon my soul. I arrived with the padre after we heard of the terrible events. We did what we could, which was far too little. Our prayers were of little use to those too agonised by their pain to hear us. Yes, I left. In so doing I have carried the guilt for the rest of my life. And now this… a son. You are right to see me as evil."

Llucia, desperate though she was to destroy him, hadn't foreseen such a response; neither had she anticipated the unsettling vestige of affection that still lay within.

"But you were the padre?"

He sighed and briefly closed his eyes once more.

"I wish that had been so."

"You were," she shouted, "you led the children, I helped you with their Sunday worship, you spoke from the pulpit. You were the padre."

"No, it was Padre Serrano, an old man, well into his seventh decade. I regret to say, he had very little cognition of the days of the week, let alone of the work within the church at Sant Cristofol. I was one of his lay helpers, a volunteer. He was taken advantage of by those involved in the events that destroyed your family. I should have reported his incapacity long before, though my weakness and fear prevented this."

"And afterwards," said Llucia, "when you cared for me?"

The bishop stared at her, tears once more welling in his eyes.

"At first you were very unwell. You had seen terrible things. I lived in Mao; I was a stonemason, a very different life. But I paid for your lodgings in Alaior and for the care you received there. We spent lots of time together, you became stronger. Then, slowly, my feelings for you changed. My guilt at my hopelessness began to turn into love. You were a young woman, a beautiful woman. I was not yet a priest, though the age difference and the way our love progressed… I knew it was wrong."

"Wrong?" she blurted. "Wrong? You left me, having given me hope. You left me to have my son alone, to rebuild a life, a family, a future. I've achieved that and far more, but for much of it I've lived in a hell you helped create. You left me."

His head dropped once more, acknowledging her anger.

"I have no wish to deny any of what you say. I left you. The church authorities were cautious to distance themselves from any scandal. I knew this later, but at the time, I was naive. Padre Serrano had little knowledge of what had happened around him, and I was easily persuaded to enter the monastery in Valencia, that my sins be assuaged, my life become of some worth. I grew into the man of office you see today, shackled by eternal shame, only momentarily alleviated by the work I can do for others."

"And my son?" asked Llucia.

"Our son," replied the bishop, gently, "I had no idea. I should have done. I cannot try to deflect from my cowardice. Of course, I should have been concerned. I have never forgotten. Before I found the church, you were my only love. But yes, at the time, I ran."

"To Palma," said Llucia.

"Eventually, yes, I arrived here, as have you. A long journey for us both."

Llucia prided herself upon her planning. She'd learnt to be the mistress of detail and strategy, a deal-maker, and where that was not possible, a force that could not be resisted. But in this moment, conflicted as she was by the long-buried emotions of the heart and the realities of a thwarted reward for her loathing, she felt stymied; exhaustion cascaded through her body. The years of toil to right injustice had brought her here, as much adrift as the man whose treachery had so inspired her to fight.

"Oriol… our son. Please, what is the help he needs?"

They were both consumed by the circumstance of their situation, but it was the bishop who pressed for clarity. The irony wasn't lost on Llucia.

"He sailed for Alexandria many weeks ago, a journey he's made many times over the years. This was to be his last. His trade there and the dangers of the Mediterranean, now that the war is building, have made the ventures less reliable."

"His ventures?"

"We have an agent in Cairo from whom we buy sugar. We ship it back through Mao and then sell it on. A significant amount we keep for the villages, for our workers. They have come to rely upon us for this and other food, particularly during harder times. They cannot depend upon the authorities."

"A noble trade indeed."

"It may appear so," replied Llucia, "but it is Oriol who is the generous one, not his mother. He sees it as his, and therefore our, family's duty. I, on the other hand, can only see dependency and a day of reckoning when we cannot sustain the benevolence."

"He is a nevertheless a man of great goodness."

"Would you expect any less from your son?"

Unlike before, there was less bitterness in her words.

"I have some influence still, which I will use," he said.

Her plan had been to expose him for the evil he was, and then use this to lever his compliance. But here he was, taking the initiative without any thought for his own conflicted position.

"Do you know of his arrangements?"

"Oriol is his own man now," she replied, "and I have willingly passed my responsibilities to him. But I still make it my business to be informed, though would not admit that to him."

He nodded.

"He has travelled by vessel: *The Adelphi*. It's at least a week overdue in Alexandria. We have well-tried arrangements for being informed, and there has been no sighting whatsoever."

"This boat; it's reliable?"

"The Andreassens are old and trusted acquaintances of ours; their fleet of vessels, their contacts, are all dependable."

The bishop pondered for a moment.

"I certainly remember the family name." He hesitated.

"And...?"

"They remain a prominent Jewish family, I believe, generous too, with their gifts on this island."

"Is there a problem?"

"I know very little other than I hear that they are strong advocates of the Jewish cause in Palestine, and that they have the tacit trust of both the British and the Ottomans."

"So, shouldn't that help?"

Llucia was puzzled by his reticence to come to the point.

"I believe it also makes them subject to the qualms of either side; it's a dangerous position to be in."

"You will help."

Llucia was instructing once more, but the serious intent etched on his face dispatched the requirement for a direct response.

"I shall ensure that those I trust will check the port for any news. When Oriol arrives..."

Llucia interrupted him.

"If Oriol arrives."

"Llucia…"

… a compassionate smile, a gentle reassurance, and now the use of her first name. How she had loved this man.

"…when Oriol arrives," he repeated, "I shall ask that his care is uppermost in their minds whilst he is ashore."

"Will he not be alerted?"

"Those I know there are driven by love and by righteousness. They will do the correct thing and I assure you, will be impossible to spot. Please, I ran from you once. I shall not run again."

There was a knock on the door and this time it only partly opened. Somewhere behind it a chastened Padre Serrano.

"I am sorry to remind your Excellency," he whimpered, "but you are due to be at the Església Sant Nicolau in half an hour."

They looked at each other, and for the briefest of moments, both thought for a way to extend their conversation.

"When I hear, I will get a message to you. You too have a padre as your secretary, I believe?"

She almost smiled.

"Llucia, I understand that you will carry the hurt I caused you for the rest of your life, that I cannot be forgiven. You may have thought I would deny your words, that you would need to balance my compromised state against the price for helping Oriol. But you have brought me the greatest gift, the chance to help our son… and the joy of seeing you again."

Those eyes had regained some beauty. Even through the venom, she still wanted to believe in him.

"When Oriol is home," she said quietly, "then I will start to know again what trust really means."

He rose and gently bowed. There was no greater desire in his heart than to hold her, but the deeds of his younger heart could not be unlocked. He moved towards the door, fighting returning tears. He pulled on the handle, about to leave, before gently turning one last time.

"I want you freed from the burden of grief I have caused you. All those things you believe about me I deserve. I pray that finally I can act in love to serve you, and our son, as I should have done all those years ago."

The door closed and she crumpled in her chair, convulsed by her loss.

"The report goes on to say that the boat was tended by a smaller supply vessel whilst laying a mile or so offshore, and that it then set off on a north-easterly bearing."

Brigadier Regis-Templeton looked around the table at the hastily called meeting. They were an unusual grouping, even by the Bureau standards. Whilst the majority were regular army intelligence officers, there were also trusted civilian officials, including Moussaabey, and what HQ would generally refer to as a 'rag-tag of disorderly others', by which they meant academics such as Lowthian and Grice-Farquharason.

"There are a number of things about this that may be significant. Firstly, the route they were taking would lead them to the coast of Palestine, somewhere between Haifa and Ashkelon, both places from which we have formal intelligence about suspicious interactions between Turkish forces and unnamed vessels anchored offshore. Secondly, few captains in their right mind would willingly take their boat towards a hostile territory controlled by our enemies, across waters crawling with naval sea power."

He began to cough somewhat uncontrollably, and an aide passed him a glass of water. After a few moments, he apologised and regained the thread.

"The boat was what we would call a 'drifter', used for fishing in their hundreds in British waters. Some, though, made their way to other destinations, particularly as they aged."

"A bit like us, sir," interrupted one of the older officers, to the amusement of the others.

"Yes, indeed," said Regis-Templeton, amiably rolling with the sentiment, "this one though, seems to have found a Balearic home. From the shore, the name that could just about be made out was *The Adelphi*, though we must accept that may not be accurate."

Lowthian and Moussabey shot each other a startled look; it was the very name Smith had whispered to Nooney.

"If it is indeed so named, then we believe from the records of purchase held by our people that it belongs to a group owned by a Jewish family in Mahon, in Menorca, the Andreassens. This may be significant."

The Brigadier nodded across the table to Lowthian.

"Colonel, if you would…"

She opened a folder in front of her and began to speak.

"We work with many agents to support the military push. One such asset, also Jewish, is becoming particularly prized. He has convinced London that water can be found below the desert."

There were guffaws of laughter from all sides of the table, though Lowthian was noticeably not amused. She waited for the outburst to die down and then stood up and moved a few feet back from the table, placing herself in front of the map wall that ran the length of the room. As she did so, something of a reverential hush fell upon those gathered. Her reputation as an intellect with a mind for military solutions had spread throughout the officer classes stationed in Cairo, as had what had appeared to most as her idiosyncrasy – that of being a woman.

"It takes 20,000 gallons of water a day to enable a brigade to operate in the desert. That is the bare minimum. For the last two years, we have built a network of pipelines connecting water sources from the Sweet Water Canal to the Suez, and then onward to operations in the Sinai. Where this hasn't been feasible, we've built railway lines. You will all most likely know this. You should therefore know that many parts of this network are vulnerable to attack by the Turks or their surrogates. If we are to have confidence that the push through Sinai and on towards Jerusalem will be successful, we shall need to have accessible and easily defended water supplies along our route of attack."

"Beersheba has great big bloody pools of the stuff," said a Major from the Anzac Mounted Division, "so, surely we'd be better to focus on a quick strike north to capture that?"

"Yes, they have water, but as I would have thought you'd also know, nowhere near enough to sustain the capabilities we need in the field if we are to drive the Ottoman into submission. And you've already seen the dreadful consequences of inefficiently planned incursions along those lines."

This much was certainly true, and try as they might, none of those in attendance had expected the setbacks that had occurred at the hands of the enemy counter attacks of recent months.

"Three exploratory wells were sunk last month on the basis of this agent's information," she said, using a pointer to show their locations.

There were further knowing chuckles and shakes of the head.

"Two of them..." she paused, "...have revealed clean water from the aquifer, the third we think may also fill in time."

There was a stunned silence and an almost collective look of disbelief. Then one of the army colonels spoke up, noting what most of the others must have been thinking.

"Well, only a 'gippo' would have been able to dig those holes; it's so bloody hot in the middle of nowhere, none of our lot could have been there, so, hardly reliable I would have thought?"

There were grunts of agreement.

Lowthian gave him a stare and he began to wiggle, somewhat regretful at his observation. She'd had more than enough of the masculine banter that so often passed as 'just joshing', and determined to cauterise the source.

"'One of our lot' as you put it was there."

She stationed her gaze such that it passed right through him, as a spit through the roast.

"Me."

There was an uncomfortable silence.

"And yes, I was working alongside what you quaintly call 'gippos', and advised by our Jewish friend, otherwise I would not have been able to find the exact locations where the bore holes were needed. I rode with the Bedouin, as did other specialist officers. Those 'gippos' have been a superb source of support for the British Army, pinning down the enemy by constant harassment and attacks on their supply lines, and all despite the language and mistrust that comes from those who use such words."

"I'm sorry, Colonel, I didn't mean to..."

"In fact," she continued, "let me introduce you to one of my 'gippo' colleagues."

She pointed to Moussabey.

By now, the precise source of her ire was wishing a well would open up right below his chair.

"I'm so sorry, of course I didn't mean you, Peter, I…"

"…meant the other sort, those I see in the squares, with their funny ways, their strange language. Is that what you're trying to say?" continued Lowthian.

Brigadier Regis-Templeton admired her fearlessness and passion on this matter, but cut in to prevent any further damage to one of his officers.

"You should know, gentlemen, that the Colonel spends significant time building our support base with our Arab friends, much of it in some of the most inhospitable desert environments. Peter Moussabey has been a key ally in this task, and we should all be grateful. Please, let us all ensure the language of respect."

He looked across to Lowthian to continue, and for another few minutes she summarised, without interruption and with the complete concentration of those in the room, the nature of the well-digging work and the significant influence this could have upon the war, before handing back to the Brigadier.

"So, as you can imagine," he said, "if we could replace current supply pipelines and train-drawn water tankers with those natural underground supplies, it could energise our push against the Ottoman up into Palestine. If we'd studied our history as our Jewish agent had suggested, we would have known that water existed in these sites for hundreds of years."

He looked across the room at Grice-Farquharason.

"Tell them please if you would."

"Oh right, yes, sir."

He was mildly startled to be invited.

"Erm, yes, well… in the first century AD, a fellow by the name of Flavius Josephus, a bit of a historian of those times, described exactly this in his book about the Jewish Wars… and—"

"…we've been fighting over the same area ever since," interrupted Regis-Templeton, keen not to let too loose the academic within the Colonel.

"Of course," he continued, "if there is any suspicion about the Andreassens, we now need to examine it. Do they, for example, have links with our Jewish water diviner? Is what we are hearing and finding too good to be true, or is it all absolutely legitimate? I need your eyes and ears on this. We need to know who to trust. Is this understood?"

There was agreement all round.

"Good. And one more thing. The unit in Alexandria followed the supply vessel that met up with *The Adelphi* as it sailed into port. A fellow, clearly not a local, jumped ashore when it berthed and made his way down here to Cairo. He's being watched. The reason should be obvious by now, but I'll spell it out. If that boat is up to no good, then apart from worrying about the work of the Andreassens, who on earth could this particular fellow be? Is he a spy?"

"Do we have a sketch, sir?" asked one of the officers.

"Well, it would have been nice to get a photograph, but you all know how damned difficult this sort of stuff is; unless that is, we somehow convince him to sit for us at a portrait studio."

There was polite laughter.

"So, the best we've got is an artistic impression that you should take a look at when you leave. It will stay here, on the map wall, for the rest of the week if you need a refresher, and there's a few spare copies."

He held up the sizeable drawing, showing an average sized man, swarthy complexion, mid-thirties, well dressed in a smart light brown linen suit.

"Oh… and there was a strange thing about him that may help: he had what looked to have been a nasty gash across the middle of his head."

There was a great deal of heavy water washing within the head of Oriol Quintana. He was perched in a local coffee house just off Shari El Ghuri, in the less than salubrious El Hamzawi district, a fifteen-minute walk and tram ride from the centre of Cairo. It was a cut above the usual premises of the area and just a short amble from the cramped room at his hostel.

He was known to the locals, though his visits had become less frequent over the years. It was still an unusual place in which to find a European, even though Oriol's Mediterranean complexion and informal attire distinguished him, in the eyes of fellow customers, from their stereotype of the typical Cairo colonist.

The stools and tables at which they all sitting were mostly positioned below an awning which covered the pavement, and this, together with the narrowness of the street, provided an effective shade in which to relax. The interior also housed tables, arched over by thickened limestone walls, but cooler though this was, it was much too dark to encourage the natural Arab conviviality that thrived in such places.

The clientele was entirely male, mostly in groups, noisily playing cards, board games, or just debating matters of the day. A few were sitting alone, some reading the newspaper, others simply gazing abstractedly; it was these who heightened his suspicion.

His journey to Cairo had been plagued, even when judged against the abnormal standards of his business there. The Andreassens had skipped their routine time in Alexandria to complete business further along the coast. Then, when the launch that picked him up from *The Adelphi* reached the quayside, no one was there to meet him. Taqi al Din al-Bilal had always made a point of welcoming him ashore, offering generous hospitality in the offices at The Alexandria West Bay Shipping Company and accompanying him to his hotel or train, but this hadn't happened and the premises were locked.

So he'd made his own arrangements to travel on the express to Cairo, and developed an increasingly uneasy feeling that he was being watched. He'd suppressed this as irrational, and by the time he disembarked at the station at Midan Bab El Hadid was recovering some certitude, only to be confronted by two Coptic priests, fully robed in clerical attire, asking in broken English if he was a lonely traveller requiring accommodation.

After a night's disturbed sleep, he'd dismissed all of this as coincidence and paranoia. Though he couldn't remove so easily Elisheba Andreassen's parting words as he left *The Adelphi*.

She'd briefed him with her usual intensity about the arrangements for the return journey to Mao, insisting upon summarising to remind him of his deadlines.

"We should be back in four days, berthed as normal in Alexandria. If all goes to plan, your goods and the rest of the cargo will be in the hold, and we should be ready to sail two days following."

But there was a wistfulness about her that was out of character. As they parted, she'd held his hands and wished him good luck, health and peace.

"Should we not return," she said, "remember that what we did was borne out of goodness, and our love for the land of Zion."

What did she mean? Why would she not return and what possible greater danger could she be sailing towards than that which they had already faced together en route?

Then, this very morning, he'd received a note at the hostel that his usual contact was unavailable, that he would be meeting a different intermediary later at the rendezvous in town. Again, he dismissed his stupidity at the concern, and at the control such continuing and preposterous emotion had exerted. He'd built up years of experience in the nuances of Cairo life, on top of which, he'd survived the ravages of the sea and an attack by the German navy. To be overly exercised by such coincidences and by a few locals sat on their own in the same coffee house, therefore felt quite ridiculous, and anyway, not one of them had paid him any interest.

He'd relaxed and taken another coffee from the steaming dallah pot brought to his table by the owner. Oriol had acknowledged the man's friendly concern. Was he in mourning? Was that why he was refusing sugar with his coffee?

So, with something of a smile, he'd settled back to enjoy the spicy bitter taste of the coffee and the aromatic scents that encircled, and began to return to calmer waters. He thought of his family; what would they be doing? He longed to return to them, Turo Vell, and the poetry he loved.

He pulled out the dog-eared bundle of paper he kept in his pocket; the small pencil he always carried, and read the words:

"I met a man today.
Angered, razored, kettled by the certainties of others.
Battered on the blasted heath of his business,
His life a fishnet of uncertainty."

He stared at them, momentarily conveyed back to that well in the courtyard at the farm where these were first written. They were harsh lines. Since which, and try as he might, there had been nothing.

Surrounded though he was by the noise and routine commotion of side-alley suburban Cairo, there was now a silence returning in his head and an attached, almost discarnate sense of isolation. He began to write.

"His burden? Integrity denied. His crime? To do his best as he had always done before. But this song wasn't good enough. They judged him culpable. And left him; cursed, undressed."

Indeed, so becalmed had he become that as he left to make his way into town he quite forgot to pay attention to the movements of those around him.

Had he done so, he might have noted a Coptic priest across the street. He'd been engaged in a conversation with a stall holder but had now moved away, edging through the crowd, careful to remain as invisible as a man in a dress could be, whilst still maintaining a reasonable distance between himself and his quarry.

CHAPTER 9

"There have been some developments."

Colonel Lowthian was never one for exaggeration, though from her demeanour something was up.

They'd been called to a meeting at the office in The Cairo Sugar Association, so assumed it must be significant, though neither Laurie nor Nooney had been made aware of any late changes to their brief. The arrangements for the sale of sugar by the 'Trading Assurance Cairo' were in place; all that was needed was confirmation from Smith of the means of passage across the Mediterranean.

As soon as they arrived, they sensed that Peter Moussabey, sitting next to Lowthian across the table from them, already knew about what was coming. The Colonel got straight to business.

"Seems our sugar business is just about to become a bit stickier," she said.

A faint smile crossed her lips, though this quickly made way for sobriety. They were all in civilian guise, Lowthian impeccably so, exactly as she had been in her role as the secretary to the Company. As was normal, there were none of the usual military formalities.

"We've received intelligence that the boat Smith proposed for our cargo has been delayed."

This was news to the pair. They had led on the deal-making and were the front line of the operation; or so they believed.

"Well, we've heard nothing of the sort," said Laurie, "where has this come from?"

"That I can't tell you, I'm afraid."

There was an uneasy silence. Up until this point, both men had assured themselves that Lowthian shared every lead, that they were completely trusted. But the meddling by Major Fogge had unsettled Laurie, and as much as he detested the man, perhaps he had a point. So he didn't hesitate.

"Why not?"

Lowthian was taken aback. The Bureau section she ran encouraged a sense of comradeship by dispensing with rank and position and when it came to planning all brains, no matter how stewed, were welcome. But deep down, she knew that insubordination was only ever a stone's-throw away.

"That's the first time you've been so direct with me, Laurie," she said, "and it's something I hope never to have to reciprocate. There are parts of the picture that we can all see and deal with, but sometimes its scale becomes overwhelming and more caution is required."

Laurie was unconvinced but chose for the moment to let this pass. Nooney though, sensing a new dynamic, pushed for clarity.

"I think what we're saying is that given the planning and direction we've put into this, we should have been kept informed of everything that may affect things."

"That's what I'm about to do," retorted Lowthian, noticeably irritated. "What I can say for the moment is that the importance of your operation has increased significantly."

"Your operation?" blurted Laurie, forgetting that he had only a moment ago decided to keep his counsel.

Lowthian was now annoyed.

"Our operation if you will…'our operation'… is that better for you… is that clearer?" she spat.

Given the wilder side of her nature now uncovering, Laurie decided that yes, it was sufficient for now, and a stony silence affirmed this.

"Excellent. Now that's sorted, perhaps I can continue?"

"Our objective has been to unravel the scale and supply lines of the sugar black market, and we seem to be on the verge of a breakthrough. Two broader issues have arisen though, one of which could be explosive, the other more straightforward but of huge concern for military discipline."

She was thumbing some of the notes she'd used the day before in the emergency briefing called by Brigadier Regis-Templeton.

"It seems that the boat we've been offered for use by Mr Smith hasn't docked at Alexandria. Instead, it sailed onward towards the north-east, possibly heading for Palestine."

"Does that mean Smith will renege on the deal?" asked Nooney.

She knew that neither could be expected to see the wider complexities of the Palestinian connection, though perceived that Nooney, with his background, would be the more aware of the two.

"And how do we know all of this?" said Laurie, "Smith would have sent us word."

"He has," replied Lowthian.

She turned to Moussabey to take up the reins.

"Two days ago, I received a message from Smith via 'Eastern Telegraph' that our bird had flown, as I believe you like to say."

Laurie cast a quizzical sideways glance at Nooney.

"Charles the first, mate, 1642," he whispered, but just loud enough for all to hear.

Laurie's eyebrows raised and Nooney could almost hear his, "I know that".

"Smith assures that another vessel can be made available in a few days, equally reliable, and that our arrangements remain unaffected," continued Moussabey, "but we are less convinced of this."

He hesitated for a moment, aware of Lowthian's reticence not to exceed the brief from the intelligence meeting with the General.

"You see, every boat that sails into, out of, or past Alexandria is monitored by intelligence from the shore. There is a very efficient unit based there. They reported that our boat…"

"*The Adelphi?*" interrupted Laurie.

Moussabey nodded, "…met a smaller boat just offshore, which picked up an individual from them, a male, and brought him quayside."

"How do you know this man came off that boat? Did they actually see him pass between the two boats?" asked Laurie. "He could simply have been a member of the crew that had sailed out from the port in the first place, a coincidence?"

"That is so," replied Moussabey, "but the intelligence suggests he did transfer, and Smith himself seemed very clear when we checked such things with him to disassociate himself from any knowledge of this man. Given he appears to know everything about the movements in the port of those he trades with, this alone is curious. Those observing also described this man as of seemingly educated Jewish origin. He was carrying a suspicious head injury."

"What?" Laurie was unconvinced.

"We have a sketch."

Lowthian passed the drawing to them they'd taken from the briefing.

"Educated Jewish? Why on earth did they assume that?"

"His appearance."

"But that's ridiculous; he could just as easily be Arabic or some sort of European. And anyone with damage like that to the head could attract suspicion. He might just have banged his head on a door or got clocked in a drunken fight."

"Laurie should know about this stuff," said Nooney, "he's from Worcester."

Moussabey seemed baffled by this attempt at humour, and Lowthian stepped in.

"This hunch was further supported by intelligence suggesting that *The Adelphi* is owned by a Jewish family."

"Well, so what if he's Jewish?" said Laurie, still unaware of the potential ramifications of such information.

"We cannot ignore the chance that those aboard are plying their trade on behalf of the Ottoman in Palestine," continued Lowthian, "seeking favour for a post-war advancement, for influence; who knows? Maybe even towards a pro-Jewish position."

Nooney, though, wasn't so sure.

"On the boat on the way over, one of our officers briefed us about how the Ottoman had treated their Jewish locals. No better, it seemed to me, than some of the things they'd escaped from elsewhere."

Lowthian nodded, pleased that she'd judged his broader comprehension of these matters correctly.

"Some though, will see the Ottomans as the more likely victor of the war in this part of the world," she replied, "the power that unlocks a Jewish homeland in Palestine. If that means a conspiracy between such an anti-British group, some of whom may be on that boat, and our enemy, then we need to know."

"So, who are we helping, Jew or Arab?" asked Nooney.

Laurie went to speak, but refrained: he couldn't help the thought the answer to that question was 'ourselves'.

"All who will settle for peace," replied Lowthian.

"Blimey, best of luck with that," retorted Nooney, though discomforted immediately by the impact his lack of subtlety may have had upon Moussabey. So close had they become with him, so reliant were they upon his support, that they'd begun to lose sight of his situation.

"We walk a tightrope," replied Lowthian. "We need all our friends to help us. But if this individual from the boat is a spy, it could place in doubt the credibility of the plans to advance across the Sinai and into Palestine."

It was an astonishing statement for both men to hear. Their work to track the sugar subterfuge had, it now seemed, become a significant adjunct to the major military objective in the Middle East. Little wonder that Lowthian had been so reluctant earlier. It took a moment for the impact to settle.

"The good news," said Moussabey, attempting to lighten the moment, "is that Smith remains firmly committed to our deal, so congratulations, gentlemen."

"You were the important link, Peter," said Nooney, still somewhat concerned by what might have appeared as his insensitivity, earlier.

"We have all played our part," he replied, "and maybe in the doing, we've hooked a bigger fish."

"Talking of which," said Lowthian, "there is a second matter, this time relating to military personnel, which makes such a task even more difficult."

"Is it that some of them aren't very bright?" said Nooney, and this time everyone laughed.

"Regrettably, that is something of a constant," she replied.

"No, quite the opposite, I'm afraid; it appears that our intelligence-sharing isn't secure."

Nooney was aghast, though seeing Laurie noticeably less so, suddenly remembered their conversations about 'who to trust' that at the time he'd dismissed as irrational. Maybe he was on to something?

He began to feel a sense of unease. Too many fraying ends were appearing.

"Somehow, information on a variety of matters has been leaking from the Bureau, mostly trivial until now, tip offs about searches, checks upon permits, enforcement activities relating to local low-level crime… a few artefacts that have gone missing, that sort of thing."

"Until now?" asked Laurie.

"Brigadier Regis-Templeton spoke to Peter and me following that intelligence briefing."

Neither Laurie nor Nooney was aware that Moussabey was privy to such high-level discussions: another revelation.

"He asked us about the Sugar Case."

There was a pause.

"The problem was neither of us had mentioned this case to anyone, let alone the Brigadier, given the early days of the operation and the need to be sure of our sources before directly involving others. So, we four are the only ones who know about this."

"Apart, you could say, from Smith and his assistant and our supplier at the sugar refinery," said Laurie.

"Exactly so," replied Lowthian, "but as far as they're concerned, I'm certain they believe we are a bone fide operation, and would have no interest in exposing us. And as Peter says, we appear to have hooked that fish."

"Plus, of course, whosoever they may have talked to, Arab or European, innocently though that may have been. It could have somehow blown our cover," continued Laurie, unwilling to acknowledge Lowthian's thinking on a potential source of the leak.

"Unlikely in my opinion," said Moussabey, "I've worked with Smith before on other matters."

Once again, Laurie and Nooney exchanged glances as this was also news to them.

"I think I can judge the man well enough to know that despite appearances, he is very discrete. Idle gossip would cost him his business, and maybe much worse."

"And then there is myself and Nooney," said Laurie.

Lowthian shot him a look of mild annoyance that implied her complete faith in the pair should even be questioned.

"There's never a closed door when we're working in the Bureau," he continued, "not least because they don't shut properly. It would be pretty easy for some of our planning to be overheard, or our documents seen when we were elsewhere."

"Despite what you might think, we're very fastidious about such matters," retorted Lowthian, "nothing is ever left unsecured, I see to that, plus, the staff in the section are trusted completely."

"All the staff?" asked Laurie.

"Go on?"

"That's quite awkward," he replied. "I have no evidence, just a suspicion."

"You mean Major Fogge?"

For a moment the four of them said nothing, leaving Fogge's name complete with its two 'g's' and one 'e' resting in the ether.

"I've said before, Laurie, feed him drivel to help pass his time, he's a hopeless case, born imperiously deluded. He's probably told you to watch out for myself and Peter, something he says to all those he thinks he can impress."

"He was aware of our journey to Alexandria," said Laurie.

"I'm not surprised."

Laurie shook his head in amazement. He'd banked the information lest it set hares running, and yet here was Lowthian batting away his fears almost dismissively. And she knew? She could also sense his confusion.

"You didn't tell me," said Laurie.

"As you deal with him brilliantly," she replied, "and that will need to continue. Because of the added importance now of our operation, we'll be expected to work more closely with the regulars at HQ. It will be easier therefore, to get on with our task unhindered, if we start to play more strongly to the skills Fogge assumes he has. We shall involve him directly, enabling him to report, monitor, request on our behalf, but at all times out of synchrony with the guts of the operation."

"But he's a liability," blurted Laurie, "you've said that yourself."

"That's true, but potentially a useful one."

"How on earth will the operation be safer with him more closely involved?"

"As I said," and she smiled, "you deal with him brilliantly."

The tram Oriol had planned to catch was late, so the comforting quiescence he'd hoped it would provide began to evaporate at a greater rate than the sweat from the now enforced trot-cum walk: he couldn't afford to be delayed for his meeting. Familiar though he was with Cairo, how useful the short-cut across the gardens beside the Convent School near Midan Abdin would prove remained to be seen, and in the dry, intense heat his light trousers, hat and linen shirt were soon gluing to his body.

He paused for breath on the cooler corner of the square, concerned about his harassed appearance, but more so by his exact whereabouts. After a moment to reflect and still none the wiser, he headed north, reasoning that at least he'd hit one of the major parallel routes that crossed the city from the Nile towards The Tombs of The Caliphs. Once back on regular territory, he would re-calibrate.

Then, out of the corner of an eye, he caught sight of The Ministry of Waqfs on Shari Gami, a gem of a place that had long lodged in his mind as it so appealed to his sensibilities: a building in which the central purpose was to organise charitable gifts, grants, legacies of land, property and money, for the public benefit.

More pressing, he remembered that across the street from there was Shari El Madabigh. Follow this and in five minutes, even at a gentle pace, he would arrive at his meeting on time and less perturbed than he'd feared. The same could not be said for his unseen priestly shadow.

On reaching The Agricultural Bank of Egypt, he crossed the road, paused briefly to adjust his shirt and push back his hair, then entered below the archway and on through the sizeable glass doors of The Cairo Sugar Association. Once inside, despite the noise on the trading floor and the wrestle of bodies, it was refreshingly cooler, thanks to the huge fans, light walls and open windows.

He headed across to the usual desk at the back of the hall. As he did so, three smartly dressed men, two European, one Arab, together with a strikingly well attired European woman, appeared from the door that led to the back corridor. They seemed an unlikely grouping of sugar traders, much smarter and more focussed than what he had come to regard as the norm for the building. And they were silent. As they rushed past him, one of the men appeared to pause briefly to take a second look at him, as if engaging with a long-lost memory. The man then continued briskly onward towards the main doors, almost colliding in his temporary inattentiveness with a Coptic priest.

"Welcome back, Senor Quintana," said the concierge, and the distraction passed.

"Your papers, as per usual." He passed a folder across containing documents requiring his signature.

"Your Association membership updates, and of course, a fee request, I'm afraid."

Then with a polite, "please... allow me," he led Oriol through the door to the quieter pastures of the dusty corridor beyond the main trading hall, and on along to the only office without a sign on its door. This, at least, was a reassuring hint of normality. *One day perhaps*, thought Oriol, *they will at last hang a name here, something smart, such as the 'Trading Assurance Cairo' one on the office next door.*

The concierge knocked on the door, waited for a moment, and then knocked again. Eventually, there was a restrained "enter" from somewhere within and Oriol was shown through, to be met by a stout man of middle age in an uncomfortably tight and oddly inappropriate

The Poet Laurie Ate

tweed suit, sitting awkwardly behind a Davenport desk. His hair had been heavily brilliantined and licked militarily flat. There was a scalpelled parting down the middle. All of this sat above a tiny nose and thin moustache. He made no effort to stand, and even less to make eye contact, was on the short side, and his feet didn't quite reach down to the floor. He mumbled something to Oriol which he interpreted as to 'take a seat', so he did as bade and settled into the only option – a distressed and weather-beaten fanback armchair, incongruous in both its appearance and positioning, some distance away. The man bore no resemblance to his usual contact 'Jones', who was much taller, thin with rimmed spectacles, and most distinctly a man blessed with *plein de bonhomie*.

After a few moments of awkward hush, Oriol decided to take the initiative. His spoken English was perfectly acceptable by now, though the slower the response in conversation the more confident he felt.

"Mr Jones, he is away?"

The man continued to study the desk top. Perhaps it was the way he had phrased the question? He tried again.

"I had your note but expected to meet Mr Jones as well?"

He smiled to encourage a response. Still nothing. But then, looking more closely he could see that the man was shaking. One of his hands was holding the desktop for comfort, but the other had wandered across to some paperwork, which was now gently vibrating.

"Shall I be meeting Mr Jones today?" he asked again, determined to get something of a response and at this and with some effort, the man at the desk began to speak.

"No."

Oriol waited for more, but nothing seemed imminent.

"Perhaps I have come to the wrong office?" He got up to go, at which point the man shot upright like a cocked trigger, and looked directly at Oriol.

"Eaton," said the man.

At last, thought Oriol.

"That's very kind, but I have had some food and a coffee."

The man looked at him, his eyes glazing faster than camel scat in the desert.

"Eaton," he said again, almost firmly.

Oriol was becoming more confused; perhaps his English wasn't improving after all.

"No, I am not hungry, but thank you."

This time the man placed his feet onto the decorative pedestals that hugged the sides of the desk, and heaved himself upward, hovering towards Oriol at an angle that mirrored the slope of the Davenport's writing surface.

"Eeeeyyyyaaatonnnn," he mouthed, slowly, volubly, "that is my… name." He pointed animatedly towards himself.

He continued to roll his lips around the sounds a few more times in the slow way Oriol recognised as a characteristic in those who considered themselves superior. In this case, the additional purpose of the overemphasis was to entice understanding from a limited foreigner.

Oriol laughed, both at the pomposity and confusion.

"Of course, now I comprehend, you are Mr Eaton. I am pleased to meet you."

He extended his hand across into the void between the two, assuming it might be construed as an opportunity to make amends for any perceived glitch, but instead, Eaton sat transfixed and dithering, occasionally nervously tapping his head.

"I thought you were asking me if I had eaten," said Oriol, still trying his best to be amiable, to explain politely to the imperious ass why there had been a misunderstanding.

Nothing.

"The English language; so many words with different meanings," he continued.

Again, there was no response.

He was now exasperated by the shenanigans and eager to establish the credibility of their arrangements. If this trade was to fall through there might just be enough time to arrange alternative transactions with other contacts before he had to return to Alexandria to meet *The Adelphi*.

The whole journey had become fraught with danger, and now this: pure farce. Enough was enough.

"Mr Eaton, you are wasting my time. If you have the normal trade papers and have arranged that I meet Mr Jones, then good. If not, goodbye."

This had an immediate effect. It wasn't that Mr Eaton was incompetent, it was more simply that he was petrified. The thought of the deal sliding from his newly trusted hands forced him into a babbled reaction, and he began to speak, though by now his legs were also tapping time.

"I am sorry, Quintana," he said, adopting an almost military style of address, "I have the necessary papers from Jones for you to sign. Tomorrow we shall take these to our meeting with him."

"Why is Mr Jones not here? I always meet him when I come to Cairo."

Eaton seemed thrown by this.

"Erm… funeral."

"Oh, I am so sorry. Somebody he was close to?"

"Ah, yes… his father."

"What, his father was here in Egypt?"

"Oh no, not at all, died in blighty."

"Where?"

"Blighty… England."

"So Jones is in England?"

"No, his father is in England… well in a way, buried there… in a grave…"

Eaton began to make digging movements.

"Yes, yes, I know… so where is Jones at a funeral?"

Eaton was struggling; he hadn't been briefed on this. Sit at the desk, keep things to a minimum, get the document signed and bring him to the meeting with us tomorrow. Keep it simple, don't give anything away.

"In his room."

"His room?"

"Yes, he takes time to pray for his father every year on the day of his funeral."

He made a praying sign, just in case it helped the increasingly troublesome explanation.

Oriol was temporarily speechless. The detailed planning of his trip, the risks he and others had taken, the years of effective contacts in Egypt, all trivialised by this man. What was going on?

"Show me the papers," he instructed.

Eaton squared them up and pushed them towards Oriol, who by now had moved closer to the desk. He leafed through them, intimidating the wilting frame of the emissary, before sitting back down and methodically analysing the detail they contained. To his relief, they were in order, exactly as he had routinely received from Jones. Why had this taken so long?

"Pen," he barked to Eaton who speedily obliged.

He signed both copies and passed them to Eaton, pointing out the place for his signature, lest he be confounded by this task too. Even then Eaton made a clumsy mistake, crossing out his first attempt on one of the copies and starting again, so both were also initialled and dated, one copy kept by Eaton, and the other, the one containing the correction, by Oriol.

"So, 40 tonne sacks of sugar are to be transferred to Alexandria tonight, in the usual way. Is that correct?"

Eaton nodded and things were now easing with Oriol driving the arrangements, though it still felt very odd.

"And the other forty, the remaining payment for my services on your behalf?" he inquired, checking out Eaton's understanding of the mechanics.

"Shipped on to you once we receive news that you have safely arranged for the transport of our artefact, and that it has reached Madrid."

His swift reply surprised Oriol and he started to relax a little. The dimwit that inhabited Eaton seemed at last to be getting a grip. It was the customary practice for his services in transporting works of art and other precious items to be paid for through the currency of sugar, and he was relieved that this, at least, did not require his explanation.

"The artefact," inquired Oriol, still checking Eaton's credibility, "how will that be arranged?"

"As normal," he replied, now more lucid.

"First, the exchange with Jones needs to take place, then you will meet our friends from the loading team at Pont Limoun Station, and they will ensure the item is secreted within the sugar. The sack will be identified with the usual coding, but in every respect will appear identical to every other."

"And the last two numbers of the code?"

"27."

This indeed was exactly the routine. Customs officials in Alexandria were too hard pressed to undertake a thorough check of all goods being loaded into the hold of every boat. However, if pushed by the British to do so, they would comply, and the trade in sugar had become more dangerous for anyone involved in unauthorised activity. Huge amounts were now routinely being smuggled, causing price hikes and lost tax revenue, so there was a particular state of alert when these goods were loaded. The fact that Oriol's trade was arranged by a British company operating out of Cairo had meant that in the past it would have been nodded through, but those times had gone and even the British were beginning to suspect that their own people weren't necessarily playing by the rules.

"Good," replied Oriol.

"So, when is the meeting with Jones?"

"Tomorrow at ten."

"Here I presume?" Eaton hesitated, as if his pithering was about to return.

"Erm… no, we have decided upon a different venue."

"What?"

"We have a space on the third floor of the Sednaoui Department Store, just off Khazindar Square. We believe the exchange we need to make with you will be easier there, in plain sight, so to speak. An item of art, a fashionable piece for the home, being purchased just as anyone would expect at the counter in any such store. And anyway, to return here twice in two days might draw suspicion."

Oriol pondered the arrangement for a moment, considering it unusual. On the other hand, Eaton was right; he had never used The Cairo Sugar Association for the secretion of such an item on his many visits previously, so this alternative proposal made some sense. Though he wasn't a complete fool.

"We shall actually meet on the ground floor," said Oriol.

"No, it must be at the counter on the third where there is exclusive privacy for the handover of more expensive items."

Eaton was almost becoming assertive.

"It will be the ground floor. Jones will need to stand at a counter in the middle of it and when I am ready, I will introduce myself – but it will be in a very public space."

"But he ordered me. It must be on the…"

"Ordered?" replied Oriol.

"Those in a business of this nature usually request. The Jones I know is a very convivial person. I can't imagine him ordering anyone to do anything; it's not in his nature. Surely only soldiers order?"

Eaton's face flooded with an inner terror. Of more importance now, was to ensure that Oriol actually arrived. Bugger the exact location for the trade.

"Yes, yes… understood, I agree that makes sense, middle of the ground floor. I will tell Jones."

"Good," replied Oriol, though deep inside he knew it wasn't.

Are you still sure about them? his mother had asked that night as they sat together in the farmyard. She was talking of the Andreassens, but this could now equally apply to Jones and his previously impeccable deals. Were he to actually attend in the morning, he would need to be prepared, certain this wasn't an entrapment.

"And tell Jones to be properly prepared., Do you understand?"

Eaton nodded.

"I shall wait no longer than five minutes, and the handover of the item will need to be done immediately. Much as I appreciate Jones's company, after today, the sooner we are all on our way the better."

Again, Eaton acknowledged him, keen to ensure that the arrangement remained in place.

"And one more thing: tomorrow I shall meet just Jones, no one else, and especially not you. Is that clear?"

A brief flicker of resentment crossed Eaton's face, but quickly passed. Oriol picked up his papers, turned, and without any thought to shake

Eaton's hand, walked out of the door, back along the corridor, across the crowded trading floor and out onto Shari El Madabigh.

This, his last journey to Cairo, had become increasingly bedevilled.

CHAPTER 10

"Don't get your balls in a knot, mate." As ever, Nooney cut straight to the heart of the matter.

"We're here in this lovely spot, army rations, enough water in our bottle for an overnight, and we have each other for company. What could be better?"

The squalid ground-floor squat in which they were encamped, smelt of animal faeces and worse. They'd discussed potential origins for the odour but couldn't agree upon the specifics. Laurie had suggested cats; he'd noticed three or four strays shoot out from behind the rolls of thin carpet stored against the walls, only to be corrected by his good friend.

"Rats for sure, the size of cats, though."

Laurie squirmed in disgust.

"Blimey, Laurie, back home we grill the ones like them on a weekend; beautiful with a bit of mustard."

"Very funny, Nooney. What a god-awful place this is."

They were cooped up in a shop half way along a narrow street, more of a back-alley to Laurie's mind, that led towards St Nicholas Orthodox Cathedral. Right opposite was a hostel, smarter by far than the place they were occupying, but still not looking like much.

The terrified family who owned the place had been put in lockdown at the close of business, confined to their living space on the floor above by the heavy-handed mob sent by Major Fogge. The noise this had created at the time must have alerted half of Cairo.

"You've got too used to the fancy life at The Grand Continental, that's your trouble," continued Nooney.

They were on the official surveillance directed by Colonel Lowthian, monitoring the hostel frontage for any movement by the spy from boat 31; intelligence passed to them by Moussabey, confirmed he'd returned to his room there in the early evening.

Were he to leave by the front, they were to follow and intercept him if they felt the need; but otherwise, simply trace his movements and contacts. The rear door of the building was covered by regular Military Police, operating from the street there and to all intents and purposes patrolling normally, checking passes, intercepting traders, warning drunken troops. On the inside was the night manager, a reliable source and on a healthy British retainer.

Laurie was sitting on a low wicker stool, peeping out from behind the shutters of their fetid grotto, across towards the hostel. The front door was haltingly illuminated by an old gas light hanging uncertainly above it, and one half of the double door was open to the interior. Inside he could just make out the reception area and its apparitional attendant.

"Going to be a long night," he said, "so we'll need to take turn and turn about."

Nooney shuffled across beside him and gently prised open one of the slats.

"Blimey, hours and hours of looking at that. What we need is the bloke over there to tip us the wink if our friend is about to leave, turn his desk lamp up or something."

"I did suggest that," said Laurie, "but Lowthian made it clear that all the calls for this operation would need to be led by Fogge. No chance, therefore, of such sensible planning."

"Strange one, all of that business about him," replied Nooney. "Guess we've got no option for now but to just get on with things."

Laurie nodded.

"Well, we've done as asked," he continued, "the arrangements with the mill are in place, so our sugar should get to Smith tomorrow, and now, here we are, settling in for a night at the Ritz. Not a bad day's work given the circumstances."

As they spoke, the late-night life of the alleyway unfolded in front of them. It was quiet. The miserable shops, house-fronts and cafés were all shuttered; just a few locals had wandered out, taking advantage of the cool night air and lambent street light to sweep the frontages of their property or just sit and chat.

Occasionally, groups of men shuffled past, some unsteadily so, heading for bed or at least a hard floor nearby. But by midnight, the only things to observe were the wild dogs that sporadically appeared, searching for rats, for love, or for the occasional deposit of dry nutritious waste.

"We're to 'stay primed', Nooney: instructions from Fogge."

Nooney smiled.

"Too right, mate. What the hell does he mean? Thinks he's that Lord Kitchener bloke from your lot. And anyway, we've been primed to his madness for a while now."

They both laughed.

"I think the best we can do about Fogge is to stay awake, work out our options."

"Well, to do that Laurie, you'll need to shut up, because most of the time when you go off on one I feel drowsiness enveloping me in its embalming embrace."

"Blimey, Nooney, you're one to talk."

"Eloquently, of course," he replied, chuckling.

For another half an hour or so, they kept up the insulting banter that cloaked their great affection for each other, all the time eyes fixed on the hostel opposite. Then, following a lull and with a developing lassitude, Laurie returned to the events of the last few days and the things that troubled.

"It worries me even more now, Nooney: we're asked to take orders from Fogge, a man Lowthian knows to be incompetent, yet seemingly he's now in charge of this palaver. Then she tells us all the stuff about the push into Palestine, and the fellow over in the hostel being a spy. It all seems a bit spurious doesn't it?"

Nooney agreed.

"Remember, she also invited herself onto the operation with Smith. First we knew was when she told us at the last minute."

"To be fair, Laurie, she was brilliant, and her Arabic was a clincher."

"Maybe, but it's as if she no longer trusts us. And she didn't like being challenged to explain her actions."

"Well, she is a Colonel," said Nooney. "I mean, for all their protestations that the Bureau is a democracy of minds it's still a slave to protocol."

"Then there's the Moussabey stuff – did you know he was part of the high-level briefings meetings?"

"Of course not."

"I really like the man and respect him, but it's unsettling. I'm not even sure he would have let us in on the conversations he'd been having with Smith had we not pushed. He obviously knows that man more than we first realised."

"Well, Smith is a slippery one for sure, Laurie, which is why it's been good to have Moussabey at the front of things. He has legitimacy, and on top of that, probably faces the biggest losses of us all if things go wrong."

But Laurie persisted.

"And this spy business… we're to believe that fellow holed up across the alley could be working to undermine the British effort; seems pretty flimsy stuff to me. If anything, on that same basis, it could be Moussabey and Smith that are doing that."

Nooney was becoming alarmed by the growing pile of supposition his friend was assembling.

"Hold your horses, Laurie. Flimsy? Could it be that you, the policeman from Worcester, is the one who's hanging on to the flimsy evidence?"

"What do you mean?"

"All those things you've just mentioned might be a bit strange, but equally, they could all just be coincidences which your mind has turned into worries."

Laurie frowned.

"You need to use a bit of the old 'Occam's Razor' if you ask me," he continued.

Laurie looked at his friend in bemusement.

"Is this something else you're going to addle my brain with, Nooney?"

"An old English Friar, mate, boring as hell he must have been to come up with this, so perhaps he's a long-lost family member of yours."

"Nooney, watch it."

Laurie was never sure whether all the stories Nooney told were true, but they were generally so persuasively disclosed that he liked to think they were.

"In a nutshell, Laurie, he proposed that if you had a hunch about something it was more likely to be true the fewer the assumptions you had to prove. The simpler the better, so to speak."

"So, when was this great idea proposed?"

"Blimey, Laurie, do you think I carry loads of trivia like this around in my head all day?"

Laurie raised his eyes.

"1327."

"That's a lie; you've just made that up."

They both started to laugh.

"OK, well maybe ten years either side, but that's the date alright."

"So, you're criticising my thinking by quoting some old religious type from the seventh century?"

"He was big in his day you know, Laurie, quite the Isaac Newton he was."

He could see that Laurie remained unconvinced.

"Well, in your little ramble, you listed so many things, none of which we'd have a cat in hell's chance of establishing, that I'd say it would be difficult to lend any credibility to your concerns."

"And?"

"So, what I'd suggest is that you try to stop worrying."

For a moment or two, they continued to scan the street scene in silence. Maybe, thought Laurie, his friend was right. Fogge's stirring of the waters about the trustworthiness of the Bureau had said more about the Major than about Lowthian or Regis-Templeton. So, in the grander scheme of things there was perhaps a certain genius in allowing this man some role; but why now, just as the seriousness of the operation had escalated? He trusted Nooney's counsel, but the feeling of unease persisted.

"But why hadn't she told the Brigadier about our operation?"

Nooney rolled his eyes at the ongoing analysis, but didn't contradict.

"Hey?" repeated Laurie. "Why not? It's as if she and Moussabey may have had something to hide. It's not as if we weren't onto something in Alexandria with Smith. And yes, I know, Fogge's a buffoon, but he knew all about what we were up to, or purported to, at least. He as good as warned me about Lowthian and Regis-Templeton. Why? What was in it for him? What if he actually was onto them?"

Nooney continued with his inquisitive gaze, though now less willing to deny the validity of what he was hearing. He could see the cogwheels continuing to gyrate inside the investigative mind of his friend, and felt less disposed to suppress his own burdens about the turn of events.

"I must admit," he said, "I was surprised when we held our last meeting at The Cairo Sugar Association. We didn't need to and it was risky. It would have been much easier at the Bureau."

"Shite!" shouted Laurie, causing Nooney to almost levitate in shock.

"Keep the noise down, mate, for pity's sake, what's wrong with you?"

"Sorry, Nooney… just that you reminded me."

"What do you mean?"

"Have you got that sketch?"

"Sketch?"

"You know, of the spy; the one we 'borrowed' from Lowthian's office."

Nooney remembered he'd taken a copy from the few pinned to the Bureau wall and buried it inside in his jacket pocket. He fished it out and passed it to Laurie, who immediately stood, holding the image up against the window, levering a few of the higher slats open so that the moon and street lighting filtered through.

"Laurie, have you lost your mind? Shut those damned slats; we'll be seen."

There was no response and Nooney shouted again, as loudly as he dare, this time pulling at Laurie's leg.

"It's him, bloody hell, it's him," shouted Laurie.

"What's him? And for pity's sake, keep it quiet."

"The bloke in The Cairo Sugar Association."

"What?"

"On the way out from that last meeting there with Lowthian and Moussabey, I saw this bloke," he held up the sketch, "dressed smartly, bash on his head, just as in the picture; it's what caught my attention. Mediterranean complexion as well. He was standing at the reception desk as we came out from the office. I looked straight at him, thought I knew him. I almost went to speak, but it didn't seem right at the time. You've just reminded me. It was him. I'm sure it was him."

Nooney admired his friend's intuition. This sort of recognition was his bread and butter, his job back home, and so he didn't doubt the assertion. The connections were starting to smell.

"You know, on second thoughts, Laurie, it could be that Occam's Razor might be a bit too blunt a tool for the situation we're in."

Laurie stared at him.

"What I'm saying," said Nooney, "is that on this one occasion you might just be right. There are too many things that aren't adding up."

Laurie was relieved, and yet troubled that maybe he'd convinced his friend.

"I hope I'm wrong, Nooney, for both our sakes. The question is, what to do?"

There was now a gravity to their circumstance that previous certainty and conceit had denied. Daring action required confident options.

"We do absolutely nothing," said Nooney, "whatever goes on out there in the next few hours, we keep out of it."

Laurie was staggered. Nooney was the last man to shirk a responsibility, and the first to find a way through a problem.

"Do nothing?"

"If stuff goes off, we take part but lose the scent."

"What, you mean deliberately hang back?"

"I'd call it more of an inability to keep up, become outmanoeuvred."

Laurie was aghast.

"We can't do that, we're under orders; we can't back off a situation like this, we have a responsibility."

"So, what's the worst that could happen?" asked Nooney, "we get shoved back into the regular army, back to the barracks, because we really aren't that good at catching a spy?"

"But they'd know."

"Know what? That we lost the trail of our friend from over the way, that we cocked up the Sugar Case, that we, too, were really quite incompetent?"

"But we'd know, Nooney, we'd know."

For a while, neither man spoke, bound by an overwhelming sense of melancholic solemnity. They continued to peer across at the hostel, notionally on the lookout for the spy, but convinced now that the only surety that had absconded was that which they once called 'truth'.

"We've done bloody good work on this case," said Nooney eventually. "We've earned the right to be informed. If we're not to be let in, then our only protection is to dispense with the in-built naivety our superiors depend upon, and use our strengths."

"And what are they?"

"Well, Laurie, without the people like us, those who consider themselves imperious tend to get a bit dizzy. Sometimes they can even take to their bed."

Laurie smiled. Nooney was only saying what he believed. His whole life had been littered with such battles.

"Until we are certain of what we're involved with, let's be a little more considerate of our own positions, the same way the lot above us are. Let's play by the same rules."

The great thing about Nooney was that in his calm and understated fashion, he always managed to find a route that pointed skyward. He was also fair-minded and respected the honourable notions that dominated Laurie's head.

"I can see I've shocked you."

"A little," replied Laurie, "it's not that I don't agree with your logic and I'm relieved you're confirming my concerns. I'm not going crazy after all."

"Forget the 'going', mate; you're crazier than a thistle-slinger in a frock shop. But in my book, there's great joy in madness."

Laurie cheered.

"It's just that there is a duty, Nooney, even in the ridiculous circumstances we're in, to do our best, to leave the concerns behind us until after the events of today are sorted."

Nooney grinned.

"Of course mate, you're right."

"What? I am?"

Laurie had expected more of a fight.

"Well, I know you well enough, Laurie, to trust your instincts, even when we're stuck in a stinking hole like this."

The mood had lightened considerably. Even the street dogs had turned in for the night. All the two had for company as they peered across the alley was the odd rodent that scuttled along the pavement into the drains, and the occasional shrouded rocking of the night manager beyond the open half-door opposite. It would have been futile to expect any signal from that quarter should the spy decide to move. There was nothing for it but to remain vigilant, and blunt the onset of somnolence by whispered conversation, much of it dominated initially by Nooney.

"Blimey, Nooney, do you ever listen to yourself?"

"I try not to, Laurie, unless I'm on my own, and then I worry what others are missing. I'm good value though aren't I?"

Laurie smiled, and for a moment they remained silent.

"What are you going to do, Nooney, when all this is over?"

"Have a bloody great sleep and a brew of tea."

"No, you basket case. I mean when you're back in Auckland."

"Onehunga, mate."

"Near enough hey, Nooney? Onehunga then."

"Well, there'll be plenty of vacancies for a bloke if I make it back, given how many Kiwis have been slaughtered at the front. So, I might even try to get a lecturing job at the University."

Laurie admired his ambition and the confidence he expressed; this was far beyond his own expectation in life.

"Do you think this lot's been worth it, Nooney?"

"Well, I guess that all depends. We believe we're fighting for liberty, don't we?"

Laurie nodded.

"The thing is, liberty arrives too cheaply for some. They remain ignorant to the sacrifice upon which it was founded, but when it's threatened they cry and scream."

"But we have our governments, Nooney, the King, an order to things."

Nooney let out a shriek and then clasped his mouth, realising it was he who was now making the noise.

"Sorry, mate. It's just that if that's working so well, why is it that you and me are sat in this shit-tip right now? Why is it that our blokes at the front are used like fodder? And why the hell are we still tip-toeing around those incapables who assume they have entitlement over us? Tell me?"

He had a point, but these were the thoughts that normally lashed at Laurie's soul.

"You're starting to sound like me now, Nooney. But we all have a voice, a say in things; surely you trust in that?"

"Maybe. But I can't imagine a future in which we tolerate the sorts of things that are happening today."

"Blimey, Nooney, I haven't heard this from you before. You've definitely been in my company for far too long."

Nooney grinned.

"Sorry, but you asked. It's good to stay wise to the consequences of ignoring those who might treat us as fools, and not take it for granted that there will be a better tomorrow. We have to work at it, not just spout on."

There was a silence; they were both becoming very tired.

"What about you?" said Nooney, eventually, "what do you want?"

Laurie pointed to his head.

"Peace up here would do nicely."

Nooney smiled.

"Well, at least you're a little closer now."

Laurie pulled a face.

"Harmony and chaos, mate," said Nooney, "you have to experience the latter to fully value and work for the former."

Despite the words from his friend and the continuing focus upon the building opposite, Laurie was now desperately struggling to stay awake.

"You could move to New Zealand."

For a moment Laurie thought he'd misheard. But he could see Nooney was serious.

"What chance have I got of doing that? There's no way. I couldn't afford to do it."

"There's assisted passages, Laurie, happened all the time before this lot started. You'd get a job easily enough and a house for the family."

"My wife wouldn't contemplate it, Nooney."

"Have you asked her?"

"Of course not, I've never thought about it."

"Will you?"

Laurie hesitated.

"Ah, there you go, I bet you make all the decisions in your house, it's what a bloke does. Ask her, you might be surprised."

"But the children."

"What about them? They'll get real jobs, land. It's a bloody beautiful place. And…"

"And what, Nooney?"

"We'd still see each other. We're half a world away, mate, but we don't have to be."

Laurie was exhausted now, though ashamed to admit it. But the conversation and the camaraderie had enchanted.

"How on earth did we end up here, Nooney?"

"What the hell?" he replied, smiling gently. "What an experience we've had, hey? If this was my last day on earth I couldn't be happier. You get some shut eye, I'll take the first watch."

And with that, the conversation ceased. Despite everything, there was a job to be done, and daylight was just a few hours away.

A huge sense of relief enveloped Laurie. He shifted from the stool and across the room, fashioning some bedding against a wall from a few of the smaller and less odious carpet rolls. Some sleep would help matters, and there was at least the reassurance that he and Nooney remained a team. Whatever they would face, they would do so together and in trust.

Oriol had been awake for at least an hour before the dawn. The Azan was in full flow, and the faithful were following its enticement to their first prayers of the day. It wasn't this that had disturbed him: he'd nodded off for a few hours during the night, only to be periodically awoken, as the nightmare of drowning at sea and the fate of the Andreassens left him covered in sweat and feeling cursed. And in these more wakeful moments, the spectre of his mother Llucia's warnings, and the nagging list of coincidences that had plagued his time ashore in Egypt, hung heavily.

He'd passed some of the time deep in thought about the day ahead. There hadn't been any message about the boat. If necessary, he'd hole up in Alexandria and await another vessel from the Andreassen fleet. Either that, or he'd track down Taqi al Din al-Bilal at the Alexandria West Bay Shipping Company to arrange for a different passage back to Mao.

As for the meeting with Jones, he'd arrive well in advance, survey the scene for anything that troubled his senses. If all was well, the deal would be completed and he'd be off. But if anything was awry he would abort, no matter the financial loss, and leave unnoticed on the slow train.

An hour after first light, he slung his bag across his shoulder and checked out. He was thanked by the desk manager with a warm shake of the hand; a first time for everything, he thought. He squeezed through the half-opened door and into the bright morning light. It was already cloudless and fiercely hot and the street was busy. He'd be lucky to get a seat at his usual café.

There were hawkers plying their wares, something he'd not experienced near the hostel before. Where were the British and their policing today? They'd been around earlier, banging on the door of a shuttered shop opposite. From his room he'd noticed two Europeans, dressed a little like himself, being dragged unceremoniously out of the premises and frog marched away. Probably a brothel, he'd thought.

As he pushed his way past the bodies, heading for his coffee, he came upon a sizeable crowd, laughing and cheering at a street performer, and he stopped to take a look. A man, regaled with colourful scarves, was singing loudly, whilst a goat performed a balancing act on top of a small bottle. Then, a dog that appeared to have a leg missing leapt up onto the backside of the man's donkey, and balanced on two of its three available legs, tongue hanging to one side, howling. To further hoots of joy, a small monkey appeared from below the man's shift, removed his fez, and proceeded to fleece the crowd for donations, most of whom happily obliged.

The performer caught his eye and waved, and the monkey rushed across whipping away his white boater before he could respond. The crowd thought this hilarious, and for a moment Oriol joined in with the fun, grinning widely, proffering a note in exchange for the return of his headwear.

Such unexpected fun lightened his mood, and even the café seemed quite empty and suspicion free when he arrived.

"No sugar," said the owner in his best English, smiling in recognition.

Oriol thanked him but on this morning there was less time to linger than he would like, and he was soon away along Shari El Ghuri, on through the maze of back alleys, to the tram stop at the Arab Museum in Bab El Khalq: he wasn't going to risk another delay, and so had decided upon this longer walk and then the faster direct tram to Opera Square.

As he disembarked from his ride into town, he congratulated himself upon his efficiency. There was still an hour before the meeting with Jones, more than enough time to be convinced of the safety of the exchange. So he strolled towards the Sednaoui Department Store, taking the shadier east side of the street, eventually settling on a seat that offered an excellent view of the store frontage. He took a newspaper from his bag and spread it across his legs, to all intents and purposes, just another businessman enjoying an early morning break.

He'd been vigilant and despite his previous misgivings, nothing had seemed untoward. Indeed, he'd enjoyed the morning, rather as he had on previous less troubled visits, and chuckled at the thought of the monkey. From time to time, he peered beyond the newsprint and across to the store. There was a guard at the door graciously welcoming each customer as they entered, even bowing to a group of Coptic priests. He relaxed. Everything appeared spectacularly normal.

"You've been a silly boy, Laurie." Sergeant Wirrall wasn't impressed.

"Not only that, you've caused your Kiwi friend here to get caked in the mess as well."

"Not so, Sergeant," interrupted Nooney, keen to protest the unfairness of the circumstances.

"We both agreed that…"

"Shut your mouth, Nooney. You're under my charge here, not the fancy pants Bureau bunch you've been used to. Barracks from now on, get used to it."

Laurie had been interrupted a few hours earlier from his slumbers on the floor of the carpet shop by an unpolished troop detail from the Regiment. They'd kicked the door in and manhandled both him and Nooney back to the Bab El Hadid barracks, depositing them in a secure room next to Captain Hillary's office.

"How many times, Laurie, have I told you to watch out, that you'd cop it if you kept behaving like the irritant you were when you first arrived here?"

Laurie remained silent.

"Well, well, now there's a turn up, for once you're speechless," continued Wirrall with undisguised sarcasm. "What wonderful progress we're suddenly making."

"Sergeant…"

Nooney had no 'previous' with the Sergeant when it came to peril and believed he might bring some gravity to the situation.

"What?"

"I can explain."

"Nooney, you could probably explain camel fart to an organ grinder, but it still wouldn't wash."

There was a moment of stillness, the realities dawning. Nooney's earlier suggestion that they follow the route of incompetence to escape from their difficulties now seemed judicious.

Sergeant Wirrall circled, eyeing them as a farm hand would a damaged sheep. He was on his own, having ushered the rest of the collection party away.

"You're here at the request of the good Major," he hissed. "Major Fogge, a good friend of yours, Laurie, I believe?"

He smiled and pushed his nose close to Laurie's face.

"He and the trusty Captain Hillary are currently engaged on manoeuvres in the town, important work apparently, though they haven't seen cause to involve myself in the matters."

There seemed a sense of enmity in the statement and this alerted both men.

"Seems that you're to remain here in this secure area until they return from whatever their little mission is."

Laurie and Nooney glanced knowingly at each other, and this was duly noted by Wirrall.

"Yes, it seems that every man and his mother-in-law knows about the action, save for those most likely to be of some bloody use."

He continued to circle them slowly. As a professional soldier, he'd had years of experience building up a fearful suspense in his men, and few had ever resisted his gentle menace. These two though were an exception, and he quietly admired them for it. He stepped back and eye-balled them again.

"Now, for just a moment, try to imagine a situation, a blessed situation I would say, in which you two malcontents were nowhere to be seen."

"Sergeant?" Nooney's shocked response spoke for them both.

"So that upon the return of those two prestigious officers, it would appear to them that you had ignored instructions to remain in this locked room, and somehow found a way out."

Hope piled back in.

"Maybe it was that you'd mistakenly thought I'd asked you to help with back up and that I'd not really meant to lock you in. It's generally easy for you pair to cock up instructions."

He moved to the low army-issue desk and lowered himself gingerly onto the three-legged stool beside it. He began to suck in air between his teeth, creating an indelicate and piercing low level whistle. He seemed to be enjoying himself, as if there was a sense of relief, of liberation almost.

"Ah, lovely seat this, more comfortable than it looks. The number of times I've stood where you two are now, listening to some poor devil or other being admonished for his inabilities, by an officer whose own insufficiencies were wider than the Nile. Nice seat mind you, more comfortable than it looks. I could have got used to all of this myself, the furniture, the room."

He smiled. Laurie and Nooney could hardly believe what they were hearing.

The Sergeant placed his hand inside a pocket, and pulled out two keys, making a show of placing one on the desk in front of him. He eased himself back up and walked past them towards the door, leaving them facing eyes front.

"Time for me to take some men shopping; there's a new place not far from those lovely gardens, bit expensive. I might find Mrs Wirrall a new hat for church."

He opened the door, and they heard a key being placed into the lock.

"And of course, how on earth could you possibly be expected to follow me discretely from a distance, given you're about to be stuck in here?"

The door shut, three turns of the locking mechanism confirming their confinement. The two men turned and stared at each other in amazement.

"Are we both thinking the same thing?" said Nooney.

"What, that this is a set-up?"

"Maybe, but given his manner, couldn't this be a genuine invitation?"

"To end up incarcerated for disobeying orders?"

"Come off it, Laurie, where's that sense of honour you mentioned? He doesn't trust his masters, either."

Laurie went to the desk and peered closely at the key.

"Hell, mate, it's not a murder weapon you know."

Laurie stared at his friend but thought better than to respond.

"If this works, it's shit or bust," continued Nooney. "I'm happy to back off though if that's what you want."

There was no chance of that by now though.

"You're right," replied Laurie, "better to fly than fall."

They waited for a few moments, listening for any signs of a guard outside, before Laurie picked up the key, moved across the room, and with three nervous turns of the lever, unlocked it. Then, after taking care to secure it behind them they were off and past the disinterested sentries at the front gate, following the tail of Sergeant Wirrall.

"Not too close, mate," said Nooney, "the mood he's in he might just turn around and decide to arrest us. Maybe he's been on the moonshine?"

Laurie smiled.

"I know where he's going."

"You clever arse," replied Nooney.

"We both know what's along this street, Nooney."

They had crossed Midan Bab El Hadid and were keeping pace with the distant Sergeant and his army troop, south along Shari Nobar Pasha.

"We'll come out at Opera Square and The Grand Continental Hotel," he replied, "they're great digs there by the way, you should try them."

"Yes, yes, but what's opposite the hotel?" persisted Laurie.

Nooney twigged.

"Ezbekiya Gardens."

"Absolutely, the very same 'lovely gardens' Wirrall alluded to. And what lovely new shop is found on the way down there?"

Nooney's eyes lit up.

"No, you don't mean…"

"You've got it, the Sednaoui Department Store," replied Laurie.

"The place Smith loves?"

"And Lowthian?"

"If you're right, mate," said Nooney, "we could be heading to quite a party."

Oriol had entered the Sednaoui store a good thirty minutes before the agreed rendezvous with Jones. His instincts told him there was nothing to worry about. There were no military or police, the place was abuzz with customers, mostly the Cairo well-heeled, and there was an air of routine familiarity in the behaviour of the staff. None looked overly observant or on edge. He'd carefully checked the three ground-floor exits from the road, and again, surreptitiously, once inside, so that nobody would be any the wiser as to his motives. The side door on the north of the building, wedged open to encourage a cool draught of air, made the most sense by which to exit when the time came. It was unattended and had the easiest access onto Shari Nobar Pasha and the nearby railway station.

He'd made it to the fifth floor and was leaning over the crafted steel barriers, surveying the scene below him. The building was designed with the gesture of space as its template. Each floor circled around the huge central atrium, supported by a beautiful steel column of elegantly woven steel. There were enormous chandeliers and expensive smells. Walking into the store was like entering a beautiful opera house, minus the seating. The whole thing was topped by an enormous internal glass roof decorated in the art nouveau style, through which light flooded. It was a building that meant to impress.

The large ground-floor sales area far below was covered by upscale carpets and imported, and extravagantly priced, European glassware. At its centre were fine arts items, and these were already flying from the shelves. This was an intoxicating place, one in which the Cairo nouveau riche could engorge themselves. And in the very heart of this expanse was the unmistakable frame of Jones, walking calmly between the sales desks to his pitch, smiling and nodding confidently to those around him. Oriol watched as he slid beside the assistant who was busy with an existing customer. He appeared known to those in the store, and no one had seemed the least bit confronted by his presence.

In their past encounters, neither he nor Jones had shown any curiosity about each other's means of existence or background, though Oriol had once let on that he wrote. What counted most to them both was the bond of trust borne out of their successful trades. Jones benefitted from the discrete transfer of his precious artefacts to Europe via neutral Spain, and Oriol from the payment 'in kind' of sugar. Jones always stressed he was securing the art works for future generations, and Oriol in turn, that the sugar helped save his people. He was content that at least one of them was telling the truth.

He took his time to descend the stairs between floors, checking at each level on Jones, and scanning the building for anything out of place. Once on the ground, he confirmed his initial assumption about the choice of exit door and browsed the street for anything untoward. Fully convinced, he made quietly for the meet with Jones, determined that within a few short minutes he would be on the return leg back to Mao; his work in Cairo finished for good.

As he approached the sales desk, Jones had his back to him, speaking to a customer. He didn't need to see the face to know that this was indeed the man he'd come to see. The exuberant confidence and charm with which he was advising a female client was sufficient. As she thanked him in her best English accent and turned to leave, Oriol spoke.

"Good morning, Mr Jones."

The very tall figure of a sharply suited English gentleman whipped round to greet him. Behind his rimmed glasses was the sculptured boyish face of a man permanently excited by the japes of his day.

"Good heavens, Mr Quintana, what a pleasure to see you. It's been far too long." He grabbed Oriol's hand and shook it with a grip and sincerity that both flattered and disarmed.

Oriol went to respond, but as normal Jones wanted the stage.

"I'm so sorry about the confusion over our need to meet here. Eaton told me he may have thrown you. Typical of him, I'm afraid. Decent chap but caught something exotic down town, rather knocked some of the stuffing out of him. Not to worry, you're here now."

Oriol went to speak again, but Jones was on a run.

"Can I get you some tea, scented water maybe, biscuits? Oh, by the way, what a fool not to have asked, was your journey over here to your liking? I know the Med can be a bit rough at this time of the year."

Oriol had forgotten quite how overpowering Jones' affability could be.

"All very good, thank you," he replied, "and I've only just had a coffee."

"Jolly good," Jones responded, "hope you found a good spot; there are some really unforgivable Arab coffee houses off the squares. Can't imagine what they boil in those damned pots."

Oriol smiled; he'd also lost touch with how obnoxious Jones could be.

"I have the paperwork from Eaton, and I'm afraid I'm on a very tight schedule. So, what I'd really like is the item you have for me."

Jones was a little taken aback; he'd clearly been hoping for a little more jabber, but business was business.

"Oh right, yes, well, of course. I'll get to the point."

He bent below the sales desk and with both hands pulled out a hemp bag that was tied by string and fixed with a bow. There was clearly some weight to it, and it was the size of a very large serving tray. It was much bigger than the easily secreted items Oriol normally dealt with, and Jones could see that he wasn't too pleased.

"This to be the finest piece I've ever entrusted you with," he said.

Oriol recognised the bluster and smiled. He knew where the real power lay in this relationship.

"I am very clear about this, Mr Quintana. So much so, indeed, that it will merit extra worth when we next settle our account with you."

Oriol remained unmoved by the blarney. He didn't require an enticing incentive, not least as there wouldn't be any future reunion.

"May I?" he asked.

He lifted the item, and his suspicions were confirmed. It wouldn't fit into his bag and would therefore need to be carried individually to the station. Concealing it would be even riskier. Something of this scale hadn't been part of any previous deal.

"Not possible, I'm afraid," said Oriol.

Jones knew that Quintana was no man's fool, but hadn't expected this turn of events.

"Oh, come now, I'm sure that once sewn into your sugar sacks and packaged, it will transfer seamlessly, so to speak."

Oriol checked to see if Jones was going to smile at his own joke. If so, it wasn't that funny, given the time it would take him to unpick, bury the item, and then re-stitch sugar sack 27. It was quickly apparent though that the comment had been witlessly conceived.

"This has never been part of any deal," said Oriol. "An item as weighty as this will bring greatly more suspicion, not least added weight, upon my shoulders. I'm not prepared to take that risk."

Jones was now becoming nervous. A tiny bead of sweat appeared from underneath his heavily greased hair.

"But this really is a masterpiece, Mr Quintana. It's something we can both take a pride in liberating."

Oriol remained unmoved and wondered at his interesting choice of words.

"Let me show it to you." He began to undo the bow, hoping to confound any protest by the magnificence of the art within. But Oriol was having none of it.

"I'm sorry, Mr Jones. Our business together has been a pleasure, but I'm going to have to leave this with you. I'm sure you can arrange for the paperwork to repatriate the sugar you've advanced me back to your company."

He turned to leave, and Jones panicked.

"Quintana, please, wait, Quintana…"

Oriol paused and looked back at the flustered, and now deathly pale, beanpole.

"I've clearly made a misjudgement. Please, I'm sure there's a way to see reason over this."

Oriol paused whilst Jones sought for a suitable option that might convince his agent of transport to remain within the broad tenor of their agreement.

"You're a poet I think, if my memory serves me right from a previous convivial discussion."

This was the second time in a few weeks he'd been called that and it sounded good.

"Perhaps you'd be interested in a gift from me to, shall we say, make up for my indiscretion in this my misconstruing of the situation?"

He bent down to his shoulder bag and pulled out a time-battered tome, placing it upon a counter. It was *The Odyssey of Homer*. Oriol picked the book up, carefully examining the preface and title page. This was one of the earliest published volumes, *Translated from the original Greek, printed for Bernard Lintot, 1725, London*. He'd read that they existed, but never dared to believe that one day he'd hold one. He gently leafed through a few pages, unable to comprehend his good fortune. Didn't Jones know how precious this was?

He could hardly contain himself and continued to look through the book, in fact, so ponderously that Jones seemed to develop a nervous facial tick. Dominance retained, he casually nodded his agreement, though not wishing to give anything away or reveal any joyous bewilderment at his good luck. Jones, on the other hand, was ecstatic.

"Oh rather, jolly good, yes indeed," he exclaimed, relief coursing through his body. "I'm so pleased that book is going to such a fine and deserving home."

He went to place it inside the sacking with the other precious item, but Oriol stopped him.

"You were going to show me the artefact."

"Ah yes, of course; excuse my rudeness."

He removed the sacking to reveal a thin and ragged slice of limestone, onto the smooth side of which was carved an image in the style of many such items found in excavations around Cairo and beyond. Jones' eyes glazed with wonder at its appearance.

"There are two magnificent images," he said, "here…" He pointed to an impressively adorned female profile, "and here…" A smaller male figure surrounded by exotic birds.

"Atum, one of the creator gods of Egypt, and Hatshepsut, the greatest female Pharaoh of any Egyptian dynasty and a much maligned figure. Probably three and a half thousand years old, a piece of great beauty, priceless."

He continued to gawp at the relief fragment, almost unwilling to let it pass his grasp.

"I need to make my departure," said Oriol, a hint of irritation in his words. Still Jones lingered.

"Mr Jones?"

"Ah, yes of course." He lifted the relief as gently as he could back inside the sacking, retying the string.

"I look forward to being reunited with this when I get back to England, when things get back to normal."

He smiled at Oriol,

"That will be a good moment, Mr Jones, but it will I suspect, not be the 'normal' to which you were so used."

He picked up the relief, which was just as heavy as he'd anticipated, and placed it somewhat awkwardly inside his bag.

"Have a good journey, Mr Quintana. As always, it's been a joy to entrust you with the things I hold most dear, and I look forward to our next engagement."

He proffered his hand, and Oriol managed an awkward wrong-handed shake, given his right arm was already tightly affixed to the Egyptian consignment.

"Indeed," he replied with as much emphasised indifference as he hoped the Englishman would understand.

He headed for the door. As he did so, a commotion began at the main entrance, and his instincts locked in. Head down, he moved quickly but without apparent urgency, less this attracted attention, directly to the north exit. The door was still wide open, a fresh breeze was blowing though it, though people were rushing in past him now to see what was happening. Once out in the open, he risked a brief turn, and saw a group of British soldiers noisily barring the doors, including the one he'd just passed through, though none of them appeared to pay any heed to him. As he walked away towards the station, he checked behind him. To his relief, the invasion party seemed more intent on examining the store interior than the street. It was yet another troubling coincidence, though it took his mind off the weight of history below his arm.

Once assured that he was safe from their attentions, he stopped, partly in fear allayed, but also to gather breath. He carefully rested the Egyptian load on the floor and knelt to rearrange his shoulder bag. As he stood back up, two European business types brushed past him, walking urgently towards the store. They're in for disappointment, he thought.

Nooney felt a shove and almost stumbled into the doorway of the 'Buccellati Photographic and Bibliographic Store'.

The irony wasn't lost upon him; he'd spent hours in this place when on day rest from the barracks, so a push in this direction wasn't entirely unwarranted.

"What the hell did you do that for, Laurie?"

"Quiet, Nooney, keep down."

"What's the matter with you, mate, are you off on one again?"

"It's him, the bloke in the sketch."

Nooney needed no further explanation.

"You sure?"

Laurie peered back along the street. Their spy was now standing upright, a bag slung across his back, a load of some sort, possibly a box, clasped uncomfortably to his side. He was walking away from them towards the square and presumably the station.

"I think you're right, Laurie."

"We should split up. I'll follow him; you go to the store."

"No chance, mate."

"What?"

"Have you seen what's going off down there?"

There was now quite a performance unfolding outside the Sednaoui store, and they could just about make out the voice of Sergeant Wirrall ordering his men to disperse a crowd that was beginning to gather.

"Right, but again let's keep our distance," said Laurie, "I'm sure he's headed for the train." They followed, advantaged by this certainty.

He was though, particularly adept at losing himself in any congestion, and keeping a distant tab upon him became increasingly awkward, particularly once they approached Midan Bab El Hadid.

"We'll need to figure this out," said Nooney, but as normal his friend had arrowed in on the task and was now more concerned about losing the spy than starting a dialogue.

"Laurie, we need to make sure we've got back up."

"Laurie," he said again, "can you hear what I'm telling you?"

But Laurie pressed on and Nooney, knowing only too well that his advice would appear an unnecessary restraint, gave up to their fate, certain as ever that they would find a way through.

He followed his friend across the square, avoiding the traders and their carts, listening out for trams. They crossed the central area where he used to meet with Manoli and his performing monkey and momentarily recalled the scene as he and Laurie had defied the British Amy's attempts to discipline the Arab crowd. They'd survived that without a plan, they'd do the same here.

"Have you got your pass, Nooney?"

Laurie was speaking again.

"Yes, of course I have."

"I think we're going to need it."

The crowds were now mostly behind them, and they rested briefly by a large palm tree next to a tram stop, which gave them some cover. They watched as the spy continued into Midan El Mahatta, turning right towards the goods yard at Pont Limoun Station.

"Looks like he's talking to the Arab guards," said Laurie. "Why's he there? I'd swear he would have carried on to the main station?"

"Obvious, mate."

Laurie screwed up his face.

"What?"

"Just look at what he's carrying. He needs to conceal it somehow. Too bloody big for the Alexandria express."

"We're going to have to follow him, Nooney. Once we know what we're up against, one of us can get word."

After waiting for a few minutes, they walked casually across to the station barrier outside the guardhouse at the front of the Pont Limoun goods yard. An Egyptian official came out and they showed him their Military Police passes containing their rank, Regiment, and photograph, signed by British Army GHQ. He seemed unwilling to accept this, obstructive even. Laurie was just about to argue the point when a couple of orderlies, noticing a second European visitation within a few minutes, wondered over. Upon seeing Nooney, they both broke into broad smiles and proffered their greetings.

"Some of my old friends, mate from my time on permit checking back in the square," he said, replying as best he could in his broken Arabic to their welcome.

They spoke to the official, and he lifted the barrier, though he still appeared displeased by their presence.

They moved into the yard, following a path with the goods shed to their left and a single line siding, empty save for three open-sided trucks, to their right. As they came level with the end of the shed and peered inside, a gang of labourers could be seen hard at work above an engine. A few of them turned to look at the two Europeans, but seemed disinterested, sufficient for Laurie and Nooney to conclude that the man they were following was unlikely to be found with them. Nooney nodded ahead, towards a second shed. It was bigger than the first, had two sets of railway lines going into it, the nearest of which was empty, but the other had at least a dozen trucks exposed beyond the shed doors, and as far as they could tell without revealing themselves, maybe another six or so inside.

"This is more like it," whispered Laurie, "look at those molasses waggons."

He nodded towards the long-barrel waggons that composed the bulk of the rolling stock.

"Not going to be able to hide anything in those," replied Nooney.

"Agreed, but look the other way."

Nooney inched his head around the door to the shed, and towards the end were more waggons, though this time low-sided. They were being tended by three Arab workers, who were loading sacks, possibly of grain, or even sugar. And next to them, working at close quarters with one of the sacks, was the now unmistakable figure of their man. By his side was his bag, and next to it the crumpled sacking that had been around the item he was carrying.

"He's hiding stuff," whispered Laurie excitedly. "Look, he's hiding stuff between the sacks."

"Or inside them," said Nooney.

"We're badly positioned here," continued Laurie, "let's get a vantage point from below those." He pointed to the molasses waggons.

"On my shout." Laurie held his arm aloft until the Arab workers were otherwise focussed, then signalled for Nooney to scramble across the line. He quickly followed, and for a few minutes they lay there, silently cowered flat between the rails below the waggons.

Once convinced they'd been undetected, they began to inch forward, scrabbling awkwardly towards the unsuspecting foursome working on the front waggon. They crawled as close as they dare, stopping just a few waggons away from their objective, listening to the Arab conversation now clearly audible. Nooney indicated he couldn't make out anything they were saying. As for the spy, he was either silent, or had gone.

"I'll lead out," whispered Laurie, indicating towards the side of the waggon they were below.

"What?" replied Nooney, even more quietly but comically confused, "and appear like a bloody genie out of a bottle?"

Laurie smiled and gave a 'thumbs up'.

"But we don't have any way of knowing if they're armed, and there's no back-up," he continued, mouthing the words almost silently.

"Nothing to worry about," replied Laurie, "I have my pistol."

Nooney was incredulous. The thought of Laurie with a pistol was more alarming than the potential that faced them in the waggon ahead.

"No worries, Nooney," shushed Laurie, sensing Nooney's concern.

"What do you mean?"

"I still haven't been issued with any bullets."

They both started to muffle the laughs errupting from deep within. Nooney fought back the tears appearing in his eyes, whilst Laurie waved his hand rapidly at him to try to stop the hilarity becoming apparent. Neither man could explain to themselves why in such a desperate moment they were so convulsed, save for the great affection they held for each other.

From their position below the rail truck, they'd counted three sets of legs. When the fourth set dropped down, they waited until the moment they all turned to walk away from them, presumably towards an office at the rear of the shed, and quietly edged from below their hiding place.

As they stood, one of the men ahead of them checked his pockets, and realising that perhaps he'd left something, turned to go back. Upon seeing the two Europeans, he let out a shout and jumped in startled surprise.

The other three turned around and stood stock still, transfixed by the vision of two oil-stained businessmen, no more than twenty feet away, staring back at them. Then, bizarrely, one of the Arabs pointed at Laurie and waved.

"Blimey," whispered Laurie, "it's the fellow from the shite detail I led at the barracks, the one we saved from being lynched."

Laurie waved back and smiled, and the other two Arabs nodded in acknowledgement, though less engagingly. Only the European with the scar on his forehead remained detached.

"British Military Police," said Laurie, and he moved a few steps ahead of Nooney towards the four men.

"There is nothing to be concerned about; we're just carrying out a few checks."

Nooney did his best to interpret in his broken Arabic, though noticed the European of the group move his hand towards his pocket.

"Stand still," he commanded, pointing to the man, who for the moment obeyed, though it was clear to both Nooney and Laurie that his body language shouted run or fight. Laurie moved a step closer again, raising his arms gently, beckoning for calm.

"There is nothing for you to worry about," he repeated, smiling to add further assurance.

Just then, the sound of rifles being cocked in unison cracked from some way behind them. The three Arabs, well practiced in the realities this threatened, shot their hands up into the air and shouted in terror. The European on the other hand stood perfectly still, calm even.

As they turned, the all too familiar aural displeasures from Captain Hillary washed towards them.

"You pair of morons," he yelled, "you dumb-headed arseholes."

He was standing as far as they could tell, judiciously positioned behind his guard of men, all of whom were pointing rifles directly towards both themselves and those that they had just been about to apprehend."

"Captain Hillary, I can explain," shouted Laurie.

Oh no, thought Nooney.

"I knew from the moment I set eyes on you, you little shit, that you were a troublemaker. The only explaining you'll be doing will be from behind bars."

"But, Captain, we are just about to—"

"Hit the floor or you'll cop a bullet. That's an order."

"Captain Hillary, there's no need, this is under control. We can—"

"Now," raged Hillary.

Laurie ignored the instruction and turned towards the terrified Arabs and their accomplice. It had worked before, and would do so again. As he did, the European made to move his hand to his pocket. Laurie went to move towards him but was hit from behind by a huge impact to the centre of his back, accompanied by the crack of gunshot.

His head hit the floor, and for a moment there was a complete numbness, no sound, no vision, just the strangest of smells. He rolled onto his back and as he looked upwards the most idyllic blue sky appeared in the bottom of his eye line; on the top though there was only blindness. There was no feeling at all in the rest of his body other than the suppressed sensation of being held, and a dull awareness there were people around him.

And then, very gradually, the distant whisper, the return of noise, became the shouts of men frantically issuing instructions, muffled by the beating bass of his own heart, and the elephant snort through his nostrils.

He was turned onto his side.

"Can you speak, mate?"

He heard that alright. The blindness in the tops of his eyes was now more like a mist, and he could make out a figure holding him. Pain started to thump from the middle of his back, and the inside of his head rolled like an empty oil bin. He could move an arm, even see his chest. There was blood. He was heaved into a seated position, and could make out beside him a huge pool of blood, broken bone-like chunks of shell, slices of offal.

"Well done, mate, that's it, keep going, just sitting you up."

It was Nooney. It was going to be alright.

"Nooney," he mouthed, and through the fog he heard someone say, "He's talking, Captain."

"Nooney," he said again.

Then the smell hit him: burnt flesh. Suddenly, his inside was unwillingly alive, reactive. He vomited, falling to one side, but just about able to use an arm to help prop himself. He vomited again, this time pulling his hand up to his mouth to wipe away the contents of his stomach, covering his face in so doing with a compress of warm blood and splinters from the floor. His sight was clearing, and he began to make out the appalling stew that hung from his chin and across his body.

"I'm sorry about this, Nooney," he moaned slowly, twisting his neck towards his friend.

Holding him was a startled soldier, himself covered in the blood and vomit from Laurie. Bent around were others, eyes laden with fear and pity, each man seemingly unable to speak. Laurie summoned the meagre supplies of strength left in him, and again shouted to his friend.

"Nooney?"

Again, the soldier holding him said nothing, averting his eyes from Laurie's face. One of the others in the group muttered a response, but so quietly he couldn't hear.

"Nooney?" Laurie whispered again.

This time the response was clear.

"I'm sorry, mate." They parted to reveal the contorted body lying a few feet away.

It was face down in a heap, angled so unnaturally as to instantly shock. The trousers and shoes were intact, but the jacket and shirt had been mostly stripped from above the waist, burnt black around their frayed edges, next to which the skin was shredded and scorched. There was more blood, some still gently trickling to the floor, and a huge hole where the neck had once been. Above that, there was no distinct feature, just a cavern of fractured bone and puss where the head had sat.

Laurie stared through the scene, unable to comprehend the appalling vision. It was Nooney's gear alright, but someone must have been wearing his shoes and trousers. Where was he? Was he fooling around again? This was one of his jokes. This must be one of his damned jokes and Nooney, it just wasn't funny. Not one little bit. Nooney, stop it, Nooney.

"Nooney, Nooney."

"We're sorry, mate."
They struggled to hold Laurie down.
"Nooney, no, Nooney, stop it, don't do this."
"Get a medic," somebody shouted, "get a bloody medic."
Laurie vomited again.
And then blackness.

CHAPTER 11

Colonel Mildred Lowthian was sitting alone in her rooms at The Grand Continental Hotel. The sun had settled some hours past and the metropolitan night-life of Cairo was breaking over Opera Square. She'd often relax outside on the balcony, absorbing the perfumes from Ezbekiya Gardens, the erupting music, and the bustle of high-end stalls. But tonight the glass doors were closed and the windows shuttered: there was no desire for even the remotest observance of the jubilant gatherings across the way.

To be a woman such as her should have been joyous. Loved and freed by liberated parents and as academically qualified as a woman could be, she should have been lauded by those around her; or so Brigadier Berrington Regis-Templeton had said.

He'd been instrumental in her recruitment, recognising her skills and the way she'd earned the respect of the Arabs she worked with. He'd also protected her as best he could from the enmity her gender, intelligence and brusqueness caused amongst the older staffers.

"She's no woman, though," one dismissively intoned at a meeting of the General Staff; an observation that seemed to meet with much agreement.

And now she felt marooned. He'd warned he was to return home, adjudged unfit to serve, lungs afflicted by the gas from his earlier war. But it would be months away, a year even.

And there was his promise: nothing need change between them.

"I shall write. When all this is over, we shall still be able to see each other."

But she knew from bitter experience the deceit contained within such loving sentiment. A wife, children and land would predominate his remaining years, whilst her talents and usefulness would be contingent upon the vagaries of other male overseers.

All this and now Nooney. She'd witnessed enough slaughter and inhumanity to fill a dozen lifetimes. But her incredulity at the scene that morning at Pont Limoun Station, the disgorged physicality, the smell, wouldn't leave her.

Nooney was special. And there was an agonising pain and guilt about his death, which she alone owned.

There was a knock at the door. She ignored it. For once, despite the years of selflessness, she could not be ready for further demand. But it persisted, and eventually out of respect to some deeply embedded inner duty, she responded. It was Peter Moussabey's wife, and she was holding a large basket covered by a linen cloth.

"Hanna, what a lovely surprise."

They embraced awkwardly, what with Hanna's encumbrance and her own lie.

"Food," she exclaimed triumphantly. "I thought that as you were unable to join us tonight with Berrington, I would at least do my best to show you something of what you were missing."

Lowthian laughed, her camouflage now in place.

"Please, do come in; as you can see, I'm quite alone."

The smiles were mutual, and Lowthian suspected her absence may have pointed to a 'romantic other'.

"I'm afraid I wouldn't have been good company tonight; it's been a very difficult few days."

Hanna concurred. Her husband had struggled, too. He'd said very little, but she understood that grief was at its core.

Lowthian wasn't one for small talk, and she found she discomforted most women when expounding, even gently, upon anything remotely approaching her many convictions. Hanna Moussabey was different though; a good friend and an equal. She bore no truck from supercilious men, nor settled for subordination. She too had travelled, and was a leading light in her community. All of this, as she would jokingly chide her husband, whilst raising four independent young women.

Her company was precious, and they were soon settled and engaged with talk of family and the scarcity of sugar. Lowthian's mood lifted briefly, and the conversation moved on to matters of fairness and the ends required to attain it; a subject close to both their hearts but which they felt stymied to reveal when in the company of others. Time spent with Hanna travelled quickly. Eventually, though, the directness of the trauma that had infected Lowthian entered their exchange.

"I have seen many tragedies in my life," she said, "but this one has taken something of a hold of me."

"Peter has obviously not said anything specific," replied Hanna, "but he too has suffered, I know."

"A good man has died," continued Lowthian, "maybe needlessly."

"Maybe?"

Lowthian understood her surprise. When indeed was such a death ever justifiable?

"And I feel that responsibility."

They sat for a while, quietly, waiting for the words.

"Did you think that this could happen?" asked Hanna.

"No," replied Lowthian, bowing her head, almost as if the thoughts contained within it were too burdensome to support.

"Quite the opposite. We are meticulous. Recently, things have been much better; there's been a new optimism. This could destroy everything."

"And what about the good man you mention?"

Lowthian couldn't summon an answer, and Hanna, for her part, had never understood how the military mind rationalised death. There was a lengthy lull.

"It turns out," said Lowthian eventually, "that this war isn't just about fighting the enemy we can see, but the ones within our midst."

Hanna was becoming troubled by the messages. She admired the Colonel greatly, but despite the sorrow in her loss, there was a harshness about her. She'd expected some emotional element in response, some sensitivity to the circumstance that had so troubled. But her friend appeared more attached to the mechanics of the man's death rather than the humanity within it, and that didn't sit easily.

"You will know this only too well, of course," continued Lowthian, keen to navigate towards a different conversation, "your family deserves a secure future, but for you, too, there must be that question of trust."

From another mouth, this statement would have appeared kindly. From Lowthian, and in this frame of mind, it suddenly held a hint of menace; unintentional perhaps, but present nevertheless.

For the first time since their friendship had blossomed, Hanna began to question Lowthian's words. Perhaps it was the fact they normally met in the company of her husband and the Brigadier. Or maybe this was just the way a woman with her life experience, fighting to be heard amongst earless authorities, had learnt to cope with emotion. In its suppression, she therefore appeared so unwittingly singular.

"Such an elusive concept is sewn into our very existence," replied Hanna. "We trust family, precious friends, and above all, God."

Lowthian smiled.

"All we meet though in this world if we build walls," she continued, "are others just like ourselves; those who speak the same, believe the same, reinforce our values and prejudices. But we should be better. The life I demand for my daughters is an independence to choose, to be free, without fetter."

"From what I saw of Germaine on our recent visit, I judge you to be well en route to that end," assured Lowthian.

The mention of her oldest daughter jolted. Lowthian knew a great deal more about her and her family than she did of the Colonel. She knew so little of her background, a strange situation for such good friends.

An irrationality began to eat away at her, tempering her thinking. What if the Colonel took against the Moussabeys? Was the relationship she believed they shared really genuine, or was it a necessary adjunct to the British wheels of control?

"Hanna, are you alright?"

"Hanna?"

"What?… Oh, sorry," she replied eventually, inwardly admonishing herself for being ridiculous.

"No matter," replied Lowthian. "I was asking because of what you said the other night about being part of a country for all Arabs. It was both beautiful and compelling."

"Peter believes that the British will leave our government stronger when this war is finished, that they will honour the service and sacrifice he has made, that we will be secure, better off."

"And you?" inquired Lowthian.

"I believe the British will do what is best for them, and that this may not translate in the way Peter hopes."

"In what way?"

"When you leave, Peter may be strung up from the nearest tree."

Lowthian was shocked. This was her good friend, never taken to exaggeration. She'd underestimated Hanna's passion, her fears, as well as her ability to dispense with the verbiage that all too frequently surrounded the desire for honest exchange.

"I cannot believe, Hanna, that we shall leave Egypt without a functioning government, where your rights to live freely will be protected."

Hanna laughed, dismissively.

"Rights?" she rasped. "It's overriding force we need. This alone will maintain the peace. Rights are what the ditherers, the intellectuals and the 'already saved' can talk about."

Lowthian was feeling increasingly unsettled. She'd been welcomed, and then in time trusted by the Arabs she worked with. There were encouraging signs the top brass were beginning to appreciate the role they could play in defeating the Ottoman. But perhaps in so doing, she'd overlooked those already within the British orbit; people like the Moussabeys, reliable supporters of the war effort, those who would be the necessary and dependable agents of post-war change.

"I hope dearly that you are wrong, Hanna. We are builders and friends rather than oppressors."

"You are indeed a dear friend," replied Hanna, "and it pains me to say these things. I know the sacrifices you've made for our country. And I know that you have placed yourself in grave danger, that you could have chosen a very different route. But you appreciate clarity; you asked earlier about truth; well what works here is position, status, and money... and of course the people you know, the sect, the tribe you belong to. How I wish it was not so, that if only we could be... more British."

They both smiled at the intentional irony.

"Our farms are now estates you helped set up. But those who once worked their own land are landless as a result. Our cotton is sold to your mills at the lowest prices and our sugar becomes mysteriously too expensive for our people... yes, you have saved us from the Ottoman, but in doing so have transferred us to a different dependency."

Lowthian recognised the sentiment. Each day in Cairo, she saw unimaginable poverty. She also saw opportunity and a better future. She admired these people. Some, though, would continue to suffer, such was the way of these things.

"You asked me once, Hanna, how long it would take for Egypt to be truly free. I couldn't answer then, and I can't now. What I do believe is that with those such as you and Peter here to build the country, there is always hope."

Hanna stared at Lowthian, attempting to withhold her inner pain from an innocent.

"We cherish our friendship with you, remember that. Our lives are immeasurably better for the protection you offer. But know this. The action that drives most of those you see around you, here, in the street, is fear. Fear of what happens when you leave, fear of reprisal, fear of saying the wrong thing, being of the wrong faith, the wrong colour, fear of our own people. Whilst my words may not be those you wish to hear, whilst they may pierce, they are nevertheless spoken as my truth."

Lowthian remained muted, unable to fill the silence. Had she been Hanna, she would almost certainly have said the same.

"I am deeply sorry," continued Hanna, "for the loss of such a good man, for the grief of his family, his friends. You must not isolate yourself in blame. I doubt greatly he would wish for that."

"But there remains an undeniable fact of our circumstance. At the end of this war, God-willing, you will be able to return to your home, your family and freedoms. I though, will be losing everything."

"Why have you waited until now to tell me this?" asked Laurie.

He was sitting awkwardly, leaning on an ungainly army-issue walking stick, wedged by this and his steel chair between the wall of the room and his bed. He'd spent ten days in the south wing of the Army Hospital at the Heliopolis Palace Hotel, receiving round-the-clock treatment, before being transferred back to this, his more familiar base in the tiny windowless room in the basement of The Grand Continental.

He'd expected the attention would slacken, but if anything the opposite was true. His days had been filled with treatment and, increasingly, rehabilitating physiotherapy. It hadn't escaped his attention, injured though he'd been, that he was indeed a very important patient. He didn't want for a thing.

His sight was now fully returned, and the headaches from the severe concussion had passed. Three ribs had been cracked by the force of Nooney's shove that removed him from the line of fire, and a bullet had clipped his right shoulder, chipping the clavicle and damaging some deltoideus muscle. This, he was told, was one of the two fired by the spy, the very same that had struck and killed Nooney. He was still in pain, but with each passing day his physicality was returning.

What would not leave, though, was the blackness. From the moment his eyes opened and despite the kindly personal attentions, the waking day seemed filled with futility, and the certainty that he had killed his friend. Until now.

"Nooney's death was needless," said Lowthian. "I've taken until now to process the actions and examine the conspiracy I've described, searching for an excuse to ease my conscience. But there's nothing there I can take comfort from. On the basis of our intelligence, there was a collective misjudgement."

She hunched her shoulders momentarily, something he'd never associated with her, as she was in so many ways quite immortal.

"On this occasion," she emphasised, "we didn't take proper account of the madness of the human condition."

Even in his overwhelmed condition, Laurie was able to codify her remarks. His friend had been shot dead in a moment of avoidable insanity.

Were this to be the denouement of their time in Cairo, the bitterness would endure. But there would be an occasion for recompense, of which they were now both sure.

"Major Fogge has paid me three or four visits," said Laurie. "I was out of it for at least one of them, but I believe he still rambled on anyway."

"He's been given the responsibility by GHQ of cleaning up this mess," replied Lowthian, exchanging a knowing glance, "he will need all the help you can give him."

"I have a very limited memory of what happened. Fogge said that had it not been for Captain Hillary's presence of mind, I too would have been killed, maybe others."

Lowthian stared back at him, straight-faced. She clearly had other ideas.

"There is no way I could ever conclude that either," continued Laurie, "but—"

"...you must nevertheless agree with the presumption," interrupted Lowthian, "and remember what I've told you before about Fogge. It will be necessary to play along for now."

"The spy," continued Laurie after a moment of reflection, "what's he like?"

"His name is Oriol Quintana. From the papers he had on him, he trades from Mahon in Menorca. He's been a frequent visitor to Cairo, knows the sugar trade inside out. It's amazing we didn't bump into him at The Cairo Sugar Association."

"Ah... but we..."

Laurie stopped; he'd keep the sighting he'd made there to himself for now, though what he'd said to Fogge from his hospital bed was anyone's guess. Lowthian waited, then assumed the pause was somehow related to Laurie's condition.

"The paperwork he held," she continued, "it all seemed to be in order. Everything signed off, lots of British permissions given to him. He seems on the surface to run a legitimate business. We're checking it, but if he is a spy, he's got an unusual eye for rule-following."

"Why the shooting then?" asked Laurie.

"That's the madness I referred to. He must have panicked."

"Panicked?"

"Yes, apparently you and Nooney rushed him."

Laurie hung his head and despite the presence of his female Commanding Officer, tears cascaded down his cheeks.

Lowthian waited for his emotion to settle. She'd considered she might try to soothe him, place a hand on his uninjured shoulder, speak quietly to reassure; but she was as incapable of giving such succour as was he of receiving it.

"There was one strange thing about him, though," she said quietly, and only after a few minutes when she thought it right.

"In his bag of possessions was an old poetry book, and a notepad on which he'd scribbled various writings. When he was asked about it at the interrogation, all he said was that he loves poetry."

"And the scribbles?" asked Laurie.

"We have a few in the Bureau who have had a shot at interpreting the Spanish, but it's in a dialect, he calls it *Menorquin*. It doesn't make much sense, but again he says he himself is something of a poet, and it's nothing more than verse he was composing. Nevertheless we've got a team trying to break any code."

For the first time in weeks, Laurie smiled. How Nooney would have appreciated the irony. In trying to protect his friend, he'd been gunned down by a poet.

"It's alright, mate," Nooney would have shouted, "just lying here within a hearse, ducked the Turks but killed by verse."

There was another pause between them which embarrassed neither, their collective contrition and grief louder than any words.

And then quite suddenly Lowthian broke the silence.

"We are very similar you and I," she said.

Laurie was shocked. He, like all of the men, held her in the highest regard for her courage, tenacity and intelligence. But her status and background could not have been more different.

"We both lost our father when we were young."

Laurie was stunned. *How on earth did she know that?*

"We both had to make our own way, overcome obstruction."

He gawped at her, now almost open-mouthed.

"Yes, you will be asking how I would know these things, let alone how I could make such comparisons. As I have told you before, it's my job."

He remained speechless.

"I'm telling you this as no one else will; you deserve to know, especially now. Why do you think you were chosen to join the Bureau? Why did you become such a friend and colleague to Nooney, one of our best men? Why have you been trusted so?"

Laurie shook his head. He had no armoury that could assist a reply.

"Nooney knew it; we all recognised it, and you should at least be aware of it; you belonged here. You will therefore forever be burdened, haunted even, unless you learn to assuage the mistakes and the regrets that mask your many triumphs. I said earlier his death was needless. So, it would also make his life here to have been inglorious should you continue to bear a responsibility for its ending."

Laurie struggled to discern her words. They were reassuring, almost tender, spoken as if from a friend, not a Commanding Officer.

Trust was a delicate thing, too. Like love, once questioned, did it still really exist? Nooney had cautioned he retain his confidence in her. He was a man he both trusted and loved.

"When you lead, you choose the responsibility to try to make something better, to look up not down. You also choose the pain of judgement. To reflect is therefore noble. But to allow self-pity, well, that's lamentable."

"I needed a good friend to remind me of this recently," she continued; "I simply pass this to you, as I am sure Nooney would have done."

She wished him well and left. The day was no longer quite so dark.

The Poet Laurie Ate

"My name is Father Daoud Emam; I am here to see your prisoner."

He passed his papers of authority to the Military Provost Staff Sergeant who examined them somewhat ponderously, cross-checking with a list he had on his desk. The priest cut an imposing figure, tall, athletic and assured. But this didn't entirely deter the Sergeant.

"It says here that you'll also provide a personal affidavit from Brigadier Regis-Templeton, Army Intelligence. Do you have that?"

The Sergeant made no secret of his disdain. He may have said he was a Coptic priest here to minister to the interred, but the foreigner incarcerated in the cell was the worst sort, one who'd killed a soldier.

Emam reached into a pocket within his vestment and proffered the credential requested. He hadn't expected to be asked for this further confirmation, and the letter of authority wasn't from the Brigadier even though it was signed in his name. But to all intents and purposes, it seemed to do the trick. And at any rate, if challenged, it would only have been a minor inconvenience to secure the real thing, such was the way matters worked amongst the flock to whom he tended.

"You'll have to submit to a search," grunted the Sergeant, miffed that Emam had the necessaries and that this was all that was left to him to cause delay.

"Before my men do this, I must ask, will they find anything they shouldn't?"

"Only my God," smiled Emam, "though please be warned, he is likely to embrace them warmly with his blessings."

The Sergeant's face remained blank, and he indicated to the two Military Policemen beside him to commence their work. But before they could start, Emam raised his hand.

"Please, wait."

The search team looked hopeful.

"Would you hold my bag whilst I am being so carefully felt." He passed his leather case to the Sergeant, who was by now distinctly unamused.

A few moments later, the bag was thrust back to him, and he was escorted through the office and to the cell where Oriol Quintana was being held.

"Fifteen minutes," barked one of his sidemen, "and in English; he can speak it well enough when he wants."

Emam smiled down at the man and stooped to enter the cell, the thickening sound of eternity in his ears as the iron door thudded shut behind him.

The space was small and hot, and smelt of the faecal bucket prominently positioned on the floor. There was a tiny barred window looking out onto the exercise yard, but apart from that, no apparent means of ventilation. Below this was a small desk-like wooden table and connected seat, the sort that might be common in a schoolroom. Along the adjoining wall was a steel bed, firmly fixed to the brickwork, impossible therefore for use as a projectile, yet seemingly equally impractical for its intended purpose. Sat at the far end of this and propped against the wall, was the man he'd come to see.

Oriol was dishevelled, and even though the light wasn't the best, Emam was surprised. In the street, he'd followed a well-dressed businessman, confident, and courteous to those around him. Here, though, was a shell of that man. He wore the same trousers, but they were stained and crumpled. There was no shirt, just a vest, and the neatly manicured hair now unkempt, hanging across his forehead, partly obscuring the scar, his face bleached of all prospect.

To Emam's surprise, Oriol started rubbing his stubble-free chin.

"Despite it all, I think a shave still improves a man," he said, grinning despite the pain of his circumstance.

Perhaps there was a chance for this man after all, thought Emam and he introduced himself.

"Father Daoud Emam, from St Nicholas Cathedral in El Hamzawi, just off Shari—"

"...Shari El Ghuri," interjected Oriol, "I know it well."

Emam was relieved. There was a spark in the man, though he hadn't expected quite such a response.

"And I also know you too, I believe," he continued.

Emam looked on, distracted by the response but eager to encourage the dialogue.

"I now know why it is that wherever I have been in Cairo since arriving, there's always been a Coptic priest nearby, eager to help me."

Emam smiled.

"We are a caring group."

"And my welcome party at the station when I arrived?"

Emam affected not to understand, though Oriol knew otherwise.

"I must apologise," said Emam, "sometimes our concern for others pushes us to an ebullience that would shame even Salome."

Oriol grinned.

"How are you?" asked Emam.

"In need of a lawyer rather than a man of God," he replied, "particularly one who has been following me through the streets."

"I must be slowing down," said Emam. "So sure was I my presence was invisible that when you began to walk quickly that day, I needed to run to keep up. You have been an exhausting quarry; have you no respect for an older man?"

Oriol shook his head gently and pursed his lips. He enjoyed the priest's humour if not the circumstances that had led to the visit.

"Have you been treated well?"

"You need to ask?" replied Oriol, his mood changing. "I have witnessed a man killed in cold blood, been arrested, roughly treated, interrogated for hours on end, my possessions stolen, incarcerated here in this hell-hole, my rights denied me, and accused of being a murderer."

He looked angrily at Emam.

"If that is being treated well, then yes, I am having the time of my life."

"Was it you who betrayed me?"

"Betrayed?" Emam looked directly at Oriol.

"What was there to betray?"

Oriol sat quietly for a moment, the uselessness of his position intruding once more.

"Fancy one?" asked Emam, as he pulled a cigarette out of his bag.

Oriol was surprised, but declined.

"Do you mind if I do? Normally I might desist, but I think in this case it might even help with the smell in here."

He was an odd one alright, thought Oriol.

"Why are you here? I have said everything I can possibly say to those fools who taunted me at the interrogation."

"I am here to help you," replied Emam.

"By spying on me?"

"It is you who is considered to be the spy, not I," said Emam. "My behaviour is based in faith."

Oriol grimaced.

"I am not a religious man in the way you might wish."

"Neither am I," replied Emam.

"You are a Coptic," said Oriol.

"Does that word disqualify me?" replied Emam. "Surely a man such as yourself, would recognise that to place such a label around a neck is about as useful to our understanding as a writer without paper."

Emam reached into his bag and pulled out the notepad Oriol had used for his poetry. He passed it to him and gazed at the amazement on his face.

"How did you manage to get hold of this?"

"Well, it wasn't because I am a Coptic priest."

"But this was taken from me by the British?"

"And now they have no use for it. Their greatest code breaker tried every method known to the intelligence community and concluded there was no sense in what you had written. So in that respect he was convinced that you were either quite mad…or, of course, a poet."

Oriol smiled again. The priest was still confusing, but even in his incarcerated state he recognised in him a fellow traveller.

Emam passed him the pencil that had also been taken from him.

"Lead. It has such a powerful use beyond the bullet," he said.

"Weren't you searched?" asked Oriol.

"Bodily yes, but the Sergeant held my bag politely before returning it." He winked. "And anyway, they are not necessarily the brutes you may believe. They are as afraid as all of us in their own way."

He pulled out *The Odyssey of Homer* from his bag and passed it to Oriol, who despite his distrust was unable to mask his delight. He took the book and held it gently for a moment, reminded that beauty still existed in his world. Instinctually he opened to the front page, checking it was the edition placed into his possession, from what now seemed so long ago.

"It is the same one confiscated from you, the 1725 edition," said Emam, "something of a literary jewel. They see no reason to deprive you of it."

He was indeed much more than a priest, thought Oriol.

"It would take a literary Philistine not to realise the significance of this book," continued Emam, "but then I believe that even in Cairo's most prestigious and recently opened shopping establishment such people can be found."

Oriol closed the book, cradling it to his chest as a mother would a babe. But this priest?

"If this is freely given, then I thank you for your compassion. But if you wish this to be a gift that compounds my assumed guilt, then here, take it back." He handed the book towards Emam.

"Please, they are yours to keep," he assured.

"So, you work for the British?" asked Oriol.

"I work for peace, wherever that takes me," replied Emam.

"So, does your faith help you understand why an innocent man is told he is a murderer?"

"No, but does the day blame the sunlight for the heat? We are all linked and dependent. I believe there is always a reason, always a way."

"For me the way is always love," said Oriol.

"Then you have also found faith," replied Emam, "in every act of that love you describe."

This priest was indeed different, almost irreverent. He hadn't inquired about the shooting at Pont Limoun Station, or contradicted him when he protested his innocence. He knew a great deal about the circumstances of the event, and must have the ear of the British. Yet his were the only soothing words since the arrest and interrogations, and he appeared a free spirit.

"At the time of that poor man's killing, I was about to return to Alexandria, my work completed. My only crime was to be a few days later than expected in meeting up there with my passage back home across the Mediterranean."

"Have you news of that?" inquired Emam.

Oriol didn't answer, and for a moment there was disappointment. Maybe all the priest really wanted was information, after all?

Emam though breathed a little more deeply; Oriol was, it seemed, unaware of the news about *The Adelphi*.

"I am not asking for such detail to incriminate you, if that's what you think," he said, "and I can see from your face that you are unaware of events."

Oriol was thrown by the comment.

"Events?"

"I organise food handouts across Cairo, so I liaise with the British for permissions with regard to this and for my work with the Coptic community. I am therefore familiar with the operations at Alexandria more than might generally be realised. After all, I am 'just a priest'. Mostly, this relates to the trade of food and supplies, but also on occasions for the carriage of Coptic refugees."

"Refugees?"

"We are often seen as outsiders and unwelcome, our homes destroyed, possessions stolen. Egypt had become a safe haven, though this war is changing that."

Oriol shook his head. Everywhere he looked, there was struggle.

"So I am privy to news regarding any events that affect this work."

He paused.

"What is it you need to tell me?" Oriol could sense some foreboding in the priest's tone.

"The boat *The Adelphi*… I must tell you what others have left unsaid… that there has been no news; it is as if she has disappeared."

Again, Oriol looked at the priest, feigning disinterest. He trusted the Andreassens to cope with whatever came their way.

"Which means," continued Emam, fully aware of Oriol's position, "there is a chance she may be lost."

The words burnt into his heart, as well as his pretence to indifference.

He doubled up, shattered, and buried his head in his hands, locking his ears and eyes. All he could imagine was the dreadful vision of their sinking, and the returning dream of his own drowning.

"I am sorry," said Emam eventually and with gentleness, "I thought maybe you had been told. There is always hope."

Oriol thought back to Elisheba's last words that had accompanied him since their parting weeks earlier.

"Is it really a life without passion?" How he'd admired her.

Again, a long silence intruded. Then Emam moved towards Oriol and picked up the notepaper and pencil from the bed. He scribbled something on it and placed the paper back. After a moment or so Oriol dragged himself up and slowly focussed on the paper beside him. There, in clear Menorquin, was written:

I know you are innocent. You will need to trust me.

The priest had already surprised, but this was beyond any expectation.

Emam put his finger to his lips, moved back, tearing away and screwing up the note before putting it back inside his pocket.

Then he spoke again, but this time in Oriol's own tongue.

"Keep your counsel, stay strong," and winking once more, "have faith." He smiled.

"How do you know my—"

"…language?" interrupted Emam.

"As a boy, my family fled from the leftists and the catholic extremists terrorising mainland Spain. We were saved by the openness of your islanders. My family found a home in Ciutadella. I might be your long-lost older brother."

Again he smiled, but this time broadly.

"I must go, but please, remember the things I have urged."

He stood, rearranged his garment, and placed the leather case over his shoulder.

"I shall see you again soon," he said, returning to the use of English, "if you need reassurance that I come in love then page 34 of your book has a verse that will help. Please, enjoy what you find there, and believe in it."

He banged upon the cell door and after a short wait a guard appeared from along the corridor.

"Thank you so much," said Emam, as the Military Policeman stood to one side, to allow him to pass, "it can be so confining in these small places don't you think?"

"Oh, I almost forgot."

He still had the pencil in his hand, and turning, he threw it back to Oriol, narrowly missing the bucket.

"It's a sign," said Emam, "shit really can be avoided."

The Policeman seemed taken aback, but then assumed he'd misheard.

A little while later when the daily round of checking, cleaning and feeding had met a routine pause and the solitude of his cell had returned, Oriol picked up the book and thumbed through to page 34. There, almost matched to the page colouration and size and fixed tightly into the binding, was a letter. He removed it from its attachment and carefully unfolded it.

'From His Excellency Paulinus, Bishop Emeritus of the Diocese of Arage, Valencia.'

My Son,

I pray that this letter finds you in the very best of health and good fortune, though I fear the possibility that may not be so.

I have asked my dearest colleague, Father Daoud Emam, to offer you his greatest pastoral works to assist your security and safe return to those who love you most dearly. He was an impressive young man when I first met him during my days at Sant Cristofol, and he has grown in God to be the greatest of servants to the people of Cairo. I beg you to seek his assurances.

My son, I failed you once before. I do not intend to do so again.

I look forward to the time you can be reunited with those who love you dearly.

Paulinus.

Oriol read and re-read the letter, feverishly, unbelievingly, wishing to be convinced of its authority. An imprimatur from a man such as Bishop

Paulinus seemed implausible, though gratifying. The mention of Sant Cristofol only served to deepen the questions in his mind.

Having memorised it, he tore it into strips and placed it next to the bucket. If it was both sincere and genuine, then it was remarkable. If it was another wasted promise or duplicitous, then it might at least serve some practical purpose.

"Ah, Lance Corporal Laurie, thank you for struggling through your pain to be here this morning. We are so grateful."

As ever, Major Fogge fizzed with the genial excitement of a boy who'd just been given a new toy by his nanny. But the blandishments had long worn thin, and attendance had hardly been optional.

Laurie was back in the same tiny office at Army HQ at The Savoy where he'd first met Fogge in what seemed like a lifetime ago.

"So glad to see you looking so well," continued Fogge, beckoning Laurie to sit.

"My dear chap, it's been such an awful time for you."

Laurie stared back at the man he'd once simply thought of as an amiable fool. Making his way to the meeting had been something of an effort. His shoulder was feeling easier, the dressings and medications now removed. There was still a pain in his back where the ribs had broken, but it connected him to Nooney and he was in no rush to lose it. Physically, he was returning to good shape, emotionally, though he remained stranded in gloom.

"Can I first of all say how saddened we all were by the awful tragedy surrounding Lance Corporal Nooney."

Laurie looked at the faux face accompanying Fogge's words and merely saw a leer. To Fogge's left, cramped on a stool against the Major's wicker chair, was Captain Hillary, barely able to tolerate the presence of Laurie let alone offer him any pretence towards compassion. The communion was completed by the enigmatic Sergeant Wirrall, propped uncomfortably next to a standing lamp, and pressed tightly against the corner of the room in the only space left available.

"Terrible business. None of us had foreseen these events would end so tragically."

Laurie fixed the Major with a piercing stare, his anger heightened by the pretentious inference towards collective grief that Fogge's words implied.

"As he was on an attachment with us, I've written to Nooney's Commanding Officer with the New Zealanders, and of course to his parents."

Laurie had already promised himself that in such an event he would rectify the damage by his own letter at the first possible opportunity.

"I've thanked them on behalf of the King for the selfless way he gave up his life to save others."

Laurie knew the score by now, and how this was all working. He was still too numb though for the rage within him to flow, and anyway it wouldn't help with the final service he'd pay his friend.

"You said some interesting things, Laurie, when I visited you in hospital, many incoherent of course, but some that I was able to note and pass on to the investigating team. It helped them, I believe, in unpicking the workings of the prisoner."

"Things, sir?" said Laurie.

He had no idea what they may have been, nor whether or not this was just another ploy by the Major to involve him more personally with Nooney's killing, but either way, it wouldn't work.

"You don't remember, dear chap?" said Fogge, encouraged.

"Why, the good Captain was with me to ensure nothing was missed, two heads and all that sort of stuff, don't you know?"

"I am told I spent time at the Heliopolis Palace," replied Laurie, "but as for whom I saw or what I said, I have no memory whatsoever."

"Well, that's no matter, Laurie, no matter at all. In fact, it's probably best like that; it will help things move along."

Laurie was sure it would.

"Turns out we popped a spy ring, one that could have blown our chances of capturing Jerusalem right out of the water."

"Sir?"

Laurie maintained his disassociated air, made even easier now by the turn of events.

"Christmas you know, Laurie. Allenby is hoping we can take Jerusalem from the Ottoman by Christmas."

"Allenby, sir?"

Fogge paused briefly. Laurie had been through a shock or two, but he seemed even slower off the mark than when he visited him in his hospital bed.

"Yes, you know Laurie, the new Field Marshall."

Laurie peered back at him, expressionless.

"Oh well, no matter, nothing for you to trouble yourself with."

"Don't trust the little creep, sir," hissed Captain Hillary, unrequested and quite audibly.

"Thank you, Captain, there is no need for that."

"I think there is, sir, if you don't mind my saying."

"But I do, Hillary," replied Fogge, irritated by the Captain's persistence, "I very much do. Be quiet. Do I make myself clear?"

"Yes, sir," responded the upbraided sidekick, testily, "you are always very clear."

Laurie had no desire to be part of this, but it nevertheless felt the perfect dialogue. Cracks were appearing.

"Take no notice of Captain Hillary's humour, Laurie, he means nothing but good. None of us have really been ourselves since this incident."

Fogge seemed to take a few deeper breaths, as if he was trying to remember what it was he needed to tell Laurie.

"The trial, sir?" said Sergeant Wirrall.

"Yes, yes, thank you, Sergeant, I was coming to that."

Fogge was too vain to recognise his own choleric disposition or *irascibilis*, as he would have put it, but it was now very much on show.

"I can tell you that following his interrogation and the collation of evidence, all of which were carried out by myself and the Captain under the good offices of Brigadier Regis-Templeton, the assailant was found guilty of spying for an enemy agent and of the manslaughter of Lance Corporal Nooney. The findings were affirmed by the office of the Provost Marshal in accordance with the laws expressed in The Army Act, and—"

"...is he dead?" interrupted Laurie. Fogge was taken aback.

"Dead?"

"Was he shot?"

"Laurie, what do you mean?"

"That's what spies get, sir, especially those who murder."

"Well... manslaughter, dear boy, you see..."

"Murder," retorted Laurie.

Fogge had never seen Laurie like this. He'd always been a difficult man to call, but never one so eager to see the demise of another.

"Listen here, Laurie, I know you've taken this show badly, but it's important we do things by the rules. Do you understand?"

Laurie remained poker-faced.

"Sir."

"That's good. You should know that we do not believe from the evidence presented that the spy was aiming to kill Lance Corporal Nooney. The judgement was that it was more of a defence mechanism on his part; the gun was accidentally discharged. Of the spying, there can be no doubt. He came into Alexandria on a boat that trades with the Ottoman in Palestine, and with a crew who worked with the Turkish leadership in Haifa."

"So he will be shot then, sir?"

"It's not as easy as that, Laurie. He's a Spaniard and therefore a neutral."

"What, sir? Does that mean our bullets would pass right through him, that he has special powers?"

"What?" Fogge was becoming mystified by Laurie's behaviour. This wasn't the man he knew.

"Sir, I warned you..." said Captain Hillary trying to intervene, but he was quickly rebuffed by Fogge's irritated stare.

"No, Laurie, it means we can't shoot him because we'd upset the bloody Spaniards and that might just bring even more problems our way. Do you understand?"

"Yes, sir, understood... good, so... we can't hang him either?"

"No, man, damn it, neither can we hang him," Fogge shouted, and even Captain Hillary seemed taken aback.

"I'm not sure Lance Corporal Laurie is well, sir," said Sergeant Wirrall interjecting as quietly as he could, "he doesn't seem to be himself."

"Thank you, Sergeant, you're right."

He tried again.

"What I'm saying, Laurie, is that in a few weeks' time, when you are stronger, we would like you to be part of the party who escorts the spy to Suez, on the Red Sea…"

Laurie looked perplexed.

"…the first part of his journey to a life of incarceration in Australia."

"Ah, that's good, sir, though I thought we'd stopped doing that in the 1860s?"

"They won't notice another one I'm sure, Laurie, and anyway, one less for the exchequer, hey?"

For the first time, Fogge felt he was getting through.

"Will you be fit enough for it do you think?"

"I will, sir…"

"…fitter than a butcher's dog in fact, Major," replied Laurie.

Fogge creased his eyes in bewilderment. This wasn't the Laurie he'd jousted with, but concussion and shock did strange things to people.

"Good man, Laurie," he said optimistically, "that's more like it."

"Probably best for now if we leave it there, though maybe you still have a question?"

"Just checking then, sir, he's not to be drowned either?"

"No, Laurie," replied the Major, trying to stay calm.

"So, expiration in any of its forms isn't to occur at any stage?"

Fogge could barely contain himself, but the words of Sergeant Wirrall and his increasing concern for Laurie's health and state of mind restrained his response.

"That's right, Laurie, expiration in all its forms is completely ruled out."

"Thank you, sir."

"That's all good then, Lance Corporal Laurie."

"As I guess a life sentence incarcerated in Australia must be even worse," said Laurie.

Fogge turned to Sergeant Wirrall, his patience exhausted, and asked him to see that Laurie got back to his room at The Grand Continental.

"Keep a close eye on him please, Sergeant," he said, wearily, "and make sure he's progressing satisfactorily."

The Sergeant and Laurie saluted and left the office.

Once the coast was clear, Fogge turned on his Captain.

"I will not keep reminding you about your position in the grand scheme of these things."

"He's playing you for a fool," replied Hillary.

"He's still unwell, and maybe that's for the best in the circumstances," said Fogge.

"Who says he's unwell?"

"The medical people."

"They've released him. Nothing about any madness."

"Madness?" replied Fogge. "I'd call it a kind of acerbic melancholy. Shakespeare was full of it."

Hillary gawped.

"Oh really, Hillary, for a Balliol man you are so obtuse. What did you study again?"

"Mathematics."

"Ah, that would explain it."

Hillary nervously tapped his head with his hand, feeling for his cap which was actually on his lap. He wasn't going to have any of this, but the hesitancy his societal positioning had riddled him with was far stronger than his mettle, and Fogge continued.

"Do I really need to remind you about who the fool in all of this really is?"

Hillary avoided Fogge's direct gaze, though he clearly had a view.

"Fortunately, he seems to have a very hazy memory of things, a characteristic you might wish to emulate."

There was menace in the sneer and Hillary remained silent. For now.

CHAPTER 12

For the past two weeks, Laurie had returned to light duties. Colonel Lowthian had ordered his recovery to be monitored by a physician normally assigned to the officers. He was to concentrate on rebuilding his strength. So he took her at her word, undertaking increasingly long walks before the sun was high, re-familiarising himself with the sights and aromas of the city, repeating the circuits just before nightfall. During the heat of the day, he rested, wrote to his wife and children, and thought.

His apparent special status ensured that the only official requirement of him was to write a report upon the events surrounding Nooney's death. There appeared to be no rush for this submission, as his faltering and therefore unreliable memory had been acknowledged by those who seemed to need to know. And anyhow, it transpired the spy had already been tried.

Despite appearances, though, he was beginning to fully comprehend the course upon which he was now set.

"I doubt if your submission will be justiciable anyway, dear boy," Major Fogge had said on one of his visits.

Laurie had no idea what he meant, nor cared, especially as Fogge had been full of his usual instinctual insincerity. As his strength returned, though, so too had his determination to honour Nooney, whatever the means.

So, as much as he would have liked otherwise, it was with this sense of duty he'd agreed to Fogge's request to meet the local man who was to lead the spy's escort party to Suez. The place chosen for this was St Nicholas Cathedral, an unusual choice he'd thought, but then again, this was the Bureau. More daunting was its location just a short walk away from the carpet shop where Nooney and Laurie were ensconced on observation the night before the killing.

"I was expecting to see a military man," said Laurie, as he sat on a hard pew at the back of the building.

Sitting a few spaces away, close enough to speak but sufficiently distant to prevent suspicion of association, was the not entirely unfamiliar face of Father Daoud Emam.

There had been dozens of others in the building when Laurie had entered earlier, paying respects, conversing quietly or praying. But it was Emam, standing near the altar and in front of the iconostasis, upon whom he'd fixed. He'd last spotted him in what now seemed like another lifetime: he was the Coptic priest who'd acknowledged Moussabey that day at The Cairo Sugar Association, as they'd all left a meeting of the Trading Association of Cairo. And after a few moments in the cathedral, it was this same priest who'd moved, quite unnoticed by others, to sit just along the way from him.

"Well, I'm wearing a uniform of sorts," replied Emam.

"That's open to interpretation," said Laurie, and Emam smiled.

"As with so much in this world," he replied, waving his arms gently around, as if embracing the cathedral's interface between human scurry and the eternal mystery.

He was pleased Laurie's reputation for obduracy had survived the trauma of Nooney's death.

"Do not be put off by the imagery that you see around you. Saint Nicholas is a hero to us all, the most giving of men. Who wouldn't want to be constantly reminded of that?"

Laurie ignored the invite to saintly magnanimity and pointed to the brilliantly coloured triptych by the altar, crowded with ornately dressed figures, heads garnered by halos.

"And all those people in those paintings?"

"For the Orthodox," replied Emam, "religious imagery represents an opportunity to embrace universality. We prefer a crowd. In death, as in life, we expect to be surrounded."

"No wonder I stood out then when I entered," said Laurie, "no room for the unorthodox?"

"Well, I hope that like me, the people you see here work with need rather than denomination."

"And what is your need?" asked Laurie.

It was normally Emam who assessed this in others, so he knew that Laurie's response was deliberately designed to challenge.

"The same as yours," he replied, disarming the directness.

The priest stood, beckoning Laurie to follow him, and they walked from the building and out to the street. They were soon back amongst the narrow alleyways that radiated from the cathedral, and the throng and noise of Cairo street life.

Below the protection of the protruding balconies within the narrow maze it remained fiercely hot and hoarse-dry. Yet Laurie felt strangely liberated. Even Emam's obvious alertness for any sign of an unwanted tail brought him a returning impulse for purpose. The uncertainty he'd wrestled with since Nooney's death was leaving him.

"Where are we going?" asked Laurie.

"To the prison cells to visit a Spaniard," replied Emam.

Laurie halted. Despite wariness his better instincts towards the priest had prevailed. Maybe though he'd been mistaken.

"Are you mad?"

"Mad enough to want to help you."

Emam commenced walking, and after a moment's hesitation Laurie followed.

"What if I don't want your help?"

"Then consider this, an innocent man does."

"And who is that?"

"The man the British want us to transport to Suez for his onward incarceration, for causing the death of your friend."

"Us?"

Laurie had momentarily forgotten that the meeting in the cathedral had been specifically arranged at Fogge's behest, with the man who was to guide the escort party.

"Beyond Heliopolis the route can be treacherous. I know the desert, and for all their technological advancement, even the British are a poor match for an unhappy camel. In the past, Colonel Lowthian accompanied me. I hope that qualification will put your mind at rest."

Laurie remembered she'd relied upon local guides during her route finding work for the military, and that one of these had been a Coptic priest.

"And anyway," he continued, "be assured he is neither murderer nor spy."

"So who fired those bullets?" asked Laurie.

"Well, your pistol was one of the exhibits."

"What?"

"A bullet had been fired from it; one other was left in the chamber."

"That's ridiculous; I was never issued with any bullets, that I do remember?"

Emam looked at him somewhat quizzically, and a frustration surfaced.

"Nooney will tell you…"

Laurie stopped himself before finishing, realising the futility and cruelty in the momentary delusion that his friend was still alive.

"I know that, too," replied Emam, pausing before exiting the alleys and onto the busy Shari El Sikka, "and that's exactly why we need each other."

They boarded the tram at the crossroads with Shari El Surein and took the direct route to Heliopolis, thirty minutes to the north-east. Laurie waved his 'Tramways Du Caire' pass at the conductor who frowned resentfully, reluctant to allow him passage. Emam had already taken his seat, his religious credentials more than sufficient.

"Heliopolis," he shouted to Laurie, who, so reminded, proffered his other 'Cairo Electric Railways and Heliopolis Oasis Company' pass, which seemed to satisfy. He moved along the tram and sat down next to the priest, an odd couple amongst the mix of everyday Egyptian life.

"It's an important man that has two passes," said Emam.

"I'd forgotten this route out to the new town," replied Laurie. "I only used it a few times with Nooney as generally we travelled from Pont Limoun."

"A place I thought we best avoid for the present," replied Emam, with a kindness that seemed genuine.

He was still something of a mystery to Laurie, but the route to resolution lay in whom to trust, and for now the priest had proven nobler than he could have imagined.

"I'm sorry," said Laurie," I don't even know your name."

"Father Daoud Emam." They shook hands, raising a few eyebrows from those around them.

"I am sure that we radiate a degree of unfortunate entitlement," said Emam, aware of the onlookers.

As the tram rattled towards the open spaces and parklands of Abbasîyah and the edge of old Cairo, it quickly emptied. Few of those who'd boarded in the centre had either the means or the reason to travel onward to the more elegant neighbourhoods, let alone continue beyond to the palatial surroundings of Heliopolis.

The two men hardly spoke on the journey. Laurie's mind was elsewhere. His visits to the new town had been frequent and mostly inglorious, dealing with curfew-breaking soldiers who'd failed to make it back to barracks from the pleasures of central Cairo. Neither he nor Nooney enjoyed locking up the mostly adolescent, but bitter experience had taught them the harm such indiscipline could cause. So it was a necessary labour.

As the tram pushed on from Abbasîyah along the final and marginally inhabited stretch towards the town, it reached speeds approaching 40 miles per hour, slowing momentarily to pass by the British and Egyptian cavalry barracks, before one last sprint into the 'city of luxury and leisure'.

The grandeur of the place had almost overwhelmed him at first. Heliopolis was a world apart from the intense excesses and noise that accompanied Cairo life. The boulevards were wider than anything he'd ever seen, and the buildings, though recent, were more consistently elegant and outwardly ageless. The architecture had distinctive and classical Oriental and Arabesque influences, as befitted the requirements of Cairo's wealthiest.

The largest were palatial and home to Egyptian and European business barons, government grandees, and most notably the Sultan, Hussein Kamel. And amongst all of this was the imposing Heliopolis Palace Hotel, a building that rivalled Cairo's finest, and where, in its commandeered role as a military hospital, Laurie had recently spent such a concussed time.

More curious was the multitude of religious buildings. He'd never seen a mosque before arriving in Egypt, but here their domes and minarets seemed to be everywhere. And there were dozens of synagogues, temples and churches, including the huge catholic basilica that dominated the Heliopolis skyline. There was a tolerance of religious choice that he hadn't expected. His journey to this land had been driven by honour and virtue; a determination to serve his country. He'd thought little of what Egypt would bring him beyond disease, dehydration and distrust. Yet increasingly he'd been enlightened by its complex society, that in duress had learnt an awkward sort of resilience, and in its desire for the tolerance and optimism represented by these places of worship.

The tram halted at the end of Shari El Ahram and the few remaining passengers disembarked. Most of them seemed to head towards the Heliopolis Palace Hotel. Even though its former glory had now been supplanted by a crowded army hospital, with tented extensions stretching out across the formerly manicured front lawns, it still needed maintenance and cleaning.

"Shall we go to the racetrack?" said Emam, taking care not to miss a step as he alighted.

"Why not?" replied Laurie; "is our spy also a jockey?"

Emam laughed.

They headed off in the direction of the huge basilica, and the street widened even more. At Shari Ramses they turned towards the Heliopolis Race Course, and though still a ten-minute walk away, the well-drilled lines of the 3rd Australian Light Horse Brigade encamped there were clearly visible.

Laurie sighed.

"You know the camp?" inquired Emam.

"Far too well."

He didn't feel the need to explain.

"We shall enter in a more direct way than perhaps you've been used to," replied Emam.

As they approached the two-storey domed Byzantine building that sat at the end of the street, Laurie saw more fully what he meant. It was the casino building and in some senses a smaller version of the catholic basilica; but hugely more significant for those military men who'd lost their shirts gambling there.

"Shall we?" said Emam, and to Laurie's surprise, he led up the limestone steps to the large panelled doors at the entrance, where he was greeted like a revered friend.

"You know this place?" asked Laurie.

"Of course," replied Emam. "I am privileged to meet such wonderful people."

He could see Laurie's confusion that a priest might grace such a spot.

"Where better to meet the needy?"

It was approaching midday, so the building, officially at least, was closed. They were led through the main floor past the mostly empty gaming tables and bar, and out onto the concourse and garden to the rear. To one side of this lay Luna Park, clearly visible with its swing cars and Helter Skelter, now silent. A large wall screened the remaining sides of the garden from view.

Their eager assistant had gone on ahead to a small gate, neatly camouflaged within the back fence. He unlocked it, revealing before them both the huge hustle of military humanity and the enormous scale of the army camp. They squeezed through the space and onto the racetrack, Emam graciously thanking the man, who in turn crossed himself and bowed, closing the gate behind them.

"Enter ye by the narrow gate?" said Laurie, and Emam grinned.

"Matthew 7, a personal favourite of mine, too," replied Emam. "Are you really quite convinced that you're an unorthodox believer?"

They moved across the track, taking care to avoid military practising cavalry drills, and headed towards a large water tower standing high above the town of army huts. Below it stood the headquarters building.

"You're sure we have permission to be here? It's an odd way to make an entrance," said Laurie.

"Of course," replied Emam, cheerfully, "…I work to keep all doors open."

The headquarters were securely guarded, along with the other activities housed within a wooden building, but it was many times larger. The long and regular lines of billets that radiated away from it accommodated over a thousand men, though at times the camp swelled to twice this size as divisions moved here to prepare for onward mobilisation to Sinai. Very often these temporary newcomers had to make do with a tented village on the fringe of the racetrack, but for now the place was as quiet as Laurie could remember.

Emam showed his permissions to the outer guard and they were allowed through, up the steps, and onto a second checkpoint, where Laurie was also required to confirm his paperwork. One of the guards looked at him sympathetically, and for a moment it threw him.

"Tough one, mate," he said, in an accent Laurie took for Australian. But he noticed the lapel insignia and realised he was a New Zealander with the Anzac Mounted Division.

"Lance Corporal Nooney was one of our own. Do what you have to, mate."

Before he could process a response, he felt Emam pushing him inside. They were led through a number of small and stiflingly hot offices into a darkened holding area, where a further check was undertaken, this time including a search of their clothing.

"Tomorrow at 7 am," replied the Sergeant at the desk, after Emam had inquired about the following day's preparations, "and no camels thank God, just four of the Horse Brigade fellas, all reliable, two pack donkeys and their Arab minders, your good self, sir, and anyone the British send us, for what good that will be worth."

"Well, I can confirm this one will be of great value," Emam said, smiling and indicating towards Laurie. The Sergeant seemed unconvinced.

"Lance Corporal Laurie," said Emam, and there was an immediate change in the Sergeant's demeanour.

"Please, excuse me, I had no idea it was you."

By now, it was clear that he had some status with these men. It must have been his association with the killing; he was the bloke who was there when it happened, the one Nooney had taken the bullet for. And it was obvious that in these surroundings at least, the man to be transported to Suez on the morrow was as guilty as hell.

Civilities of sorts completed, the Sergeant beckoned them through an archway behind him, and there facing them in a cell… was Oriol Quintana.

He was standing, hands clasped around the bars of a locked door. He could hear he'd had visitors as his cell was no more than a large cage, making his every movement and utterance observable from the outside. Around it was sufficient space for a guard to patrol, and two others were stationed at the entrance to the room and facing the prisoner.

"I see you were expecting us," said Emam, cheerfully, pleased that at first sight Oriol looked much brighter than when they last met. He was certainly cleaner, his grubby clothing replaced by army issue trousers and a civilian jacket.

"I am to be more presentable for my journey," joked Oriol.

"Ten minutes, then that's it," said the Sergeant.

"You may talk freely through the bars to each other, but the guards must remain, I'm afraid."

Emam nodded, and the Sergeant returned to the office.

"Anyone for a cigarette?" inquired Emam, proffering his smoke case to the surprised ensemble.

"My quarters are less odorous than at our last meeting," said Oriol, smiling, "so I shall continue to resist."

Laurie scrutinised the Spaniard's face, the eyes in particular. In his world they were the entry to intention. He'd seen this man at close quarters moments before the shooting, sensing none of the animus that would lead to the destruction that followed. But during the darkness of his recovery this had tormented: how had he so misjudged?

Yet here, within the complex immediacy of this their second fleeting moment, and the guilt of Nooney's death, there remained a dogged and recurring consciousness: that try though he had to convince to the contrary this so-called spy had no designs to kill.

"This is Lance Corporal Laurie," said Emam by way of an unnecessary introduction; "he will accompany us to Suez."

The two men stared at each other, neither really knowing what to say.

Had it not been for this man, Laurie knew that Nooney would still be alive. And were it not for the Englishman stood once more in front of him, Oriol knew he'd be home at Turo Vell, rather than facing the end of his life.

"I am sorry for your loss," said Oriol eventually, breaking the silence.

The words hit Laurie like a hammer. They were spoken quietly and from a man already condemned. He'd expected to hear resentment, hatred even, but not humility.

"We move tomorrow," said Emam, wishing not to inflame the pain they both bore. He needed to maximise the short time they had together.

"We shall use horseback, maybe less than three days to get to Suez if we are lucky with the desert. You are able to ride?"

Oriol nodded.

"Were you able to reflect upon my last visit?" Emam inquired.

Oriol perfectly understood the question, and that nothing should be said to alert the guards.

"Indeed," he replied quietly, "particularly the good wishes from my father. I had no idea that he held me in such regard."

"Be assured of that," said Emam.

"I will let him know of the joy his words brought, and the hope that one day you will all be together once more."

Oriol looked at the priest, hoping desperately, despite the coded words, for more. But even in this necessarily obscure exchange, they had given some confirmation and comfort.

"Perhaps, therefore, you will allow a short prayer?" continued Emam, raising his eyes expectantly, his face hidden from the guards behind him.

This was an instruction rather than a request, and Oriol followed the priest to his knees.

"Hold my crucifix, my son, as we pray to Saint Nicholas for safe passage."

Everyone in the room bowed their heads and Emam began to speak in Latin. Oriol took hold of the large wooden crucifix passed to him through the bars, though still firmly attached by its leather tie to Emam's neck.

For a while, Laurie looked passively on from behind the priest, trying to establish the familiar within the inexplicable mystery of the prayerful message.

But then, little by little, he recognised the slightest of changes in flow. Emam had begun to introduce snatches that were less recognisable, more resonant, a form of dialect that sat uneasily within the already impenetrable Latin. To Emam though, this was simply his native Menorquin, sufficiently plausible to the untutored ear as to be a natural part of the latinesque meditative pulse of the prayer within which it was hidden, but which nevertheless the prisoner would understand.

The more Oriol heard, the more he tightened his eyes in disbelief. What the prisoner was receiving from this amazing man was far beyond the spiritual; he was being given instructions for the days ahead.

As Emam raised the tone he took firmer grip of the prisoner's hands, cupping them around his own so that he could, unseen by the others, open up the crucifix. Inside was a thin piece of paper. He carefully manoeuvred this into Oriol's palm.

When he was sure these actions had been completed and understood, he tailed off the volubility he'd brought to the ceremony, rested for a moment's silence, and then stood, slowly raising Oriol with him with one final tight squeeze of the hand.

"The Latin may have sounded unfamiliar to you, my son," he said, "but be assured that the words contained promises from Saint Nicholas that you must truly believe."

He stared again at Oriol, who, though somewhat reeling, bowed as if truly blessed.

"Now, I must leave you for a few minutes to finalise the arrangements for tomorrow, but you may speak with Lance Corporal Laurie if you wish.

If either of you have any hatred in your hearts, it must be left with those prayers to St Nicholas."

There followed an awkward moment. The guards were still present, but here was Laurie, otherwise alone and face to face with the man he'd intended to hate, yet with whom he was required by decency, if nothing else, to communicate.

He struggled, gagged by guilt and confusion. What possible words would suffice for a man who'd witnessed the brutality of Nooney's killing, whose innocence he wished to believe, but whose deeds had led to the bloodied slaughter at Pont Limoun? The very same man who'd also expressed remorse for the killing of his friend.

"You are a poet?" asked Laurie, wondering immediately why he had said something that in the circumstances felt so senselessly trite.

Oriol was taken aback, not least that his literary abilities had again been referenced.

"I try," he replied eventually.

They looked at each other. One of them would need to engage, make the effort to fill the space, fulfil the obligation required of them by the priest.

"It helps, particularly now I find myself in such unusual territory."

"And you?" he asked Laurie, who was still troubled by the crassness of the conversation he'd initiated.

"I enjoy reading it, yes," he said, after a moment's hesitation, "though writing it is beyond me."

"I doubt that," replied Oriol, "you may just need to look more closely."

Laurie's face must have betrayed a flicker of emotion. Coded language had become a way of life for him in Cairo, and this wasn't about to change. There was another uneasy pause.

"It may help you on the journey to Suez," said Laurie, awkwardly.

"And aboard the prison ship to Australia and incarceration?" asked Oriol.

It appeared an accusation rather than a question. Laurie remained silent.

"You are right," said Oriol, "there is no answer to this that can be openly explained."

There was no sign of a return of the priest, a man barely known to either but whose confidentialities had bound them both in an unspoken tryst. So Oriol pursued the theme that had befallen them.

"Art," he said, breaking the awkwardness.

"Art?"

"You have so many talents in your country. Constable, Turner," continued Oriol, "they are well known to us."

Laurie was relieved Oriol hadn't interpreted his rambling as complete stupidity. But how had such a conversation as this developed with both men marooned by the unmentioned matters of life and death?

"I know of them," he replied, "they remind me of the landscapes around my home."

"Painted by your hand?" asked Oriol, smiling gently.

"I try, but I keep the outcomes to myself."

"I used a similar approach to my poetry," said Oriol, "but then I realised there was a duty to speak what was within me."

He too paused, aware of the ridiculous context for such discourse, but unable to deny the gentle uplift to his spirit this had after a month of desperate incarceration.

"Have you an artist who inspires you?" he asked. "Maybe a particular painting?"

Laurie smiled at the question. He'd supposed he would rejoice in this man's committal, but instead found himself inspired by the way he seemed to rise above his misfortune. And yet, this conversation he'd blunderingly introduced still seemed so at odds with their circumstances. What was he to say?

"February Fill Dyke," he replied eventually, "the artist is now quite famous, but he was born near my village. He understood the land and the people he was painting; he wasn't at all sentimental; he painted it all, the good and the bad."

Oriol cheered at the thoughtful response. In a different life there would be much in common.

"I am sure it is beautiful; but the title of the painting?"

"There are ditches around the village that fill with water in the winter to protect us from the floods. But the land is still difficult to work and, on a cold evening, with a falling light, and with the trees empty of their leaves, the real hardships in life for those returning from the fields become all too clear."

"It may all sound unappealing to some," said Oriol, seeing Laurie grimace, "but to my ear it captures the reality of the life I too see daily." *How the children at Turo Vell would have enjoyed Laurie's description*, he thought.

"You must believe me," he said after a short moment, "I did not kill your friend."

Laurie braced. Forced back to the bleak reality of the moment he wanted to speak his mind, to ask the questions. But he hadn't the words and the guards hadn't the patience.

"That's it," shouted one of them, "you're wasting your time with him, mate. He's had his chances. Deserves no pity from any of us."

"Step away please, Lance Corporal," said the other, more politely, "this man is to be transported tomorrow to a place more suited for his sort. I'd ignore his fine talk if I were you."

"Needs finishing off," continued his colleague, "though slowly, if you can. Leave the bastard in the desert."

Laurie backed away, face expressionless, and turned to go. The guards' attitude had been disturbing, but so too had his own conversation with the prisoner. He left the cell room and passed through the building to the entrance, where to his surprise it was Emam who appeared to be the one doing the waiting.

"Are you done?" he inquired.

Laurie nodded, and they walked together through the barracks and across the racetrack, this time using the official and heavily guarded camp entrance, out onto Shari Ibrahim. Laurie was once more deep in thought.

"It went well?" inquired Emam.

"Challenging for us both, I expect," replied Laurie, "especially the prayers."

Emam smiled.

"What if those guards understood you? They would have noticed your deviations."

Emam turned to look at him.

"In my experience," he said, "those fine men struggle with English let alone my Latin. Nevertheless, I love them dearly."

They moved on and Laurie cheered. He was beginning to like the priest.

At the junction with Shari El Ahram they parted, Emam pointing to the nearby basilica.

"I have further business," he said, "but I shall see you tomorrow morning back at the cell. Please use the main gate," he said, "as your pass will enable your entrance… whichever one of them you choose to use, of course."

Laurie headed towards the Heliopolis Palace and the tram back into town.

"Oh, you can ride a horse, can't you?" shouted Emam.

Back in the cell, Oriol sat on his bed, eating the offerings presented for his lunchtime ingestion. His surroundings, though rigorous and with intense surveillance, were far better than those he'd endured during the weeks of incarceration at the barracks. Initially, he'd attempted to find a form of medium through which to communicate civilly with the guards, but soon gave up in the face of their hostility. He had, though, been able to monitor the moments of their least alertness, and as the guards themselves sat eating, he knew that this was one of them.

He carefully unravelled the tiny piece of paper passed to him by Emam, taking it from his palm and placing it by the side of the plate from which he was eating, partially obscuring it with a scruffy napkin.

He recognised the writing. It was from his mother, Llucia Quintana. The shock was immediate. How had this been made possible; and following the one from Bishop Paulinus? The priest had confused as well as encouraged by his first visit. But now this? Surely, there could be no duplicity given the authenticity of the message?

'Turo Vell, Es Migjorn Roc'

My beautiful Son,
Your father assures me that you will be safe, that those intermediaries around you will protect and deliver you. I pray that you have the strength to endure and to believe in that promise.
We love you and long for the day you will be back within the loving embrace of your family.
Your loving mother.

He bent close to his food so that he could clean his face with the napkin and roll the secreted letter back into a tight ball within his hand. He was also able to wipe his mouth and then, without attention, his eyes. Tears of emotion had been unpreventable, though he quickly fought to restore a composure that would not draw attention.

He'd been incarcerated and interrogated for weeks, time enough for news to reach his family perhaps, even for this message to return, but who were the 'intermediaries'?

Taqi al Din al-Bilal from Alexandria West Bay Shipping Company perhaps, but he'd not even been on hand to meet him when he finally arrived ashore from *The Adelphi*.

The priest? His Minorquin words had been as comforting as they were surprising. But what authority could he possibly carry to be so involved? He was just a priest.

And his mother? She had written 'your father', but she wasn't a religious person and would never refer to a cleric, no matter what his station, in such a way. Her life had been one of distrust of the church, she even used Sant Cristofol as a useful storehouse for the family businesses.

"You're going to cop it, you murdering fucker, you know that don't you?"

It was the less pliant of his gaolers.

"All that talk with the Pom about painting and poems. You're gonna need more than fancy words and pots of paint to protect you in the desert."

"That's enough, mate," said his gentler colleague.

"You ain't gonna make it to Suez, let alone Oz," he continued.

"Enough, mate."

"That Poms a nutter and you killed his mate. He'll put lead in your legs and leave the desert to cook you."

He smiled as he said it.

"Enough!"

This time the Sergeant had appeared, and there was an instant response.

"He's a prisoner of his majesty and, absolute shit though he is, you'll do nothing further to enlighten him with your thoughts in his remaining time with us. Do you understand?"

The guard stayed tight-lipped, anger in his eyes, though he acknowledged the instruction.

"Sergeant."

The guards returned to their positions around Oriol's cage, and the Sergeant to the office. A repressed normality returned. The weeks of turmoil, the concoction of hope and despair had taken their toll. He lay down on his bed, enfeebled by exhaustion and an overwhelming hopelessness, unable to care about the morrow. It was no longer mattered that he knew it was to be his last.

CHAPTER 13

Laurie awoke just before sunrise, though his gloomy basement room at The Grand Continental remained consistently timeless. As he made his way through the hotel foyer and out into Opera Square, the cool chill of the early morning and a piercingly low sunlight announced the new day. He felt physically well now and surprised by the inner calm recrudescing through his veins. He longed for home. Yet the greater yearning was to right the injustice of Nooney's loss: the next few days would be critical.

Following his meeting with Emam in Heliopolis, he'd returned to town and visited the army store within the bowels of The Savoy. The essentials for his forthcoming desert journey had already been assigned and were laid out on a table before him: a light scarf to protect the neck and head from the sun and wind-blown sand, a grey cotton shirt, khaki shorts, knee-length socks and boots. A long woollen overcoat was hanging from a rail nearby.

"You'll need that," he was told, firmly, "otherwise you'll freeze during the night."

In a back pack at the end of the table was a flimsy rolled up ground sheet and two water bottles, across which had been rested a bayonet knife and a Lee Enfield 303 rifle. This time, though, there was to be none of the previous folly; he was handed a body belt with five fully-laden cartridge leather pouches, which were to be strapped over his left shoulder and diagonally across his chest and abdomen.

How Nooney would have laughed.

"No no. Don't let him use it," he would have pleaded, "he couldn't hit a camel at ten yards."

So he looked quite the fighting man as he made his way around the corner to Shari Imad El Din, jumping aboard the first tram of the morning to Midan Bab El Hadid. Once in the square he hopped off and dashed across to the Heliopolis line that ran directly from Pont Limoun. On this day, there was to be no room for sentimentality. He caught onto the open rear of the last car as the tram departed, brandishing his Cairo and Electric Railways and Heliopolis Oases pass at the conductor, who ignored him completely.

For reasons he couldn't fathom, he felt triumphant, even though little had been achieved. But he felt back in control, and well in advance of the 7 am rendezvous at the Australian Barracks.

For ten minutes or so he relaxed, and given the desert crossing that lay ahead, enjoying what was likely to be the last of any fresh breeze for some days. But just as they were gaining speed passing through the Ghamra district and with Heliopolis and the camp no more than a few miles away, the tram shuddered to an emergency halt. Some of the passengers were thrown from their seats but quickly regained themselves, and for a brief few moments the mostly unbruised remained politely seated, observing the pleasantly grassed gardens of the nearby Girls' College and the views beyond to the new city. Then, word came down the tram from the driver that seemed to greatly agitate.

"Bloody British Army," shouted a plum English accent attached to a briefcase, "doing their damned manoeuvres across the farmland and the waterway. Why, as if the Turks are going to paddle along that in broad daylight, unannounced?"

And sure enough, as Laurie and the passengers strained their eyes towards the Ismailia canal to the north, men on horseback and armoured vans could be seen rushing to take positions along the dyke, leaving nothing to chance as they prepared for the forthcoming push into Palestine.

What they hadn't accounted for was the newly rebellious tram brigade, mostly local, but with a sprinkling of European volunteers, who vehemently objected to their journey being halted. In no time, those most able were down off the tram and formed an inchoate charge towards the British troop lines still crossing the track, fifty yards away. Whoever had planned this early morning exercise for less than grateful soldiers had significantly underestimated both the reliability of the Cairo Tram timetable and the passion of its clients.

As they charged, the British forces parted, more in amazement than confusion, yielding ground to the howling group and its prominent briefcased Englishman. Keen to take advantage of their position, the raiders waved furiously back towards the tram driver to follow up their advance. After some hesitation, and with the encouragement of abusive advice from those aboard, he engaged forward traction and nudged cautiously towards and then onward through the British lines.

Rout accomplished, the triumphant marauders scrambled back aboard to rapturous cheers, accompanied for good measure by generous hand gestures and Arabic profanity towards the bemused troops.

The English accent and his briefcase stood up and graciously bowed to his carriage, acknowledging their plaudits for his treacherous yet successful role in the action.

"What bloody idiot could have organised that without consulting the Tram people?" he shouted across to Laurie, "God help us if he's put in charge of anything serious."

Just then, the stony-white bespectacled face of Major Fogge appeared on the track in the disappearing distance, as the tram gathered speed once more. Laurie shrank into his seat to avoid any chance of recognition. This wasn't the time.

The unannounced interruption, distracting though it was, had pushed Laurie for time. When the tram eventually pulled into Heliopolis, he leapt off just before Luna Park and ran hard along Shari Abd El Munim, sweating under the weight of his kit and the beat of the early sun. He passed the casino, slowing to a more dignified pace as the entrance gates to the camp appeared. He presented his pass at the guard house and was

The Poet Laurie Ate

allowed straight in, just as Emam had said. Not only was he known, he was also expected.

"Do your job, Lance Corporal," said the soldier who checked him through, "he deserves everything he's going to get."

Two or three others looked his way and nodded their support. Nooney really was a popular man, even with the Aussies. The prisoner, on the other hand, was dead meat.

As he approached the headquarters building there was already a gathering of men and horses. Four soldiers were mounted and clearly ready for the journey. Between them was Oriol, a forlorn-looking figure compared to the previous day, hunched over his mount, holding the reins but manacled by the wrists to two of the men either side of him. Standing and talking to two Arab guides and next to the pack-mules was the priest, but before Laurie could speak, he heard another familiar voice.

"What time do you call this, Laurie?"

Sergeant Wirrall was alert as ever and on his case.

"Ten minutes to seven, Laurie, ten minutes to seven. You're late again."

Emam turned around and greeted Laurie with a cheerful grin. He was already enjoying Wirrall's sense of purpose.

Though temporarily thrown by the Sergeant's presence, Laurie stuttered to protest his innocence: after all, he was still on time. But there was more to follow.

"Don't you try it, Laurie. I've heard all the excuses I ever want to hear from you."

"Yes, Sergeant," replied Laurie, surprised yet strangely comforted by the appearance of a man who'd helped in his inimitable way, and whom he hadn't seen since Nooney's death.

He knew that Wirrall wouldn't waste energy on small talk.

"In case you're wondering, think of me as Major Fogge's man on the spot. He asked me to keep an eye on you: and for what it's worth, I don't blame him."

So much for sentiment, thought Laurie.

"He also told me, of course, not to mention any of that to you, so I bloody well won't. Do you understand Laurie?" Indeed he did.

Emam coughed.

"Gentlemen, if we may?" He signalled to them both to mount.

Laurie had undertaken basic training with the mounted arm of the Military Police in Cairo, in case of eventualities, so knew how to perform this efficiently. Wirrall on the other hand, had never sought to trust any form of transport he couldn't walk around once aboard, and so it was left to the priest and one of the guides to slide his foot into a stirrup and heave his stout body onto the saddle. The rest of the party held back from laughter, but he was very aware of what they were thinking.

"I know you bloody lot are smirking all over your faces, but just be glad you're here watching an old soldier, rather than in the trenches."

There was little malice in his voice though and they, in turn, knew of his valour on the Western Front; if anything, their respect for the man grew.

So this unlikely party containing the prisoner, four guards, two local guides, the priest, Wirrall and Laurie, shuffled off through the camp, out through the main gates, and on into Heliopolis.

They crossed onto the wide boulevard of Shari El Ahram passing by the front of the basilica, and then turned south-eastward, beyond the splendour of the Sultan's Palace and into the desert fringe.

For the best part of an hour they trotted gently, cautious of Sergeant Wirrall's equine inexperience, following what looked like a disused tramway. Eventually, they came to an isolated but working Tram Depot, warily crossing over the many rail junctions that brought traffic to this outpost.

Just beyond, Emam called a halt. Wirrall's horse, though, hadn't been so instructed and brushed into one of the guards.

"Whoah steady, Sarge," he shouted, and Wirrall waved an apology.

Emam mouthed some instructions to the guides and then turned to the party.

"Ahead of us is the old Indian Mailroad," he said, pointing to the hard-based ballasted sandstone route stretching into the far distance.

"Built by the British to connect them with the Red Sea before the Canal to Suez was completed. Today, it still serves a similar purpose, though of course," and he patted his horse, "we must trust to the four legs below us, not wheels."

Emam knew the soldiers were experienced and reliable, and the guides completely dependable. But here, no more than a short way into their task, he was already concerned for the safety of Wirrall, Laurie and the prisoner. All three would be liabilities in this environment.

"You must drink from your first bottle," he instructed. "Enjoy, as the water is only gently warm."

They did as bade, grateful for the chance, though it crossed both Laurie and Wirrall's minds as to how long these supplies would last. Emam had assured them all before they set out that they would have enough water to get to Suez, though he had added that, "by then it will taste disgusting."

It was already very hot, and after only a few moments in their stationary position the flies began to gather about them and their animals.

"Remember," continued Emam, "as we move on, we must stay close. The wind from now on will start to pick up the sand. It is easy to become blinded, so I shall tell you when we need to tie-up to each other. We will be following the Mailroad but do not be deceived by the calm of what you presently see; any of you lost in such conditions and at any time beyond this point, should consider themselves already dead."

"Blood hell," grunted Wirrall, below his breath.

"Your rifles will save your lives should we be threatened…"

By whom, thought Laurie? Most of the local tribes were supportive, or so Colonel Lowthian had intimated. And surely the enemy wasn't probing so close to Cairo?

"…so keep them protected from the sand. Place them within your saddle holster or covered below your clothing. Always."

Wirrall nodded affirmatively, and even the guards seemed assured, having at first had serious misgivings about a priest guiding the party.

Emam could see that further detail might help Laurie and Wirrall.

"There are water towers along the route that once fed the railway. They are still filled regularly by the British in case of future need, though there is no guarantee they have done this recently. And of course, our local friends who use this route for their flocks may have occasionally borrowed some of those supplies for their goats. Needs must in a war."

He smiled.

"We shall stop at each one if water is available and take advantage of it ourselves. If, however, it's foul, we shall need to manage with what we've got."

With that, he turned his horse and led off, continuing with further shouted instructions as he did so. These weren't obvious to some of the group.

"What did he say at the end? I didn't catch all of that," said Sergeant Wirrall, now taking advantage of his unintentional alignment alongside Laurie's horse.

"He said it's just during the cool of the morning and the night that they are at their most dangerous," replied Laurie.

"Dangerous? What's he on about, dangerous?"

Wirrall's focus momentarily shifted from the worrying instability of his means of carriage.

"Snakes and scorpions," replied Laurie, to Wirrall's obvious alarm.

"Poisonous?"

"Apparently," said Laurie.

"If it moves and it's bigger than your hand, its bite will kill you for sure, apparently."

The Sergeant shuddered. This wasn't his natural terrain.

For a couple of hours they continued with their gentle progress, though an intense sun had soon meant the need to cover themselves against the burn with scarves and coats. Nothing, though, could prevent the combined discomfort of sweat wherever clothing touched skin, and the invasive effect of sand. And there was the harsh dryness that began to roughen the tongue and crack the lips.

Wirrall, on the other hand, seemed more challenged by his posterior.

"I'm sure my arse is seizing up," he shouted to Laurie, "if that saddle of yours is better than mine I'm 'aving it when we stop."

Laurie looked enviously ahead at Emam and the Arab guides. Their loose robes and head scarves were all perfectly attuned to the conditions,

The Poet Laurie Ate

and they were such natural horsemen. Despite Emam's warnings, they were some way ahead, whilst he and the Australian guards were hung at the back, shepherding Sergeant Wirrall.

As for the prisoner, he'd remained in the same hunched position since the journey commenced, handcuffed, tethered to his escort, yet otherwise ignored. He was little more than a commodity to be dispatched.

It was time.

Wirrall had attached himself to Laurie's horse by a line. So he undid the tie, passed the rope to the Aussie soldier at the rear and kicked on up, drawing next to the guards flanking Oriol.

"How ya doin', Lance-Corp?" asked the friendly voice, in an accent he immediately recognised.

"New Zealander, hey?"

"Proud but poor," replied the soldier with a friendly smile. "There's two of us on this patrol, most folks think we're Aussies, so we usually just keep quiet about our superiority." They both laughed.

"Good to speak to you at last, mate," he continued, "decent to meet the bloke who tried to help Nooney."

Laurie was beginning to understand the closeness amongst the New Zealand troops and their familiarity with Nooney's demise. It would, he hoped, make the task ahead easier.

"There's still unfinished business to sort," replied Laurie.

"Did this bastard go for you as well then?" asked the guard.

Laurie nodded.

"Nooney bought it. Should have been me."

Oriol stirred from his distant world. He was hearing a very different Laurie from the one he'd met in his cage the previous day.

"Oh, will you just look at that," said the guard on the other flank scornfully, "he's alive after all."

"You two from the same place?" asked Laurie.

"You're right there, Nooney's patch, just outside Auckland. Private Bestic, by the way, attached to the 3rd Light Horse."

"So you're from Onehunga?"

"Blimey, mate, you know your stuff," said Bestic.

"I had a good teacher; Nooney told me all about his life, even said he'd help get me a job there after the war if I was brave enough to try it."

"Be proud to have you, mate," replied Bestic, "and by the way," he said, and nodded across to the other guard flanking Oriol, "he's Private Halbert. Much shyer than me but a born killer." The New Zealander's and Laurie laughed.

"Give me just a moment alone with this bloke, I say," said Bestic.

Oriol lifted his head slightly, his eyes open just enough to see across to Laurie. The priest's Menorquin words from the previous day were still ringing in his ears. But this dialogue was alarmingly at odds with the comfort they had given.

"Well, that might be arranged," said Laurie.

Bestic grinned.

Then, just as suddenly, his face blanked. Laurie, it seemed, was entirely serious.

"You reckon?" he asked, needing to check.

"Well, why waste all this effort to Suez?"

Halbert started to shift nervously in his saddle.

"You could be right," replied Bestic, now less confident, and beginning to regret the conversation he'd opened.

"After all," continued Laurie, "he's just a dead weight. Whatever any of his glories were, they're long gone."

He leant across and shoved Oriol, who shirked to one side, gripping the horse's neck.

"Just look at him. He's pathetic."

"Yeah, you're right there, mate. Probably wishes he wasn't so handy with that gun now, hey," said Bestic, unsure as to how to lighten the conversation.

"I didn't kill the man," whispered Oriol.

"Blimey, he can speak," said Bestic, "shall I give him a biff in the mouth, mate, so we can carry on our chat?"

"I have never shot anyone," continued Oriol in a barely audible whisper.

"Well, will you just listen to that," said Bestic, "and we all believe him don't we?"

The Poet Laurie Ate

He spat with some force over the prisoner. Most of the phlegm landed on the horse, but a sizeable amount stuck across the Spaniard's shoulder and neck. Within moments the area began to crawl with airborne life.

"I've heard he's a poet," said Halbert attempting distraction, worried by the way things were headed.

"Oh, so he's a word turd is he?" howled Bestic. "I've heard it all now."

"I want you both to know that I'm going to take good care of him," said Laurie, "very good care indeed. So much care in fact that he won't need to concern himself about his life in Australia, or even the need to make it to Suez."

The two New Zealanders exchanged worried glances, and Bestic appeared momentarily perplexed.

"What, you mean you're going to—"

"Nothing to worry about," cut in Laurie.

Halbert, the more sensitive and attuned of the two guards knew exactly what Laurie was inferring. But his colleague was less cognisant.

"You're going to sort it?" he said, eyes now squinting in alarm, "you mean you're really going to finish him…"

Laurie raised his hand to shut the New Zealander up, and put a finger to his lips.

"As I said, there's nothing for you to get agitated about."

Bestic's earlier bombast had now deserted him. As much as he hated the prisoner. all he could see was his own time in the slammer.

"Maybe, come to think about it, you should take a step back, mate, let it fester for a while."

Laurie frowned, a look of rage creasing his face. Then, just as suddenly, he burst into a smile, freaking out Bestic who pulled back accidentally on the reins causing his horse to buck.

"All I'm saying is," said Laurie, as things settled, "be gentle with this man. Make sure he doesn't go all soliloquy on you… and I'll do the rest."

He pulled back to rejoin Wirrall, leaving the two New Zealanders alone with the prisoner and their increasing state of astonishment.

"What you prattling on about up there, Laurie?"

"Just checking they're dealing properly with the prisoner, Sergeant."

"Watch your step with those two," he said, "they have axes to grind they do, I can smell it. We've to make sure the spy gets to Suez in one piece, and that's what we'll do."

"Yes, Sergeant."

"And don't forget, I'm definitely avin' your saddle when we stop."

It was another hour before the Sergeant had his wish. They'd halted sometime earlier at the Basta El Shlhîb water tower. But it had been empty of all but the most fetid supply. Even the donkeys had rejected it. So Emam had decided to push on to the next at Basta El Dihier, and here their luck, of sorts, was in.

"Ten minutes," he'd instructed.

The two Australian guards set about climbing the weather-riddled ladder straddled between the tower's corroded metal legs. They unhooked the worn leather piping from the elevated tank before carefully guiding it down to the hollow beside the track. The water was both hot and odorous, but palatably so, and as the trickle began to flow from the pipe into the newly appearing yet modest oasis, the animals surged forward to gain a prime spot. So much so that it took some restraint from their mounts to establish control, as well as avoid Wirrall's onrushing horse.

"Damn this beast," he shouted, "I'm 'aving your horse as well, Laurie, do you hear me?"

The party took advantage of the brief respite to dismount, quench their thirsts and ablute, though Sergeant Wirrall could hardly walk let alone squat. Needs completed, they were about to get back to the horses when an alarm was raised by a guide. He'd climbed to a rock promontory high above the track to scout the horizon, and was frantically gesturing back to them with his arms.

"We must move," said Emam, with an urgency that suggested trouble.

They quickly remounted, even Wirrall, and moved off towards a bend in the Mailroad less than a mile ahead. There, protected from view by the valley side, they pulled up again.

Emam instructed a guide and one of the Aussies to accompany him back on foot, and crouching as low as possible, they edged slowly towards a vantage point just below a gentle crest in the track. After crawling the last few yards, they lay completely still for several minutes, binoculars trained on something beyond the rise.

"We have company," said Emam, once they'd scuttled back to the group.

"Company?" asked Wirrall.

"Bedouin. Maybe an hour away from us at the most, as many as ten of them, and a lot of goats."

"Friendlies?"

"Possibly," replied Emam, "but we cannot afford that risk."

"We've got a valuable cargo with us, Sarge" clarified the Aussie. "We can't stop to find out whose side that lot are on."

"But they've got goats," said Wirrall, "they're hardly likely to storm after us."

"That's correct," hissed Emam, irritated for once, "but even four of those men deciding we are of interest would be a problem. After all, we are not all as expert as they in these conditions." He fixed Wirrall square in the face.

"You have a recommendation, then?" replied Wirrall, aware of the mild rebuke but completely unconcerned by it.

"It will be some time before they reach the water tower. They will stop and water the goats. By then we can be well beyond their sightline along the Mailroad."

"But they would still catch up with us if they desired," replied Wirrall.

"Not if we deviate from our route."

There was a moment's hesitancy. Convinced though the group were of Emam's abilities, they'd become accustomed to the straightness and relative safety of the track, and its attendant promise of water. The notion of detouring meant uncharted desert and a terrain of which they were less confident.

"In a few miles," continued Emam, "there is a route south-east, towards the Ugret El Naga' hills. I know it well. It will enable us to join up with the Mailroad closer to Suez and is unsuitable for a party of goat herders. If we take it, we shall soon know whether they are following the route to market... or us."

"And what if it's the latter?" Wirrall needed the detail.

"We shall have the higher ground, the advantage."

"We shall also be stuck in the open with the night drawing in," replied Wirrall.

"The land towards the hills will give us the shelter we need. Tomorrow, all being well, we shall be back on the Mailroad and only slightly delayed."

"Won't those Bedouin know from our tracks what we're up to?"

"If they've no interest in us they'll be glad we're out of their way. We also have expert help to hide our tracks," he said, and pointed to the two Arabs.

Sergeant Wirrall was notionally the senior man of the party, though savvy enough to recognise both his inexperience in desert fighting and the limitations caused by the throb in his lumber area. So he wasn't in any way minded to dismiss the information he'd been given.

But to Laurie's great surprise, he asked for his opinion.

"The priest knows this terrain like the back of his hand," he confirmed.

Wirrall paused for a moment. It was quite clear to everyone by now who was really in charge; the priest had earned their respect. Wirrall, above all else, was a realist. The option presented had seemed reasonable, and he nodded his consent.

He also made a mental note to start compass bearings from the point at which they departed from their route. After all, he was an old soldier.

"We must therefore proceed with some speed," said Emam, and whilst the subsequent trot seemed to Wirrall like a wild gallop, to those guarding Oriol it was far too sluggish.

"Can we go a bit quicker?" shouted Bestic, concerned by the increasing jeopardy. "Even my horse is getting the shakes."

"It's the old Sarge," whispered Halbert.

"Or this bag of deadwood," said Bestic, pointing to the hunched prisoner, "he'll cause us all to get killed."

Oriol had refused water at the halt, and this, the gallop, and an increasing familiarity with his fate meant his head felt tightly constricted, throbbing sharply, as if knifed through.

"I did not kill that man," he mumbled. Whatever lay ahead, he needed to be true to himself.

"He's off again," said Bestic.

"I live in love," whispered Oriol.

Bestic's sensitivities couldn't cope with the receipt of such unsolicited wisdom. He grabbed Oriol hard by the neck, his nails drawing blood, and shoved him forcibly across towards Halbert, whose horse reared. The commotion caused Wirrall to momentarily forget his concerns.

"Oi, you two," he shouted forward, and the party came to a stop.

"Pack it in now or you're on a charge. Do you understand?"

Bestic was still seething, though Halbert, shocked by the potential his mate had caused for injury to himself let alone the prisoner, quickly concurred.

"Bestic?" shouted Wirrall again, though this time with venom.

"Yes, Sarge," he replied eventually, though unwilling to show appeasement in front of a convict who'd murdered his fellow countryman.

The party moved on again, but this was another unsettling moment. Wirrall was an experienced soldier. He'd survived two horrific years of warfare before transferring to Egypt; his guidance and common sense had saved many lives. The key, he'd always told his men, was to minimise the imponderables. He began to sense, though, that on this journey such ambition would become increasingly challenged.

After a nervous and seemingly over lengthy time, they eventually turned off the Mailroad and onto broken ground. The pace slowed. The Arab guides had stayed behind to disguise the group's tracks before heading off into the desert in an opposite direction. Distraction achieved, they would join the party later in the day. Not for them the concern about geography. This was their terrain. Re-locating the group would be no more difficult for them than for Laurie finding his way home from Worcester.

The Wadi they'd entered was dry as a bone, though the rounded stones over which they rode and the steep-sided red sandstone of the valley pointed to the torrent that could occur here during extraordinary rains. But the occasional Acacia Tree, listing like a winded camel, and the scattered greenery peeping from behind boulders, pointed to the infrequency of any such deluge.

As they climbed, the Wadi narrowed, and the gloom from the unrelenting hours of riding and concern for their safety slowly gave way to more optimistic buoyancy. The fractured red walls continued to constrict, providing shade and shelter from the sun and wind. Even the water left in their bottles seemed to cool a little. At each rest stop, confidence grew. A consensus developed that they weren't being followed. Even Sergeant Wirrall began to relax, bolstered by the ability he'd now accomplished to independently enable forward motion in his steer. Stopping the beast, though, was still another matter.

It was late afternoon by the time Emam brought the party to a halt. The temperature was falling quickly. He pointed to a line of caves along the escarpment ahead of them.

"Our base for the night."

They dismounted, and led their horses carefully around the boulders and across the rough scree that lay between them, food and rest.

The animals were tethered in the smaller of the caves, whilst the party settled in the one immediately beside it. There were the remains of fires across the floor, and ledges had been hewn out of the natural curves of the interior by centuries of visitors. Sleeping arrangements would therefore be more amenable than they'd feared, given such a foreboding environment. And the cave felt remarkably warm compared to the outside.

"Sandstone," said Emam, "retains the heat. Such places are valuable."

"Almost as if you have been here before," countered Wirrall.

They began to settle in for the night. A fire, built from the dry brushwood carried on the donkey's backs, was soon roaring away. Halbert led Oriol to his sleeping quarter on a ledge at the back of the cave, and attached his handcuffs to a chain. This, in turn, was wrapped and locked around one of the several floor-to-roof sandstone pillars. He offered some food, but Oriol refused it. He did, though, consume the contents of a full water bottle.

The two Australians took first watch, with Sergeant Wirrall for company. Halbert set up guard near to Oriol, and Emam climbed further above their cave position to take advantage, so he said, of a moment's solitude. Bestic and Laurie, on the other hand, scouted around in the valley just below their position for additional material that might complement the store for the fire.

"I'm going to finish him," said Laurie quite suddenly, as he hacked at the browning remnants of a large Desert Thorn bush. Bestic was alarmed. He'd tried to bury the irrational encounter with Laurie earlier in the day, hoping that the delirium of that moment had passed.

He attempted distraction.

"It's not dead, you know," he said.

"Just leave things to me," replied Laurie.

"The bush, mate, I'm on about the bush. It looks dead but it ain't."

Laurie simply stared at him. Bestic tried again.

"Full of leaves it'll be if it ever rains again. But for now, though, I grant you, it looks as if it's carked it."

"Carked it?"

"Dead, mate. But the thing is, really, it's just lurking."

"Well, the prisoner will be fully carked by the morning, Bestic."

The New Zealander hesitated, and Laurie continued.

"You said yourself, a moment alone with him is all it would take."

"Love to, mate. But there's the legalities of it."

"Not if he tried to leg it," replied Laurie.

"Hardly likely," said Bestic, "given the length of chain around him."

"There's ways. Just needs you to keep out of things."

Bestic hadn't bargained for any of this. Bluster apart, he'd never threatened more than the odd thump to anyone since arriving in Egypt, let alone agreed to be party to a killing.

"Can you do that, Bestic?"

"What?"

"Keep out of the way?"

"But it's not legal… and what's more, it ain't even right."

"Well, shall I make it easier for you?"

Bestic froze, fearing Laurie was going to threaten him.

"Now, hang on a minute, mate."

"I'll make it an order then."

"But none of this feels right to me now, Lance Corp."

"You said earlier, Bestic, what a waste of time it was to move this bloke to Suez. I knew what you meant."

"Yes, but I didn't mean…"

"What? What didn't you mean?"

"All of this… you telling me you're going to do him in?"

"You don't know that though, do you?"

"What?"

"You don't know what I'm going to do… you're just imagining things, but you don't really know."

"It looks bad to me though, whatever it is…"

How Bestic hated himself, his mouth, his boasting… what had he done to bring on this insanity?

"You said order… well if that's an order," he mouthed, trailing off, "… it's just…"

"Go on."

"…I know about the penalties for doing harm, especially if I'm the guard."

"They're the same as disobeying a lawful command," replied Laurie, "and that's what you'll be doing if you get in the way. And anyway, you won't be the guard, I'll see to that. All you have to do is keep out of my way and your mouth shut."

By now Bestic was desperate. He searched for words.

"Our orders, Lance Corp, are to get the prisoner to Suez."

"And until then they will be to use all means necessary to restrain him, should he try to escape," replied Laurie, "but because you'll neither be on duty nor awake when that happens, there'll be nothing to concern yourself with."

Laurie pushed his face closer to Bestic.

"As I said." There was menace in his eyes. "By morning the prisoner will be as completely carked as a person can possibly get. Is that clear enough for you?"

Bestic backed away, convinced now that he was in danger.

"Of course… yes, of course, I get it. An order. That's it then… whatever you say. He's a murdering shit anyway, so why should I worry?"

"That's very good, Bestic, wasn't that hard after all, was it?"

"No, Lance Corp… of course not. Let's get back to the rest, shall we, get the fire going a bit, keep warm?" Laurie, the man he'd so admired for trying to save his fellow countryman, was in fact completely mad.

Just then, two horsemen appeared, so close that they shouldn't have been missed.

"Jeez," shouted Bestic in shock, as he went for his rifle.

"Stop," commanded Laurie, "it's fine."

The Arab guides had made it back from their distraction duties with the Bedouin and they laughed loudly, cheered that they'd caught the men by surprise. They continued onward to the cave, and Bestic, spooked by the whole experience, quickly gathered the kindling and scrabbled up the slope after them.

Laurie, though, stood a while before returning, watching the sun disappear below the dimmed flicker of a very distant Cairo. Beyond the city, thousands of miles away, was home, his wife, his family. And at the other end of the earth, in Onehunga, was a family whose son would not be returning.

This was the right thing to do.

Later that night, after they'd all eaten and the first watch arrangement made, Emam moved to the back of the cave to sit next to the prisoner. Halbert had temporarily left Oriol's side to eat and was still by the fire trying to talk some sense into Bestic. No one seemed to pay him much attention, and anyway, Emam was a priest; it was natural that he'd wish to speak with a condemned man.

But Laurie, sat in a corner and apart from the others, noticed everything; the priest's body language, how he convinced Oriol to eat, to take more water, and most of all the prayers. They were of a style he'd heard previously between the two, beginning quite normally, probably in Latin, but then developing into a rhythm of language that defied recognition. Yet clearly they spoke of something, as for the first time on the journey the prisoner seemed engaged, attentive even.

Once Emam had finished his ministry, he returned to the cave opening to take in some cool air and Laurie moved across to him.

"How is our spy?" he asked quietly.

"A little better now," replied Emam, "he has at least been fed and watered."

"As have the horses."

The priest didn't take kindly to Laurie's analogy, though guessed no criticism was implied.

"And our followers?" inquired Laurie.

"Near enough." Emam smiled.

"Yourself?" continued Emam. "Is this the closest you will come to asking for confession tonight?"

Laurie was about to respond when one of the Australians piped up.

"Sarge, do we keep the fire going or not?"

Wirrall looked across towards Emam. Fire etiquette in the desert wasn't his strong point.

"Better we do," replied the priest, breaking away from his conversation, "it will keep away the creatures we do not wish to share our sleep with."

"But what about those Bedouin, won't they spot us?" persisted the Aussie.

"They are still on the Mailroad," replied Emam, indicating towards the Arab guides, "our friends saw to that."

Reassured by what he'd heard, Sergeant Wirrall went through the watch arrangements for the night. The Arab guides were to be excused; they'd done their bit. Bestic and Halbert would take the next shift once the Aussies had been stood down.

"Lance Corporal Laurie, you'll then take over at two and I'll keep you company."

"No need for that, Sergeant," interrupted Emam before Laurie could speak, "I'm awake then for prayer, so I'll sit with Laurie and keep him company. Perhaps you could follow on, see us into the dawn?"

Normally Wirrall would have overridden the suggestion. But his day's exertions meant he could hardly stand let alone remain alert, and the others knew he was owed.

"Alright then," he replied, "but make sure you kick me well in time, mind you."

With that, the party quietened, and all, apart from the watch, settled down to rest. Despite the hardness of the floor and the concerns of the day, most soon slipped into deep slumber. Laurie, though, found this impossible. His mind was too exercised by what lay ahead.

Half an hour before his watch, Laurie elbowed himself up from his bed roll, and sat for a while, silent, staring across at Oriol. The prisoner was still hunched and motionless against the back wall of the cave. To the Aussie guards on watch and in the low light thrown by the flickering embers, there was something uncomfortable about Laurie's expression, though neither thought to say anything.

After a while, he stood, slinging his rifle over his shoulder, and moved to their position. Apart from the grunting of Sergeant Wirrall, the odd snort from the horses, and the gentle whisper of a desert breeze, there was complete silence.

"You get off to sleep," he said to the men, keeping his voice low, "I'll take it from here."

"You sure?" they asked, "you're supposed to be sharing with the priest but he's outside somewhere, god knows why. You shouldn't do this on your own."

"I shall soon be joined by him," he assured, and in truth they needed little encouragement.

Within a short while they too were asleep, and once he was as certain as he could be of their genuine repose, he picked his way through the men, across to the prisoner. Halbert, who had taken it upon himself to guard the spy, had turned over onto his side, his face away from Oriol. He was breathing quietly and in the semi-darkness appeared to be in a deep sleep.

With no time to hesitate, Laurie removed the rifle from his shoulder and placed the barrel firmly against the spy's temple. He'd expected alarm, but Oriol was awake and prepared.

Laurie placed a finger in front of his mouth, then slowly lifted the rifle away from Oriol's head. He took a key from his coat pocket and held it out, nodding towards the cuffed hand that attached Oriol to the chain restraints. Slowly, the prisoner eased himself upward into a sitting position. Despite the trepidation, he took hold of the key with his free hand, and placed it as carefully as he could in the cuff lock that attached his shackled hand to the chain.

The clasp opened with a distinct thud. For a moment, both men froze. But the deprivations of the day had triumphed. Even the Arab guides remained sound asleep. Assured they remained undetected, Laurie helped Oriol inch slowly to his feet, the rifle now against his body, and in this ungainly union they wove their way silently across the cave and out into the night.

The first few steps were cautious, with the darkness and scree combining to increase their peril. But there was a decent moon, and they began to adjust, becoming more sure-footed, Oriol led the way, firmly directed from behind by the rifle still pressed in his back. When they reached the gully where earlier Laurie had harvested the Thornbush, they stopped.

"Right on time," said a voice, a few yards ahead of them, clothed inside a heavy-duty but barely visible shift.

"I was beginning to feel the chill."

It was Emam. He lit a cigarette, inhaling deeply, as if he was on a street corner in Cairo.

"What did you expect?" replied Laurie.

"Well, perhaps a bit more respect for our prisoner?"

He nodded towards the rifle, but Laurie ignored him.

"You made your way out much more easily."

"As I told everyone," replied Emam, "I would be engaged in prayer. You should try it."

By now Oriol's confusion had deepened, and it showed.

"Come, let's move on," he continued, "our charge will benefit from more certainty."

Laurie hesitated for a moment, briefly conflicted by the potential calamity that lay ahead.

"Are you ready?" The priest was becoming impatient.

"OK," replied Laurie, "yes, let's move."

"Is that an order?" asked Emam, and Laurie grinned.

"That would be futile given your higher power… however, I have the means." He nodded to the rifle.

"That is so," said Emam, "though I doubt it would do you much good."

They walked on, observing complete silence, slowly picking their way down the valley and in the general direction of the Mailroad. Initially, Oriol was able to move unassisted, but the limitations of his physical condition eventually started to tell.

"We are not that far now," said Emam. "You must keep going."

Far from what? thought Oriol. In his exhaustion and bewilderment, he had lost all care.

The valley began to widen, and in the strengthening moonlight they could pick out the outline of a gentle ridge just ahead of them. Emam stopped.

"Is this the place you agreed?" asked Laurie.

"Indeed so," said Emam.

"And beyond that ridge?"

"Freedom."

The three men stared at each other for a moment. Then Laurie broke the silence.

"And you?" He looked directly at the spy. "Are you ready?"

Oriol felt surprised he'd been asked. He was numb, save for the deepest confusion and fear.

"It's not much of a slope," Laurie assured.

Emam held his arm out towards the spy, signalling for him to follow, and he shuffled awkwardly forward. What other option was there? As he did so, he became aware that Laurie seemed to be staying back.

"Are you sure you will be able to do all of this, Laurie?" asked the priest, his voice now raised.

"I am," he said, "and you; are you certain about Quintana?" Oriol turned, amazed that his name had been used.

Emam nodded affirmatively.

"I hope very much that your worries will soon be over," said Laurie, sensing the spy's distress.

The words were clearly felt. Oriol began to sink to his knees, but

Emam wrestled with his weight and dragged him back up towards the slope.

"Please," urged Emam, "we must go. There will be no more falls on this night."

"He's right," encouraged Laurie, pointing to the ridge, "that's the last bit of up."

The priest nodded and waved, strengthening his grip on Oriol's arm, and they began to climb.

Laurie watched them for a moment as they turned, shuffling slowly together up the slope like an old married couple, the priest a cigarette-smoking man of God, and the spy, a misread poet.

Both men embraced goodness and love. So too had Nooney. It had taken a war to find them.

Just before they reached the crest, he pulled the rifle from his shoulder. The magazine was already full, so he pushed the bolt action into place and took aim. An explosive punch rang out as the bullet discharged. He automatically chambered a new round, quickly rotated the bolt handle, and released a second bullet.

Both shots would have been heard from miles away. There were just a few hours of darkness left and there was much to do. He secured the rifle and set his mind to the task of building a fire.

Back in the cave there was utter pandemonium. Sergeant Wirrall was raging like an unhinged bull.

"Where's the damn prisoner?"

"He was over there when we handed over the watch to Laurie," said one of the Aussies, eyes convulsed.

"What do you mean 'handed over to Laurie'? Where was the priest?"

"Well, I thought he was asleep."

"What? You halfwit. What do you mean 'thought'?"

"It was dark, Sarge," said the other.

"Of course it was, you fool; that's why you were on guard."

"But he said we should stand down," said the other, "that the priest would be joining him. Get some sleep, he said."

Wirrall felt he might actually be about to do some harm.

"Get some sleep', did you say, 'get some sleep'? You stupid pair of morons, if we get out of this, you're going to have more than enough time for that inside a jail. Do you hear me?"

They were too terrified to respond. They'd been followed by the Bedouin, there were shots in the night, and now this. It was all too much.

"Bestic," shouted Wirrall, trying to prioritise some logic over the madness that was engulfing them, "did you or your mate see anything?"

"No, Sergeant," replied the New Zealander.

"Was the prisoner still locked up?"

"Yes, Sergeant and I think the priest was sleeping near him, sound as babies they were."

"You think? Oh my lord," shouted Wirrall in desperation. "Why now? All these years, the trenches, the gas; survived it all only to be stuck up a cliff in the middle of the bloody desert with you lot."

He caught the eyes of the Arab guides and for a brief moment felt grateful they'd at least know what had happened. But his hope quickly evaporated as the fear and distrust in their faces became apparent. They spoke little English and his grasp of Arabic was negligible. More to the point, they too, seemed terrified. They weren't accustomed to such disorder from the British.

"How many shots?" he asked, trying to stay calm. The soldiers looked at each other.

"At least two," said Halbert.

"Four or five, I reckon," said one of the Aussies. Millard rolled his eyes.

"Where from?"

The group looked at each other.

"Where from?" he shouted again. "Above us, below us, the north-west?"

There was some hesitation.

"For pity's sake," yelled Wirrall, "where from?"

"Sounded close," stuttered Bestic.

"Reckon so," whispered Halbert.

The two Aussies shrugged; the Arabs hadn't understood.

Sergeant Wirrall rubbed desperately at his forehead, as if trying to extract some buried wisdom from his army years that would resolve their dilemma. He was surrounded by frightened incompetents. The spy had escaped, and for all he knew Laurie and the priest were the recipients of those shots.

He ordered the men to kill the fire and to take up defensive positions at the edge of the cave. The two Aussies were instructed to crawl to the horses, and to tether them out of the line of fire if they could. There was some reticence at first, but the thought of further charges should they ever survive and make it back to Cairo provided the bravado they needed.

And this was how they stayed until dawn, terrified but vigilant, awaiting an attack.

"He had a madness in his eyes," said Bestic quietly.

"Madness?" hissed Wirrall.

"Yeah, even the Aussies noticed. Crazy-like. Said he was going to finish him off."

"Who said?"

"Laurie."

"Finish who off?"

"The spy…Sargeant, he seemed to have it in for the spy."

"What? Are you sure?" asked Wirrall. "Why didn't you speak up?"

"We just thought it might be the sun, or that he wasn't used to the riding," continued Bestic, "but then he said stuff about doin' in the prisoner."

"He's right, Sargeant," confirmed Halbert. "The way he was behaving towards the spy was creepy, as if his mind had gone. Think it was his way of sorting things for his mate, Nooney."

"What?" spat Wirrall incredulously. "Are you saying those shots were fired by Laurie?"

The New Zealanders exchanged glances.

"He's mad enough in our opinion, Sergeant."

"And the priest?"

"There were lots of shots. The priest was the sort of bloke who'd try to intervene…"

Wirrall thought he knew Laurie, could work him out, keep him out of trouble, make some use of the skills he had. But this?

As the sun began to rise, the tiniest traces of smoke started to appear in the low sky, less than a mile away. The desert wind was dispersing it, mostly in their direction, and the party strained to observe any suspicious activity that might be about to emanate from its source. But even though Wirrall had the binoculars and an expertise in such matters, the lay of the land between them and any fire was unkind. So the Arab guides were tasked to climb to higher ground above the cave, to scour the surroundings for anything suspicious. But they too soon returned, their gestures indicating they'd detected nothing of interest.

But they pointed to their noses, and were agitated.

"What is it?" said Wirrall.

They spoke, but it made no sense. They continued to sniff the air and contort their face, and the more Wirrall asked them to talk in King's English, the blunter they became, slicing their throat with hand gestures.

"What's that smell?" shouted one of the Aussies from the neighbouring cave.

"Horseshit," shouted Bestic.

"No, mate, it's meat... though it's gone bad." And sure enough, creeping into both caves was a disturbingly rancid odour.

"Can't place it," said Halbert, though the Sergeant did but dared not engage.

Just then below them in the valley appeared the dishevelled figure of Lance Corporal Laurie. He was on his own and walking unsteadily back towards them.

"What the hell?" said Bestic, and he creased his eyes to focus. "He's got blood all over him."

"He's got no rifle either," added Halbert.

"Keep your guns on him," said Wirrall.

"Sarge?"

"You heard, Bestic. Until we're sure."

"Laurie," shouted the Sergeant eventually, "you alright?"

There was no reply, though he continued to walk at the same shambling pace towards them. He seemed to be carrying something.

"Laurie," shouted the Sergeant again, "answer me, man, are you alright?"

There was still no response.

"Cover me," said Wirrall, and he crawled over the protective ridge at the cave entrance with an athleticism previously well hidden, to get a closer view of the Lance Corporal.

He propped himself up behind a boulder, watching as Laurie came ever nearer, ignoring all warnings to stand still.

Eventually, Wirrall ordered the cave party to stand and train their guns on him, ready to fire.

"Last chance, Laurie," he screamed, "explain yourself now or face those bullets from behind me."

"Morning, Sargeant," responded Laurie suddenly, almost as if he was on a Sunday stroll. He was smiling wildly, something the Sergeant had never seen before.

"You alright, Laurie?"

He was close enough to the Sergeant and his men at the cave entrance to reveal the blood staining on his uniform and the armful of meat he seemed to be carrying.

"I've been out hunting," he answered.

By now, even the horses seemed spooked by the figure climbing towards the caves. His eyes seemed distant and there was a smell about him. He scrambled past the Sergeant, up over the last rock, and made for the ledge he'd left earlier. The men stood motionless, watching, dumbstruck, waiting for him to speak, but instead Laurie lifted a piece of the meat that appeared to have been cooked, and began to eat.

"It's very nice," he said, seemingly quite oblivious to the amazement he'd caused, "can I offer you some?"

"Where's the priest, Laurie?" said Wirrall.

"Back down there."

"Where?"

"By the fire," continued Laurie, "he's with the spy."

The Arab guides were now extremely agitated. They began shouting loudly, pointing at the Lance Corporal. Wirrall tried to calm them.

"Laurie, we need to know what's happened." But the Lance Corporal seemed more engaged with his food than with the terrors of the group. The Arabs indicated they were going to their horses.

"Bestic, Halbert, go with them, and take two spare horses to bring the prisoner and the priest back."

The Arabs appeared relieved they were being allowed to their mounts; the New Zealanders though seemed far less enthusiastic. Within a few minutes, they were saddled and leading their horses down towards the Wadi, whilst Laurie remained uncommunicative, distracted it appeared by his breakfast.

For an hour this was how they remained, unable to gain any real sense from him and at a loss to fathom out what had happened.

"I think he's gone barmy, Sarge, we all know it happens," said one of the Australians.

"The sun, mate, or the malarial sickness," said the other.

As Sergeant Wirrall considered a resolution to their collective fates, the two New Zealanders appeared below them, galloping wildly and without the spare horses. They were shouting incoherently, and reaching the lee of the cave edge jumped from their steers, running wildly up the remaining ridge. Once inside, they continued to rant, all sense of order lost. Wirrall struggled to calm them.

By now, though, he knew; that appalling smell… he knew…

"It's everywhere, it's everywhere," wailed Halbert.

Even though he was the more reserved of the New Zealanders he was still beside himself.

"Blood scattered all over the place, wild animal tracks, meat, chunks dragged off across the rocks to who knows where, and in the fire. It was all in the fire, burning, smelling…"

"What d'you mean?" screamed an Aussie.

"Him, mate," he howled, "he's killed 'em and…"

He couldn't finish.

"…look at him now," hollered Bestic.

Laurie was completely disengaged, resting on his sandstone ledge, picking at his meat bone.

"What, mate? Jeez, what are we looking at?" shouted the other Australian.

"What he's eating... it's down there, on the fire... the Arabs have scarpered; they knew, they knew, when they smelt the smoke."

"Knew what, mate?"

By now, all four soldiers were screaming incoherently.

In desperation, Wirrall pulled his pistol from his belt and lifted it towards the men. It had an instant effect.

"Shut the racket up," he said loudly and slowly, and he waited for a few short moments for his actions to take effect.

"That smell... we were used to it on the front."

Halbert vomited, his worst fears confirmed, whilst the other three stared at Wirrall, hoping for a gentler revelation.

"Burning flesh."

CHAPTER 14

"I warned you something like this would happen," screamed Captain Hillary, emitting a fine spray of spittle, some of which settled upon Major Fogge's immaculately creased trouser leg.

"Calm down, Hillary old chap," said Fogge, "it's nothing like as bad as you're making out."

They were in the office at the Midan Bab El Hadid barracks and the Major was lounged across a Turkish divan, trusting his colleague's rage would soon pass.

"I'm not your 'old chap' you stupid runt," screeched Hillary, holding his forehead as if seeking to reaffix it to a hinge.

Fogge was taken aback. They may have been forced into their symbiotic relationship by recent events, but even so, this really was too much.

"I say, Hillary, that's not the way a gentleman behaves."

"Gentleman? You stupid arse, don't you realise what's happened?"

"Now look here, I'm your Commanding Officer and I'm ordering you to calm down."

"You can stick your order up your jacksie," replied Hillary, "because where we're going, that's all it'll be fit for."

The Major was used to Hillary's unpredictability, but he'd hoped for a more encouraging response to the news that Lance Corporal Laurie had killed the spy.

"It's a catastrophe, I warned you about him," bawled Hillary.

"As I remember it, Hillary, you warned me he was clever and devious, but given what he's gone and done, its clear that actually he's very, very, stupid."

But still the Captain stamped around the room in an apoplectic rage, ranting obscenities and threats which in routine circumstances would have seen him locked up. But these were far from normal times, and for better or worse, he and the Major were an item.

Fogge remained silent to allow the invective to unwind, and this seemed to do the trick; the abuse receded. He poured Hillary a large sherry, which he consumed in one gulp.

"There," said Fogge gently, "nanny knows best and all of that, hey dear chap?"

Hillary slumped into a cane chair, overwhelmed by the revelation of the spy's demise and the depth of the ocean in which he now floundered.

"How did he get back here?" he asked after a few moments.

"Sergeant Wirrall," replied Fogge. "He used compass bearings to navigate his men and Laurie safely back to Heliopolis."

"And where's Laurie now?"

"In the same cell the spy was in, on the racecourse at the Aussie barracks."

"Has he talked?"

"Seems he won't," replied Fogge, "he's mostly in a daze by all accounts."

"What if he does?"

"Well, he's surely mad as a hatter, so who's going to listen?"

"And the priest?"

"Same way, most likely shot and then… well… who knows what?"

"What do you mean?" said Hillary.

Fogge hesitated.

"Well?" he asked again.

"Laurie was covered in blood when they found him; seems he was also eating freshly cooked meat."

"What? Where on earth did he get that?"

"Quite," replied Fogge, leaving the question to roam. He didn't have long to wait.

"You mean…" said Hillary, slowly sequencing the events, "that he killed the priest and…" Fogge cut in.

"…well, it's just a maybe, currently, gruesome business if true, of course. There was a trail of blood and quite a few charred remnants on the fire, lots of wild animal tracks; must have had their belly full. But no other sign of the priest or the spy."

Hillary squirmed.

"That's beyond madness," he grunted.

"Oh, absolutely dreadful, dear boy; what greater definition of insanity could there be?"

There was a moment of stillness as the Captain tried to figure out the trail of actions unfolding before him. He'd no inkling Laurie would react in such a horrifying way. All he and Fogge had desired was for the Spaniard to be out of the way.

"But there'll be questions," he said.

Major Fogge's lower lip wriggled, seemingly independent of the upper.

"That's all taken care of."

"How do you mean?"

"Brigadier Regis-Templeton, dear boy."

The name hardly reassured. The Brigadier was hugely respected, and a stickler for procedure. Worse still, he was inscrutable.

Fogge detected his reticence. These misgivings were the stuff of wiffle waffle and no more than he'd come to expect from such a disappointingly insecure man.

"He's one of us for heaven's sake, Hillary, an Oxford man. Damn shame he went to Brasenose but one can't have everything. Despite that, he seems onside…"

Captain Hillary's face blanked.

"…with all this business with Laurie," emphasised Fogge, realising he'd need to be slower and more precise. "He's going to be tried." Hillary's eyes popped.

"There's nothing to worry about, the Brigadier's appointed me to be the Presiding Officer, and one of his old oppo's, an ancient buffer no doubt, will sit in on things to ensure fair play."

Hillary needed convincing.

"It will work wonderfully. The whole thing will be over in a jiffy."

"But the evidence," asked Hillary, "surely all of that will take time?"

"There's a war on don't you know, Hillary," said the Major, scoffing gently, "and good old Allenby seems to have good a decent hold of things. So, nobody will want this to drag on. If Laurie's found to be mad, he'll be incarcerated in some out-of-the-way place. If he's found sane, then he'll face a murder charge at a General Courts Martial."

"What if he's shown to be innocent?" asked Hillary.

Fogge was becoming exasperated.

"Really, Hillary, for a man of your breeding you do disappoint me at times. How on earth could he be found innocent, given both the deaths of these men and his clear and corroborated lunacy?"

"He will need representation," replied Hillary. "The Army Act states that: there might be some clever arse from the Bureau or somewhere who knows something we don't know."

Fogge rolled his eyes.

"What on earth do you think I've been doing these past six months, man?"

Hillary stared at the Major. In truth, he'd be very hard pressed to answer.

"...I've been uncovering everything that's going on in that tin-pot office of theirs. Nobody trusts them, they're quacks and fruitcakes, the lot of them. There's nothing to be concerned about from that lot.

To Hillary, the last sentence seemed worryingly like an epitaph.

"What... you mean you've been spying on them?"

"Liaison, dear boy, that's what we call it. All sanctioned by Army HQ. And it's helped you and I along the way, has it not?"

Hillary was hardly assured. He knew the Major's vainglorious tendencies could befuddle matters, though there would be an officer to front the case against Laurie, and Fogge had excellent connections.

"Who will be prosecuting?"

"Well," said Fogge, "we needed someone with the chutzpah and élan to carry something like this off."

"Have you appointed?"

Fogge looked at Hillary and smiled.

"Why yes, of course… you."

Llucia Quintana sat on the steps of Sant Cristofol, in Es Migjorn Roca, looking across the Place De L'Esglesia towards Cami d'es Cemintiri and her farm at Turo Vell. She'd made the short journey to the village so many times, though rarely without burden. As a child, she'd been sent to seek work in the fields of others, to supplement her family's shortfalls. As a young woman, it was accompanied by grief at the loss and injustice of her parents killing and the theft of their lands; an evil that had robbed her of everything. And as an adult and then matriarch, she carried the eyes of others: those who relied upon her for benign beneficence, or despised her for what she'd achieved and controlled.

This morning was different; the affliction she now bore felt insufferable. It had been several months since her journey to Palma, with no further word about her son. She'd met with Bishop Paulinus, left letters to be sent if that would help. She believed in him; the man who'd betrayed her, left her to fend for her life. Yet still she trusted. *"I shall not run from you again,"* he'd said. Her strength had always predominated; but now she feared its failing.

The door of Sant Cristofol opened, revealing the stooped figure of Padre Alvaro Marin peering outward from the darkness, head bobbing, surveying the square and the scene below him like an enfeebled owl. She would normally have bullied him into making the trek to Turo Vell, but today, fearing the worst, she'd acquiesced to his request to meet at the church. It would have been a triumph for him, but she didn't want his bad news to be aired within the sanctity of the farm. She would need to digest it, appear strong.

"Good morning, *Señora* Quintana," he squeaked, attempting a reassuring smile though visibly apprehensive of the force sitting just below.

"Padre Marin," she acknowledged, somewhat to his consternation, as she rarely alluded to him so formally.

She followed him into the church and they settled in the same family pew as when they last met. How different those times now seemed.

"I trust you are well, *Señora?*" asked Marin.

She stared through him, unable to summon either acerbic wit or genteel neutrality. She felt close to breaking. All that remained was the finality in the message about her son that this pathetic maladjusted man had to offer.

"You indicated in your note that you had news," she said, quietly, so quietly in fact that the surprised padre needed to double-check before responding.

"Yes, this came to me yesterday from an Andreassen boat at Mahon."

He passed her an envelope embossed with the seal of *His Excellency Paulinus, Bishop Emeritus of the Diocese of Arage*.

"My instruction was to give this to you at the first opportunity."

She nodded and took the letter. He left her to go about his own matters and for a while she sat quite motionless, paralysed by the fate she dare not acknowledge.

She wasn't a religious woman: her faith had been ripped away. But as she caressed the envelope's protective wax strip, she felt an overwhelming compulsion to be held in grace, hidden even, like the letter within.

She closed her eyes, unable to fight the desolation this moment had brought. And resist though she tried, the prayers came, streaming more profusely from within her than the cascading tears.

Eventually, she began to pick at the wax on the envelope and slowly removed an elegantly handwritten letter.

My dearest Llucia,

May this letter find you filled with hope.

Our son is alive and in Cairo. My emissary there has reported irregularities that have prevented his direct return to you. In the fullness of time these will be overcome.

I shall write when I have further news but assure that he is being held in the loving arms of God.

Your servant,
Paulinus.

The relief was extraordinary. She struggled to prevent herself screaming with joy. Oriol was alive.

She pored over every word again and again. Her son would return it said. Paulinus had kept his word; her trust in him from their meeting had been justified. And he'd written those words: *our son*. Those were not loose words of faith. They were words of love. She believed him. Despite everything that had happened between them, she believed him.

But then the doubts: 'irregularities'? Oriol had never been challenged before, let alone prevented from returning. He must still be in danger. She had counselled him against this journey. She should have been stronger, forbidden it, but he was her son, obstinate, determined, confident. He got things done. To oppose would have been impossible.

"Are you alright, *Señora?*" inquired Pardre Marin.

He'd returned expecting the very worst, fearing how she might respond. For a moment, he was left hovering as she held the letter, staring ahead.

"Yes, thank you, Padre," she said eventually, now more controlled, quiet.

His shock was palpable. She'd actually thanked him.

"Do you know when this letter was written?"

"It arrived four days ago in Palma, and transferred to Mao by an Andreassen boat."

Llucia did some calculations. At best, the news from Cairo would be a month old and much could have happened since then, Oriol could be on his way back home. He could also be in worse peril. But she believed the bishop, trusted her instincts. And now this… the letter. If only their lives could be re-wound. She stood up to leave.

"*Señora*, if I may."

The padre was also troubled, and this was an opportunity that might not repeat itself.

"The artefact your son will be bringing when he returns, you were insistent it would need to be hung in a prominent position within the church, and I…"

Llucia stopped him.

"There will be no more such works for you to worry about, Padre. Those needs are at an end."

He stood, open-mouthed, hardly believing what he'd heard.

She wished him good day and left to return to Turo Vell. There was nothing more she could do now save the things she hated the most: to wait and rely on others.

Much later that same day, well after sunset and in an elegant apartment on Shari El Saqqayin in the El Nasriya district of Cairo, children's screams broke out from within the Moussabey household. Attracted by the sound of frenzy, they'd looked out from their bedroom window to the street below. A crowd had gathered. At first they'd taken little notice. But as it grew and the noise of agitation rose, they realised that they and their house were the subject of the vitriol.

Seeing them in the window, the crowd began to hurl abuse. Before long, stones and an array of other objects that came to hand were thrown. Their parents had run to them and bolted the shutters, and the house remained solidly impregnable, but despite their assurances that help would be at hand, it had taken an hour before the British Military Police appeared, their Egyptian counterparts nowhere to be seen.

Once the commotion had passed, and a guard posted, they'd all ventured outside, though the children were immediately ushered back. The street was awash with debris and would soon be cleared. But on the door and wall to the house in animal blood were plastered the words that could not be so easily erased.

'Spies, Traitors, Coptic scum'.

"The British will not desert us," insisted Peter, but Hanna was dismissive.

"You and your British sense of honour. They will not protect us, now or in the future."

"There will be guards," he insisted, but she wouldn't be diverted.

"Pah! All that will do is further advertise our status to the mob. We have been marked out. We shall never be safe here."

"Hanna, this is our home. Our children belong here. We must see this out. We cannot keep running."

"And whilst we await whatever trust you attach to the British, our lives will be washed away," she spat.

"They will not fail us," shouted Peter in exasperation.

"Then test that reassurance," she replied, voice raised in anger, "go on, find out from them what exactly is it that they will do for us."

There had rarely been a cross word in the Moussabey marriage; there were challenges enough for them as part of a minority. As for the British, Peter knew that despite his work, he held little if any sanction over them. Even his role at The Agricultural Bank of Cairo would be in question once the occupation was over. Hanna, as always, was right. She was the realist, he the dreamer.

They hugged.

"One day," whispered Hanna, "the accidents of history, of the place we were born, will become irrelevant."

"I pray that is soon," said Peter, and they kissed, making light as best they could.

They, at least, had experienced a life of possibility. But they grieved for their children. Four beautiful, innocent daughters, born to a loving family, raised to believe in the goodness of the human soul. Four beautiful innocent daughters, blessed in a faith they hadn't chosen, but had grown to love. Four beautiful innocent daughters who loved Egypt, but were now to be consigned as detested outsiders.

Laurie had been brought in great haste from his cell on the racecourse to the Midan Bab El Hadid barracks. He was to face justice. Colonel Grice-Farquharason, the officer appointed to represent him, had warned there would be little time to prepare a case, given the momentum with which the war effort was now proceeding. Allenby was within touching distance of a momentous push for victory in Palestine, and the eyes and efforts of the military were elsewhere.

But Laurie knew there was another reason for the speed of his journey, heavily guarded and in the back of a disguised police waggon: there was growing hostility towards the British on the streets of Cairo. Troop numbers were being rapidly diminished as they moved to join with the Allenby initiative. Those still left were being routinely confined to barracks to avoid agitation. So the site of a gentle prison guard procession from Heliopolis would have presented an easy a target for the mob.

"Gentlemen and… lady." Major Fogge smiled thinly towards the female court usher. "…as the Presiding Officer of the Court, I call upon the Confirming Officer to read out the offences for which the defendant, Lance Corporal Laurie, is charged."

Fogge was in his imperatorial element and waved to the officer to commence.

"The charge sheet reads that on the morning of Monday 23rd July, 1917, Lance Corporal Laurie disobeyed orders by standing down soldiers on watch, enabling him to coerce a convicted prisoner, one Oriole Quintana, together with a Coptic priest, Father Daoud Emam, to travel into the desert with him, whereupon he shot and unlawfully killed them both. And that he then attempted to dispose of parts of their bodies, most likely by burning and ingestion, leaving the rest to be dragged away by wild animals."

"How does the prisoner plead?" asked Fogge.

"Not guilty," replied Grice-Farquharason on behalf of Laurie.

"Ah, thank you, Colonel," replied Fogge.

"I should say, Major," added Grice-Farquharason, "that when it comes to the formal presentation and cross-examination by the defence Lance Corporal Laurie has expressed a desire that for the for the most part he shall be permitted to represent himself. He is more than familiar with courtroom procedure, given his background. I shall of course be here to answer the prosecution case this morning, and after that for advice should that be needed by the defendant."

Fogge was momentarily thrown by this unorthodox turn of events, though quickly regained momentum, concluding it would play to his interests.

"Yes, yes, of course. I would always advise the defendant to leave the entirety of his case to someone with such expert proficiency as yourself, Colonel," he said, smiling faintly, "but I really must respect his wishes on the matter."

He looked up, his eyes poking fleetingly over his glasses in a manner designed to deter objection, and moved swiftly on.

"And can I also confirm to the court that the Prosecuting Officer in these proceedings will be Captain Hillary. I wish it to be noted for the purposes of the record, that I am satisfied that in the straightened times in which we find ourselves, both representing officers, Hillary and Grice-Farquharason, have been adjudged to be competent and qualified to act in accordance with the regulations required by The Army Act."

Laurie looked at Captain Hillary, perched opposite him, nervously fidgeting with the cap and cane that were resting neatly upon his desk. Everyone knew that he and Fogge were the closest of colleagues. Surely there would be a challenge to this prosecuting arrangement? But there was nothing save an affirming silence.

He couldn't quite believe it. His luck was in. Thank God for Allenby.

For the first five minutes or so, Fogge ran through the seriousness of the matters in hand and reaffirmed the sincerity and clarity he would bring to proceedings.

"I will be very clear," he concluded, "we shall today establish the true facts of this case; facts which will prevail."

All of this with the regal serenity of a man who'd primped himself in the mirror that very morning, and been wonderfully pleased by what he saw.

"And I warn," he said, attempting to expand his half-pint chest, "that there will be no room for magniloquence."

Most of those gathered nodded their heads obligingly, though few had any clue as to what he meant.

"So, I call upon Captain Hillary to proceed."

Hillary stood, the pencil-legs that bore him peeping from below his khaki shorts. He placed a hand upon the desk next to him for reassurance. He began to speak, his thin black moustache dancing wildly above his upper lip, and for a while seemed supremely confident, self-satisfied even, reading from a prepared note listing Laurie's indiscretions.

"…and those cautions resulted in Lance Corporal Laurie losing some of his pay for a month. Even by then, he'd distinguished himself from the rest of the men by his outspoken challenges to those in authority. Indeed, upon his arrival in Cairo and in this very room, he was admonished by myself during a briefing of the men."

"Objection," interrupted Colonel Grice-Farquharason, "this has no bearing whatsoever upon the specific charge of which the defendant is accused."

"On the contrary," said Fogge, "such prima facie evidence will provide vital background to the case."

He nodded to Hillary to continue.

"You will also have read my own testimony about his true sympathies, as demonstrated in both his leniency towards an Arab mob, and in his unhealthy familiarity with street vendors. These actions led to charges and a week-long latrine detail, supervised by Sergeant Wirrall. I would add, that had the advice I gave to the Arab Military Intelligence Bureau at GHQ as to his untrustworthiness been accepted, we wouldn't be in this position today."

"Objection, this is all circumstantial," said Grice-Farquharason somewhat testily.

Major Fogge was having none of it.

"Look here, Colonel, you really shouldn't disport yourself with these interruptions; they aren't helping your case. Captain Hillary, please proceed."

Fogge was becoming encouraged by the Captain's performance, and Hillary beamed.

"Moving on to his time with the Bureau, despite his orders from officers at GHQ to maintain effective liaison with them, he soon became suspiciously evasive, frequently covering his tracks or playing the fool when confronted."

"Major Fogge, please…"

Grice-Farquharason was by now quite exasperated.

"…Yes, yes, alright." Nodded Fogge. "On this occasion I accept that the term 'playing the fool' which I presume you object to, is inappropriate and should be scrubbed from the record, though I for one never thought of him as anything more than irreverent towards authority."

Hillary rolled his eyes at yet another interruption, and continued.

"Again, I refer you to the written summaries of his dealings in the 'Sugar Case' which took him to Port Alexandria and work with The Alexandria West Bay Shipping Company and its Arab owner, a certain…" and he sneered, "…Mr Smith, a sometime associate of the British, though whose credentials leave much to be desired. By this time, Laurie was ensconced in Bureau operations with the late Lance Corporal Nooney, making frequent trips up and down the Nile." He looked disapprovingly at Laurie. "Some of which he even reported upon."

"Would you be so kind, Captain, to remind the court who his controller was?" asked Fogge.

"Indeed, Major, it was Colonel Lowthian. Well known to you all I'm sure as a woman officer, one whose reputation amongst, shall we say, our 'Arab friends' is second to none."

He stared around the court, pausing long enough for the insinuation to bottom out.

"All in all, this picture of unreliability, indiscipline and suspicious subterfuge presented Lance Corporal Laurie as a character completely unworthy of the trust and reliance that was being placed upon him by those such as Colonel Lowthian; a trust all the more extraordinary given the secretive and sensitive nature of the operations involved. Indeed, had he not so engrossed himself with those in authority at the Arab Military Intelligence Bureau, he would already have been imprisoned for his offences.

"Objection," shouted Grice-Farquharason, "this is circumstantial nonsense."

"Overruled," snapped Fogge, "sit down."

"Which brings me specifically to the death of Lance Corporal Nooney."

Hillary theatrically picked up a glass of water and paused awhile, enjoying the eyes of the court.

"Please, take your time," encouraged Fogge whilst simultaneously pointing a disapproving glare at Grice-Farquharason.

"On the day of Nooney's killing by the spy, instruction had been sent to where he and Laurie were on undercover operations to report back immediately to barracks. At first they refused, though with hindsight and the pattern of behaviour now uncovering before you, it would be fairer to Nooney's memory to conclude that Laurie was the lead recalcitrant of the pair. When they were finally escorted back to Midan Bab El Hadid and secured within the building to await questioning, they again disobeyed orders, eventually making their way to Pont Limoun Station, from where Laurie led a direct and deliberate action of obstruction against an ongoing operation to the arrest the spy. As we know, this led to the shooting dead of Nooney, an entirely avoidable event had it not been for the reprehensible behaviour of Lance Corporal Laurie."

He paused for another sip of water.

"What was going through his mind, you might ask?"

"Indeed," interrupted Fogge, hoping to be helpful and now excited that his protégé was operating so effectively, "are you suggesting cunning or madness?"

"Well practiced illusion, Major. Because as we all know, the subsequent... 'injuries,'" he emphasised the word with an affected gesture, "...incurred by the defendant, encouraged something of a wave of sympathy to spread throughout the men, and indeed, even amongst some of the officers investigating his case. I suggest the fortuitous period of hospitalisation he then enjoyed, enabled time and cover for his ultimate act."

"Can you be more precise please, Hillary," asked Fogge, "as I think we're all aware he took something of a knock, and that can do strange things to a chap."

Fogge smiled sympathetically at the impassive Laurie.

"Yes, sir. In this action of self-pity and spurious humility, the defendant gained the confidence of Father Daoud Emam, a local priest who does..." he stopped momentarily and corrected himself, "...I should say, *did*, such fine pastoral work with our fallen men and prisoners. The defendant so ingratiated himself with the poor man that he was given an introduction through his good offices to the incarcerated spy, Oriol Quintana, all quite contrary to regulations."

"You have the evidence?" inquired Fogge.

"I refer you to the written testimonies of Quintana's guards, both here at the barracks, and from the Anzacs at the gaol in Heliopolis. It was with such assurance in Laurie's abilities, and of course the priest's huge slice of Christian empathy, that prompted Father Emam to lobby for his attendance as part of the prisoner's incarceration party to Suez, for onward transportation I would remind, to life with hard labour in Australia. The priest had no idea, of course, of the evil intentions that lay behind the kind façade that concealed the real Lance-Corporal Laurie."

"And what do you believe those intentions were, Hillary?" inquired Fogge.

"Initially, sir, it was deception. The spy, Quintana, was described by some as a poet, though this was mostly dismissed as buffoonery. After all, anyone can write poetry. Laurie though apparently showed interest, even appeared kindly towards the prisoner. I believe this was simply because the so-called poetry this man had in his possession, even the book that he carried, contained messages from enemy sources which military intelligence failed to decipher."

"Messages, Hillary? Surely these would have been scrutinised by our people?"

Fogge was at least offering a nod as to his neutrality.

"You would have thought so, sir, though attempts to do this by the Arab Military Intelligence Bureau came to nought, the very same organisation that in such poor taste had employed Laurie."

"Objection," exploded Grice-Farquharason, "this is preposterous. The Arab Bureau is absolutely central to our work here in Egypt, an essential part of the war effort."

There were a few raised eyes around the room.

"Please, please, calm yourself," implored Fogge, waving his hand as if calming a struggling member aboard a coxless four.

"We are here to give proper justice to Lance Corporal Laurie," continued Grice-Farquharason, "not to make unfounded criticism of those who work with our Arab friends for the mutual good."

"Yes, yes, of course, but please do steady yourself," intoned Fogge, aware that on opinions relating to the Bureau he was very much amongst friends, and that Laurie's defence officer was rather too close to the matter to overly engage.

"Please continue, Hillary, you mentioned 'messages'?"

"Code, sir, instructions the spy was to use to destabilise; promises of support for those who are agitating here, specifically the anti-British Arab mob… or so Laurie and his Arab friends initially thought."

He paused to allow the message to diffuse across the fanned airwaves that permeated the room.

"So Hillary, are you suggesting that as well as a murderer, Lance Corporal Laurie is also a conduit, an agent, unwitting or otherwise, for our enemies?"

"Why else, Major, would he carry out such a heinous act in the desert? There can be no other rationale. Laurie was profiting, one way or another from his work with the Bureau, even attempting to sell sugar through a bogus trading company he'd established. I refer you to the formal documentation everyone has on that, clearly signed in his name on behalf of 'Trading Assurance Cairo.'"

He waited for a moment whilst the rustle of shifting paperwork died down.

"But this was simply a part of his brief one presumes?" inquired Fogge, helpfully.

"So it would appear. But in reality, he used this to oil the wheels of his Arab associates and, of course, to line his own pockets. He pulled the wool over the eyes of those around him whilst pretending to operate in the best of British interests."

Just then Fogge's attention was unexpectedly diverted.

"Can you ask him to get to the point?" whispered General Aukkerley, the additional officer appointed by Brigadier Regis-Templeton to oversee proceedings, and until now assumed by Fogge by virtue of his advanced years, to be compliantly muted.

"Can you get to the point please, Captain?" interjected Fogge, as if this original thought had just come to him.

Hillary glared impatiently. He knew his extraordinary competence had been more than sufficient to convince those with intellect of the validity of his case.

"I shall also therefore be very clear," he boomed slowly back towards Fogge, to the stifled delight of many in the room, "things became trickier when the Bureau let slip something which at the time they assumed to be true."

He moved to a large map of the Mediterranean positioned on an easel at the corner of the room, and picked up a long wooden pointer.

"Here we have Egypt, the Sinai and Palestine, to the north the Ottoman, Greeks and Italians."

"What's this, a bloody school lesson?" seethed Aukkerley rather too noticeably.

"...the spy's role, in reality, was driven by the Andreassen operation in Palestine, the Jewish agents who have so fastidiously supported our efforts against the Ottoman – or so they made it appear." He pointed to a number of boat-shaped markers helpfully positioned on the map across various parts of the Mediterranean.

"...he'd even travelled to Egypt on their boat, *The Adelphi.*" To emphasise this he helpfully moved one of the markers from Sicily across towards Egypt to reconstruct the journey.

"This was an Andreassen boat just like all these others you can see. He was then dropped a mile or so offshore, making his way by subterfuge to Port Alexandria, rather than risk arriving formally. All would still have been well for Quintana, had Laurie not engaged in the spy's joy of literature."

"What the hell is he going on about now?" huffed the General once more, and again rather loudly.

"What are you going on about?" aped Fogge, unaware his efforts at independence were now being audibly undermined from the sideline.

"Well, Major," replied Hillary, increasingly irritated at this questioning, "in their moments together in the jail, Laurie realised the true motives behind Quintana's poetry. Whilst the man in front of him was claiming to be nothing more than a businessman trading with Arab contacts, to the contrary, he was attempting to support the anti-British Arab network here and become a trusted supplier, probably of arms. Once that had been achieved it was his intention to trade this information onward to a lucrative bidder, most likely the Jewish nationalist movement, the real employers of the Andreassens' loyalties. In effect, they would then be enabled to 'muscle-in' on this Arab network without their knowing; take control, organise it more effectively and thereby help tie-up the British here, destabilising any future British activities in Palestine."

"What?" Fogge certainly hadn't meant to be negative, but even he was now losing the thread of the Captain's forensic incisiveness.

Hillary sighed, were they all really so slow?

"To paint this tryst at its simplest: unbeknown to the enemy who believed they were his sole employers, the spy Quintana was actually working with the Jewish effort to apparently support the British push into Palestine, which once successful would need to be undermined by Arab unrest in Cairo."

"Ah, right, yes of course..." said Fogge, followed after a few moments thought, but this time loudly by... "What?" This hadn't been the line he'd agreed with Hillary before the court case had opened.

"And you know all of that for certain, of course?" said Aukkerley no longer muted, and increasingly irritated by Hillary's growing monologue and certainty.

"Yet at the same time," continued Hillary, unabashed, "and unbeknown to the British intelligence community with the exception of Lance Corporal Laurie, he was also working with the enemy to support the Arab agitators here in Cairo, determined to cause problems for ourselves."

He smiled triumphantly, quite taken by the brilliance of his rhetoric, blissfully unaware of the blank faces that greeted him.

"Unfortunately for the spy, Quintana," he continued, "he hadn't banked upon the abilities of Laurie to unmask their developing friendship for what it was. That in effect, he knew the spy was a double-agent and that this was a threat; not just to Laurie and his Arab cronies but to his continued crookery and safety."

"Crookery?" exclaimed General Aukkerley in Fogge's ear. "What the hell's that?"

"It therefore became apparent to Laurie that unless Quintana was eliminated he would be unmasked, along with his friends, as even the so-called intelligence officers at the Bureau would eventually catch up with proceedings."

"Objection."

It was Grice-Farquharason's turn now.

"This really is an appalling misrepresentation of the available evidence."

Most of those present assumed he was about to enter into a deconstruction of the tosh Hillary had presented about Laurie.

"The phrase 'so-called intelligence officers' is a scurrilous and untruthful indictment of the work of the Bureau, and says more about his own jealousies and twisted imaginings than their magnificent activities. He should retract, and…"

Then, almost as an afterthought, he returned to the case against Laurie "…acknowledge also that it has no bearing on the matters in hand."

Things were beginning to slip, and the General was now growling. There was more to him than Fogge had appreciated.

"Retract the accusation about these officers if you would, Captain Hillary," said Fogge, "so that we can move on please, and Colonel Grice-Farquharason, can you enable us to progress more quickly?"

"I retract," said Hillary, "and accept they're 'called' intelligence officers."

The General shook his head in frustration.

"To conclude therefore, the late Lance Corporal Nooney also got wind of things, leading tragically as we all now know, to him trying to thwart Laurie's efforts to shoot the spy at Pont Limoun, attempts that led to his own death at the hands of the man he had just saved."

There was something of a commotion around the room as this observation fully landed.

"From then onwards, Laurie knew the spy wouldn't go quietly. So his only hope was to eradicate him, together with the priest to whom the spy had confessed from his jail."

There was a moment's uncomfortable silence. Fogge couldn't be sure that Hillary had finished, nor that there wouldn't be a further signal of instructive dissatisfaction from the General. Then, unwittingly, he stumbled to the question others had arrived at far earlier.

"Please do remind us again, Captain Hillary, what was it exactly that Laurie had to gain in being the culprit of such a clearly murderous act?"

Hillary rolled his eyes. *How stupid could Fogge be?*

"He expected to get away with it. Can't you see?"

He looked around the court for approbation, but none was forthcoming.

"He banked upon covering up the crime. No bodies, no murder, him acting as if in some form of demented shock, eating meat he'd claim later he'd brought along with him, just to 'beef up', so to speak, the fragile state of his bewildered mentality."

He chuckled quietly at the cleverness of his linguistics.

"Really, Major, this is so blindingly obvious."

"The man's a bloody fool, Fogge," hissed the General.

"You're a bloo…" stuttered Fogge, stopping just in time.

"Captain Hillary," boomed General Aukkerley, "you seem to have overlooked the fact that there actually aren't any bodies to speak of."

"Just the parts he was seen to digest," replied Hillary triumphantly, "together with the evidence we have that he was doused in blood and that the investigating soldiers saw human remains on that fire."

He stared wildly at Fogge, triumphantly. This was the time to push that blusterer to one side.

"Quite literally," he said, "these are the real facts about…" and he paused theatrically, "…the poet Laurie ate. I rest my case."

Fogge was both astounded and shocked, not simply at the story Hillary had concocted, but the passion with which he'd corralled the defendant's guilt. Even more striking was a personal terror; what exactly had he unleashed in his choice of prosecutor? He'd regarded Hillary as moderately bright, a trier. But the man's impetuosity and barmy logic had whizzed through his brain like an admonishment from pappa on a cold bonfire night.

This was becoming tricky.

"Get a grip, man," said the General under his breath.

The docile, ageing 'has been', recommended by Brigadier Regis-Templeton, was clearly anything but.

Fogge began to smell a trap. He needed an exit.

"Have you had a thorough medical, Lance Corporal Laurie, since your release from hospital?" he asked.

Grice-Farquharason and Laurie looked at each other in bemusement.

"I ask because so many of our good men have been affected by Enteric Fever and other desert diseases, impacts upon the mind, makes men act completely out of character, even leads on occasions to a sort of madness, if you will."

"Sir?"

Laurie had been silent to this point, though could see where this question was leading.

"Well, insanity, temporarily caused as in this case, or of a permanent state, can be used by the defence to mitigate the charges against you."

General Aukkerley raised his exotic eyebrows towards Laurie in caution. He needn't have worried.

"I was given a clean slate of good health on my release from medical care, sir, both physical and mental. I can assure you that I am completely sane."

Bugger, thought Fogge.

"One hour adjournment," he announced, "and in the meantime, I should like to study those medical records."

Grice-Farquharason nodded and passed a folder to Fogge.

And with a bang of the Major's gavel the room emptied.

Laurie, accompanied by his Military Police guards, headed straight back to the holding cell. Fogge, on the other hand, chose the sanctity of his office and the respite provided by the chaise lounge.

CHAPTER 15

There was a loud thump on Fogge's office door. He ignored it as he was sat inside a large tin-bath, dragged there and laboriously filled by an Arab orderly. He was attempting to soak some sensibility back into his bones before returning to the court. But silent resistance proved futile; the enraged Hillary burst in.

"What on earth do you think you're doing?" shouted Fogge, scrabbling for his spectacles, a sinewy arm and fingers flailing down the side of the bath like an aerial root system.

"Fuck you, fuck you, fuck you!" ranted Hillary, as if in some despotic mantra.

"Hillary," shouted Fogge once more, "you're not supposed to be here; we're in the middle of the trial. I must remain impartial."

This further incensed the Captain as he barged around the room, extending the range of his abusive vocabulary and kicking out at anything within range, including the Major's bath and favoured cane chair.

"Everything alright in there?" shouted a voice from outside and they instantly hushed, as if a lover's partner had returned home unexpectedly.

"Is everything alright, Major Fogge?" repeated the voice.

It was Sergeant Wirrall.

"Yes, quite alright thank you, Sergeant," replied the Major, "just cursing aloud, take no notice of me; it's the arthritis."

"Very good, sir."

As the Sergeant's footsteps departed, Hillary recommenced, but this time in an energised whisper.

"Impartial, you say, fucking impartial?"

His eyes were rolling, his cheeks inflamed.

"Hillary, I'm ordering you to leave this office at once," retorted Fogge, attempting to enforce some form of authoritative decorum, despite his prostrated water-bound circumstance.

"You can order all you like, you pompous dick," shouted Hillary, unconcerned now if anyone heard, "don't interrupt me again when we're back in that court, or try that sympathy stuff about Laurie." He thrashed at a pile of papers on Fogge's desk, and a few fluttered down into his bath. "Sort yourself out; you know what was agreed. Or else face the fucking consequence."

And with that he stormed off, banging the door behind him.

Fogge was left in his bath, quietly seething. Things were getting out of hand.

As they returned to the court and Laurie was free of his guards, Grice-Farquharason passed him a slip of paper.

"Just been given this by the court usher," he whispered. "Does it make any sense to you?"

Laurie began to read the first few lines.

"I met a man today.
Angered, razored, kettled by the certainties of others.
Battered on the blasted heath of his business,
His life a fishnet of uncertainty."

He beamed.

"What is it?" asked Grice-Farquharason.

"Redemption."

"What?"

"Truth of a sort… for Nooney."

The Colonel appeared even further perplexed.

"It's from the spy," whispered Laurie.

"What on earth do you mean?"

But there was no time to elaborate, nor was Laurie minded to.

"I call upon Colonel Grice-Farquharason to proceed for the defence," announced Fogge, and the Colonel, thrown but nevertheless composed enough to hide the fact, glanced towards Laurie for assurance their plans remained unchanged.

"As I've already indicated, Major, Lance Corporal Laurie has expressed the desire to conduct his own defence from this point onwards and I seek your further affirmation for this."

"Are you quite certain that's wise?" inquired Fogge, more in real trepidation now for his own circumstances than in sincerity towards the course of justice."

"I have absolute confidence Lance Corporal Laurie will represent himself with great efficacy," replied the Colonel.

Fogge had feared this eventuality since it was first mooted earlier in the morning session. His inclination then had been to count upon his command of the court and to eventually overrule it on the grounds of Laurie's incompetence or madness, avenues of escape which now seemed problematic.

He turned to face the prosecution counsel, fearful he may still be inflicted with the malicious malady displayed in his office a little while earlier.

"Are you happy with this, Captain Hillary?"

"No, sir."

Fogge was relieved; there was still at least a veneer of respect from his number two.

"He's an accomplished liar as well as a murderer, and shouldn't be enabled with the means to waste the court's time."

"Objection," shouted Grice-Farquharason.

"For heaven's sake," snapped General Aukkerley, this time with no attempt to cover his displeasure, "it's allowable in law, Fogge, so let the man speak for himself."

Fogge's face drained of its colour. With the growing unreliability of his junior officer and the increasing authority of the General, his options were narrowing. Survival became imperative.

"As you say, General, yes, of course."

Captain Hillary looked furious. Fogge had just shed any agreement they'd ever had.

"Please proceed, Lance Corporal Laurie."

"Thank you, Major," said Laurie, standing confidently and surveying the officers and administrative staff around the room and appearing anything but insane.

"Brevity is what Captain Hillary inferred, so I shall oblige."

The strength of his opening words and the confidence with which he uttered them brought a further wobble to Fogge's withering demeanour.

"You opened these proceedings by stating that the truth will prevail. Well, that is what I shall present, though it will be a very different truth from that which either Captain Hillary or yourself will recognise, and entirely free of the 'magniloquence' of which I know you are so fond."

There was a discernible leap in attentiveness amongst those gathered, accompanied by hurried whispers and stifled gasps. This man seemed unexpectedly tenacious and direct.

"Now really, Laurie, this will not do your case any good," blustered Fogge, but Laurie continued.

"I was cautioned early in my time here, that much is true. The charges were issued at Captain Hillary's behest and were a way of face-saving for him."

"Why, the lying ..."

Hillary was apoplectic.

"...Captain Hillary, please," shouted Fogge, attempting to retain balance as well as control.

"He also mentioned," continued Laurie, ignoring the barbs, "my actions during an incident in Midan Bab El Hadid, when I accompanied Lance Corporal Nooney on a routine patrol around the square. I simply requested that he, Captain Hillary, restrain from ordering our troops to fire at unarmed Arabs."

"Why you complete arse…"

"…Captain Hillary, please," shouted Fogge once more, "you must not interrupt proceedings in such a way."

"Oh, I shouldn't should I?" retorted Hillary.

The court stared, and General Aukkerley seemed aghast.

"Trying to shut me up are you?"

"Captain Hillary, please, I ask you again to…"

"Shut your mouth, man and follow procedure," stormed Aukkerley, finishing Fogge's words, "or face dismissal from the proceedings."

By now it was clear to all present that even by the challenged circumstances of the times, this hearing was becoming particularly memorable. For Fogge, though, the sands were shifting.

"We'd arrested a number of traders," continued Laurie, "who were to prove helpful to our intelligence people, though, of course, I didn't know that at the time. We ensured their safety, and the safety of our soldiers, and that was the only reason behind the action I took that day."

"Do you have any witnesses to corroborate such capacious claims?" asked Fogge.

"Well, Lance Corporal Nooney would certainly have confirmed the actions. If you read the report he wrote, which was attached to the charge sheet, you will see that he reinforced my explanation at the time."

"Of course he did," shouted Hillary.

Fogge shot him a glare and Aukkerley heaved in his chair.

"And I still have the contacts of those we arrested if needed, plus the statement from a street performer helpful to us with leads and information: a man by the name of Manoli."

"Ha, I told you he's mad," ranted Hillary, "asking us to trust bloody Arabs. Does he think we're all stupid?"

Aukkerley exploded.

"Enough, Hillary. Leave the prosecuting chair."

"But, sir…"

"Guards."

For a moment there was pandemonium as Captain Hillary was frogmarched by two Military Policemen from his elevated position as inquisitor-in-chief for the King, out through the court across the long back end of the briefing hall and into the drill yard.

"Keep your hands off me you fucking dimwits," he shouted, as they eventually left him, standing in the full sun, removed of all dignity and shade.

"I'll have you on a charge, I will, I know who you are."

"I'd go to your room if I were you, sir," said one of the men, politely.

"Or to bed," said the other. "A good lie down always helps, I find."

They turned and left him hurling abuse, first towards their backs, and then as they departed, the Cairo sun.

Back in court, the proceedings continued, though in a decidedly different vein. General Aukkerley had assumed control.

"Please Laurie, do continue," he said, ignoring Fogge's affronted expression, "we shall seek the testimony you describe. Are there other witnesses?"

"Sergeant Wirrall, sir."

Aukkerley looked at his listing paper and noted Wirrall's name.

"We shall return to this when he appears later. I'm keen though to learn of your time with the Bureau: the prosecution appear to have some misgivings?" and he looked directly towards Fogge, now slumping forlornly in his Court President's chair.

"I cannot understand that, sir," replied Laurie, "as I was actually appointed by Major Fogge himself, quite out of the blue. Captain Hillary was there too. All three of us met in Major Fogge's office at the time, and Sergeant Wirrall had escorted me there."

"So why would there be any concern in their minds?"

"No idea, sir, though Major Fogge did ask me to inform upon the Bureau."

"What?"

"He said that was his role, Liaison Officer with Army HQ."

The General turned towards the Major.

"Fogge?"

He was expecting a response but none was forthcoming

"As soon as I started working directly for Colonel Lowthian, I had to learn to be secretive. Mistakes, careless words, would cost lives. I maintained that approach on operations, and therefore excluded Major Fogge from anything other than that which the Bureau wished him to know."

"Wished him to know?"

"I regret to say, he became a useful source of disinformation, sir."

Once again, a startled hum wove its way around the court at the revelation. Fogge sat sheet-faced, staring straight ahead. Aukkerley beckoned Laurie to continue.

"It became apparent that there were reasons for Major Fogge's interests in my work that were not entirely consistent with his role."

"For example?"

"The suggestion I was involved with a company was true," continued Laurie, "the Trading Assurance Cairo was legitimately established with the full knowledge of the Bureau to lawfully trade in sugar."

"For what purpose?" inquired Aukkerley.

"Huge amounts of sugar were being lost, presumed stolen. We assumed this was to fund anti-British actions on the streets, so we planned to use this company as cover to find out how this was happening. Colonel Lowthian and Brigadier Regis-Templeton will vouch for this. Indeed Colonel Lowthian masterminded much of what we did. Her fluency in Arabic was critical, as was the support of local agents, especially Peter Moussabey from The Bank of Cairo."

"We shall hear from Lowthian shortly. Have you requested Moussabey?"

"Yes, General, but he is unwilling to attend. He and his family have been compromised by his support for us. Were we to make guarantees on his behalf, I'm sure he would accede to a further request from yourself."

General Aukkerley understood the Moussabey circumstances exactly, but also knew that to make further unsustainable promises would simply add to the dishonour this man had already felt. So he simply nodded to Laurie to continue.

"We suspected Major Fogge and Captain Hillary were far too interested in all things sugar, as I was questioned by the Major over my journeys to Port Alexandria and our Trading Assurance Cairo contacts there."

"Now, wait a minute, Laurie, you are directly suggesting that these two officers were in some way interested in subverting Bureau operations?"

"We all believed this was a possible explanation for their obstructive behaviour, General, not just myself."

"Yes, but do you have proof?"

"Colonel Lowthian will affirm this, plus I would like to draw your attention to the statement you have from Mr Taqi-al-Din-al-Bilal, owner of The Alexandria West Bay Shipping Company in Port Alexandria."

There was a pause as the General read the relevant section in the papers he'd been given by Grice-Farquharason at the start of the session.

"These clearly state that the 'Mr Smith' mentioned here, and this Arab gentleman, Mr Taqi-al-Din-al-Bilal who makes and signs the statement, are in fact both one and the same?"

"Yes, General."

There was a loud gasp around the room, though Fogge, still folded in his chair gave no hint of shock.

"Major, do you know of such a man?" asked the General directly.

"Of course not, sir," replied Fogge.

"These are serious allegations, Laurie, which alter the complexion of this court though not the general thrust of the charges against you."

"You will see that these things are linked, sir," replied Laurie.

"But Mr Taqi-al-Din-al-Bilal, whom you call Mr Smith, is not here to answer for himself."

"He is similarly reticent to Mr Moussabey, sir. Smith, or should I say Mr Taqi-al-Din-al-Bilal, knows now that our company was a front for Bureau activities, and he willingly complied with us to protect his own interests. He became very useful."

"So, he will say what you tell him to say?" asked the General.

"Not at all, sir. He has extensive and legitimate business operations across the Mediterranean; brave work I would remind. He doesn't ask any questions of those who pay him to carry their merchandise on his boats. He relies upon the British and Arab authorities for that as they authorise his cargoes, and he has all the official paperwork you could wish for."

"Major Fogge?"

The General's stare would wither a rat. Fogge was in a predicament: one that required sacrifice.

"I cannot speak for Captain Hillary, sir, he has an unpredictable streak that I have long wrestled with. I can say with absolute certainty that I have never knowingly had any association or dealings with this man 'Smith'. Hillary was the one who generally dealt with the Arabs. These are all questions for him."

Aukkerley harrumphed dismissively.

"Which therefore brings me to the spy, Oriol Quintana," said the General.

"You claim, Laurie, to have had an affinity with him, literature apparently?"

Laurie smiled.

"My main interest was in ensuring his innocence. Once I met him, yes, we talked about the things we had in common, but it was obvious he was who he said he was: a farm owner who traded occasionally in Egypt to help his family and his people, back in Menorca."

"Weren't suspicions heightened by the way he skulked ashore at Port Alexandria and those he kept company with?"

"His image had been circulated within the Bureau as a potential spy, and there was the notion that enemy code might in some way be involved within the items found on his person. So yes, it made good sense to check his story out, but as things turned out it came to nothing."

"And the priest?"

"Father Emam?"

"Indeed," replied Aukkerley, though his eyebrows had preceded him.

"My meeting with him was actually arranged by Major Fogge."

There was another hum around the room as this sank in.

"He was to be the intermediary who helped guide Oriol Quintana's guard party to Suez, he knew the desert and would help the prisoner come to terms with his fate."

"Fogge?" inquired the General.

"I can't remember anything of this," replied the Major, to Aukkerley's clear consternation.

"And there can be no doubt that Father Emam is a man of God," said Laurie.

"Is?" interjected the General, "he's dead."

"He, too, felt the innocence in this poor man, but even though the Bureau experts found no proof of any hidden code, GHQ's influence was such that he was to be treated as a spy and transported to Australia."

"What purpose was there in such a decision unless he was dangerous?" asked Aukkerley.

"That question would be better put to Captain Hillary and Major Fogge, sir, the investigating officers who recommended this outcome."

"Fogge?"

Given the Major's increasingly ghostly countenance and reticence for clarity, an intelligible response was not, by now, particularly expected.

"It was Captain Hillary," he mumbled, barely audibly, "he dealt with this man."

The General was beginning to determine a trend.

"Continue please, Laurie."

"Nooney and I were getting closer to unravelling the full complexity of their illicit dealings. Unbeknown to us and also, as it turned out, to the so-called spy, Oriol Quintana, he had in fact crossed the Mediterranean from Menorca to trade in sugar directly with the two officers, Captain Hillary and Major Fogge, here in Cairo."

There was an explosion of noise, and Aukkerley was forced to shout for silence.

"Complete rubbish," groaned Fogge under his breath.

"Quintana had no idea they were British officers, as to him, they dressed and acted as business-types," continued Laurie, once things had settled.

"His manifest papers were properly signed by The Cairo Sugar Association, Fogge saw to that, and his trade with these two business men would simply, he believed, result in a significant load returning with him by boat, one of Mr Smith's boats, to Menorca, where sugar was and remains in great shortage. It was simply a trade, nothing more, nothing less. He had made many such journeys before, all sanctioned and authorised by the port authorities, signed off as it were by the British, or under their watchfulness by the Egyptians."

"But why would Hillary and Fogge wish to silence Quintana, claiming him to be a spy, if he himself had no reason to suspect them as British officers?"

"Well, sir, they realised following the dreadful event at Pont Limoun Station that Nooney and I were close to exposing them and their illicit business activities, and that the consequences for them would be catastrophic. They could easily put the frighteners on us."

Aukkerley's face screwed.

"A latrine detail or two with the promise of worse to follow does impact the mind, sir."

"Yes, yes… but Quintana?"

"Incarceration in Australia of the man they had convinced their superiors was a spy, out of mind and as far away from the truth as it would be possible to get, would give them the freedom to cover their tracks. And of course, there were probably others out there who were acting just like them, as these two alone could not have accounted for the huge scale of sugar losses we uncovered."

There was a shocked outpouring from around the room, and Aukkerley waited, silently this time, to allow it to clear.

"But what about the shooting at the station, Laurie? Quintana, this innocent victim of the subterfuge you describe, actually shot and killed Lance Corporal Nooney."

"No, sir, he didn't," replied Laurie, "one of our lot did that."

CHAPTER 16

Laurie's revelation had caused an uproar. Even a military court could convulse in shock. General Aukkerley had ordered an adjournment until the following morning, with the main protagonists being ordered to their quarters and instructed to speak to no one; hardly a challenging imposition for Laurie in his cell. At the start of the new proceedings on the next day, Captain Hillary had been allowed to attend, banished to a seat at the side of the court, an observer rather than prosecutor. Fogge remained in his presiding seat, though it was clear to all by now that the business would continue to be driven by General Aukkerley.

"Lance Corporal Laurie, your accusation yesterday that the killing of Lance Corporal Nooney was carried out by one of our own men, was of the most serious order. I want you to reflect carefully before you speak further upon this matter, as failure to substantiate your claim will have the most serious consequences for you. Do you and your representing officer understand?"

"Yes, sir," replied Laurie. Colonel Grice-Farquharason also nodded affirmatively.

"In that case you may continue, though I must tell you that your plans to call Colonel Lowthian have been thwarted. It seems that overnight she has been summoned as a matter of extreme urgency to a new posting, and will be unavailable for the foreseeable future. This is most unfortunate given the seriousness of your case. I have made the strongest representation I can about this, but the war effort, I'm told, has to take precedence."

This was a blow, but not entirely unexpected by either Laurie or Grice-Farquharason. As for the General, he too seemed to have suspicions about such a turn of such events.

"First, we've learnt of the shoddiness of the investigation into Nooney's death. Then you informed of the apparent unwillingness of Moussabey and Smith to appear. Now this; a key witness whisked away in the dead of night. This is all most irregular."

"Please…" he nodded to Laurie, "do continue with your defence before any more witnesses abscond. But remember what I have said."

"Thank you, sir." replied Laurie.

"On the morning of Nooney's death we'd been ordered by Major Fogge to attend his office. As we were on an undercover operation monitoring Oriol Quintana, we were annoyed and suspicious. It seemed to us that the Major might be trying to throw us off the scent. Maybe they were getting closer to Quintana than us, trying to cover something up. It just didn't feel right."

"So you disobeyed instructions and deliberately left an area of the barracks you had been secured within?"

"Yes, sir, we disobeyed Major Fogge's orders, as by now we regarded him as a real threat to the operation. We thought he was up to no good, and that whatever it might be, was happening under the unwitting cover of the Sednaoui Department Store."

General Aukkerley seemed incredulous.

"Yes, sir, I know," said Laurie, "it may sound surprising, but we believed the store was about to be used by Major Fogge and Captain Hillary for one of their trades."

Hillary let out a loud hiss and rocked forward on his chair. Fogge, on the other hand, sat ashen-faced and silent.

"So we followed that hunch, made our way out of the barracks and towards the store, only to find that running the other way along the street was the very man we now know as Quintana. We followed at a distance, towards Pont Limoun Station, and hatched a plan to arrest him. After all, despite our misgivings he really might have been a spy."

"But the report papers state you stood in front of the British Troop Party positioned there that was trying to do just that," said the General.

"When we arrived at the goods yard and found Quintana, he was supervising the loading of sacks onto a railway waggon. We now know they were full of sugar. He was being helped by some local men we recognised. But there were no others around. As far as we were concerned, we were quite alone."

"Did you confront him?"

"Not immediately; we waited our time, hidden below the waggons. When we'd crawled close enough, I suggested to Nooney that we confront the group."

"Were you armed?" asked the General.

"Of sorts, sir, I had a pistol."

"And Nooney?"

"Nothing, sir."

"Quite risky then?"

"Yes, sir… especially as I had no bullets."

"What?"

"I was never issued with any, sir."

The General's eyebrows twitched in a contorted jig; up to this point, the manoeuvre could have be seen as an act of cunning and bravery. But no bullets?

"This was how we worked, sir," continued Laurie, "persuasion rather than force."

"But by all accounts at the time, Laurie, this was a spy; you weren't going to charm him into a surrender and subsequent execution."

There was a guffaw from the side of the courtroom, and the General exploded in rage at Captain Hillary.

"Once more thing and it will be you in the dock."

"It quickly became apparent he wasn't a threat," continued Laurie after things settled. "I shouted that we were Military Police and that he and those with him should stand still, that there was nothing to worry about. They seemed to understand."

"And?"

"That's exactly what they did."

"But for heaven's sake, man, the spy shot Nooney," said the General incredulously… in the head."

"No, sir, Quintana didn't have a gun. He stood there just looking at us… he seemed quite nervous, but there was no gun. And then…" he tailed off, straining to control the brutal rawness of the memory.

"…Laurie?"

"…then I heard rifles being raised behind us and Captain Hillary shouting."

"What did he say?"

"We had no idea he was there, and didn't want to take our eyes off the scene in front of us. The Captain, though, wasn't pleased, he was shouting obscenities at us, telling us to get out of the way."

"Don't you think that was a rather sensible order in the circumstances?"

"Not coming from Captain Hillary, sir. We knew that if we obeyed, he would most likely shoot first before asking questions, and there was no need for that as they were all unarmed."

"Why on earth would you choose to think that?"

"Our previous experiences, sir. And of course the next thing I remember is waking up alongside Lance Corporal Nooney on the floor, whose head I later learnt had been smashed by a bullet."

"From the spy," asserted the General.

"No, sir, as I said, Quintana didn't have a gun; he didn't threaten us in any way. We would have safely arrested him had we been left to our own devices."

"So how was Nooney shot, then?"

"In my opinion, sir, one of our own men. Unintentional possibly, as the bullet I imagine was meant for Quintana."

"But why a bullet and not a volley?"

"Someone panicked? Or pretended to?"

"But surely the men under Captain Hillary's command would know who fired."

"Not for certain, especially if the shot had come from behind them."

"Behind them? Who on earth would be behind them?"

"Normally, sir... Captain Hillary."

There was another murmur around the court as the gravity of this assertion took hold. Hillary gripped the seat of his chair, his face contorted.

"Did you actually see him shoot, then?" asked the General.

"No, sir, as I said, we had no idea the men were behind us, they must have been there hidden from view when we arrived."

"So you cannot confirm your accusation?"

"No, sir."

"Pure supposition then?"

"Well, not quite, sir. If Nooney had been shot by Quintana, the wound would have been to the front of his head, as we were facing him."

"And?"

"As I said, sir, Quintana didn't have a weapon, and the wound to Nooney... it was the back of his head that was shattered, not the front." There were gasps. "He was shot by someone from behind us."

General Aukkerley searched his papers, automatically looking for the autopsy report. Then he remembered none had been prepared. At the time, he'd though that unusual, but there was a war on and the event had seemed tragically routine; at least as reported upon by the Commanding Officer at the scene... Captain Hillary.

"There is a surprising absence of medical evidence to confirm your story," he said, after a few moments scrambling through the slim documents before him, "so this will remain unproven, particularly as we only have your word for this accusation, Laurie."

"Not just my word, sir."

"What?"

"Sergeant Wirrall's."

General Aukkerley was astounded. The realisation that there hadn't been a formal autopsy upon the deceased Lance Corporal was bad enough.

But to then have inferred that a key witness to the event had not been interviewed at the time was quite beyond the pale.

"You are sure that the Sergeant can corroborate your assertion, Laurie?"

"Yes, sir."

"Fogge? Was this man not required to give evidence by your enquiry into Nooney's killing?"

The Major shrugged.

"Fogge, that won't do," insisted the General.

"I left all that sort of thing to…"

"Captain Hillary… yes, yes, so you now keep saying," said the General. Hillary bristled and was about to protest, but Aukkerley's eyes intervened and he thought better of it.

Wirrall had been waiting nervously outside the court for his turn to give evidence, and was now quickly ushered in, receiving the protocols from Aukkerley as if they were his last rites.

"Cheer up, Sergeant," barked the General, noticing a pressed man when he saw one, "all we need is your honest testimony."

But in truth, there was thirty-five years of pensionable service to the crown at stake for Wirrall if things went wrong.

"You were at Pont Limoun Station when Lance Corporal Nooney was killed?"

"Yes, sir," he replied quietly, so much so that Aukkerley asked him to repeat the answer.

"And you saw the shooting?"

"Yes, sir," he said again, but still clearly conflicted.

"Sergeant Wirrall," said Aukkerley, "I realise that this is difficult for you. As well as the defendant, whom you will know well, there are senior officers in the room you have worked for; your loyalties must surely be tested."

Wirrall nodded.

"But I assure you that whatever you say in this courtroom, if truthful, will have no consequence for you other than our grateful thanks. You have my word on that."

"Thank you, sir."

He knew of the General's reputation, including that he was a friend of General Regis-Templeton, and that was enough for him.

"You saw the shooting?" repeated General Aukkerley.

The Sergeant cleared his throat.

"I arrived just as the shot went off. I'd earlier been commanded by Major Fogge to seal off the exits of the Sednaoui Department Store, as apparently, he was meeting a contact in there and was looking to have the man arrested if things turned sour. So I'd only just arrived at the station, having rushed to get there."

"Did you know the man he was referring to?"

"No, sir, Major Fogge kept those sorts of things close to his chest, though I saw him in the store dressed to the nines in civvies, talking with a business type in a light suit."

"And?"

"Well, the Major was always specific with me that I should 'stay alert but keep my distance.'"

"And did you?"

"Absolutely, sir, as did the spy. Our men went in to bar the doors, but in the confusion the bloke was most certainly alerted. As we now know, he also kept his distance by legging it to Pont Limoun Station."

"The men followed him?"

"No, sir, just me. I left the men to search the store and went on alone, just in case I'd jumped to the wrong conclusion. The Major had taken over anyway and I thought I'd be better off that way. So I followed my instincts and ran towards the station, though I wasn't completely sure that's where he'd gone."

"Ran?" asked the General.

"Well, more of a quick walk these days, sir, not quite as fit as I was."

"And?"

"Well, when I finally found him, there was clearly something going on. I turned around the corner of the sidings yard to see a fellow dressed in a suit, the same one as in the store. So I assumed he was the spy. He was stood with two or three Arabs and was facing Lance-Corporals Nooney and Laurie."

"Facing you say?"

"Yes, sir. I also noticed that there was a patrol of about eight men from the barracks, with Captain Hillary in attendance. They had been behind a low wall that housed some water hoses and were just in the process of standing up and pointing their rifles. Seems they may have been under cover to that point. It didn't look good, and knowing Lance Corporal Laurie as I do, I feared the worst."

"What do you mean you 'feared the worst'?"

"He's an excellent soldier, sir, but impetuous, born the wrong way round, gets into scrapes, especially with officers he doesn't think much of."

"Is he reckless?"

"Yes, sir, in terms of his own preservation. I told him, officers can be as mad and bad as the rest of us but just ring your neck in when the anger happens, or risk losing it."

"Yes, thank you, Sergeant," said Aukkerley stifling a cough, "so what happened?"

"Well, how to sort out yet another mess I was thinking…"

"…another mess?"

"Yes, sir, that was often my role in circumstances involving Laurie."

"And those involving Captain Hillary?"

"I'd rather not say, sir."

"But you must, Sergeant," replied the General, "remember, you have my word."

"…and likewise with the Captain, sir."

"And how did this mess, as you suggest, pan out?"

Sergeant Wirrall wasn't an emotional man. In his years of service he'd witnessed the most unimaginable actions and there was little that could disturb him. But he'd admired Lance Corporal Nooney, almost as a son, and his death had hit him hard. He bowed his head and tears welled.

"Nooney was an excellent man, sir," he said eventually, "it was such a needless waste of a life."

"In what way, Sergeant?" pressed Aukkerley.

"To be shot like that, sir."

"By the spy?"

The Poet Laurie Ate

Sergeant Wirrall screwed up his face.

"Laurie then?"

"No, sir, absolutely not," retorted Wirrall, "they hadn't guns that worked as far as I knew."

"Who then?"

"There was one shot, sir, and from where I was it came from our men."

"Who?"

"I can't be sure, but everyone at the front had ducked with the noise of the gun from behind them."

"Who was behind them, Sergeant?"

Hillary paused.

"Who man?" demanded Aukkerley.

"Captain Hillary."

"You f…"

Hillary was about to end his career and freedom with a stream of invective, but the General interceded, warning him yet again about his conduct.

"I don't believe any of the actions that day were intentional, sir," continued Sergeant Wirrall, once order had been restored, "Captain Hillary has had his share of ups and downs in this war like the rest of us. Whatever happened, I believe he was trying to do his best."

"And Nooney? You went to help?"

"Yes, sir, in pushing Laurie over he'd got himself in the way of that bullet, copped it in the back of the head. It was instant."

"Laurie?"

"Spark out like a light. Nooney had thwacked him good and proper."

"Were you asked by Major Fogge to comment upon what you saw?" asked Aukkerley.

"No, sir. He arrived some time after the event and said to keep schtum; that these things happen in war. Well, no disrespect, sir, but I've seen a bit more of the war than him and I'd never seen the like, but he was the Major and that was that."

The General turned to Fogge.

"Any comments, Major?"

"I presented the basics and they were accepted at the inquiry," replied Fogge, his voice muted, "...and these had relied upon Captain Hillary's recollection of things."

"But no mention of Sergeant Wirrall's testimony?"

"I had no idea he'd seen a thing."

Aukkerley blew out his cheeks.

"Wirrall, didn't you think to say something, speak to the Major, after all this was a terribly serious matter?"

"Captain Hillary made things quite plain to me as well, sir. To be precise, he told me to 'keep my great big gob shut' and that anyway, Major Fogge was 'incontinent'."

"Incontinent?"

"That's what he said, sir."

"Do you mean 'incompetent', Sergeant?"

"That's as I said, sir."

There was a tittle of laughter around the room, as much in relief at a break in the tension as in Sergeant Wirrall's assumed slip, but he knew the score.

"You see, that's exactly it, sir. I've been laughed at for years by the likes of these people," and he waved his hand to the court, "and all I've ever done is carry out orders and keep the likes of them out of scrapes."

General Aukkerley went to intervene, but something in him decided against it.

"The Captain, the Major, they think they're better, they think they're part of the bigger people who know best, that the little folk like me should feel lucky to even have a job. But you see, this war's changed all that. It's the likes of me, poor old Nooney and all the decent men in the ranks, that are the real life blood. People who have the talent if not the breeding, good people, the sort who live and die..." and he gestured to the room "...without their sense of entitlement." There was some nervous shuffling. "So this lot sat here can laugh all they like so long as they remember who it is that keeps them where they are. I said Major Fogge was 'incontinent' and I know what I mean."

There was complete silence. No one had expected the Sergeant to take such a literal approach to the assurances he'd been given, nor had they expected such precision.

"So, you won't be surprised to know," he continued, "that I overheard Captain Hillary swearing at Major Fogge in his office during the recess yesterday."

"What?" Aukkerley was startled.

"I shouted through the door to ask if all was well, but I clearly heard the Captain using threatening language, telling the Major to sort it out here in the court."

"Fogge, is this correct?"

"I tried to stop him, sir," he said , shaking his head despairingly, "but I'm afraid he was using the most peremptory form of language."

"Peremptory you say? What on earth are you going on about?" shouted the General, "you know the rules about the protocols following such a breach of discipline."

"But I was taking a bath, sir," replied Fogge obsequiously, "it was rather awkward."

"Taking a bath? Awkward, my arse," shouted the General, now incensed.

"Scumble," added Sergeant Wirrall still trying to make the most of his moment.

"Scumble?" repeated the General, wondering what on earth had now possessed the Sergeant.

"Yes, sir, Scumble is what that is, what he's just said, it's what Major Fogge does best."

Even Fogge looked bemused.

"Covering up," continued Wirrall "what I did as a kid when I was helping my old dad with his painting job at the big houses. Put a thin wash of white on top of a dodgy bit of paint work to cover it up a bit; softened it so you'd never notice there had been a problem. Scumble."

The General had heard enough. He banged the desk with his gavel, shouted at Captain Hillary to stand and then ordered him to leave the court in the close company of two Military Policemen, but Hillary wasn't going quietly. He began shouting obscenities, both at Fogge and at the court, about the injustices that were being meted upon him.

"Out," shouted Aukkerley, but still Hillary struggled.

"Doesn't alter the fact that Laurie is a killer," he screamed. "What about that, what about that?"

"Out," replied Aukkerley, once more.

"Two men dead in the desert," ranted Hillary, "murdered them both he did." His voice trailed off as he was dragged away.

For a short while, a doleful silence infected the shocked courtroom. Where was the certainty they relied upon? This, the most military of proceedings, had inexplicably disintegrated into abject legal carnage. None had ever experienced the like, especially General Aukkerley; and this was happening on his watch. He armed himself once more with his gavel, and was about to order an adjournment, as much for his own sanity as for the niceties of justice, when Laurie beckoned his attention.

"Sir, those killings Captain Hillary refers to…"

The General placed his gavel back on the desk and indicated to Laurie to continue.

"…there are witnesses waiting outside the court whom I wish to call."

"Have these been listed?" asked the General.

"No, sir, I wasn't sure they would be able to attend. But I've received a note confirming their willingness to testify."

"A note?"

Laurie asked Colonel Grice-Farquharason to pass the slip of paper he'd received the previous day to Aukkerley, who perused the contents for a few moments, eyes squinting in concentration and yet clearly confused.

"This seems to be a piece of prose, Laurie?"

"Yes, sir, otherwise referred to, or rather confused as … German code."

"What, the stuff our intelligence people were deciphering?"

"The very same."

"Witnesses you say?"

Laurie nodded.

"This is most unorthodox."

"I think you'll find that one of the witnesses is anything but, sir."

"Have they been checked?"

The General looked to the back of the court where the usher and two military officers were standing, and they nodded their confirmation.

"Fogge, any objections?"

"Isn't this non-justiciable, sir?"

The General sighed. He needn't have asked. The Major had long since lost any shred of credibility, save with regard to that which might protect his own skin: any decision of the General's would now be met with his servile compliance.

So Aukkerley gave his consent and instructed that the witnesses Laurie had waiting should be brought in for formal questioning.

The entrance doors at the end of the large briefing hall where the proceedings were being held, were a good thirty steps or so away. In the dusty gloom, two figures appeared, and there was a faint whiff of cigarette: one was cloaked, his face hidden, quite tall and slim, the other dressed in a lived-in suit, his head covered by a boater hat.

As they came closer, their faces became clearer, though their backgrounds not so. To most of the penetrating stares that attended as they were ushered to seats, they were Arabs. For a few. Though, there was something recognisable about the man in a suit.

The General pointed, asking him to take the stand and introduce himself.

"My name," he said, pausing briefly, "is Oriol Quintana."

There was a huge gasp of disbelief. General Aukkerley also seemed stunned, and it took him a few moments to restore some direction to the proceedings.

"What... the poet?" he asked.

Quintana nodded.

"Do we have proof of this?" he said, looking at the man who faced him, but seeking guidance from those who'd had dealings with the man when a prisoner.

"I can certainly confirm this," came a voice from below the hood of the witness sat next to Quintana. He stood up, removing the covering from his head and displaying what were now clearly recognisable ecumenical vestments.

"And who are you?" the General inquired.

"Father Daoud Emam, a Coptic priest," replied the man in perfect English.

Uproar returned, and this time Aukkerley's gavel swung with even greater force. It took longer to restore order than before, with the General employing several thumps to the desk, but as things eventually settled, the priest appeared to be smiling.

"These are serious matters," reminded Aukkerley.

"Which require a man with a hammer?" asked Emam.

Aukkerley grunted.

"Well," continued Emam, "quite apart from those in this room, including Sergeant Wirrall, who will so clearly recognise my friend, I have papers from His Excellency Paulinus, Bishop Emeritus of the Diocese of Arage in Spain, asking me to give my kindest protections to Oriol Quintana, the man you see before you, an instruction I most nearly failed."

The General was passed the document.

"If you need further assurance, then my Greek Orthodox brothers from St Nicholas Cathedral here in Cairo, will testify as to my credentials. Oriol Quintana and I have availed ourselves of their sanctuary for the past few weeks, since our adventures in the desert. Today brings us welcome relief."

He beamed broadly.

"Sergeant?" demanded the General.

Wirrall seemed set rigid in shocked and confounded stupor.

"Sergeant?" shouted Aukkerley again, to rouse him.

"It's them, sir, I can't believe it… but it's definitely them. I'm completely flaggerbasted."

"Flaggerbas…?" General Aukkerley quietly closed his eyes before recovering and continuing.

"Do you recognise anyone else in this room?" he asked Father Daoud Emam.

"The good Sergeant, whom I have mentioned, and of course my friend, Lance Corporal Laurie."

The General asked Emam to sit, returning directly to Oriol.

"Mr Quintana? Do you also recognise Sergeant Wirrall and Lance Corporal Laurie?"

"Yes," he replied.

The general thanked him and was about to continue, but Oriol hadn't finished.

"…plus the man across there, his face is quite distinct, though I have never seen him in a uniform."

He pointed directly at Fogge, who stared back warily, squinting over his glasses.

"What?" exclaimed Aukkerley.

"That is Mr Jones," replied Oriol, "a businessman I have traded with for several years, mostly in sugar, but sometimes other products, too."

There was uproar once more, and Aukkerley struggled desperately to rest back control, threatening the collective present that the session would be halted if such behaviour continued.

"Traded?" asked the General, eventually, some solemnity having returned.

"Everything was done through the proper authorities," continued Oriol, concerned he might become the focus of censure, "he and I ensured this, and if you need, you will be able to see all the records of our dealings. I exported to Menorca, through Port Alexandria."

"So you used the boats of a Mr Smith from the Alexandria West Bay Shipping Company?"

Oriol was surprised the General knew this.

"From that company, yes, but the man I dealt with there was called Taqi-al-Din-al-Bilal."

"The very same man we now know as a certain Mr Smith, I believe," replied the General, though Oriol was unsure as to what he meant.

"And occasionally," he continued, "I used other boats sailing into and out of there, all sanctioned by the port authorities."

"Your last boat was that owned by the Adreassens?"

Oriol stared at the General, again surprised he knew such detail.

"You were watched," explained the General, "but that's hardly relevant now it would seem."

"So where did you meet 'Mr Jones'?" he continued.

"On this occasion at the Sednaoui store, though I'd also met an associate of his at The Cairo Sugar Association earlier. It was quite an unusual meeting."

"In what way?"

"Well, he was seemingly acting as the middle man for Mr Jones, but as I had always dealt directly with Jones before, it made me wary. These are very unusual times in which to try to trade, and I had decided that this would be my last such venture to Cairo."

"Is that other man present?"

Oriol was invited to stand and take a careful look around the court.

"No, not that I can see, but he wasn't a tall man, and he appeared very nervous, kept touching his head and shouting at me when he thought my English was lacking. He had a very thin black moustache. I didn't really take to him, seemed incompetent to me. He said he was called Mr Eaton."

Hearing this, Aukkerley broke off for a moment to issue whispered instructions to a court official he'd beckoned. Then he returned to Oriol.

"Did the trade work satisfactorily for you when you met 'Mr Jones' at the store?"

"Well, he was very friendly as always, a real gentleman, but then things turned. He asked me to include an art work in the trade, a piece of Egyptian tomb-ware I believe, to be secreted in one of the sugar sacks. He assured me the authorisations were all in place. I objected and he became argumentative."

"You mean he was attempting to smuggle such artefacts to Spain, inside the sacks of sugar he was trading with you?"

"He didn't say as much, but like you, this is what I suspected. To Menorca first, then I guessed that he would want them to go onwards from Mahon, to mainland Spain, for storage until the war is over. It would eventually end up in London, I assume."

"Had this happened before?"

"Of course not. It would not be a legal trade, and I believe Egypt has already lost huge numbers of treasures."

Oriol was practiced in keeping things simple. He had no intention of shortening any trail that might lead back to Sant Cristofol and Turo Vell.

"Did you agree to this request?"

"No. I only pretended to go along with things to enable the main purpose of my visit. I would have given the art work to the authorities before I sailed."

"But you were found with a book of code in your possessions."

"Well, the only book I had was *The Odyssey of Homer*," laughed Oriol. "A gift he forced upon me to convince me of his good intent."

The General's face creased at the thought of the Bureau's greatest minds attempting to study this classic for an anti-British plot.

"But the writings you had on your person, you carried a notebook?"

"They were simply my thoughts, first drafts for the prose I was working on. I try to write."

Aukkerley consulted the writing on the piece of paper given to him earlier by Laurie.

"Is this the material that was deemed as German code?" asked Aukkerley, looking across to Laurie.

"Yes, sir, the very same," he answered, "poetic you might say."

The General shook his head and returned to Quintana.

"So you ran from the store?"

"Not at all," replied Oriol, confident now that he was actually the one directing matters."

"There was some sort of noise at the entrance, British soldiers started running in, so I said my goodbyes and left by a side door. Such disturbance isn't unusual in Cairo."

Aukkerley ignored the inference.

"I headed as normal to the station, to oversee the loading."

"Oversee? So you weren't alone?"

"There are those who work there whom I trust, people I've worked with ever since I've been trading in Cairo. They check that the right number and weight of sugar sacks are loaded, and that everything is numbered and authorised according to the manifest."

"You seem to be very thorough, Mr Quintana."

"Thank you," replied Oriol, "it is the price of bitter experience."

"Tell me," continued Aukkerley, "in which sack was the art work secreted?"

Oriol hesitated, judging the mood.

"Come now, you were arrested at the scene, sentenced to a life of labour in Australia, apparently murdered in cold blood in the desert. This is hardly a detail that should continue to trouble you."

"27," replied Oriol.

General Aukkerley shuffled through papers on his desk, opening a file and using his forefinger to find particular detail. He pursed his lips and nodded.

"As I thought," he said, "that was the sack that was found to have been torn open. There was no sign of any work of Egyptian art. I am, of course, reading from the 'report' compiled under Major Fogge's jurisdiction."

"I am only concerned about the sugar," replied Oriol, "which I legitimately purchased."

"And if true, will be honoured," replied the General. "Were you aware of being followed to the station?"

Oriol shook his head.

"Did you think that there would be British troops there?"

"There was no reason for me to be suspicious. I was simply doing what I always do when in Cairo."

"But you became involved in a shooting?"

"Two men appeared and challenged me. They were in suits and I had no idea who they were. I now know, of course, that they were Lance Corporal Laurie and his colleague, the poor man who was shot."

"Did either of those two men point a weapon at you?"

"No. I was greatly shocked to be confronted, and at the time had no idea who they were. It crossed my mind that they might be criminals. Though Laurie, the one standing nearest, did shout that he was with the British. He was trying to be calm, show authority, but it was a strange moment to be face to face with these two men so suddenly and in such a way."

"Did you draw a weapon?"

Oriol looked askance at the General.

"I have never possessed such a thing."

"So the shooting?"

Oriol took his time. It had felt a great relief to be in the court, a step closer to home, but the memories of that day still chilled.

"A group of British soldiers suddenly appeared from some distance behind Laurie and his colleague. They pointed their rifles. There was shouting. Laurie seemed to know the officer in command as he was trying to speak to him."

"What, he turned around to talk to him?"

"No. All the time he kept facing me, but he was definitely shouting back to the officer, almost as if there was an argument. Then suddenly the other man by Laurie jumped at him and there was a crack from a rifle. I expected to die. We fell to the floor, waiting for further shots, but instead heard screaming, shouts, men running, before being jumped upon by British soldiers and arrested. So began the worst weeks of my life. All I had done was to was witness a man shot dead right in front of me. Since then my freedom has been denied, terrible accusations have been made against me and lies told, and my whole life placed in turmoil."

"Do you know who fired the rifle?"

"No, but the shot came from behind Laurie and his colleague. They had no weapons that I could see."

"How did you then come to know Lance Corporal Laurie?"

"He visited me in my prison cell."

"So you had never met him before?"

"Of course not, apart from that terrible incident at the station."

"And when you met in your cell?"

"He visited together with Father Emam, weeks after the British Army condemned me to a life of incarceration. I was unsure of him at first, but I became aware he was genuinely interested in my freedom."

"Why do you say that?"

"Because we spent time talking about the beauty in life."

The General's brow creased.

"Art, poetry, great music," said Oriol, attempting to explain, "we shared a passion, a common language."

"The guards reported that you spoke in Latin to Lance Corporal Laurie."

Oriol burst out laughing, and Father Emam also guffawed from his seat a few feet away.

"Lance Corporal Laurie is an intelligent man, but I don't believe even he would have understood a word of any so-called Latin from myself. No, they were confused. The person I spoke to in such a way was Father Emam. He is also a son of Menorca, so we communicated occasionally in the local dialect, *menorqui*. He was a little out of practice, but it worked."

"It worked?"

"A plan that would serve all our purposes."

"What plan?"

"Lance Corporal Laurie realised I'd walked into a trap that he and his colleague had been setting for those from within their own ranks; officers who were taking sugar for personal gain."

"Is this true, Laurie?" inquired the General.

"Yes, sir, the accidental encroachment by Mr Quintana into our operations became an opportunity that was too good to miss. As you may now see, we'd suspected Major Fogge and Captain Hillary, but hard evidence was difficult to come by. Nooney's bullet was meant for Mr Quintana. Killing a spy evading arrest wouldn't be difficult to justify. Only in this case, the intended victim as they well knew, wasn't a spy, just a businessman who had stumbled upon their illicit activities."

"So, there was deliberate intention to remove Mr Quintana?"

"Had we not been present at that incident, sir, that intention would have been praised and rewarded, as none of this would have reached a courtroom."

"And maybe Nooney would be alive?" said the General.

The insinuation hurt… and was true. But nothing would bring Nooney back.

"Worse still," continued Laurie, determined to hide the emotion churning within, "Lance Corporal Nooney's heroics meant that I'd become a liability for them. They could probably sideline me, but with Nooney's death and Mr Quintana alive, things would be more awkward. So they planned to cover up the killing and have Mr Quintana incarcerated at the other end of the world. He'd be out of sight forever and who would care, who would ask questions?"

"But why that ridiculous ruse of yours in the desert?" asked the General. "Couldn't you just report the matter?"

"Would you all have believed it, sir?"

"Surely you could have spoken to Colonel Lowthian? She would have supported you. After all, you say she had led on the general matters in which you and Lance Corporal Nooney were involved."

"I believe that she, too, without hard evidence, would have struggled to make the case, sir. I lost count of the times she was referred to as 'that bloody woman' by officers who should have known better."

Aukkerley grimaced. He knew he may well have been one of those of whom Laurie spoke.

"But really, Laurie, wasn't there a more straightforward way?"

Laurie stared hard at the General. Even now and in this supreme moment of conviction, he hoped that what he saw in front of him was indeed an ally.

"My actions, sir, provided both Major Fogge and Captain Hillary with the misplaced confidence that their problems had been resolved, that there were no threats to their deviousness, what with me insane and Quintana gone. They could, therefore, continue to act with impunity. But as we have seen, sir, such hubris caused them to unravel before us in a way not possible had the 'ruse', as you call it, not been hatched."

"But the murders, the blood and bones… the meat? And you, Mr Quintana," said the General, shifting his attention, "weren't you at all afraid that you were about to be killed by an actual madman?"

"There were moments it is true, when I could not be sure," repied Oriol, smiling, "and it was only when I finally heard the agreed words that I totally trusted my safety to him."

"Words?"

"'The last bit of up'. They were the words he told me he would he would use when my freedom was near. I had no idea what they meant, but once I heard them as I climbed away from my captors at the cave, I knew he wasn't mad, that I would be safe."

General Aukkerley still seemed reluctant to indulge fully with the outline of events he was being presented.

"If I may?"

It was Father Emam, and the General directed he continue.

"Subterfuge. Play all the parts well enough, undertake the actions, and the mind will make up the story you require."

"Subterfuge?"

"I arranged the diversion to the cave in the desert hills," continued Emam. "The military men we had with us were, with the exception of Sergeant Wirrall, very inexperienced. Bedouin friends of mine had followed us with their herd along the Indian Mailroad, but at a distance. They knew that in the early morning in question I would require them to help me with the prisoner. They trust me. I have spent many times in the desert with them, learning from them, but also helping them as best as I am able."

"Helping?"

"Yes, General, helping them to understand the British; their ways. You see, I have my uses."

He smiled.

"Colonel Lowthian would regularly ask me to join her when she travelled with the Bedouin. We would look for routes through the desert that may help the British cause. Sometimes there would be other officers in the party too, and I would step in to make sure there were no unfortunate misunderstandings in the orders."

He could see the General was warming to his words.

"So you really do work for the British?"

"I work for love, General."

"And a certain Bishop Paulinus?"

"He too shares my Menorcan heritage. Oriol Quintana is blessed to have this man as his earthly father."

Oriol heard those words and they landed deeply.

"My friends were happy to help," continued Emam, "especially as all I required was a fire, upon which were scattered the remnants of animal meat. And, of course, when you kill a goat you spill blood. Put all this together and it was an easy task to encourage the imaginings of frightened soldiers. My two Arab guides, two of my most trusted colleagues, added to the illusion with their actions."

"So you and Mr Quintana returned unseen to Cairo with the Bedouin?"

"That's correct. An easy journey for those of us used to such ways. We have since been sitting out events within St Nicholas Cathedral, waiting for this day."

"And Sergeant Wirrall?"

"An excellent soldier," replied Emam, "he had no idea of our intentions, nor was he wise to the desert, but I knew that his skills would enable the men to get back to barracks."

The General turned to Laurie.

"I remain surprised that you chose such an option."

There was a long pause, and Laurie feared the worst.

"That said, you are clearly not a killer, not least because the men you are alleged to have murdered are so very obviously alive and well and in front of us in this court room."

He cleared his voice.

"So, Lance Corporal Laurie, I rule that all the charges against you are dropped."

A huge din broke out as the consequences of the ruling sank in. For Laurie, though, the elation that coursed through his body was soon replaced by pain and guilt. He'd dreamt of this moment since that day at Pont Limoun. But the dreadful burden remained.

"You're a clever so and so at times, mate," Nooney had said to him one day after he'd bantered his way past yet another unhelpful instruction from headquarters, "but remember, that'll make you unpopular. That lot won't care a jot for what you think, or even give you a thank you."

At the time, he'd laughed, but he knew Nooney was right.

He'd won this day for his friend, but there would be consequences.

Just then a noise erupted at the far door as two Military Police came into the room, frogmarching a bewildered Captain Hillary back into the court. General Aukkerley turned to Oriol.

"Mr Quintana, as you were speaking earlier I interrupted things to ask one of my officials to send for the man you see brought before us in court. I need to ask you just one more question and please, take your time to answer. Do you recognise this man?"

Oriol looked at the pale and broken figure before him, half held upward by his guards.

"I have never seen this man in uniform," he replied, and the General's eyebrows perked. He took a further more careful look, almost enjoying the moment.

"But I have certainly met him once before. This is Mr Eaton. I met him at The Cairo Sugar Association, the middleman I mentioned to you earlier."

Captain Hillary had by now expended every ounce of linguistic energy; indeed he was in such a state that it was all he could do to try to balance upright.

"Thank you," said Aukkerley, "that is all I need to know."

He called for a guard unit to escort both Hillary and Fogge to the cells, and once this had been completed, he formally halted the proceedings.

"The charges against Lance Corporal Laurie are to be dropped and removed from the record," he said.

"I shall arrange for a Courts Martial hearing for Captain Hillary and Major Fogge at the earliest possible opportunity."

He turned to Oriol.

"Mr Quintana. You too are free to leave this court and to continue about your lawful business. The order directing your incarceration is also to be formally rescinded. I have been told that the sugar you purchased has in fact already been sent to Port Alexandria and so awaits onward transportation at your convenience. His Majesty's Government has no wish for you to suffer any financial redress as a result of your unwitting involvement in these matters."

"Thank you," replied Oriol, the relief overwhelming, "I shall make the necessary arrangements as soon as I can contact the Andreassens. It will be good to get home."

As he said this, he noticed the looks exchanged between the administrative staff sat at the desks. Even the General looked uncomfortable.

"Have I said something wrong?" he inquired.

"No, not at all, Mr Quintana."

He paused.

"I take it, therefore, you don't know."

"Know?"

There was a further hesitation.

"We received a cable some weeks back. A boat named *The Adelphi*, the one I believe you sailed into Port Alexandria aboard, was sunk by the Turkish navy off the coast of Palestine, some five miles out from Ashkelon."

Oriol felt a pounding sickness in the pit of his stomach. He could just about manage the words he needed, though feared they were already spent in their uselessness.

"The crew?" he whispered.

"I am afraid there were no survivors."

CHAPTER 17

"That's not possible, as I'm afraid the injuries he sustained fighting the Hun have reduced his previously remarkable efficiencies."

Such was the shock of these words that Colonel Lowthian barely heard what followed.

She'd been summoned to the Army GHQ at The Savoy late at night to receive new and immediately actionable instructions on a posting. She'd protested to the table of top brass arranged before her that she was needed the very next morning as a key witness at the trial of Lance Corporal Laurie, and had requested the confirmations of Brigadier Regis-Templeton to support this. He would insist upon the paramount importance of her testimony, and his word, that of the man she trusted more than any other, would suffice.

"You should be aware he's already en route to Plymouth, sailed a few days ago."

She barely grasped the detail but intuitively, even in despair, realised this was the end.

"Yes," said another, "he'll recuperate for a while before taking over some of the training duties at the Worcestershire's, close to where he has a place. It's in the back of beyond I believe but, in the circumstances…" His voice trailed as if in some form of memoriam.

Prepared though she was by the bitter misogynistic forces that had blighted her life, the shock of this news was wrenchingly invasive. She owed Laurie her honesty to that court, and the death of Nooney still weighed heavily. But more than this, there was the Brigadier. They were close, so very close; yet he'd hardly shared a thing about his deepening struggles nor indicated the imminence of a transfer. The man she so admired, so believed, was sick and by now far away. And with him had followed another time of love.

"…left something of a mess behind him, though," continued the voice who seemed to be chairing the meeting, "what with old Aukkerley left to sweep up it's probably a good thing for everybody."

"Sir?"

"You'll not be needed Lowthian; the proceedings you mention will be over without the need for you to muddy the water. Nothing but an embarrassment for the army the whole damn caboodle, made us look like fools. Bloody good job he's gone."

This wasn't the Regis-Templeton she knew, nor the man so admired by his troops. His bravery had been undoubted, his loyalty to the men unquestionable, yet amongst this morally deficient body such pedigree seemed to have little bearing.

"You're to join Allenby's lot; you'll be properly useful once Jerusalem is taken," he said.

A further blow.

"Later tonight you're to meet up with the Aussie unit transferring to Rafah, and from there up the line, once the bash at Beersheba is sorted."

"But… why?"

"You speak something of the language I'm led to believe?"

How could these people not know of her work, the dreadful things she'd witnessed, the heroics of those she'd worked alongside, the alliances she'd forged, and the intelligence she'd provided to help shorten the war.

"A little," she replied, wishing neither to ease their ignorance nor speed her departure from the work she loved.

"But there are important enquiries still to be completed in Cairo, sir, critical work for the success both here in Egypt and in Palestine."

"Like what?" asked the General, bluntly.

His response had been insulting. Her work and that of the Bureau had always been central to things in Cairo. There had been tensions with regular army HQ, but also respect and co-dependency. Or so she'd thought.

"Well, sir, like the unravelling of the 'Sugar Case'. At last, we can control this business efficiently, reassure our Arab colleagues, provide a way for them to operate in readiness for when we are gone."

The brass looked at each other and there were mutters. She recognised a few of the faces, but she'd rarely dealt with them directly; that was the cushion Regis-Templeton had provided. But he was gone and she, the specialist in intelligence, had glaringly failed in her alertness to the possibility of the circumstance she now faced.

"You will be needed in Jerusalem," insisted the voice. These people you get on with, they will respond more easily in Palestine with you there as back-up. Apparently, we've got to put to rest the bloody Crusades reputation we seem to have, and it's people like you who can help with that."

She felt dumbstruck by his ignorance. He really had no understanding or interest in her existing role or contribution. She would simply be more useful and convenient as an interpreter, out of the way, elsewhere.

"This is a compliment, Colonel," he insisted.

It certainly didn't feel that way. It felt more like the end of a world she'd worked to create; one that now seemingly never existed.

'These people', he'd said. She thought immediately of the Moussabeys. What if they could hear such sentiment?

"There will need to be one almighty slice of delicacy in negotiation to get the various parties to settle with us, once we enter the city."

"And we're going to need your skills in persuasion," said another.

"To represent the Arabs and their cause?" she asked provocatively, and there was further mumbling.

"Cause?" responded the main brass acidly, "peace should be enough for them for now I would have thought."

And in that her conviction of honour, of promise, the currencies by which she had traded, departed.

"You travel tonight, join with the Aussies at Heliopolis. Collect your paperwork on the way out."

The voice had heard enough.

"Remember, this is an order. Count yourself lucky to be free of all this lot."

"Sir?"

"The Intelligence Bureau, Lowthian." He stared at her, eyes almost spitting bile.

"It's being reorganised, brought back into Army GHQ where it should always have been. This recent stuff you've been involved with, even you must have recognised the whole place was almost feral."

The blows kept falling. Her work had been essential to the war effort, and to the peace and security of Egypt. Even Allenby had been pleased to use its outcomes.

"But, sir, the Sugar Case, we still have a chance to close down the illegalities, the Bureau is essential to…"

"Damn you, Lowthian." They really had had enough.

"What your meddling fools uncovered was a British operation that smoothly ensured the safe passage of sugar back home. Well, we thought it was smooth until your lot stumbled upon it. Thank heavens there are still avenues out there we can use."

"Sir?"

"Why do you think we've spent so much time helping with such businesses here? Hey?"

She looked blankly back at him.

"To make certain the poor bloody starving hordes back in blighty have something to sweeten their lives."

"But, sir, there are officers who have been…"

"Been what, Lowthian?"

"Well, sir, works of art have also been smuggled…"

This was too much, and there was an explosion.

"Been what Lowthian? Hey? Been what? Don't give me that twaddle. Smuggled, smuggled you say? Bloody saved is what I call it woman, saved." He stared directly at her, a rage in his cheeks.

"All they were trying to do was their bloody job." He paused. "Exactly what they were ordered to do, that is until your bloody lot stepped in."

"But sir, a man died, surely…"

Her voice trailed as the full horror began to reveal itself.

"War, Lowthian, strange things happen. We lost one of your men, but I assure you, one way or another we won't be losing those other two fools who ran that show, not even with Aukkerley's inevitably blithering interferences."

She stood motionless for a moment. There were words she wished to say, but they wouldn't undo the magnitude of the deceit now paraded before her: a treachery in which her own noble self-delusion had played an all too significant part.

"Tonight, I tell you. Now go."

"You will soon be back with your loved ones," said Laurie.

"So long as the German U-Boats allow," laughed Oriol.

They were sitting inside St Nicholas Cathedral, almost on the very pew where Laurie had first met Father Emam, and close to the quarters Oriol had hidden in following his return from the desert. The priest had gone outside for a cigarette, so they were quite alone.

"Thank you," said Laurie, as he pulled out the scrap piece of paper from his pocket that Oriol had sent to him at the start of the court proceedings. It contained a completed poem.

"This will stay with me."

"As will you, my friend, you saved my life," replied Oriol.

He paused for a few moments, still hardly able to believe the trajectory of this, his final journey to Cairo.

"I am sorry," he said eventually, "Lance Corporal Nooney's death was avoidable."

Laurie nodded, taking some time to reply.

"He was always a showy so and so," he quipped, yet smiling, "he would have loved the pathos that surrounded his death."

"He was the best of men," continued Laurie after another pause, "he taught us all to see the brightness out there, to look for the strength to deal with the bewilderments of our earthly life."

"It must be the surroundings," said Oriol, gazing around at the opulent interior of the building, "you're sounding like the priest."

This time the laughter was strong, almost uncontrollable, drawing disapproving stares from those arriving for private prayer.

"Will you continue to write?" asked Laurie after a while.

"I have no option," replied Oriol, "it's in me; there's nothing I can do about that."

"You?"

Laurie winced, a desire long suppressed.

"You must promise me you will at least try," continued Oriol.

"I shall," he replied, and he waved the poem he'd been given, "especially as this has again inspired me."

"Again?"

"You may not realise the power of your words. They spoke to me in a way that mouths cannot."

"I am greatly honoured my friend that you should say that," replied Oriol, though Laurie wasn't finished.

"I was born into an unspoken expectation of obedience and submission. Some found escape in drink… others perhaps just a touch of madness." They smiled; the memories of Laurie's dramatics in the desert were still so fresh.

"Instead though," continued Laurie, "can you believe it? I discovered… a library."

Once again, they burst into laughter.

"But it saved me. Your poem took me right back to that building, to the words that poured from those books; helped my release. That place taught me reason had to be fought for, that ignorance could never be an excuse… and it's caused me a great deal of trouble ever since… even in the desert."

Oriol smiled. Such thinking had indeed caused them both grief. Neither, though, would admit to regret. He was overwhelmed by his survival and the company in which he found himself, courtesy of the unholy happenstance of art and war.

"How old were you, Laurie, when you started to read like that?"

"Eight."

Oriol nodded his head in wonderment.

"Well, yes," he said cheerfully, "it explains a lot of things about you."

"You know," he continued, "you were so fiercely unpredictable as we rode into the desert. I knew of our plan, but your madness was such that I expected things might still end in our destruction."

Laurie stared at him for a moment, as if this revelation had come as a complete shock.

"I must tell you, honestly," continued Oriol, "I wasn't sure that I would survive to the top of that sand hill."

In truth, Laurie knew that in that moment he too was lost. But had he failed a second innocent man, any shred of personal worth, of virtue, would have died too.

And so somehow he'd prevailed.

They sat silently, staring into the spiritual surround, lost in thought and a peace that had, for so long, been absent. Eventually, Laurie unfolded the paper he was holding and read the words once more.

I met a man today.
Angered, razored, kettled by the certainties of others.
Battered on the blasted heath of his business,
His life a fishnet of uncertainty.

His burden? Integrity denied. His crime? To do his best as he had always done before. But this song wasn't good enough. They judged him culpable And left him; cursed, undressed.

The pain had fractured his very soul. Seared by hades heat, manacled, broken, denied by those who'd been friends. All that he knew was banished, lost behind those lines he no longer saw, Picked up, played with, discarded.

To see a life stripped so bare Is to visit a crime. A man so duty-bound, so honourable yet now foregone. What cost to them that a course should be charted, Less pity and love itself be drowned?

What point at which their sensibilities align, To leave at least some meat in his broken and cockled shell? Some chance that his stem of service, trust, hope and care, Be left with at least some seed?

Instead they built fences, Circled inward against his heart, suffocating, unsparing, denying all chance of re-growth, Lifting him from life as if forked from some muddied sod, Then heaped to rot and dry.

I wished him what I could. There were no words of comfort or support with which I could tend his seeping wounds. No prizes for his future, that could banish the blackness of his eternal night. Nothing, zero. Paradise lost.

I met a man today, Thrown by grief to the pit he'd spied which others had dug, pursued by their certainty. They had ticked their backs, filed their defence, through his destruction. And for what?

"Ah, at last, you are praying."
Father Emam was back, smelling of Woodbine cigarettes, his favourite British brand, and irreverent as ever.
"Poetry," said Laurie, "though I would call it prayers, too."
"It's almost time, I believe," said Emam, ignoring for once the opportunity for philosophical discussion, and looking towards Oriol.
It had been agreed that a rapid exit from the country would be in the best interests of everyone, and so a passage on a British frigate sailing to Mahon had been arranged: a sensible solution to the misunderstandings Oriol had suffered. Father Emam would accompany him to Port Alexandria to fulfil his promise to Bishop Paulinus.
"You are indeed my father in many ways," said Oriol, smiling graciously towards Emam, "the closest I have ever come since losing my own; though Bishop Paulinus did call me 'my son.'"
"Well, maybe there is still a chance?" replied Emam, "his excellency will surely have his reasons."
"Father?"

Emam did not reply, and neither did Oriol pursue, though he was temporarily perplexed.

"Will you be accompanying me, too?" joked Oriol, looking at Laurie.

"I'm afraid not," he replied, "I've been ordered back to barracks at Midan Bab El Hadid. After all, I'm a Military Policeman. I shall doubtless be spending the rest of my days in Cairo checking passes amongst the traders and being spat at."

Oriol was surprised, especially once he realised Laurie wasn't joking.

"I'm required to keep my head down, and anyway, things are hotting up here... we no longer seem quite so popular with the locals."

"You say, 'required'?" asked Oriol, somewhat startled.

"To wait out the war, keep quiet. It will be difficult," he said, and they both grinned, "but I have a family and a renewed duty to survive, and then, who knows?"

Oriol Quintana shook his head; what a waste, what a complete waste.

Aware of the pressure of time and the need to change the tone, he stood, crossed himself and bowed towards the altar and the munificent St Nicholas.

"Following the events of my journey here, I feel I should seek help from whatever source," he said, smiling broadly once more, before hugging Laurie. "You have saved my life in more ways than you might imagine."

"A pity I had to eat you first," replied Laurie, and once again the laughter abounded.

"Any more of this and I shall need another smoke," said Emam.

Oriol picked up his bag, checking that his notepad and copy of the *'Odyssey'* were present, shook Laurie's hand and bade him farewell.

"Maybe we shall meet again?" he said, before moving off with Emam, turning just before reaching the large Mediterranean oak doors of the cathedral and shouting back, "in this world or the next." Then, along with the greatest adventure of Laurie's life, he was gone.

In Palma, Padre Perez, secretary to the Diocese of Arage knocked on the door of his master's room as was normal each day at first light, and waited. He'd expected the summons to enter, which generally quickly followed, but this morning there was none. He knocked again and still there was no response. He was wary of entering: the bishop had recently been sleeping much longer, but something troubled him.

So, he plucked up courage and eased open the door. The living room was empty, though the large full-length windows that led into the garden and then onto the sea front were open, banging gently together in the early breeze. He closed them quietly, and thinking that Paulinus might still be asleep, edged through the door to his bedroom. But that too was empty, and when he turned on a light, the spartan bedding lay immaculate and untouched.

He rushed back to the windows and through them into the garden, thinking that maybe he'd inadvertently missed his master, seated and unseen perhaps, meditating on the day ahead. But there was no sign of the man so loved by those for whom he cared.

Padre Perez felt a growing concern. Everything in Paulinus' modest quarters was as it should have been, save for the windows and his inexplicable absence. As he headed for the door his eye caught the sealed letter, placed in the middle of the bishop's desk and held down by a heavy wooden crucifix. On it was written an address, *Llucia Quintana, Turo Vell, Es Migjorn Roca, Menorca.* He ran into the corridor to raise the alarm.

That evening a fishing boat returned to port with the body of an unidentified elderly man. Around his neck was a cross, and on his finger a bishop's ring.

It had been two years since the fall of Jerusalem. Laurie was sitting at home in the tiny kitchen of the Police House in Kempsey, having returned to his wife and family and the formerly distant routines of pounding the beat.

Cairo had become increasingly troublesome and he was pleased to be done with the constant vigilance this had required. So, it should have been a joyous time. He was back where he belonged; loved, respected and above all else, safe.

But he sorely missed the closeness of Nooney's friendship, his colleagues from the Bureau, and the freedoms that had allowed him to fly. He'd returned to his job, secure for now, though suffocating by comparison to his work in Egypt. How could he explain that life? Who would understand the guilt he must outrun?

And now this: a letter from Cairo, addressed in immaculate handwriting and admirable English.

The source was unmistakable: Peter Moussabey. This man had risked his life and those of his family to assist the British. He'd kept in touch during the remainder of Laurie's Military Police service in Cairo, unofficially, and on an increasingly ad hoc basis. And typically he'd also used his bank's connections to send Laurie's eulogy to Nooney's parents in New Zealand. But the pair had drifted apart, mostly the result of Laurie's own pretence of indifference; the Moussabey's were most surely a beautiful and deserving family, but the thought of more compression upon his conscience from their impossible position was overwhelming.

He picked up the letter and began to open it, and there, momentarily, was Moussabey; comically absurd on the train to Port Alexandria, then in that ridiculous first meeting with 'Mr Smith': and in a glance, it was the Moussabey who was generous and loyal to a fault, supporting his and Nooney's work, praising them to their officers. He was a courageous, yet humble man.

Cairo, 23rd August, 1919.

My Dear Laurie,

I know that you have left Egypt suddenly without leaving your home address, and unfortunately no one in the barracks knows it, but by luck last night I had a visit from Lance Corporal Wesley (now a Sergeant) and he gave it to me.

I hope that you have arrived in good health and all your family are in 1st class health ('Tamam').

Well, Laurie, is that the way to forget your old Peter without writing a word, even a post card? ('Maalesh').

Everything is changed in town, and in the barracks. All the old L/Cpls are actually Sergeants and all the rest are new men and I can say they do not know about police business. The 2 Civil Clothes men are now Swan and Balmain.

Great difference, Laurie.

As regards the business, it is very bad… no trams in town since 14 days… the Bank is to be amalgamated, no more jealousy now. But those who helped the British are to pay a large price. We pray for the best.

I shall be obliged if you could send me a testimonial (which will remain anonymous) for what I have done for you during that year together. Colonel Lowthian does not answer my request and of course I cannot ask poor Nooney. It will be very useful, especially as you know how to write such things.

The future here is uncertain.

I hope to hear soon.

Yours sincerely,
Peter.

P Moussabey, Agricultural Bank of Cairo.

And Laurie, if you need anything from Cairo, let me know ('Salam alaykum').

Hidden within his otherwise gentle prose was the clearest message; the Moussabeys were in grave danger.

Laurie's new world had followed him home. Perhaps, though, it had always been there?

He searched for a pen and paper and began to write.

INDEX OF CHARACTERS

Laurie: Thomas Laurie, born in 1882, a village policeman at the start of the war, married to *Eveline*, 5 children, sent to Egypt following his enlistment in 1916 into the Worcestershire Regiment, transferred to the Military Foot Police based in Cairo.

Eve Laurie: Born in 1882 and married to *Thomas Laurie*. Full-time mother of 5 children and living in the tiny Police House in a Worcestershire village, alienated somewhat from the norms of village life by her husband's role.

Captain Hillary: Oxbridge educated, officer in the Worcestershire Regiment, junior colleague to *Major Fogge*, though, unlike him, experienced the Western Front. Based in Cairo.

Brigadier Berrington Regis-Templeton: 9th Viscount Littleworth, landowner from Littleworth Hall near Worcester, senior officer in the Worcestershire Regiment, serving in Cairo since 1916.

Sergeant Wirrall: Experienced soldier, served with Captain Hillary and Brigadier Berrington Regis-Templeton on the Western Front before transferring with them to Egypt.

Nooney: John Nooney, born in Onehunga near Auckland, North Island, New Zealand, 1876. Sent along with the Anzac troops to the staging-post camps in Egypt, and following training co-opted into the Military Foot Police in Cairo, serving there since early 1915.

Manoli: A local street entertainer in Cairo.

Llucia Quintana: Landowner on the Mediterranean island of Menorca, owner of Turo Vell farm near the village of Es Migjorn Roca, mother of *Oriol Quintana* and matriarch of the extended Quintana family (see the *Quintana Family Tree*).

Padre Alvaro Marin: Catholic Priest at Sant Cristofol in Es Migjorn Roca, Menorca.

Oriol Quintana: Born to *Llucia Quintana* in 1886 in Es Migjorn Roca, married to *Estel*, with three children *Ignacio, Maria, Aina*.

Peter Moussabey: Cairo local, and part of the management team at The Agricultural Bank of Cairo. Fluent English-speaking assistant when needed to the British Army, hence the anglicised name (see also *Hisham bin Moussa*) for the convenience of the British.

Hisham bin Moussa: The actual Arabic name of *Peter Moussabey*.

Colonel Lowthian: Mildred Lowthian, Archaeologist, working for the Intelligence section of the British Army in Cairo.

Hanna Moussabey: Wife of *Peter Moussabey*, mother of daughters, *Germaine, Madelaine, Marcelle* and *Andrie*.

Germaine Moussabey: Eldest daughter aged 15, of *Peter* and *Hanna Moussabey*.

Colonel Noah Grice-Farquharason: Noah Grice-Farquharason, an academic by background, working for the Intelligence section of the British Army in Cairo.

Mr Braggot: Farmer, near Worcester.

Gil: Son in law of *Llucia Quintana*, married to her daughter *Isla*.

Isla: Born in 1890 to *Llucia Quintana* and her then husband, *Biel Alexander* (see Quintana Family Tree). She is married to *Gil*.

Bishop Paulinus: His Excellency Paulinus, the Emeritus Bishop of Es Gara in the Diocese of Arage, based in Palma on the Mediterranean Island of Mallorca.

Elisheba Andreassen: Boat skipper and manager of the *Andreassen* family businesses based in Mahon (Mao), Menorca and sister of *Mattityahu Andreassen*.

Mattityahu Andreassen: Brother of *Elisheba Andreassen*, her junior in the *Andreassen* family businesses.

Major Fogge: Oxford educated, privileged background, army hobbyist. Member of the British Army General Headquarters (GHQ) team, attached indirectly to The Arab Bureau.

Padre Perez: Secretary to the Diocese of Arage and assistant to *Bishop Paulinus*.

Padre Serrano: The old Catholic priest of Sant Cristofol, a predecessor to *Padre Alvin Marin*.

Taqi al Din al-Bilal: Also known as **'Mr Smith'**. Entrepreneur, owner of the 'Alexandria West Bay Shipping Company' based in the Egyptian Mediterranean port of Alexandria, 120 miles NW of Cairo.

Father Daoud Emam: A Coptic priest, and much more.

Private Bestic: New Zealander, attached to the Australian 3rd Light Horse.

Private Halbert: New Zealander, attached to the Australian 3rd Light Horse.

General Aukkerley: Near-retirement General working at British Army GHQ.

LLUCIA QUINTANA FAMILY TREE

Llucia Quintana, b 1869.

Had a son out of wedlock, **Oriol** *(1886).* **Oriol** is ***the only son*** she gave birth to.

Married **Alexander Biel, 1889,** children *Martina (1889)* and *Isla (1890).* There had been suspicion he'd collaborated with those who took the Quintana lands. He died in a fall in 1890 and with no other offspring, so she inherited his extensive farmlands near Alaior.

Married **Pau Carles, 1891,** children *Arlet (1891) Sofia (1892)* and *Jana (1893).* Carles died at sea on a smuggling trip in 1895; there was little sadness from the many he'd traumatised. His previous offspring were illegitimate, so Llucia inherited his farmland around *Ferreries.*

Married **Hugo Barrera, 1897,** *producing Abril (1897) Ona (1898) and Paula* (1898). By now Llucia was a significant landowner. As the immediate neighbour to Llucia's parents 'lost' farm at Turo Vell, Hugo 'buys' the farm when it's placed at auction, confirming via his will her possession of both this and his existing farm He dies in 1898, shortly after the birth of Llucia's twins.

Married **Eric Farregy, 1899**, an old farmer in need of care, who dies a year later; there are no offspring. His huge estate, including houses, passed to Llucia.

Married **Arnao Reus, 1902**, producing *Juanita (1904)*. A very old banker with assumed links to the criminal element in Mao and a man with the ear of the British, Turks and Spanish, he disinherited the four legitimate children from a previous marriage due to trust issues. Llucia, therefore, inherited his vineyards, properties and cash assets upon his death in 1905.

Llucia's ten children from the above (9 girls and 1 boy by the time of this story) have mostly found partners with whom they have offspring, so by 1916, aged 47, in addition to her ten children and their spouses, Llucia has 15 grandchildren – all girls;

Oriol married Estel producing *Ignacio (1906) Maria (1907), Aina (1908)*
Martina married Ramone producing *Tina (1908)*
Isla married Gil producing *Anna (1906)*
Arlet married Raimon producing *Julia (1911) Paula (1914)*
Sofia married Josep producing *Carmen (1912) Marta (1914)*
Jana married Artur producing *Vera (1913) Candela (1914) Adrian (1914)*
Abril married Eduard producing *Jacinta (1913)*
Ona married Teodor producing *Alexandre (1915) and Caterina (1916)*

INDEX OF HISTORICAL REFERENCES

General Haigh: Senior officer commanding The British Expeditionary Force on the Western Front.

The Arab Bureau: An arm of the Cairo Intelligence Department, it was established in 1916 to co-ordinate British Policy in the Near East. As part of this activity, it worked to obtain information about enemy intentions and operations, as well as challenging any enemy propaganda. It focussed significantly upon support for 'The Arab Revolt' (against the Ottoman Empire) that commenced that year, with a view to enabling an Arab state that stretched from Aleppo in Syria to Aden in Yemen. There was a good degree of indecision within the British Army and Government as to the intentions of the various Arab groups, plus an overriding desire to maintain British access to Suez, and therefore the most efficient access to India and the East. This may have undermined the efficiency of the Bureau, which was eventually disbanded in 1920.

Alfred Lord Tennyson: 1809–1892. The poem referred to by a character in Chapter 3 is entitled 'Tears, Idle Tears' and was written by this English poet in 1847. He remains one of England's most famous poets.

Casimiro Sainz: Spanish artist, 1853–1898, who produced many landscapes. His picture, the *Banks of Manzares*, referred to by a character in Chapter 3 of the book, was one of many such canvasses he produced in his life. He was in poor health for long periods and died relatively young. He relied greatly upon the support of others to enable him to both continue and sell his work.

Hatshepsut: The second female Pharaoh of Egypt, reigning for 22 years, 1479–1458 BC, 5th Pharaoh of the 18th Dynasty.

St Thomas Aquinas: Italian philosopher, priest, theologian, 1225–1274.

Aristotle: Greek philosopher and polymath, 384–322BC.

The Agricultural Bank of Egypt: Opened in 1902, arising from the diversification of the National Bank of Egypt, founded in 1898 supported by British investment.

General Allenby: Senior Officer commanding the Egyptian Expeditionary Force, June 1917 until the completion of the war. He was elected Field Marshal in July 1919.

Homer: Presumed author of the Iliad and Odyssey: epic poems of Greek literature assumed to relate to different periods of classical Greek history as far back as 1148 BC and the fall of Troy; widely regarded as one of the greatest poets and authors in history.

Djemal Pasha: Commander of Southern area of Ottoman Empire during 1915–18.

Ishmael Pasha: The Khedive of Egypt, 1863–1879: removed under the British Protectorate.

Cylopes: Giant one-eyed creature of Greek mythology, 5th century BC.

Nonnus of Panopulis: Greek poet living in Roman-dominated Egypt, 5th century AD.

Dionysiaca: Ancient Greek epic poem in 48 books mostly on the life of Dionysus and written by Nonnus of Panopulis.

Purification Society: Egyptian movement, prominent in Cairo in the early 1900s, to distinguish boundaries between acceptable pleasure and vice.

Sednaoui family: Escaped Ottoman persecution in the 1870s, and with a talent for salesmanship, established the Sednaoui Department Store as the most prestigious in Cairo.

Nubar Pasha: First Egyptian Prime Minister, 1878, served on two other occasions, concluding 1895.

Shepheard Hotel: Established by an Englishman of the same name in 1841, it became a favourite haunt for English and other foreign visitors to Cairo.

Enigma Variations: Music written by internationally acclaimed composer Edward Elgar 1857–1934, who lived near Worcester for much of his life. The piece, completed in 1899, Elgar described as 'to my friends pictured within'.

Steam boat service from Mahon: Steamboats in general were becoming a favourite with the rich post-1848. By 1917 such forms were becoming more available from Mahon.

The Gran Hotel, Placa de Weyer: Completed in 1903, designed in modernist style by Catalan architect and politician Domenech i Montaner.

Eglésia de Sant Nicolau: Built by 1349, and a steady walk away from The Gran Hotel.

Flavius Josephus: First Century Roman-Jewish historian, born in Jerusalem, who commented on access to water in his book on the 'Jewish Wars'.

Eastern Telegraph: The Eastern Telegraph Company founded 1872 enabled messages to be communicated across continents as well as between cities such as Cairo and Alexandria. The Company relied primarily upon sub-marine cables.

Occams Razor: Franciscan Friar William of 'Ocham' 1287–1347, a man with an apparent 'razor-like' mind, is attributed with this notion that if you have two different propositions presented about something that both seem plausible you should prefer the simpler one. Logic suggests this is preferable to over-complication, as this is more likely to increase the variables, which in turn may lead to failure.

Jonathan Swift: Anglo-Irish author, satirist, political activist, 1667–1745.

Provost Marshal: The Military Provost was established in 1855 to take responsibility for the preservation of good order, army discipline and the resolution of local policing issues, across all areas where troops were stationed.

Army Act: Frequently updated, the 1916 Army Act would have been the most relevant to this story. It provided the formal guideline for justice, and was implemented as far as the circumstances of war allowed.

Transporting prisoners to Australia: The practice of sending prisoners from Great Britain to Australia formally ceased in 1868.

Cairo Tram Pass: There were two tramway systems in operation in Cairo, the 'Cairo Electric Railways and Heliopolis Oases Co' and the 'Tramways Du Caire'. Lance Corporal Laurie would have been provided with passes for both in his civilian undercover role, his travel entitlement described as *valuable en 2me Class jusqu'au date.* They would be numbered and hand signed by *Le Directeur*, with a page of regulations in both Arabic and French, stamped in Arabic. Both passes would require a photograph and brief description; for example, '*Delivree au L/Cpl T Laurie, agent secret de l'A P M*' (British Army Provost Marshal). Remarkably, 'agent secret' as an open description meant exactly that, though more likely inferred that they had 'special duties'.

Benjamin Williams Leader: Worcester-born artist, 1831–1923, he first exhibited the picture *February Fill Dyke* at The Royal Academy in 1881.

ACKNOWLEDGEMENTS

The Poet Laurie Ate is a work of fiction, created entirely from my imagination. It sits within an historical backdrop, and I'm grateful to those individuals and organisations expertly familiar with the times, whose commentaries have inspired and informed the colour palette within which the story is set. Any misjudgements or errors in this respect are therefore entirely of my own making.

BIBLIOGRAPHY

Military Crimes 1914–1918 British Army, by Chris Baker, www.longlongtrail.co.uk

A Line in the Sand, by James Barr, published 2011, by Simon and Schuster UK Ltd.

Agrarian Change and Industrialization in Egypt 1800–1950, by Peter H Bent, published 2015, by University of Oxford.

Sex Work Regulation and the Colonial Order in Late Nineteenth-Century Cairo, by Francesca Biancani, 2016, www.globalurbanhistory.com

The Fateful Year: England 1914, by Mark Bostridge, published 2014, by Penguin Group.

Woodbine Willie: Taking God and Cigarettes to the Front Line. A Report on the inspirational life of The Rev Geoffrey Studdert, BBC News North West, 4th June, 2014, by Jerry Chester www.bbc.co.uk

Peasants In Revolt – Egypt 1919, by Ellis Goldberg, published 1992, International Journal of Middle East Studies, Cambridge University Press www.jstor.org

Press/Journalism (Middle East): International Encyclopedia of the First World War by Benan Grams, 2017, www.1914-1918-online.net

Padre Who Offered A Light To Servicemen. Church Times report, 4th March, 2009, by Jonathan Gurling. www.churchtimes.co.uk

1914–16 and The Egypt and Palestine Campaigns, by Stuart Hadaway, published 2014, by The History Press.

Pyramids and Fleshpots; The Egyptian, Senussi and Eastern Mediterranean

Campaigns, by Stuart Hadaway, published 2017, by Pen and Sword Books Ltd.
Seven Pillars of Wisdom, by T.E. Lawrence 1922, first formal publication 1935, by London Jonathan Cape.
The Role of Military Intelligence in the Battle for Beersheba in October 1917, by James Noone, Studies in Intelligence, Vol 62 No 1, www.cia.gov

Map of Cairo at the time of this story:
The streets, tramways, and many of the places referred to in this story can be found online at *'The General Map Of Cairo'* held by the *'Library of Congress, Geography and Map Division'*, researchable via the following link; https://www.loc.gov/item/2009580102/ Citation: Egypt. Maṣlaḥat Al-Misāḥah, General map of Cairo. (Cairo: Survey of Egypt, 1920)
Please note the Rights and Access requirements of the Library of Congress.

A note about the anglicised use of Arabic place names:
Streets and places in the story have been given the anglicised version of the Arabic, which to the best of my knowledge would have been in use at the time by the main characters in the story. The Arabic spoken by the characters has also been anglicised.

I also wish to thank the following:
'The Worcestershire Regimental Archives' and *'The Worcestershire Regiment Museum Collection'* have been a source of documentary help and a place to examine first-hand, via the permanent exhibitions, the military clothing together with some of the equipment used by The Worcestershire`s in Egypt.

*'*The Worcestershire Regiment Archives' can be found at **The Mercian Regiment Museum (Worcestershire), Dancox House, Pheasant Street, Worcester, WR1 2EE.**

*'*The Worcestershire Regiment Museum Collection' is housed at Worcester City Art Gallery and Museum, Foregate Street, Worcester, WR1 1DT.

'*The National Archives*', Kew, Bessant Drive, Richmond, London, TW9 4DU www.nationalarchives.gov.uk

'*The Great War Forum*' www.greatwarforum.org

Individuals:
Robert Pooler, who as Police History Researcher for the Worcestershire Police Constabulary, provided information helpful to my understanding of village policing in World War 1.

The seed of the story was laid years ago, when as a child I was told my grandad, *George Percy James (1882–1972)*, had been a Military Policeman in Cairo. I was mesmerised by the very idea he was able to travel so far in those days, and to such a seemingly exotic place. Many years after his death, I started to research his life, helped by the primary resource material he'd left from his time in Egypt between 1916 and 1919. It was the evidence from this, my own coincidental visit to Cairo, and then to Mahon in Menorca, that nudged me towards the subsequent story. The more the plot developed, the more too, in my mind at least, the parallels with our current world revealed themselves.

So, I am thankful to him for the inspiration his life provided, and for the beautiful way he wrote from Cairo to his family back in England, at a time when it might be thought that men like he could not display such tenderness so openly.

The painting *February Fill Dyke*, referenced in a dialogue between two of the characters in my story, is by Worcester-born artist Benjamin Williams Leader (1831–1923). First exhibited at the Royal Academy in 1881, it's one of the many landscapes he painted, and has hung in the main atrium of Birmingham Art Gallery for as long as I can remember. I have my parents to thank for taking me there when it wasn't such an easy thing for them to do; and for instilling in me, and now through me my family-who may not necessarily be so keen, the instinctive need wherever we find ourselves in the world to visit a gallery.

Art inspires, potentially for life.

I am grateful too for the encouragement of my family and friends, which has been so important to confidence, as at times even I thought it a very odd thing to be spending so long inventing a story.

The Editor

The greatest thanks I can give go to my Editor, Elaine Stephens. Without her none of this would have been possible – quite literally.

All I had to do was write the book. Elaine had to read through it many times, suggesting changes to the flow, corrections, narrative refinements and structural changes, most of which I sensibly took on board. There have been numerous edits. Characters have been refined, some even slung. If you don't like what you read, well, at least count yourself lucky you missed the first draft.

There was a lot of laughter: and (fortunately) I do prefer her direct approach to editorial trouble shooting. In all of this she was trying kindly, supportively, and occasionally even tactfully, to get the very best work I could produce. Quite a challenge. I am in her debt.

And finally

Even though the story itself is fictitious, the events occurring at the time were overwhelming. Lives were changed in an instant; millions were killed, many millions more were casualties. Incalculable numbers of family members and friends were permanently blighted by the huge scale of the loss. Economies and livelihoods were destroyed. None of the combatant or occupied groupings involved escaped the carnage. Genocide occurred during the war; a Pandemic and eventually a great economic recession followed.

How people living through these times must have hoped it would be the last time such horrors would be allowed to happen.

Surely, the world would learn?

Ash James

The Poet Laurie Ate ©Ash James 2024 www.ashjamesarts.co.uk